<u>**Writing As: J. Risk**</u>

REALMS BOOKS:

THE ALTEREALM SERIES
1 *The Huntress*
2 *The Seer*
3 *The Empath*
4 *The Witch*
5 *The Chronos*
6 *The Warrior*
7 *The Telepath*
8 *The Healer*
9 *The Kinetic*

THE SOLRELM SERIES
Coming soon:

Concealed

GEMINI LEAGUE
Coming soon

Dark Moon

A note from the author:

So many have wanted Noah's story. This one was a
hard one to write, I had to take more breaks than I
normally would. I think everyone will be happy with
where it goes. I hope so.

I'm forever grateful for the support this series has
gained. It makes all the struggling with characters
and timelines worth it. (a lot of struggles)

Xox

Jacqueline

FURY

Animal Senses Series Book 8

Jacqueline Paige

He rubbed his hand over his chest, feeling the familiar ridges of the scars under his shirt. He could still hear her screaming the day they brought her to the house. She wasn't screaming for her own welfare though, it was for him, to let him go, stop hitting him. He could never understand why she did that. It would have made things worse for herself fighting against them. He dropped his head down almost to his chest and closed his eyes, he knew all about that, what fighting back brought.

Opening his eyes, he zeroed in on the job he was supposed to be doing. Removing panels, taking out dents, and prepping the equipment for painting. It wasn't exactly a hard task, but he was used to it. He got most of the jobs in the shop that didn't involve engines or moving parts. He rolled his head from side to side and tried to alleviate some of the tight knots so movement would be less painful. He didn't mind the jobs they gave him; he had no desire to understand the complex workings of engine parts. He'd learned to work a few of the rigs, and he did that well, so that got him out of the shop from time to time where he could go to sites and feel like he was doing something.

Putting the wrench on the nut, he gave a test tug on it to see if it had *melded*, as Jake called it, to the bolt. That seemed to be common with the dust, grime, and heat the equipment was exposed to three seasons out of the year. He had to yank on it three times to get it to loosen. Noah glared at the next one, he had enough frustration inside him that he could do this for a day before burning off only a quarter of it. The next two were easy, the third one wouldn't budge. Snarling at it, he gripped the wrench tighter and put all his anger into it. It gave way and his hand went into the panel. Looking down he saw he'd broken the bolt clean off instead of undoing it. One more thing he screwed up. With a growl, he slammed his hand into the panel.

The music stopped suddenly.

"Aren't we supposed to be taking the dings out of it, not adding more?"

Noah looked over his shoulder to see Cooper standing there. He was up on his feet now, with a cast and crutch to make sure he behaved for a few more weeks. If it had been him, he wouldn't have lasted a week, never mind the entire time Shaelan tacked on 'just to be sure."

"Thought maybe there was a rock concert going on in here. One with loud, angry music." He started across the floor toward him.

ANIMAL SENSES
1 *Heart*
2 *Scent*
3 *Passion*
4 *Courage*
5 *Solace*
6 *Faith*
7 *Spirit*
Coming soon:

8 Fury
9 Pride
10 Torment

MAGIC SEASONS ROMANCE
1 *Beltane Magic*
2 *Solstice Heat*
3 *Harvest Dreams*
4 *Autumn Dance*
5 *Winter Mist*

Dreams
Three steamy stories that started with a dream

Curses
Two tales of curses.

After the Silence

SINGLE TITLES
Solitary Witchling
Salvation
Café Serenity

Coming soon:
Outcasts

Chapter One

She turned and looked at the small window, it was night again. How long did that make it? A month, longer? She'd lost count. The only thing she was thankful for was no one else was down here with her. That was good for the other women. Did they ever have more than one locked up at the same time? She couldn't be sure.

Emersyn sat up and tugged on the collar around her throat. She should be used to it by now, but it still felt like it was choking her, even though it wasn't. After wearing it for years, you would think it would feel like it belonged there. She closed her eyes and shook her head slowly, how could anyone get used to that?

The reason it was there was enough to constantly remind her that her life was not her own. It had not been hers since she was a child. Over the years the images and memories of freedom had faded. She remembered the boat trip and the excitement of being in a new country. Her parents, she remembered them dancing to be there. She knew she used to run outside and play, knew that somewhere out there she had a mother, father, and two older brothers, but she could no longer see them inside her head. There was just an emptiness where those memories with family should have been. She'd held onto her mother's smile the longest, but now with it was gone, there was only a void left behind.

Getting up, she lifted the chain that weighed down her ankle and moved slowly toward the window. It was the only thing she had to focus on. The lights were off, and the basement was dark through the night, the only thing she could do was look out the small window, level with the ground, and hope to see something. Anything.

The pain shot up her leg from the swelling caused by the cold metal rubbing against her ankle bone. The throbbing was endless. She didn't know why they kept it on her, where was she going to go? The door was bolted shut, and the window, even if she could reach it was too small to get out. Of course, if she hadn't attacked her captors on more than one occasion, they would probably allow her more freedom. There was some part of her that made her fight back, even though she knew the consequences of doing it.

There was snow falling tonight. She inhaled a shaky breath. Another year had passed. Winter was on its way. Aspyn's fifth birthday would be soon. Putting her hand over her chest, she clutched the fabric covering her heart while she silently asked the universe to watch over her baby. If she closed her eyes, she could see her pale blue eyes and a cheeky little smile. She *had* to be okay. It was the only thing that got Emersyn through each day. Her baby was the *only* reason she had to keep breathing. Born into a life with no freedoms, yet when she smiled all the terrors faded away.

She was okay, she decided. There was no other possible outcome in her mind. Her little girl was a fighter with an attitude much bigger than her little body. A tear rolled down her cheek as she remembered when Aspyn had punched that man, her father, in the face for upsetting her Mommy. She would survive the cruelties of their world; of that she was certain. Aspyn didn't know it yet, but she was guided by the spirit of her animal. Emersyn's mother used to say that and now she had no choice but to believe it was true.

Opening her eyes, she blinked, had someone just gone past the window? She started to move closer only to stop when the chain reached its end too soon. She looked around, there was nothing in the room to throw at it to draw their attention. She considered yelling, but that would only alert her guards upstairs and she didn't need that.

How long had it been since he'd come and shown her pictures of her only reason to live? She couldn't be certain but thought it might have been longer than his normal taunting visit. She bit her lip, not even sure if it was a good or bad thing, but she desperately wanted to see the pictures proving that their daughter, she scowled—no, *her* daughter was well.

Without blinking, she stared at the window, hoping to see someone outside it again. Anyone that could get her out of here. Away from this world, she'd been stuck in for far too long. Other than the first few years of endless houses, she'd always been here. Many women had come and gone from this house in that time, but Emersyn was still here. She didn't know where they went or what happened to them, this was the only place she could loosely call home. She cut off any further thoughts when she saw more feet moving by the window.

"You be brave, Aspyn, Mommy's going to find you one day, and no one will separate us again." She whispered in a soft breath.

The sound of footsteps upstairs had her turn and look at the door. Was he here? Did he bring her daughter back? Each time she heard movement up there, she thought the same thing. Maybe he realized that holding their daughter hostage and trying to force her cycle to come back was impossible. If a woman had that power the world would be a *much* different place.

The sounds grew louder, there was something wrong. No one in this house was ever that loud. Grasping the chain, she rushed to the back corner of the cold-tiled room and crouched down beside the cot. In the darkness, she focused on where she knew the stairs ended, waiting. Were they moving the women? It wasn't unusual to do it at night. Would the others get to keep their children? The sound of the lock opening on the door at the top of the stairs echoed like a hammer on metal in the silence.

She closed her eyes and dug deeper for the courage to stay quiet as heavy boots hit the stairs. If she could just pretend to be compliant, just once—maybe they'd let her keep her daughter with her.

Opening her eyes, she watched in the dark as the outline of a large man appeared before her. A light hit her face and then moved around the room. She was momentarily blinded by it and unable to see who it was.

"One in the basement," his tone was low, and frightening in the dark space, "chained to the fucking wall. Do we have bolt cutters?"

Her heart started pounding in her chest. Bolt cutters? What was going on?

"Send him down here."

She listened as he moved around the room, afraid to speak.

"Watch your eyes. I'm turning the light on."

Chapter Two

Noah bolted upright and freed his legs from the blanket. He was covered in sweat and his heart was racing so fast he couldn't breathe. Wiping his hand over his face, he blew out a breath. *Just a nightmare. I'm not there anymore.*

Swinging his feet to the floor, he breathed slower and rested his face in his hands. He was glad this op had allowed him to have his own room. Rubbing his jaw to ease the tense muscles, he looked around the tiny space. Okay, so his room had been a closet at one time, but it was just him and he didn't have to worry about waking others as he fought the demons in his sleep and woke up ready to run—or fight

Grabbing his shirt, he yanked it over his head and jammed his arms into it. There would be no going back to sleep now. There never was. Once they started, they didn't ease up and allow any sort of rest. The only thing he could do was take his body to the point of exhaustion and hope for a few hours of dead sleep before they returned. Thrusting his legs into his jeans, he stood up and zipped them. Coffee and fresh air and he'd be ready for the day.

He moved down the stairs silently, making sure not to wake anyone else in the house. Being part of this team had given him purpose, one he was proud to have. They also ripped off all the scabs on old wounds and made him relive it all again, over and over.

Glancing at the door, he made sure it was closed and he wouldn't wake Illias—if in fact the man ever slept because it didn't seem like he did. He used his phone to light the way into the kitchen and found a coffee pot already on and almost full. Someone else was anxious for the op to start too. They were supposed to go in last night, but the other teams weren't all in place. Four hits at the same time spread out all over the map, was a logistical nightmare, or so they'd been told. He left all the planning to those with minds for it. His mind was filled with fury, hate, and violence—all hidden beneath the torment.

Taking the cup, he went out the back door and looked toward the woods. He was more comfortable with this location than the last few. Fenced-in yards brought back too many memories of closed-in spaces. It was also nowhere near where they were going, but the planners had decided it was safer to stay further away, so here they were.

As he was raising the cup to his mouth, he heard something coming from the bush at the side of the property. He held his breath until Blair and Kobie stepped out of the trees. At least he knew who else was up. He moved away from the back of the house, not caring if he was barefoot in the light snow on the ground.

Blair motioned to the cup, "you didn't drink all our coffee, did you?" He grinned.

Noah shook his head, "just starting now."

"He'll drink the pot before you can get your cup out of the cupboard," Blair informed his mate.

Kobie swatted Blair's arm, "you don't exactly share it with anyone either."

Blair faked a hurt look, "hey with all the bodies in the house now, I'm lucky if I get half a cup."

Noah grinned, he didn't envy Blair, having all those people around him all the time. He did feel a few pangs of jealousy, however, at the thought of *having* that many of your own around you. Taking a sip, he relished the burn on his tongue.

He couldn't think about his own family right now, not when he needed to stay alert and functional.

"I'll sneak in and get you a cup." Kobie kissed his cheek and then walked away.

Blair looked down at Noah's feet and raised an eyebrow. "Nightmares again?"

Noah nodded. The problem with sharing a bunkhouse with the men at Ed's meant there had been no way to hide it from them. "Just being back here—" he shrugged one shoulder, "there's no way to escape them."

Blair nodded, even though his expression said he could never fully understand. "The delay has me antsy."

"Yeah. Better to follow the entire plan than a piece of it I guess." He took a sip and watched the snowfall from the branches of one of the trees. "Good area to run?"

"It's not home, but it's all right."

They both turned when the door opened, and Konner Flores came out. He carried a cup in one hand and a water bottle in the other. When he was closer, he held the cup out to Blair, "Kobie was on the phone and asked if I'd bring this to you."

"Thanks." Blair took it and glanced at the house. "I wonder who is having what crisis now?"

Noah noticed Konner smirk, then take a drink so it wasn't obvious he did. "At least you're not there trying to delegate tasks with the building."

"I'm thankful for that." Blair smiled, "so many women overseers."

Konner pulled out his phone and looked at it. "Speaking of crisis," he held up the phone, "if you'll excuse me."

Blair pointed to the trees, "nice deep section of river that way if you need it."

Konner followed where he pointed, "good to know."

They watched him walk back toward the front of the house, the phone against his head. "I can't believe he left his mate at home."

Noah turned to look at him, "bringing her back here

wouldn't end well."

"That's true." Blair looked at the house again, "you going to be all right?" He jerked his chin in the direction of the house, "I should go see what drama is happening now."

"I'm good." He smirked, "have fun with your drama."

Blair rolled his eyes in a playful manner, "it's not drama that scares me now. Quiet is apparently bad with that many females and kids."

Noah chuckled, "I'm sure Daisie will wrangle those boys and keep them in line."

Blair started walking backward away from him, "that's what scares me." He laughed and turned toward the house.

The amusement on his face faded as soon as his friend went into the house. He turned back to the trees. Even the thought of shifting here, in this area, and going for a run had his muscles tense and his mind screaming not to. He had to wonder if that inner voice was ever going to go away. If he was ever going to feel safe shifting into what he was meant to be.

"Noah."

He turned around to see Calum standing at the door. "We're going to make breakfast, most of the house is moving now."

Turning around, Noah started back. The sooner they went over the plans meant they could get back on the road and get to where they needed to be. Tonight, couldn't get here fast enough for him. He looked forward to breaching another holding house that belonged to Aiden Tomas. Somewhere inside he knew it wasn't his fault, the things he'd been forced to do, but he felt dirty like he had a lot of sins to atone for. That conflict alone was what made him decide he would be part of this team until they ended Tomas. After that, he didn't know, he couldn't see past it to think in the terms of the future or living.

Chapter Three

Noah stared at the picture Illias held up. His heart seized inside his chest. Normally he'd stay in the back and keep quiet. Planning things like this weren't for him to do, he was just here to follow the plans laid out before them. This time, he couldn't stay silent. Before he knew it, he stomped over and ripped the photo from his hand, and spun to glare at Calum, "*this* is the house we're hitting?" His breath caught in his throat.

Calum gave Blair a quick side glance and then turned back to him. "It is."

Noah turned the photo around and stared at it. This was the house in his nightmares. He saw it awake too—every door had the potential in his mind to be *that* door. Every time he walked on wooden steps that sounded hollow; he was right back there. His hand was shaking as he tried not to crumple the photo. He looked at Blair. "Kobie stays outside for this one." He didn't know Gia or the other woman from the Incursion team, Sloane, but he looked at both for a second, "*none* of the women should go in *this* house." He held up the photo and then spun around and tossed it on the table in front of Illias.

"Why?" Blair's expression was a mix of concern and shock.

"Because it's—" he stopped and looked at Kobie and then at Gia, he knew they wouldn't even consider staying outside unless they knew the truth. Blowing out a breath, he sent the other woman an apologetic look, "it's a breeding house." It was much more to him, but that was all they were getting.

"I'm sorry, a what?" Kobie got up and looked at the photo and then at him, "like a," she waved her hand around.

"Just trust me, okay, you don't want to go in there." He didn't want to go back in there. "There are some scents that no amount of cleaning can mask." A low growl came from his throat.

"You were a guard there?" Konner leaned back against the wall, not looking as concerned as the others in the room.

"Briefly." He couldn't let the thoughts intrude, the ones of his last time at that house. He wore the reminders of that time in his skin, forever.

"Did you—help?" Sloane got up and came over to the table and looked down at the photo. "Help them," she glanced back at him, her baby blue eyes zeroing in on him like he was the devil himself.

"No." Noah chuffed and lifted his shirt up and turned slowly for all to see, "and I have these to prove I disobeyed." He could tell by their expressions that they understood what the scars on his chest and back meant. Shaelan looked aghast. Deacon looked pissed off. The only one that didn't react was Sloane, and it surprised him, but he didn't know much about her. He was sure she had her reasons to repress a reaction. Yanking the shirt down, he turned slowly and looked around. "The women should stay outside, if there are any inside, they should see *women* when they're coming out." He looked at Blair and then at Konner. "Don't touch them if they can walk on their own, don't walk behind them—give them room." He nodded, hoping he didn't need to say more.

Kobie gave him a heartfelt look and then nodded, "we can keep watch outside."

Noah felt relief. Knowing they wouldn't go inside meant a lot to him. He inclined his head in a silent thanks to her and then went back over to stand at the back of the group.

"I'll hang back outside, with Creed on overwatch," Bear said quietly, "without Jesse and Evanna here, a few more on watch could be good."

"It's a high-traffic area," Illias told all of them.

Noah stood frozen in place, staring at the house on the other side of the fence. Inside his head, he could hear the women pleading with him to help them, to get them out. He'd thought about it many times but could never act on it. Did that make him a coward? He still didn't know. So many were brought here. Young women from different clans, mature enough to carry a child, but before their first change. He remembered Devin and Rayne's faces when he explained it to them during their first meeting to discuss what he knew. He'd never discussed it with anyone else since. Not until today. Calum and Blair had followed him when he'd stormed out of the house, to help—there was nothing that could help. The last night at this house was the one that fueled his nightmares, and he knew always would. Unable to breathe after the planning was settled. He told them about his time in that house and when he was dragged from it because he finally found the one that he was willing to risk his life to save. Her pale green eyes haunted his dreams and powered his nightmares. They'd said she was his mate and he'd wondered so many times if she'd known he was her mate and if she ever forgave him for not saving her. He rubbed his hand down his throat like the collar was still there, the one he was forced to wear from that day until the day the team rescued him.

"You up for this?"

Noah jumped and turned to see Blair standing behind him, a watchful look on his face.

He nodded. "Yeah, just," he waved a hand beside his head, "ghosts."

Blair rubbed his hand over his hair, "well, let's free those ghosts then."

If only it worked that way, he thought. "I'm ready." He adjusted the piece in his ear and realized there were voices coming through it already.

"I'll follow you in." Blair adjusted his own earpiece, then pointed to the fence.

Before he could overthink it again, Noah hopped the fence and move quickly to the back of the house. He glanced down at the small window as he went past it, hoping there was no one down in the basement at all. Moving with sure steps, until he reached the back door, he crouched low so any guards on the other side of it couldn't see him through the window beside it.

He didn't take his eyes off it as he felt Blair move up behind him, then to the other side of the door. "We're at the back." He said quietly for all on the line to hear.

"Creed landed, so there's an all-clear." Sloane's voice came through the earpiece, soft, but tinged with a lethal edge.

Blair nodded to him.

Noah moved back from the door and lowered the dart gun out of his way as he braced to kick the door beside the door handle.

"Breaching in three, two," Deacon counted out over the mics, "one."

Noah used all the frustration of his nightmares to power the kick that shattered not only the locking mechanism but a good portion of the door. Blair moved fast to hold the door and stay down out of the way as Noah went in and aimed at the chair, he knew a guard would be sitting in, trying to stay awake. The man's eyes rounded in shock, and he lifted his hands high. As soon as Noah saw the thick band around his throat, he lowered the dart gun. "On the floor." He rasped, fighting the emotion trying to bleed through his resolve to do this right and not fall apart. He'd been that man, but experience had taught him that not all that wore the collars could be trusted.

"One for pickup at the back door," Blair said as he knelt and bound his hands behind his back.

"I got him." York came through the door in the hall and toward them.

"Need a hand upstairs."

York lifted the man to his feet, and they disappeared back through the doorway.

"Coming out the front with two for the center" Calum's steady tone informed them.

Blair held Noah's look, trying to assess his state of mind.

"I'll take the basement." He said to him, then heard his own voice echo in his ear.

Blair gave him a quick nod and moved to go help Konner upstairs.

Noah moved along the hall, into the kitchen like he'd been here yesterday, knowing nothing had changed, it never did. When he reached the basement door, his throat threatened to close when he saw the bolt lock was engaged. Someone was down there. The last time he'd seen this door was when he was dragged up from below, barely conscious. His body had finally reached the point of numbness, and the lashes no longer felt. He remembered the blood running down his chest but didn't know it was real. This door, on the other side of it, was real.

Reaching into his pocket, he pulled out his flashlight and slid the bolt across before he could start remembering more. The smell of fear and unbathed body odor hit his nose before he could take the first step down. His cat tensed, remembering with him how evil this place was. His cat had been his only comfort through this, but both were prisoners.

He forced his feet to move until he reached the tiled floor below. Moving the flashlight slowly, he was relieved to see there was only one down here. "One in the basement," he informed the others. Stepping around the support pole, he shone the light on the wall, hoping he didn't see what he knew was going to be there. "Chained to the fucking wall." He growled, "do we have bolt cutters?" He checked the rest of the area, just to be sure she was the only one down here.

"Bear can rip it from the wall." Calum's voice was without emotion.

"Send him down here." He turned to where he knew the light switch was. "Watch your eyes. I'm turning on the light." He told her and flicked the switch without delay.

"On my way," Bear announced.

His nose told him that she'd been down here a long time, which was odd, to say the least. A few days was usually the length of time they were kept down here. He stuffed the flashlight in his pocket, and went toward her, not giving his mind time to recount the past—again. There was no need for it, he would later in his dreams, and the next day and forever after that.

He couldn't look her in the face, he just couldn't do that. "It's okay," he tried to assure her, but knew it never could be, "I'm here to get you out." He kept his eyes on the chain connected to her ankle, it was swollen and bruised, confirming she'd been down here a long time. Still avoiding looking at her face, he held out his hand, "can you get up? Sit on the mattress while we get that off you?"

A shaking cool hand was placed in his. He squeezed it lightly, hoping to offer her some form of comfort, even though he knew no such thing was possible. When she sat stiffly on the cot, he dropped to a knee to check out her ankle.

"I remember you."

Noah's head popped up and he looked into the very same green eyes from his nightmares.

"You tried to save me." She whispered with a hoarse voice that hadn't been used in a while.

Noah's cat stilled; his muscles locked up with tension. It was her. The one they said was his mate. He swallowed, trying to find his voice. She was alive and was right here in front of him. He blinked and opened his eyes wide. She was real.

Chapter Four

"What are we looking at?" Bear came bounding down the stairs. "What the fuck." He came over and looked at the chain attached to the wall. Picking up the chain, he looked down at Noah, "watch this doesn't fly out and smack her."

Noah jolted into action and quickly knelt on the cot, placing his back between her and the wall. If the chain went wild, it would hit him and not her. He looked down at the dark hair of the woman and wanted to reach out and touch it, do something, offer her a silent apology for failing her years before. He couldn't believe she was still here in this house. They never stayed here long.

"Okay, here we go. Just hope it's not reinforced on the other side." Bear's voice was low and focused.

Noah heard the wall give way to the force of the man standing beside him and then the chain clatter to the floor.

"Three women and children coming out." Konner's voice startled him; Noah had forgotten what was happening outside of this space.

"We'll get the chain off once we're outside." Bear stepped back and then looked down at her, "can you walk?" He moved closer.

Noah got off the cot and placed himself between her and the other male. "Go help outside." He barked at him.

Bear shrugged and turned without comment. "We're going to need to get the chain off her ankle." He said into the mic.

"Bring her out, I'll deal with it." That was Deacon's voice.

Noah looked down to see those green eyes focused on him.

"Wait, you're taking me out of here?" She stood up and then winced in pain when the weight was on her ankle.

Noah grabbed the chain off the floor and wrapped it over his arm, and then bent and scooped her up into his arms. His cat started moving inside him, in a way that made him think it was trying to get closer to her. He didn't have time to figure it out, he had to get her out of here.

She wrapped her arms around his neck, but still held herself stiff. "I can't leave." Her voice shook, "I have to know where Aspyn is."

He moved up the stairs, in an awkward way, they weren't very wide. "The others are being brought out."

"Is she here? Did they find her?"

The panic in her tone felt like razors slicing into him. He stopped at the top of the stairs, bracing himself with his shoulder, and hit the button on his earpiece. "Is one of them named Aspyn?" He asked and then started to walk through the house to the front door.

"Just getting names now," Kobie said in reply.

"Doing the last sweep, looking for secret doors and shit." Blair's voice came over the mic.

"No Aspyn."

Noah clenched his jaw, he didn't know who Aspyn was, but he'd find her. Anyone that had helped her to get through this was now important to him. "What's your name?" He'd almost forgotten that was one of the first things they were supposed to find out.

"Emersyn." She said quickly, "uh, Knox. Emersyn Knox."

The way she said it, he knew she hadn't used her own last name in a long time.

He turned to fit through the front door. "Emersyn Knox." He said it over the mic.

Deacon came jogging toward them as he went down the driveway. "Let's see what we're dealing with." He hunched down so he could look at the lock holding the chain around her ankle. "I can do that." He motioned to the van where Shaelan stood. "Get her sitting and I'll get this lock off."

Noah didn't want to let go of her; he didn't want the other males near her. His teeth were clenched so tight, it hurt as he forced his body to move to the van and set her in the doorway.

"I want to start an IV as soon as you get that off." Shaelan's voice broke through and the state of her health took precedence over the war inside him. A war he didn't know how to fight.

Deacon turned to Gia, "I need something fine and..."

"Oh, I know." She turned and darted toward her van.

Noah was crouched down beside her, still holding the weight of the chain in his hands. He picked up her foot and gently rested it on his knee. Emersyn was looking around at the others, clearly searching for this Aspyn.

"The house is clear." Blair's said over the coms.

He looked at her again, wanting to tell her, but he was afraid to with the panic on her face. Grinding his teeth, he kept his mouth shut. He wanted the chain off and her to at least be in Shaelan's care before he told her Aspyn wasn't here.

"Okay, here we go." Deacon knelt beside him and leaned over her foot.

"That's a handy skill."

Noah turned to see Calum smirking as he watched Deacon without pause pick the lock attaching the chain to her ankle.

"It wasn't until now." Deacon said slowly as he focused on the lock.

When the weight of the chain in his hand changed, Noah looked to see if she was free.

"I need five minutes," Shaelan said to no one in particular.

Noah turned to see Creed was still perched on top of the house.

Calum waved his hand in a circle telling him to do a circle of the area and check that it was still clear. "We'll get the others loaded up." He turned on his heel and went to the van behind them.

"Emersyn," Shaelan said in a soft voice, "I want to put an IV in, you're very dehydrated."

Emersyn's head snapped around to look at her. "I can't—leave." She shook her head, "I have to be here when he comes back..." She gave Noah a panicked look.

He stood up slowly, "we'll..."

She jumped out of the van and hobbled toward Blair as he came out of the house. "Where is she?" She screamed at him, her voice cracking. "What have you done with her?" She reached him and threw herself at him.

Blair caught her and held her, looking down at her with shock on his face.

"I'm sorry. I'm sorry." Emersyn pulled from his grasp and slid down him to drop at his feet. Grasping his pant leg, she sobbed, "I'm sorry. It won't happen again." She looked up at him, "I'm trying. I really am."

The chain slid from Noah's hand as he got up. No one else was moving. Blair looked around at everyone, a gobsmacked expression on his face. Noah started toward her slowly, not wanting to startle her.

Blair bent forward, placing his hand on her shoulder, "Hey, it's okay," he crooned, "we'll find her."

Emersyn jerked back like he'd hit her, and she scrambled to her feet. "You're not him." She put her hand over her mouth, a high pitch wailing coming from her throat. "Oh my god, you're not him." She spun, meeting Noah's concerned look as he came up beside her, "how am I going to find her if I leave?"

Noah looked at Blair, his expression said to fix this. If he had a clue, he would have gladly. "Emersyn, we'll find your friend..."

"My friend?" She gasped, "Aspyn is my *daughter*." She jerked her head around and looked at Blair again, "I thought you were her father, I'm sorry." She put her hand over her forehead, "I haven't slept, I just," she motioned to him, "in this light you look like him."

Noah watched all the color drain from Blair's face. He looked from him to Calum who was moving toward them from the other side. Noah's chest hurt, he felt lightheaded as the pieces fit together slowly in his head. His cat went from wary, to unsure then rage. She had a child. Someone had touched what was theirs.

Gia and Shaelan rushed by him to reach Emersyn.

"We'll find her." Gia said as she placed a hand on her shoulder, "trust me, these men *will* find her."

Emersyn looked at her and then to Shaelan, who was nodding and putting her arm around her for support.

"We'll find your daughter," Shaelan said in a soft tone as her eyes flicked to her mate, telling him he had a new mission.

The tears rolled down Emersyn's cheeks, making her green eyes glisten like emerald gems. Noah sucked in air when he realized he'd been holding his breath. He watched the women lead her back to the van and help her inside it.

"Fuck." Blair hissed out a breath. "Lindon," he said in a whisper.

"Yeah," Calum confirmed and then just stood there.

Noah spun on his heel. He went over to the van and looked inside as he picked up the chain. Shaelan was putting the IV in Emersyn's arm as Gia spoke to her in a quiet reassuring tone. Spinning on his heel, he walked to the other van that Webb and Sloane were standing beside. He meant to hand him the chain to stow in the vehicle, but as he reached it something inside him cracked wide open and he lifted the chain and brought it down on the van like he was wielding a whip. The sound of it hitting the metal only made his anger more intense as he did it again and again.

"Hey," Strong hands stopped his arm in mid-air.

The fury blinding him cleared and he looked to see Blair yanking the chain from his hand.

"It's good, bud, we got her out." He nodded, a wary look on his face.

Noah jerked his arm out of his grip and stepped back, raising both hands in the air so he wouldn't hit him or anything else. "It's not good, Blair." Noah shook his head, "not in any way." He pointed to the van the women were in, "she's, my mate." He whispered it, momentarily shocked to say it out loud for the first time, he pointed to his chest, "these scars, these reminders," he gave Calum a warning look to stay back, "I got these when I failed her years ago, when I tried to *free* her from this," he slapped his hand toward the house, "vile place." Each syllable was spat. "I. Failed. Her." His voice cracked, "and now," he looked at the men standing around him like they were going to try to subdue him, "I have to find her daughter that *your dead* brother fathered," he huffed out a breath so fast his chest felt concaved, "against her will." He whispered the last words and then just stood there looking at the van that she was inside. The expressions on the faces of those standing nowhere near him told him he had just broadcast that through his mic for all to hear. Panting, he stepped back. When his back hit the van, he slid down it to crouch on the ground. Dropping his head into his hands, he tried to remember how to breathe. His throat felt raw, his chest sent pains through his entire body. He was shaking so hard he couldn't move.

Someone peeled his hands from his face and held his look with fierce determination. It was Kobie squatting in front of him. She held his look with a level expression. "I can't even grasp what you've been through," she said in a hushed tone, "are going through." She released his wrists and gave him a hard look, "but right now," she pointed to the van, "she doesn't need to see this." Her soft tone changed, "right now, she needs to find strength in those around her." She leaned back from him further, "you need to get up. Go to her and *be her* strength." She nodded her head slowly.

Noah sucked in a breath and nodded his head quickly, internally chastising himself to get his ass off the pavement and stand up. Calum walked away, his phone against his ear. Straightening to his full height, Noah took a deep breath and then nodded down at Kobie. He glanced at Blair, wanting to give him an apologetic look, but couldn't find the emotion to do it. Bear held out a bottle of water to him, he took it and looked down at it. "Where would your brother take her?" He opened it and drank it down fast.

"I don't know, but we'll find out." Blair looked at Calum, then turned back to him. "He's probably filing Devin in," rubbing his hand through his hair, he sighed, "I guess questioning those that ran with Lindon would be a good place to start."

Noah crushed the empty bottle in his hand and held it out to Bear. "They better do that fast." He turned to the van Emersyn was in, "before I do it." With long strides, he walked to the van.

"Change of plans." Calum's voice came through the earpiece. "Noah, Blair, and I will be going to a safe house, everyone else proceeds with original plans."

"Only Knox I can find in the registry isn't in a local clan." Illias' voice sounded in Noah's ear. "I'm just packing up. I'll dig more after I move and get back to you."

Noah looked inside the van to see Emersyn leaning back in the seat, her eyes closed. Her black hair was hanging limp and unwashed around her face, the evidence of her lack of care and sleep was clear by the hallow darkened rings around her eyes, but despite that, she was the most beautiful woman he'd ever seen. He climbed in quietly and sat on the seat the furthest from her.

"She'll be okay for now, until we get to the house," Shaelan told him quietly, compassion bleeding from the expression on her face. "I'll see you there." She got out of the van and closed the door.

The front doors opened, and Gia and Deacon climbed in at the same time. Gia adjusted the mirror and looked at him through it. Noah jerked his chin letting her know he had himself under control now.

"All right, let's get to the house," she said in a light tone, "and get Emersyn a nice hot bath, and clean clothes."

Emersyn opened her eyes and looked at her, but she didn't say a word in response. Turning her head, her gaze connected with him. There were no words he could speak to reassure her that her life was somehow better, that the past was gone, so he just held her look and hoped that she could understand, somehow, that he wouldn't rest until her daughter was back in her arms and Tomas and all those responsible for the torments she'd suffered were erased from the planet's population.

Chapter Five

Noah stood in the small yard and looked at the house. Inside the three women were looking after Emersyn. His mind was stuck on a loop, replaying six years ago when he'd first seen her, that part was nothing new, but now it had an extended play version adding seeing her chained to the wall. When he'd looked into her eyes in that basement, all his nightmares and dreams came true in one moment.

This house was small, and he had no idea how long they were going to be there, but eight people inside were going to have the walls closing in on him. It had been three hours and Illias still hadn't gotten back to them about her family. He didn't know if she wanted to go back to her family if there were surviving members, but if that's what she wanted, he'd make sure it happened.

Family. He blew out a breath. He still hadn't spoken to or seen any of his own. Shaking his head, he kicked at the ground with the toe of his boot. It was worse than that. Ed had told him to come to see him when he was ready, and that had never happened. He didn't even know if his parents were both still alive. How could he ever face them? It had been his responsibility to watch over his little sister, Carlene and he'd failed. The last time he'd seen her sweet little face, she was four and it was when the men that had taken them pulled her from his arms.

Spinning around, he glared at the fence, he wanted to go for a run, his cat was demanding it, but this area wasn't in the middle of nowhere and he didn't trust that he wouldn't end up killing some neighborhood dog in a blind rage.

Blair and Deacon had gone back out to get groceries and other supplies. He shook his head because that wouldn't look out of place in this small town, two large men roaming around the grocery store together. Deacon looked like a burly lumberjack and Blair, some kind of playboy rockstar.

Calum came out the door, a somber look on his face. He walked toward him, his eyes scanning Noah, assessing him. "Shae says her ankle will be fine in a few days."

Noah nodded; his guts were too tense to speak.

"There's a few minor scrapes and bumps, but nothing serious." Calum stopped and crossed his arms over his chest, holding Noah's look.

"Scars?" He could barely say the word out loud, the thought that her body could be marred like his own made it hard to breathe.

"Some," Calum jerked his chin in his direction, "nothing like yours."

Noah blew out a quick breath and nodded some more. "Good."

"Deacon and Gia will be leaving when he gets back." He moved over to the fence and crouched down, resting his back against it, "Konner called on route home, there are two members of Deacon's clan being smuggled across some borders tomorrow."

"Smuggled across borders?" He'd hoped for a distraction from the cycle of self-loathsomeness stirring in his head, this was a good one.

"Yeah, Shep knows about them, but this isn't being done through the regular channels." Calum watched him for a long moment before continuing. "There are some issues with the treatment of clans and ambassadors not being allies."

Noah gave him a hard look. "Ambassadors with the Alliance?"

Calum just nodded.

"I don't know how any of it works," Noah shrugged, "not really. Issues in other countries really aren't my problem." He rolled his eyes, he had so many problems, most of them were internal that his mind couldn't even begin to process the workings of the organization he was now with.

"It's all of our problems now." Calum stood up and glanced at the side of the house. "What's happening with Tomas we are pretty sure stems from other countries."

Noah stared at him for a second, trying to process what he was saying. "Tomas is working with other countries?"

"That's the way it's looking now."

Noah reached up and rubbed his hand across his forehead and then squeezed his temples, hoping the pressure in his head would go away. Opening his eyes, he looked at him, "what's being done about that?"

"To be determined." Calum waved his hand around, "we're just focusing on close to home right now. Until we can pin down some help on the other side of borders."

Noah nodded, "yeah." He looked at the house for the hundredth time, wondering how they were doing inside. "How did, uh, the other teams do?"

"Success on all fronts. Twenty-two women and children. Fifteen males."

Noah looked back at him, noting the way he said males, meaning they were guards or collared and doing Tomas' bidding. "Any of Tomas' people?"

"No." His tone was low.

Noah's muscles tensed. If those that worked with Tomas were out there, the damage they would cause other shifters would never end. "When are we going to go after them?"

Calum blew out a breath, "not until we find all the locations they're holding our kind." He shrugged, "if we go after the top people, then the lower ones will panic, and we'll never find them or where they're being held."

Noah nodded; it made sense. "We've gotten almost all the places I know of." He lifted his hands and pressed on either temple; the pressure was bad today.

"Before our last break, they found ledgers and records…"

Dropping his hands, Noah looked at him again, "of?"

"Where ours were being shipped or came from. One of Konner's clan members helped to decipher it."

Noah squatted down, mostly of his own accord, before his legs gave out. "This is never going to end."

Calum moved closer and placed his hand on his shoulder, giving it a light squeeze. "We'll end it, we just have to move slow and carefully, and not rush it."

Noah nodded, keeping his eyes down.

"You should go rest for a while, we're here until things are sorted out."

Standing up, Noah rolled his shoulders, trying to get the muscles to relax, even just slightly. "I won't rest until I know the plan."

Calum studied him silently for a few moments. "When was the last time you slept?"

Noah attempted to shrug it off, "before the ops, I'm good though, just don't like being on hold."

Calum smirked, "get used to it, we're going to be doing a lot of it for a while until we figure out each stop."

The van pulled up to the house, and both turned to watch Blair and Deacon get out.

"I'm going to tell Deacon the good news." Calum looked amused; Noah had no idea why.

Noah looked at the fence again, his cat didn't want to go for a run now, but he did. Rubbing his hand over his chest, feeling the ridges of the scars under his shirt. His cat, according to Coop didn't behave the same way as most. His cat was afraid to come out and didn't understand that he wasn't going to get beaten when he came out. Noah had no false hopes of ever being normal, with or without fur.

"Kobie and Shaelan are getting some food happening in there."

He turned to see Blair coming toward him. He wasn't hungry, never really was, but he understood he needed to eat. "Great." He mumbled, hoping it sounded more enthusiastic than it did to his own ears.

"I thought you'd be in there talking to Emersyn." He shrugged, "she's a little shaky, but open to conversation."

Noah frowned, not sure how he felt about Blair talking to her. "There's not much to discuss until we have an idea of where to find her daughter."

Blair braced his legs wide and crossed his arms over his chest, "but she's your mate."

Noah held his look, waiting for him to say more.

"Even before I knew about that with Kobie, I wanted to see or talk to her all the time." He cocked his head to the side, "don't you want to go in and talk to her," he shrugged, "see her?"

Noah looked at the ground, flicking his eyes to look at the other man a few times before exhaling the breath he held. "I'm sure she's fine. Shaelan is a good healer."

Blair made a scoffing noise, "I don't get it, she's your mate."

Noah needed him to drop it, just walk away. "What good is me being in there going to do?" He squeezed his eyes shut for a second, trying to reign in the anger building inside him. Opening them he looked at the house, "yeah we're mates, but there is no happily ever after here, Blair." He shook his head, "what do I have to offer her? Seeing me is just a constant reminder that I left her behind six years ago to be abused."

Blair opened his mouth and then snapped it shut. Shaking his head, he looked at the house quickly, "so you're going to find her daughter and then wish her a happy life and go back to Ed's?"

"I don't know yet."

Blair raised his eyebrows and opened his mouth to speak, but before he could, Calum called them from the door.

"Foods on, come inside so we can try to sort some things out."

Noah stood there, his gaze locked on Blairs, waiting to see if he was going to continue.

Blair gave his head a shake, "I'm here if you need to talk." Turning he went back toward the door that Calum stood in, watching him.

Sucking in a deep breath, Noah clamped down on demons trying to make him think of the day he'd first seen Emersyn Knox. Exhaling, he started for the door with long strides. They weren't going to win this time, he had to focus on figuring out where her daughter might be held. Despite what she'd been through, her child was a part of her, and she would never have a chance of some kind of normalcy without her.

Noah sneered at the thought of what he was going to do to the people keeping her away from her mother. They may wish for death when he was done with them.

Chapter Six

Emersyn sat on the small couch, her foot propped up on pillows, and watched the interaction with the others. The ice pack on her ankle was helping to dull the ache but she found without the pain, she had no distraction from thought.

"Are you sure you don't want more to eat?" Shaelan peeked her head around the door of the kitchen and smiled at her.

"No. Thank you." She hadn't eaten much, but she felt too full. It had been a long time since she'd had that much food available to her. She frowned down at the mug in her hands, she wasn't even sure how many days had passed since someone had come down to feed her.

Was she really free? Keeping her gaze on the liquid in the cup, she went over the night before in her head. He'd came and freed her, that wasn't a dream. Lifting her gaze, she looked over to where the man, Noah, stood. He'd been standing there by the window since they'd all eaten. He hadn't said a word or looked at her, but he'd freed her. He was her mate; she'd heard him say that while they were trying to take her collar off. She frowned and raised a hand to her throat, checking once more it was gone. It still felt like it was there. When her fingers brushed over the chaffed skin, she smiled despite the discomfort of touching it.

Turning her head, she looked at him. "Thank you." She said in a hoarse voice.

His head snapped to look at her.

"For-for freeing me." She offered him a helpless smile, "I don't think I said that."

He just nodded his head a couple of times and then stood there, muscles taut, silent, and watching her. His brows were furrowed, and the angst bled from his eyes when they connected with her own gaze. "How's your ankle?"

His voice was deep and softer than it had been when she'd heard him talk at the meal. "Numb right now."

His head moved slightly again, acknowledging he'd heard her, then he turned and looked back out the window again.

Shaelan came into the room. "Are you feeling up to a few questions? We need to figure some things out and you may be able to help."

Emersyn looked at her. "About finding my daughter?" She straightened.

"That and a few other things."

The caring look on her face, made Emersyn's voice fail her, so she nodded and started to shift off the couch.

"No, you can stay there, I'll just sit on the floor." Shaelan came over and sat down. "Some of this is for the Alliance, piecing things together sometimes takes many perspectives."

The Alliance? It was real? She'd heard whispers about it before. If she had to answer questions to get her little girl back, she'd do it until no voice remained.

"How old is your daughter?" She opened a notebook and set it on her lap.

"Aspyn will be five this winter." She glanced to see Kobie come in and sit in the chair on the other side of the room. The tall man that looked like her baby's father came in and stood beside her, leaning against the wall. She still couldn't believe how much he looked like Lindon. Dragging her eyes away from him, she looked back to Shaelan, her expression was patient. "Uh, I don't know her birth date, just that the snow was deep when she was born."

Shaelan wrote something in her book. "Had you shifted before you had her?"

Emersyn shook her head. "I've—" she looked around to see the other man had come into the room as well. "I've never shifted."

Shaelan turned and gave the man, Calum, a quick look. "The collar prevented it?"

Emersyn lifted her hand to her throat, having to check once more it was truly gone.

"You already know that Shaelan," Noah said in a low voice.

She gave him a quick look and nodded, before writing more. "I know, Noah, but we have to keep checking in case other methods are used."

"Like drugs?" Emersyn added.

"Yes," Shaelan nodded.

"I was given a choice, drugs or a collar." She put her hand on her stomach, "I was pregnant, so I chose the collar."

"I see." She looked to Calum again and the expression on his face when he glanced at her told Emersyn they were mates.

The thought made her look back at Noah. He wasn't looking at her, just staring at the floor in front of him.

"Are you able to share more details? When you were taken and," Shaelan lifted her hand, "the events after."

Events? Emersyn wanted to laugh but didn't. She lifted the cup and took a sip of the tea, while she thought of how to tell these people what she'd been through. "I was eight. There were a few of us taken, we were," she sighed, "being kids, playing too far from the village." She shrugged, there was nothing to add to that. Once she had a normal life and was a normal child. She cleared her throat, "they took us to a camp," she looked down at the cup, finding it easier to speak without looking at the compassionate look on Kobie and Shaelan's faces. "Uh, it was in the mountains, buildings with many beds in them," she frowned, "barracks, I think they called them."

"Do you know where in the mountains?"

She looked up to Calum and shook her head. "No. I don't remember the trip there. I think they drugged us."

"Please continue."

Dragging her gaze away from the large man, she turned back to Shaelan, "we were treated well, games, food," she blew out a breath, "the women watching us were nice." She blinked, trying to recall what any of them looked like and couldn't. "We were grouped in; I think what clan types we were from."

"How many were there? How old were you when you left?"

Closing her eyes, she took a deep breath and tried to stay calm. She opened them again but looked at the pattern on the couch and not at any eyes filled with pity. "I can't be sure, twenty, maybe."

"How long were you there?"

"Fifteen, I think," she shrugged, "we didn't really celebrate birthdays, so I can't be sure."

Shaelan nodded and wrote it down. "Were you taken somewhere close?"

Emersyn shook her head, "no, we went on a boat," she grimaced, "I was sick the whole trip." She paused when Calum and Blair exchanged a look, "then, uh, a plane, then to the house." She looked away from them back to Shaelan, "not the house you got me out of, another one."

"Okay." Shaelan looked over at Noah, "sounds similar, minus the boat trip."

He crossed his arms over his chest and looked at her, a cold expression on his face, "there were no games for the boys."

"True, and we know they separate the boys and girls into different camps." She said quietly as she watched him.

He watched her for a long awkward moment, "at least I know my sister was treated well for a while."

"Your sister was taken too?" Emersyn shifted to look at him more easily and discovered her ankle wasn't as numb as she'd thought.

"Yes. She was four." His tone was empty as he said it.

"I'm sorry." It was an automatic response, but she meant it. "Have you found her?"

He shook his head, "no."

"She might be in the records, Noah," Kobie offered him, a soft look on her face.

He turned to Calum, "I didn't even hear the names of others that were got out."

"I can get them for you." He pulled a phone out of his pocket and started tapping the screen of it.

"What was her name?" Emersyn wanted to do something to make him feel better, she'd encountered a lot of women over the years and for the most part, she remembered all their names. It gave her something to keep her mind busy.

"Carlene." He said it in a soft breath.

If it weren't for her exceptional hearing, she may not have heard him. Taking a ragged breath, she quickly looked away from him. It was an unusual name. She had known a Carlene; she was a few years younger than Emersyn and she'd tried to shield her when possible. She had never been considered healthy. "I'm sorry." She forced herself to look over at him, "she was quite sick, I don't know with what, but she didn't make it." A tear rolled down her cheek, and she swatted it away to hold his look and offer him at least that. The truth, the knowing—to end his wondering.

Noah continued to stand there and look at her. "How old was she?"

Emersyn frowned, trying to recall her own age at the time. "Uh, I was around seventeen, so fifteen? I can't be sure." She sucked in a breath and needed to offer him more than that. "She never," she blinked back tears, "she was never—abused." It was the only word her mind would allow her to speak

His brows knit together for a moment as he looked at her, then he closed his eyes briefly and nodded his head in a jerky motion. "So, before they," he sucked in a rough breath and nodded again, "thank you. At least I know now." He turned back and looked out the window.

Shaelan cleared her throat and stood up, "I'm going to make more tea. We'll talk more after that." She rushed from the room. Calum turned on the spot and followed her out.

Blair moved over and placed his hand on Noah's shoulder for a second and then turned away. "I'm going to grab some air."

"I'll come with you." Kobie jumped up and followed her mate out.

Emersyn sat there and looked at how stiff Noah held himself, his shoulders squared as he stared out the window. Her chest was tight. Setting the cup down, she pushed the ice pack off her foot and swung her leg off the couch. Wincing at the sharp stabs shooting up her leg, she clenched her teeth together and stood up. Her ankle burned, but she didn't care and dragged the heavy foot across the floor as she half-stepped, half-hopped over toward him. When she was close enough, she braced her hand on the wall. "I'm sorry. I probably could have told you in a kinder way."

He turned his head and looked down at her. "You shouldn't be on your foot." His voice was barely more than a whisper. He glanced down at her foot, then back up to her face. "I think I already knew, somehow."

Emersyn nodded, "there's a feeling deep in the pit of your stomach and you just know things." She couldn't argue with that, she'd lived it for years watching women come and leave, never to be seen again. She reached out to touch him, and then froze, her hand a few inches from his arm. She couldn't do it. Dropping her hand, she made a fist and held it tight at her side. "I know Aspyn is still alive. I feel it."

His eyes weren't brown or green, but a mix, making them look amber in spots. Right now, they were observing her face in a slow manner that had her holding her breath. "Please sit back down and rest." He held out his hand to her.

Looking at his hand, she unclenched her fingers and placed it in his, so she wouldn't have to put too much weight on her foot. "Do you," she sucked in a breath as the burning continued, "have any other family?"

"Yeah." His grip on her hand was gentle, but something told her that if her step faltered, he wouldn't let her fall.

"You can let them know now." She glanced up at him as she turned to sit back down, "so they can have closure." She watched a haunted look enter his eyes, and his jaw muscles twitch.

"I haven't spoken to them yet." He said barely more than a whisper.

"You should. A parent needs their child almost as much as the child needs them." He held her hand until she was completely sitting, then knelt to lift her foot back up onto the couch.

His gaze moved over her face again, then released her foot and leaned back from her. "I was supposed to be watching out for her."

Emersyn grabbed his wrist before he could stand up. "You were a boy and the people that took us are to blame, not you." She shook her head, "never you."

He looked down, shielding his eyes with his long lashes. "I'll go get you a fresh ice pack." He grabbed the other one and stood up. Before she could say a thing, he was out of the room. In a moment of weakness, she wanted to cry for him. She would have too, cried for the little boy that blamed himself for his young sister being taken, but she knew if she opened the dam, it would be too hard to close it off again. She had to keep it together and help these people find her daughter.

Chapter Seven

Noah perched on the windowsill and watched her. Shaelan was checking her throat and ankle again. He didn't know what she was putting on it, but the stench he'd be able to taste for days at least. Everyone had come back except Calum—who was on the phone. Noah was trying to avoid the sad looks Kobie kept giving him, so he watched Emersyn instead.

She was doing a good job hiding how freaked out she was right now, but Noah saw every nervous twitch and how she flinched when anyone in the room moved. Tomorrow it would hit her, the fact that she was really free. If he remembered right, the nightmares held off for about a week—right after the exhausted sleeping phase wore off.

He hoped, for her, she was spared them. How anyone could make a new life and put all that out of their mind, he didn't know—but he wished it for her. The nightmares and fear of sleeping to go away. He hoped for his mind to let it go and not fill his head with thoughts of worthlessness and defeat. Those thoughts came to him hundreds of times a day, and functioning like they weren't happening was draining, emotionally and physically.

Emersyn was doing great, but he saw all the little tells that marked her as both a victim and survivor. He knew her only chance at a semi-normal life was if she had her daughter, and he was going to do that for her. He was going to do that for Carlene because the compassionate little girl he remembered who talked to flowers and wild creatures would want that from him.

"Sorry," Calum came into the room, "Illias called with information, and I had to go over it with Devin." He turned and looked at Emersyn. "He found your clan. You're originally from an island in South America. Your parents and brothers are still there."

Noah watched relief fill her, but it was brief.

"The problem being," Calum continued, "is if we reach out to them, we run the risk of alerting those that are working for the very people we're trying to shut down."

"Don't contract them." Emersyn blurted out, "I can't—I don't," she looked down at her hands, "it's safer for everyone if you don't," she looked back at Calum, "for now."

Calum nodded slowly, "that leaves the issue of where to send you."

"Send me?" Emersyn looked from Calum to Blair, then Noah, "I'm not going anywhere until my daughter is found." She motioned her hand to encompass the room, "if you're finding Aspyn, then I'm staying with you."

"It might be easier for you if you went to the campground where Rayne…"

"I'm *not* going to another camp." She gave Blair a hard look.

"What about Ed's?" Calum looked to Blair.

Noah scowled, "you plan on tossing her into the bunkhouse with all of us *men?*"

"She can use one of the guardhouses at our place," Kobie glanced up at Blair, "then she's with her own kind at least," she gave Emersyn a welcoming smile, "there's lots of room to run when you decide to shift."

The mere mention of shifting made her stiffen.

"It's a bit chaotic there," Blair spoke in a soft tone while looking at his mate, "especially with all the extra families now and kids…"

"There's children?" Emersyn looked at Kobie quickly, "other children for Aspyn to play with would be wonderful."

"Then it's decided." Kobie gave Blair a big smile and then looked at Calum. "She's coming with us."

Noah watched Blair's expression change from shock to contemplation. There were so many people there now. Noah volunteered to do menial things around Ed's to avoid being on the task force at Blair's while construction and endless chattering people were. "It's a bit," he caught the warning look Blair gave him, "busy over there." He motioned to Emersyn, "it might be overwhelming." He knew at first, that he couldn't do a lot of people, still couldn't some days.

"Oh," Shaelan turned to Blair, "you could move the trailer Jesse used to the back by the trees."

Blair rubbed his hand over his hair, "that would save kicking Cale out of his place."

"As long as I can be outside, I will be fine."

Noah watched Emersyn as she said it. He knew all about closed-in spaces and how bad the demons of the past were if it was dark and had no windows.

"Okay. Now that we've settled that." Calum glanced at Blair again, with amusement in his eyes. "Let's figure out where your daughter is." He gave Emersyn a slow appraising look, "why was she taken? How long ago?" His expression softened, "anything you can remember might be relevant."

Emersyn clutched one of the pillows to her chest, Noah wasn't sure if it was out of fear or comfort, but his cat stirred inside him showing concern. Noah clenched his jaw and tried to communicate that now was not the time to have an opinion.

"He thought I was," Emersyn swallowed and gasped a breath like she was struggling to remember how to breathe, "he thought I was purposely doing something to prevent my cycle—because I've never had one."

"That's ridiculous." Kobie stood up, "there's no way to prevent it," she scowled, "if there were, I'd know."

Blair smirked.

"Bad living conditions, inadequate diet, and poor health seem to be common with those we've found that have never had their cycle." Shaelan said in a matter-of-fact tone, "that's likely the reason," she assured Emersyn.

"I tried to tell him it wasn't anything I was doing."

"Him?" Noah said it out loud without meaning to.

Emersyn turned to him, and he could see the fear in her eyes before she said his name. "Lindon." The sorrow in her eyes felt like it was burning all the way to his soul—if he had one. "He-he," she turned to look at Blair, "looks a lot like you."

The change in Blair's demeanor was immediate and severe, it sucked all the air out of the room. "He *was my* brother." He spat.

"Was?" Her voice cracked with emotion. "He's dead?"

Blair held her look, "I killed him for crimes against our kind and killing our parents."

"He's dead." She whispered. Her eyes glistened with tears as she looked around at each person in the room.

Noah felt his blood heating with fury as he watched her. Was she going to miss him?

"He'll never be back." She closed her eyes and leaned back, exhaling a loud and very audible breath.

Relief. Noah took a quick breath and blew it out to settle himself. Not miss him. Relief that he's gone.

Emersyn's eyes popped open. "What about Aspyn? How will we find her if he's gone?"

"She wasn't with him." Noah said quickly, "there were no women or children with them at that house."

"Was the house in a city?" She turned to Calum. "He wasn't keeping her in a city. I know that from the pictures he showed me." She shook her head, "he came every few days and showed me pictures of her on his phone, her playing in a creek or-or walking on a path, there were no buildings in them." Jerking her head, she looked at Blair, "I thought he was punishing me by not coming back for so long..."

"How long were you in that basement?" Kobie was on the edge of the chair now.

"I'm not sure, it's hard to keep track." She looked down at the pillow and squeezed it in her arms, "I thought maybe a month, but it could have been longer, I can't be sure."

Noah looked at Calum, "what happens with the phones and personal items after we get them?"

Calum was looking at his phone, "I'm finding out right now." He tapped the screen of his phone a few times then held it out in his hand. He'd put it on speaker.

"I'm a popular man today."

He'd called Illias.

"Illias, what happens to phones when we take down a location?"

"Didn't see that question coming. We do a deep dive into them and then dump everything off them onto a secure server to weed through them when there's time—which there hadn't been lately, why?"

"We need photos from Lindon Elden's phone."

Emersyn was staring at the phone, her eyes wide.

"Is that the one Blair eliminated?"

"It is." Calum's gaze flicked to Blair briefly.

"Okay, two seconds, and I'll be looking at them—what am I doing with them?"

"Can you send them to my phone, Blairs," he looked over at Noah, "and Noah's—we're trying to track down a young girl that was taken."

Illias made a clicking noise, "there's more than one child on this. All blonde, blue-eyed gems…"

"Send them all," Calum stated with a cold tone in his voice.

"Will do. It's a large file, so I might just pop them into a data file all of you can access and I'll send a link."

"Whatever works."

Noah's phone beeped at the same time as Blair's. He took it out of his pocket and opened the message. The room was completely silent as the others looked as well. Noah held his breath and quickly scrolled through the photos. He stopped at one of a cute child with snowy white hair. Her eyes were as light as Blair's, but the shape of them and her high cheekbones were just like her mother's. He pushed away from the window and went over to Emersyn. "This is Aspyn." It wasn't a question.

She gasped and reached out to clasp his hand in both of hers so he couldn't move the phone away. "I haven't seen this one."

"She looks like she has a little sass to her," Blair said.

Emersyn smiled and glanced at him. "Oh, just a bit." She swatted at the tear on her cheek. "Are there more?" She looked up at Noah.

The way she looked up at him, with such sorrow and hope in her eyes caused pain in his chest. He dropped down to one knee and turned the phone around. "Let's look."

She leaned closer to him, her scent smelled like home, he noticed with awe—or it would have if it wasn't smothered with fear, anxiety, and grief. He paused on each picture of Aspyn so she could look at it as long as she wanted.

"Calum?" Illias was still on the phone. "I can take the last known locations of that clan and see if anything in the pictures matches any topographic charts with the water, creeks, rivers—"

"Do that and send Devin a list of all of them. Raymond Hardy is having discussions with the men we found with Lindon, so send any information he can inquire about."

"All right, I'll get on that. How long are you staying there?"

Calum turned to look at Emersyn, "we're heading to Blair's in the morning."

"Got it, let me know when you're on the road so I can have the tracking app warmed up."

Shaclan smiled, "you think someone is stupid enough to try for us when we're with Calum?"

"Dumb people happen, Shaelan. I'll be in touch." Illias hung up.

Shaelan turned to Emersyn, "they'll find the location." She then turned to Calum, "we need to get her a phone or tablet or something, so she has the pictures of Aspyn."

Calum studied her for a moment, then nodded. "I'll see what's in the gear in the van."

Noah looked back to see Emersyn looking at the phone, a mother's pride on her face.

"She's really cute." He said and meant it.

A real smile lit up her face, "and isn't afraid to use it."

Kobie laughed and patted Blair on the chest, "guess she has something in common with her uncle."

"Hey," Blair gave her a hard look, "I can't help how good I look."

Kobie laughed more and then went into the kitchen.

"You are her uncle." A note of surprise was in Emersyn's voice. "I said I would never admit out loud that he was her father, but he's gone now."

Blair blew out a breath, "I don't even remember the clan, but I think it's time I introduced myself to them."

Calum raised an eyebrow. "You going to add more buildings?"

Blair winced, "hell no. I said I should introduce myself, not bring them all home."

Calum looked at him for a long silent moment. Noah wasn't sure what the look meant exactly, but he suspected it wasn't going to be as easy as Blair thought.

Chapter Eight

A long drive, without windows, was not what Noah needed. Normally he managed to cope with them, having the operation to focus on or the results of them, this time the source of his torment was sitting across from him beside Kobie. He could feel her tension, the anxiousness of riding in the vehicle, but she said nothing. He supposed the very idea that she had to endure this as part of a chain of events to get her daughter back was the reason why. She spent long moments looking at the tablet that Shaelan had put the pictures on. As sick as it was, he envied she had something to look at to distract her. Of course, being as it was her abducted daughter made him feel like the lowest form of being on earth for thinking it.

Kobie leaned over and looked at the tablet in Emersyn's hand, "she's beautiful."

Emersyn smiled, that kind of smile only a mother could have. "she's been my everything since the day I found out I was pregnant."

Shaelan turned in her seat, "was it a good pregnancy?"

Emersyn smiled, "only if you consider throwing up for nine months good." She sobered, "I felt like I was enormous by the end."

Noah looked at her flat stomach. He'd held her in his arms when he carried her out, there was no extra anything on her body. His cat moved inside him, almost chastising him for thinking about her body. Noah blew out a breath and leaned forward, holding the edges of the seat in a tight grip. "Where exactly are we?"

"Still a good two hours out," Calum answered without taking his eyes off the road.

"Should be a few good spots to stop and go for a quick run in this area," Blair said, a little louder than necessary.

Noah watched Calum glance in the mirror at him. Something was supposed to be exchanged in that look, but Noah was too distracted to figure it out. He was all for them stopping and him being able to get out of the van and breathe some fresh air. From here all he could see was the light snow falling on the windshield and the hypnotic, yet annoying swipe of the wipers going back and forth.

"I'll message Illias we're making a quick stop," Shaelan said as if it was already decided. "I wouldn't mind stretching my legs."

Calum glanced at her, "out of things to read?"

Shaelan laughed softly, "no, that will never happen, I just need a little air." She turned and looked at Emersyn briefly.

Noah wondered if all the others trapped inside the can on wheels were also picking up on the anxiety coming from Emersyn. He didn't blame her, not at all. If it were his child out there somewhere he'd be broadcasting a whole lot more than anxiety. He scowled and dragged his gaze from her, again, the chances of him ever having children of his own were pretty damn slim. What did he have to offer a child? Nights of restless wandering, moments of short temper, or the hours of self-loathing that brought him down so fast he never had time to prepare. No, he wouldn't put a child through having to live with a basket case for a father. He braced his weight as the van turned a corner. Not that he could ever do what was necessary to have one in the first place.

"Here should work. We can see far enough to keep watch." Calum said as he stopped the van.

Blair whipped the door open so fast that it startled Noah.

He was right behind him in climbing out. Taking a deep breath, he filled his lungs with fresh air. As he processed all the scents around them, he moved his eyes slowly to check out where they were. To the left was an open field, so not a good place to go, there was no telling how many eyes could see that field. On the other side were trees, not a thick grouping, but would still allow for some movement.

He turned to see the others were already out of the van. Emersyn stood there taking slow breaths, hugging the tablet to her chest. He moved his gaze down over her slowly, she could use more weight on her, he thought, to round out some of the hollow areas that captivity had carved into her body. "I'll…"

Blair smacked him on the back, "go for a run, and blow off some of that crap you're projecting."

He turned and looked at him.

"Seriously, your angst slash rage slash depressing vibes are suffocating me." His expression changed and he gave Noah a more understanding look. "None of us do windowless vehicles well," he shrugged, "but you haven't been for a run in at least a week, so go," he motioned to the trees, "let the kitty out to play so I can breathe for the rest of the ride."

Noah frowned and glanced at Kobie, on her face was her 'understanding female' expression, she nodded her head and then smiled at him. "We'll stay here with Emersyn." She glanced at her, "maybe borrow the bushes over there for a quick moment."

Noah looked to where she pointed, then what she was saying clicked inside his head. "Maybe a short run." He mumbled. Turning, he went to the other side of the van to strip down. He visibly jumped when he stopped and saw that Emersyn had followed him.

"Sorry, I didn't mean to startle you." She said quietly. "Um, I wanted to ask you to-to help me when we get where we're going."

Noah's spine stiffened, he would do anything she needed, he owed her that. He nodded.

"I want to try and," she looked down the front of her, "let my cat out, I think."

He could feel the fear coming off her and stepped closer to lightly touch her shoulder. "I get it." He held her look, "it's beaten into us to not shift, then the," he looked at the marks on her throat, which he hoped healed as his had eventually, "collar makes sure we don't."

"How does it feel? Finally, being able to free them?" She was shaking. He dropped his hand away so he would do something completely asinine like hug her.

"I won't lie, it scared the hell out of me the first time after I was," he frowned, "free." He nodded, "but there's nothing like opening up and running when you're in that form." He offered her a smile, that felt more awkward than anything thing he'd ever done.

"I always wondered." She whispered. Forgetting there were no consequences now for speaking about such things was hard for him too for months afterward.

"I'll help you," he motioned to the van, "Kobie will, and Kelsey, you'll meet her when we get back," he swallowed the lump in his throat, "she helped me that first time, I freaked right out."

Emersyn's eyes rounded, "I never imagined doing it, never mind with so many of my kind."

Noah sucked in a breath, then regretted it when he took the scent of her anxious excitement into his body. "They're good people, Emersyn, every last one of them at home." He looked at the ground, home, he'd never called it that before.

"I'm glad Aspyn will be coming back to a much better place than she left."

Noah looked up to see Calum standing at the back of the van in cat form, the expression in his eyes easy to read and telling him they didn't have all day.

Emersyn turned and then gasped, "you are so beautiful." she smiled and stepped closer to him and then stopped, "I've never seen anyone this close after they shifted."

Calum glanced behind him and then looked back at Noah.

He cleared his throat, "we don't want to be stopped here too long..."

"Oh, yes of course. I'll go sit with Kobie." She gave him a stiff nod and walked back around the van.

Noah exhaled a loud breath and then nodded at Calum, letting him know he'd be right behind him in a moment. He'd have to clamp down on his animal, otherwise, he would probably run the last two hours to get back to Ed's. As he stripped off his clothes with stiff movements, he realized he was looking forward to the mayhem back home. He even missed Jake and his odd sense of humor, not that he'd ever tell him that. Ever.

Shifting without hesitation, he went around the van and glanced at Emersyn, her gaze moving over him, and then she was smiling at him. That fueled a bigger need to run it off as Blair worded it. Scenting the air, he had no problem picking up the direction Calum and Shaelan had gone. He bound in that direction without pause. He'd make sure Emersyn got her daughter back and yeah, he'd check in on them and watch over them, likely for the rest of their lives, but even his cats' thoughts confirmed they weren't able to be a proper mate to anyone.

Chapter Nine

Emersyn scrambled to sit up as she fought to catch her breath. Her heart was beating so fast that her whole body was vibrating. Where was she? Kicking the blanket to the floor, she stood up and looked at the other empty bed. The trailer. She was in a trailer at Kobie's. Blowing out a breath, she focused on calming down. The light-headedness made her sway as she moved to the front of it. Bracing her hand on the wall, she closed her eyes and tried to erase the images from her mind. The pains in her ankle served as a distraction long enough for her to reach the small couch and sit down. Turning, she moved the curtain and looked outside. There were no tall fences or buildings anywhere to be seen, just nature and a light dusting of snow, making it bright and new-looking. It was new to her, all of it. She wasn't in that house or, she touched her neck, in that collar.

Leaning back, she closed her eyes again and took a deep breath. It had been dark when they got here last night and after the long drive of trying not to freak out, she'd been too exhausted to care where she slept.

Her stomach gurgled with hunger, reminding her that she'd been too tired to eat as well. Sitting up, she looked down at her ankle and scowled at it in a silent chastising that it was going to cooperate and allow her to move around freely. Freely. She smiled slowly; she was free. She could step outside anytime she wanted to.

Jolting, she looked around for the tablet. Getting up, she leaned against the counter beside a sink and looked back to the bedroom. It was on the small table between the beds. Blowing out a breath, she limped back to get it. As she reached it, she noticed someone had plugged it in. She knew it wasn't her. Noah, she didn't know how she knew, but it had to be him that did that for her, so she could continue to look at Aspyn. Removing the cord, she hugged it to her and turned around.

Stopping beside the little fridge, she opened it far enough to peek in, hoping for something to drink at least. Her hand shook as she did it, going into the cupboard or fridge was against the rules unless you were told to. Clenching her teeth, she hissed out a breath between them, she forgot, again that she was free. Putting the tablet down, she yanked the door wide open.

She stared at the contents with awe, it was full. Not of sealed trays of premade foods, but fruits, vegetables, and store containers she didn't recognize. She felt giddy. Fresh food. That had been so rare in the last nineteen years. Grabbing an apple and bottle of some sort of juice, she set it on the counter behind her and then moved her hand, hovering over the containers and reading them. It took her a minute to sound out the word. Yogurt. She had no idea what it was, but she was trying it.

Closing the fridge, she turned and looked at the cupboards and small drawers. Opening the top one, she grinned to see forks, spoons, and knives. She hadn't eaten with anything but a spoon in many years. Of course, that was her own fault, she had tried to stab a guard with a fork. Clicking her tongue, she frowned and then opened the container, did she need a fork for yogurt or a spoon? Upon seeing the contents of it, she nodded, "spoon it is." Taking one out of the drawer she closed it and hopped to the table and stretched to reach the items on the counter to put them on the table. A note stuck to a small machine on the counter caught her attention. She scowled at the words. Turn. On. For coffee. Eyebrows raised, she pulled it off and pushed the button. She'd never had coffee, it wasn't allowed in the houses, but she remembered older women always saying how much they missed it.

Settling down in the seat, she watched the machine as it gurgled and made coffee. Picking up the yogurt, she looked at the picture on the side. There was fruit in the picture, but when she looked in it, there was just a white substance. Stabbing the spoon in, she stirred it around and was delighted to see the fruit was hiding at the bottom. Taking a bite, she moved it around her mouth, it was an odd taste, not bad, just nothing like she'd had before. Swallowing it, she decided she liked it and took another bite.

Emersyn walked around the yard, slowly, careful of how much weight she put on her ankle. There was no injury that would keep her inside today. She stayed close to the trees, avoiding buildings and the areas they were building. She didn't know the rules of where she could go or shouldn't go, and she didn't want to do anything to make them regret bringing her here.

She was amazed that she could stand in one spot and smell so many things at once. The smells of nature were so new to her, that she was sure she'd never get tired of them. Years of the old house smells needed to be purged from her mind.

Facing the trees, she took a deep breath and realized the scents of others came to her. Three if she wasn't mistaken, two she didn't know, but the one she did. Noah was out there. If she hadn't recognized his smell, she would have gone back to the trailer. There was no mistaking the male scents that were out there and she wasn't ready to face unknown men.

Even with Noah among them, her body still shook as she fought to continue standing where she was. Before she could decide what to do, three men walked out of the trees. A tall redheaded man was pulling his shirt over his head. He said something to the one walking beside him and even Noah smiled. She hadn't seen him smile at all before now. It didn't erase that haunted look from his face, but he seemed a different man when he did. She sucked in a breath, trying to figure out what to do when she noticed he hadn't yet put his shirt on. Her eyes locked on the marks on his chest. They were old and white welts, but they were plain enough among the muscle to see clearly. An image flashed in her mind, and she put her hand over her mouth to stop the cry of anguish that wanted to come out. She remembered that day when she was taken to a new house. Remembered it so clearly all the emotions came back with it. How could she have forgotten that night? Stumbling back a few steps, she tripped in a rut on the ground and fell backward.

All three men rushed toward her. Emersyn scrambled backward away from them as they got closer. The redhead stopped and said something to the other man, who stopped on the spot, but Noah continued until he reached her. He dropped down into a crouch and held a hand toward her.

"It's okay, Emersyn, we're not there." His tone was soft and soothing. "Jake and Cale won't hurt you."

Moving just her eyes, she looked at one and then flicked them to look at the other man. they looked upset, but not in the way she was used to. "I—" she swallowed, trying to prompt her voice to work, "I remembered that day." She whispered it, afraid if she said it too loud the pain would come back. "You fought all of them to get to me. To free me." A tear rolled down her cheek. She looked at the lines and welts on his chest. "Look what they did to you."

Noah dropped to a squat and held his hand toward her again, "it will never happen again."

She searched his eyes and saw it there, an unspoken oath that he would never let her be harmed again. Swatting the tear away, she took his hand and let him pull her to her feet. She pulled her hand away, unused to physical contact, but then she looked at his chest again, and sorrow filled her. She wanted to cry for him. Without knowing why, she stretched her arm out and placed it on his chest, just the fingertips, and touched a wide scar above his heart. He inhaled a sharp breath, and she looked up to see if it hurt him. The expression on his face said so much that her chest tightened. She saw fear in his eyes, the kind that she knew only too well. She pulled her hand away and grasped it in her other one so she wouldn't bring him more pain. "I'm sorry."

"It's fine." His tone was flat, telling her that it wasn't at all.

She swallowed, trying to take the taste of anguish out of her mouth. "I thought they killed you." She inhaled through her nose and looked back up at him. "The last time I saw you they were dragging you out of that house."

He stepped closer and lifted his hand like he wanted to touch her face, then stopped and dropped it to clutch his shirt tight in both hands. "They tried." The muscle in his jaw pulsed.

Emersyn didn't know how long they stood there, their gazes locked on the others, silently reliving the commonality of their tortured past, but it filled her with both sorrow and strength that surprised her. They'd survived it.

Someone cleared their throat and made both turn away from the other. She looked from one man to the other, the emotion on their faces was the kind that only those that had been free their entire lives would have. Compassion and pity.

"I'm Jake." The dark-haired man smiled in a friendly way. He motioned to the redhead, "this is Cale." The other man bobbed his head in a greeting. "Uh, I'm sure some of the women will have breakfast started," he looked toward the house, "if you're hungry."

Emersyn shook her head, "I ate some of the food from the fridge." she paused, watching their reactions carefully, hoping it was all right that she did. None of them so much as blinked at that, she looked back to Noah, "and I like coffee." She smiled at him.

Noah smirked; it was small, almost undetectable. "I remembered they don't allow coffee in the," he glanced down at the ground, "houses and thought you might want to try it."

"I like it with sugar." She told him with a smile.

"Me too."

She turned to see Jake look horrified.

"No coffee." He jolted as if someone smacked him. "That's," he made a strange noise, "I can't." he shook his head.

Noah looked at him, "ignore him. He thinks he's funny."

"I don't think, I know," Jake said with a smile. He stepped backward, "Nice to meet you, I'm going to mooch some coffee from inside."

The other man, Cale didn't say anything, just smiled at her and turned to the house.

"Are you staying here to help, Noah?" Jake called to him as he walked.

Noah turned, "no, I'm going over to the shop to give Gage a hand."

Emersyn watched them leave, "the shop?"

Noah scowled, then moved with fast jerky motions to put his shirt on. Jerking it over his head, he looked down at her, "Yeah. It's across the way," he pointed, "five minutes. We work on big equipment."

She wasn't sure what that would entail. "Is that where you live?"

His brows creased, then he gave her an abrupt nod, "I'll, ah," he turned on his heel, "see you later."

Emersyn watched as he moved with long strides to a truck and then got in and left without so much as a backward glance. His ghosts may even be more to bear than her own, she decided. Inhaling deeply, she turned back to the trailer, she needed to see her daughter, see the innocence and joy—it was the only thing that kept her going.

Chapter Ten

Noah turned up the volume and stood there for a moment. He didn't know the band or any of the words, but the hard beat vibrated through him and helped him feel like he could breathe. Turning around, he tapped the wrench against his leg as he walked. It was a menial task he'd been given, but it was something to do. Anything was better than putting that look on Emersyn's face repeatedly. The fear and timid expression on her face when she looked at him felt like knives being jabbed into his chest. It was his fault, he knew that. Seeing him brought it all back to her. He should have gone for a run here, had intended to, then the next thing he knew he was pulling to at Blair's.

He rubbed his hand over his chest, feeling the familiar ridges of the scars under his shirt. He could still hear her screaming the day they brought her to the house. She wasn't screaming for her own welfare though, it was for him, to let him go, stop hitting him. He could never understand why she did that. It would have made things worse for herself fighting against them. He dropped his head down almost to his chest and closed his eyes, he knew all about that, what fighting back brought.

Opening his eyes, he zeroed in on the job he was supposed to be doing. Removing panels, taking out dents, and prepping the equipment for painting. It wasn't exactly a hard task, but he was used to it. He got most of the jobs in the shop that didn't involve engines or moving parts. He rolled his head from side to side and tried to alleviate some of the tight knots so movement would be less painful. He didn't mind the jobs they gave him; he had no desire to understand the complex workings of engine parts. He'd learned to work a few of the rigs, and he did that well, so that got him out of the shop from time to time where he could go to sites and feel like he was doing something.

Putting the wrench on the nut, he gave a test tug on it to see if it had *melded*, as Jake called it, to the bolt. That seemed to be common with the dust, grime, and heat the equipment was exposed to three seasons out of the year. He had to yank on it three times to get it to loosen. Noah glared at the next one, he had enough frustration inside him that he could do this for a day before burning off only a quarter of it. The next two were easy, the third one wouldn't budge. Snarling at it, he gripped the wrench tighter and put all his anger into it. It gave way and his hand went into the panel. Looking down he saw he'd broken the bolt clean off instead of undoing it. One more thing he screwed up. With a growl, he slammed his hand into the panel.

The music stopped suddenly.

"Aren't we supposed to be taking the dings out of it, not adding more?"

Noah looked over his shoulder to see Cooper standing there. He was up on his feet now, a cast and crutch to make sure he behaved for a few more weeks. If it had been him, he wouldn't have lasted a week, never mind the entire time Shaelan tacked on 'just to be sure."

"Thought maybe there was a rock concert going on in here. One with loud, angry music." He started across the floor toward him.

"I busted the bolt." Noah looked back at it.

"Isn't the first, won't be the last." Cooper stopped beside him and looked from the bolt to him, "figured you'd be over at Blair's now that your girl's there."

Noah snorted, "I'm gone so much now, I want to help here when I'm around."

Cooper nodded his head slowly, a sober expression on his face. "What's eating at you?"

Noah shook his head and held up the wrench. "Nothing, I…"

"Don't lie to me, kid, my leg is damaged, not my senses." He inhaled, "I could smell the fury coming off you as soon as I stepped in the door."

Noah exhaled, slumping his shoulders. "Emersyn saw me without my shirt this morning and it brought back memories she should never have to think about again."

"For you or her? You can't control what a person thinks." He tilted his head, "unless you have some mind power hoodoo none of us know about." He smirked, "do you?"

Noah looked down at him, not even sure if he was being serious. "No."

Cooper smirked, "didn't think so." he moved closer and examined the bolt he'd snapped off, "easy fix once the panel is completely off."

Noah bobbed his head like he agreed but found he didn't care much about it.

"I was going over later to meet your girl. Calum told Gage she's got a strong spirit and is holding it together well considering…"

"She's not my girl."

Leaning on the panel Noah was trying to work on, Cooper took off his hat and rubbed his almost bald head, "she's your mate, then she's your girl."

Noah shook his head, "I'm going to find her daughter, help her get back to her family," he paused, not even sure if she'd want to go back. He hadn't even spoken to his parents yet. "If she wants…"

Cooper put his hat back on, "so you're going to walk away from her and her little one?" He frowned for a second, "is it because the child isn't yours?"

Noah couldn't mask the surprise. "No." He shook his head, "I don't care about that," he sputtered, "well, I mean she's related to Blair and despite what her father did," he shrugged, "she's a child, it's not her fault."

Cooper's serious look lightened, "right, so it's not that."

Noah liked Cooper, and had since he first met him, but the man confused him often. Talking to him was like he was searching for a loose thread, and once he found he just kept tugging on it until things started to unravel. It was unnerving to be the recipient of one of Cooper's talks. "Look, Coop," he realized he'd never called him that before today, "I appreciate what you're trying to do..."

"What am I trying to do?"

Noah waved the wrench beside his head, "get in my head and give me some kind of pep talk."

Cooper raised one eyebrow, "Is that what I'm doing?"

He's looking for that thread now, Noah thought and almost smiled, "you don't want to be in this head, trust me, it's not a good place..."

"Because you've endured hell?" The man showed no emotion as he looked him in the eye.

Noah opened his mouth to answer...

"And survived it." Cooper waved his hand at him, "and are still surviving it."

Noah braced his one hand against the panel and looked down at the floor. It was a trap, he knew it was, but couldn't figure out exactly how it was. Shaking his head, he looked at him, thinking he had the answer to stop this right now, "it's a mess, Coop, some things can't be fixed." Noah huffed out a breath, "what I went through," he snorted, "what she went through..."

"So don't fix it."

Noah closed his mouth and looked at him, stunned that he'd said that. "Well—that's what I'm saying it can't be..."

"Sometimes when something is broken beyond repair, you have to give up trying to fix it and start thinking about the parts that aren't and that can be helpful for other things."

Noah sucked in a deep breath and looked at the other man. He made no sense. None that he could see.

"Neither of you is ever going to forget what you've been through, there's no miracle pill out there that could ever do that, so you have to start working to figure out how to live despite it."

The breath he'd taken came out all at once, leaving him speechless for a second. "You don't get it, there is no despite it—we are a constant reminder to each other," he set the wrench down before he tossed it, or beat the metal he was supposed to be fixing, "we're just supposed to look at each other every day and *feel* it all over again?" Hands on his hips, he shook his head and then glared at him, "I can't even close my eyes and sleep without going through it every single night..."

"You're not saying anything I don't know." The older man's expression changed to understanding, "I share that bunkhouse with you, I hear you tossing around at night. I know you bolt out of that bed like it's on fire. You might think you're suffering in silence when you pace around outside screaming at the stars inside your head, but I hear you." He nodded, "We all hear you."

Noah stepped back, a sweat breaking out on the back of his neck. Of course, he knew they'd all hear him with their exceptional hearing, but to admit it, that was different.

"You're not in it alone anymore, kid, I've been waiting for you to see that, but your skull is pretty thick I guess." Cooper inhaled slowly and then let it out, "we can't take it away or change it, none of us will ever know what it's like what you lived through, but we're here and we're waiting to help however we can."

Noah felt like his throat was tightening, his emotions were reaching the point he wouldn't be able to stop an outburst. He needed to get outside.

"That's what family does, kid, we stick with you no matter what." Cooper glanced at the broken bolt, "you think we keep you around because you're a handy guy with a surplus of skills?" He smirked. "And we keep Jake for his chef skills too."

Noah snorted; Jake couldn't even make toast without charring it. "Fuck, Coop, it's a mess. I'm a mess." He felt his eyes water and didn't care. "How did it come to all this?" He shook his head and fought the urge to just slide to the floor and sit there. "The Alliance, I know they're good, I just—how did it end up harming so many..."

"Come on." Cooper waved his hand to the back doors, "let's go sit out back and watch Gary try to park the rigs brought back without crushing anything."

Noah looked at the task he was supposed to be doing.

Cooper gave his head a shake, "we have all winter to make them all pretty again. Let's go talk."

Noah blew out a breath, feeling like he'd somehow failed, again. "I know I'm not good with engines and that, but I'm trying, Coop."

"No one said you weren't and really, we don't care." He motioned to the door again and then looked at him with that look, the one that said it wasn't a request.

Sighing, Noah turned and headed to the door.

"I'm going to explain where all the shit went wrong, kid, so take notes and pass them on to anyone else that needs to hear it."

Chapter Eleven

Cooper watched Gary as he hopped out of one rig and went toward another. "I used to work for the Alliance." He glanced at him, "when I was young and rambunctious like you boys." He smirked like he was lost in memory for a moment. "I found my mate, loved her—" his expression changed, "but she loved another, so I put all my woe into helping the Alliance keep order." He rolled his eyes; both knew the failings of that.

Noah forgot to breathe as he processed that. Cooper had a mate out there.

"It was Kelsey's mother." Cooper said softly, "and I don't go spreading that around." He took off his hat and looked at it, "there are just some things that are best if few know." He looked at him and Noah nodded, still trying to think past the surprise. "When she was killed," regret filled his eyes, "I know it because of Aiden Tomas' father and his lot of assholes." He nodded his head slowly, "I had to decide if I was going to watch over Kelsey or continue to help the Alliance."

"You chose Kelsey." It was a stupid thing to say.

"I did." Inhaling slowly, he put his hat back on his head, "I told you that part, so you'd see that I understand with mates and that." He gave him a hard look, "knowing them and walking away isn't an easy road to travel, you understand?"

Noah nodded, he understood more than he wished. For six years he'd seen Emersyn's face haunt his every moment of living.

"Yes, you understand that part good." His expression lightened, "I figured you'd be over the moon to know she was alive."

Noah felt like he'd smacked him, "well—yeah, I'm happy she's alive, of course, I am."

"Good. that's a start." Cooper turned and watched Gary put the loader in drive, then move a few feet and put it in reverse again, shaking his head, he huffed out a breath. "My father and grandfather worked with the Alliance, way back." He shrugged a shoulder, "none of us knew how bad it really was or was going to be."

Noah leaned on his knees and watched him, not wanting to interrupt with comments.

"Before the Alliance, each clan had their own laws, looked out only for their own," he paused, a faraway look on his face, "things were pretty bad from what I understand, clans feuding, a lot of fighting going on," he lifted one shoulder, then dropped it, "everyone wanted more territory and shit like that." He finally looked at him, "our numbers were strong then, you see, there were as many of us and there were one-forms and in most cases, we stood side by side and no one cared if we grew fur or had skin." He shook his head, "those that didn't know, never would, we blended with the one-forms like there was no difference."

Noah heard a crunch of metal and looked to see Gary jumping out of the rig and glaring at it. One more ding for him to fix, he thought.

"We should keep count," Cooper said with a smirk, then sighed again. "The hunting of our kind started to get bad, like hiding in the hills kind of bad." Cooper waved his hand in the air, "with cars coming along and communication getting faster, we were no longer able to live side by side with them and be safe."

Noah watched him and listened, he'd been denied clan life for too long, and he felt he needed to know the reasons why and if anyone could lay it out for him, it would be Cooper.

"One clan went to another, then they to one, and so on until all these waring shifters finally realized they'd have to work together to survive." Cooper snorted, "of course, more fighting among us went on for a few years after that because each clan figured they were the best to be at the head and lead all the clans through this." He smirked, "the bigger shifters thought they'd be the best at it because of their size, or the strong ones their strength," he gave him a quick glance, "I'm sure many lives were lost trying to prove all that." He rolled his eyes, "but in the end, a vote was decided on," he looked around like he was thinking it through, "which was a lot more complicated back then, right, you couldn't just call someone up and do a video phone call thing," he shook his head, "the logistics of how they did this worldwide in a time where you had to ride a ship for weeks to get from one side to the other," he nodded, "that there is commitment, and if they hadn't none of us would be here now, we'd all be extinct, know what I'm saying?"

Noah nodded but didn't say anything.

"So, the voters chose the wolves, now there's more than one kind, so at that point, they had to kind of group us into categories right, like cats, wolves, all the bears," he waved his hand around, "then it was decided each clan still had their alpha's, and the alpha's had a second, or seconds in some cases," he shrugged, "they would represent with the Alliance." Cooper frowned, "the name just suddenly made sense to me." He grinned, then sobered again, "There were a lot of battles over the vote, as you can imagine, but I wasn't there so I don't go presuming who did what." He held his look for a second before continuing. "It was decided that there would be Ambassadors in each country that kept watch on things for the leader or Devin's kin that was at the helm." Cooper sat there for a moment and then finally sucked in a breath and continued, "shit started going south when the one-forms started having wars of their own, communicating got harder, and countries had to start looking out for themselves more and more because it was too dangerous to travel for many years at a time as the one-forms battled over," he shrugged, "this isn't a history lesson, you can research that shit." He grinned briefly, "a lot of ours died in those wars too, we were still trying to blend for the most part." His expression was haunted for a moment, making Noah wonder who his family had lost in the one-form's wars. "Anyway, with the distraction of global wars, other factions were able to establish a foothold on things in life, like the novelty of having a pet shifter, and such." His jaw clenched for a moment, "by the time the Alliance clued in, it was out of control." He turned to look at Noah, taking his time searching his face, "we didn't know it was a worldwide problem, you understand? We thought the Tomas family just had a few friends scattered about and that's how they were pulling it off." He gave him a hard look, "but as you know, your girl isn't from this continent, so you know it's not as simple as stopping one man's organization in one country."

Noah's stomach knotted, "yeah, I've been hearing bits and pieces from the teams, so I have a pretty good idea of the whole picture." He rolled his head from side to side; the ever-present knots were tight today. "I just need to know that we're getting somewhere with it."

"Here? We are. You ask Calum the numbers, he'll tell you." He looked at him with a softer emotion on his face, "we're really proud of you boys doing what you're doing."

Noah's eyebrows went up.

"You and Blair, rolling in those places and getting ours out, damn proud." Cooper jerked his head to the side and looked in Gary's direction again as he took off his hat and rubbed his hand over his head. "I know you'll succeed." He said it softly and then put his hat back on, "but now, after you fix that mess in the shop, you need to get your ass over to your girl and help her." His expression was dead serious now, "I'm not saying mate her up or anything, but be there." The creases around his mouth were enhanced as he scowled at him, "she's never known freedom or what the world is like with all its gadgets and things," he gave his head a shake, "she must be missing her little girl something bad too, she's going to need someone to lean on, Noah. Someone that understands where she's been."

Noah opened his mouth to tell him that it couldn't be him. What did he know about being a parent, hell, what did he know about helping others, he could barely get through the day himself.

"You'd rather it be one of the other guys? How about that Cale boy, he's got a good soul in him, a friendly disposition— you'd rather it be him looking out for her?"

Noah's cat was paying attention now, in fact, it felt like it was trying to climb out through his chest. "No." It was more growl than word when it came out.

Cooper nodded his head once, "good. Now go get that panel off so I can fix what you broke, then get your ass back over to Blair's and help there, so you'll be handy if she needs you." He stood up and then looked back down at him, "and for god's sake stay away from the saws and nail guns."

Noah dropped his head and couldn't help smiling. He'd almost taken his hand off with the skill saw the first time he tried to use it. Standing up, he looked at the other man that meant more to him than he'd ever be able to express. "I'm just not a tool man."

Cooper laughed, "oh I know, but you are a fighter and that's what is most important right now in our world." He held his look and Noah wasn't a hundred percent certain, but it looked like pride on the older man's face. Had anyone ever been proud of him before? "I know you'll find the right way, just like I know you'll be there the day Aiden Tomas is brought down." He nodded his head again and then started to walk away. "You need an instruction book on how to drive those?" He yelled in Gary's direction.

Noah watched him go over to give Gary an ear full. It wouldn't be a demoralizing thing, not with Cooper, he'd smack him down a wee bit, then build back him back up again so he'd be a better man when he was done.

Blowing out a breath, Noah walked back into the shop. He didn't know if he could be over there with Emersyn all the time, what if she didn't want to see him? Was he supposed to creep around and stay out of sight? How was he supposed to find out what he should or shouldn't do when he was around her? He could talk to Blair. If anyone knew, it would be him, he was good around females.

Noah went over and picked up the wrench and looked at the nut still stuck inside it. Females. He blew out a breath, he still couldn't handle being near any. His heart sped up so fast when one of the women over there even looked at him. How the hell was he supposed to be there for Emersyn when he couldn't breathe? Growling low, he looked over at the stereo. Music wasn't going to fix anything, but at least if it was loud enough it drown out the volume of his thoughts temporarily.

Chapter Twelve

"You want to pay attention, so I don't nail your hand to the board?"

Noah jerked his chin back to look at Blair. "Sorry." He moved his hand out of the way.

After it was up, Blair turned to look over where Emersyn and Daisie were hanging sheets on the clothesline. "We have a dryer." He looked at Noah, "but the fresh air smell is better."

Noah shrugged, "clean sheets, fresh air or not work for me."

"Right." Blair shook his head, "then they bring them in and toss them in the dryer anyway because it's too cold for them to dry properly." He sighed. "She's good for her right now. Daisie."

Noah looked back over at them. If anyone could soothe the pain and worry it would be Daisie. The child was a walking wonder to him. She saw the good in anything, somehow. He wished he could have half the faith in things that little girl did. "Yeah." He glanced around, there wasn't anyone close to where they were working. Now might be the only time to catch Blair alone. "I was, uh, talking to Coop earlier—"

Blair turned to look at him briefly as he double-checked the measurements for the next piece. "Is everything okay?" He frowned, "well, beyond the obvious shit I mean."

Noah shrugged, not sure now how to ask him. "Yeah, he was telling me about his past, to help me, I think."

"His past. Shit, I've never heard him talk about his past."

This surprised Noah, why would he tell him and not the men that grew up here?

"Listen, I know Coop's talks are cryptic, or they feel that way," he smirked, "I went to him for help when..."

A door slamming had them both startle and turn. Nichelle was stomping toward them, the expression on her face made both men freeze and watch her.

"What now?" Blair said under his breath.

She zeroed in on Blair before she reached him, "did *you* know I don't get a graduation?" She flung her hands up, "because we're on lockdown from some psychopathic idiot?"

Blair opened his mouth and then snapped it shut so hard Noah heard his teeth click together. "Graduation? You just started the..."

"Not for *that*." She spat at him, "I finished early, the normal program for the high school requirements." She stopped a few feet from them, "I worked my tail off to do it too. Eight months early and now I find out that there is no graduation for me," she put her hands on her hips and glared at him.

When a female stood like that, it never ended well for whomever she was focused on. Noah stepped back a step, panic forming in his guts.

"Isn't graduation in the spring? Usually?" Blair asked her hesitantly.

"Yes." She enunciated it thoroughly, dragging out the s sound at the end. "But not for me, not now, not then." The hands came off the hips to wave around, "I should be on a stage, smiling, wearing one of those stupid caps with the tassel thing, but I don't get that. The Alliance has pulled *strings*," she made quotes marks in the air, "for special certificates." She dropped her hands back to her hips and gave him a hard look, "do I get to walk across a stage and be recognized for all my hard work?" She paused and Noah looked to Blair, he wasn't sure if he should answer or not. "Nope. I get a box and glitter in the mail. What the hell do I need glitter for?" She growled and it wasn't a sound a young female made, it was from her animal, and it sounded like a warning in Noah's ears.

Blair cleared his throat and took a step closer to her.

"You," she pointed to him, "are going to talk to the king and fix this."

Blair stopped moving.

Noah glanced around wondering if there was anyone close by for backup. He saw Kobie was standing near enough, but she didn't look concerned, she watched Blair like he was being tested at this moment. His cat stirred; he could feel the young tiger inside her now too.

"I will see what's going on." Blair's tone was soft and soothing, and Noah had no idea how he could do that right now. Noah wanted to go kill something to make this girl happy.

"If you want a stage and presentation, honey, then you'll get it. All the others that have earned it will as well." Blair stepped closer to her now, placing his hand on her shoulder. "Even if we have to build it ourselves." Blair glanced at Noah, and his expression said to back him up.

Noah opened his mouth and had no idea what to say, the panic inside him starting to smother him. He nodded his head and hoped that would be good enough at this moment.

"See, Noah agrees, you'll get your stage and graduation."

Just like that the young woman was disarmed as her shoulders slumped and the cat he'd sensed seemed placated. Noah looked at Blair, really looked at him, and had no idea how he'd managed that with a light touch and a few words.

"I'll get it sorted." Blair confirmed, "but right now I need someone to round up the kids for their afternoon online classes."

Nichelle nodded, giving him a quick smile. "I knew you'd fix it." She looked at Noah and smiled and he quickly forced his mouth to form a smile. "I'll herd the kids." She turned on her heel and darted across the yard.

Blair blew out an audible breath and rubbed his hand over his hair. Kobie was walking toward them now, she had one of those mate-only looks on her face and Noah went right back to feeling uncomfortable.

"Did you know about this?" Blair asked her.

"We just found out when Beth called." She glanced in the direction Nichelle had gone. "She's worked hard. Considering she's had no family support, it's nothing short of amazing. She's smart," she smiled at Blair, "and has decided she's going into the medical field."

Blair huffed out a breath, "that's," he frowned, "that sounds expensive."

Kobie chuckled, "it's going to be complicated." She stopped close enough she could rub her hand over his chest. Noah had noticed all the mated females seemed to do this a lot to their men, he didn't understand the significance of it, but every time it seemed to settle the man down. She stretched up and kiss him on the mouth, "you did good," she smirked, "I was ready to strip and go after her."

Blair groaned, "yeah me too." He motioned to Noah, "and his cat was ready to wage war."

Noah's eyebrows went up, he hadn't realized his emotions were broadcasting that strongly.

"I better go help with the kids." She kissed him again and walked away.

Blair dropped his head down and blew out a breath again.

"I don't know how you do it." Noah confessed, motioning around them, "deal with all this."

Blair grinned, "I have no idea." He turned to watch his mate walking away, "I suspect the love and guidance of my woman has a lot to do with it." He nodded his head a few times agreeing with his own words, "sorry, what were you saying before the wrath of Shell descended upon us?"

Noah blinked, he'd forgotten they'd been talking, or he'd been trying to talk.

"Noah. Blair."

He turned to see Calum standing in the drive. He waved them to come over.

"He looks serious," Blair said and started going in that direction.

Noah sucked in a breath, trying to change gears *again* and make his body move to go over. His mind started churning out possible reasons Calum wanted to talk to him. Noah's cat was still close and just as unhappy about the false alarm to fight. With luck, he thought, maybe Calum had someone they could go kill or chase down. Noah's heart thudded hard in his chest. He needed to focus and put the brakes on. He could never let his cat lead, not ever, it would be a trail of blood if he did. All those years it wasn't just Noah that suffered, his animal did too. They'd both lay there in pain at night, Noah unable to accept what he was a part of and his cat desperately needing out. No, there was no way his cat would ever be driving this body, not if it killed him to keep control.

Chapter Thirteen

Noah stared at the phone, then looked at Blair, who had an expression that said he wasn't seeing the connection either. They were on a call with Illias, Devin, and the King.

"The third message is pretty much the same," Illias said, "again it's from a public phone in a little town I could barely pinpoint on the map."

"The clan has to be nearby." The King summarized.

The call had started with Illias telling them they couldn't find Blair's brother's clan's location. They'd been moved and had been off the radar for a few years. The men that had been with Lindon Elden were being less than helpful with its location as if they weren't sure of it. None of it made sense. If they came and went with Lindon, how did they not know where it was located?

"The things in the photos fit, mostly." Illias said in an annoyed tone, "but I can't be sure."

Illias had stumbled across three messages left on a system that hadn't been used by the Alliance for a few years, but the line was still active. Only a clan that wasn't in constant contact with the organization would use it.

"Play the first message again," Blair said as he zeroed in on Calum's phone.

"One sec."

Noah moved closer, like being a foot closer to the phone was going to make some sort of difference.

"Here we go," Illias said in a hushed voice.

"I hope this is the right number. My grandmother had it." A woman's whisper came over the phone. "My name is Mckenna Stein, I am from the Elden clan—we need *help*. We can't continue like this. I go on supply runs Tuesday, every week, and can meet someone behind the general store in Dastin. Please send help." The line went quiet.

"I did some digging and when the Elden clan were *with* the Alliance there was the family name of Stein on the list," Illias said. "As you heard, message two she's getting, uh, annoyed and the third message has some very colorful language in it." Illias cleared his throat.

"When was the third one left?" Calum asked in a quiet voice.

"Two weeks ago."

Calum turned to look at Blair as he spoke, "let's hope she's still watching for us, it may be our only way to find them."

"And Emersyn's daughter." Kobie leaned closer to Blair.

Noah crossed his arms over his chest. "When can we go?"

"Can you send the location of *Dastin* to everyone, Illias? I can't even find it on a map." The king said.

"Yeah. It's not on most maps, I used the public phone to figure out where it was." He chuckled, "not many public phones left out there."

"That's good, sounds like a pit stop on a road and won't be filled with people to sound the alarm." Blair hugged Kobie against his side.

"Calum, you think we should send a team in?" Devin asked.

Calum was silent for a moment, "no, I don't think we should go barging in with a whole team, at least not at the start."

"What are you thinking?" The king asked.

Noah looked at Calum, he respected the man a great deal, and it seemed everyone else did as well.

Calum's jaw clenched a few times, "Shaelan wants to go back to Konner's and check on the twins, so we'll be without medical assistance if it's required."

"We can send someone else with training," the King said, "I was already looking over the teams before this call," he cleared his throat, "Blaise Morgan from the special ops team has field training for medical needs, and having her team training on-site might not be a bad idea."

Calum nodded his head slowly, "I know Blaise, she's also from a tiger clan, so that fits well."

Blair stiffened, "I don't think we should take…"

"I'm going." Kobie said before he could finish, "*my* people are now yours and that goes the other way too, Blair. These *are* your people, even if you hated your brother, so they're mine now too."

Blair looked down at her, a lot of emotions going through his eyes. Noah didn't know how he managed not to voice any of them. He simply inclined his head. "Okay."

The King made a muffled sound that to Noah's ear sounded like a chuckle. "I will leave the selection of who is going up to you."

"I'll get back to you with the details." Calum said, "but let's arrange to have more of Kenzo's team nearby for backup." He motioned to the phone, "I can only figure there are more that followed Lindon there or this woman wouldn't be trying to find help instead of the clan walking away."

"Agreed." The King said.

"I'll call Kenzo once we get a map and location." Devin said, "what's the travel time, Illias?"

Illias blew out a breath into the phone, "I'd say, a day and a half, maybe two from Blair's location. At least if you want to stay off the radar everywhere, otherwise, twenty-four hours with some tag team driving."

Calum nodded, "we'll start making the arrangements." He glanced at the door, "I have to call Konner to come to pick up Shaelan before we go."

There was a note in his voice, that Noah had never heard before. Worry. As far as he could figure out it was the first time the mated pair would be separated.

"If you'd like to go with her..."

Calum cut off the king, something Noah would never do. "No, I'll be with Blair and Noah, we don't know what we're walking in on and I wouldn't feel comfortable not going."

"Very well. Keep me informed."

Calum nodded. "I will, Shep."

Noah didn't hear the goodbyes; he was too busy trying to keep his cat on the inside. They had a location that Aspyn was likely at and from the sounds of it more than just that little girl needed help. He felt he owed it to Emersyn and all those living in that clan to bring them—what? Justice or freedom, he couldn't decide.

"Noah."

He blinked to see Calum looking at him.

"Are you going to tell Emersyn we found the clan's location?"

Noah opened his mouth and then looked at Blair, not sure why they were all staring at him.

"I'll come with you," Kobie said, her facial expression switched to that understanding look women got.

Noah just nodded, feeling like he missed something important in the last few minutes.

Blair smirked, "relax, you're bringing her good news." He glanced at Calum for a second, "the look on your face is like you're telling her the family dog got run over by a car."

Noah scowled, "And what if her daughter isn't there?"

"Illias said the pictures lined up." Calum offered.

"Even if she's not, you're giving her hope, Noah, and that's the most important thing right now," Kobie said as she opened the door and held it open for him.

Noah swallowed the lump in his throat, she was right, even if she didn't understand that hope was something that lead to disappointment and pain more often than not.

Chapter Fourteen

Noah walked with slow hesitant steps from Cale's little cabin. He hoped Kobie assumed he was taking smaller steps for her benefit, but one thing he'd realized about her early on was that she noticed everything.

"How are you doing?"

He looked down at her but didn't make eye contact. "I'm good."

She smirked, knowing it was a complete lie. "It must be hard, having her here." She gave him a focused look like she could see inside his head, "all the memories must haunt you even more."

He was uncomfortable enough just walking with her, he didn't want to talk about the horrors of his life with her. "It's a challenge." He finally said, hoping she would just let it go there.

"I can't imagine it. What it would be like to see Blair and then not for so long—the uncertainty and everything." She grinned, "I didn't even want to be mated, but I couldn't stay away from him either." She made a point to make sure he noticed her looking up at him until they made eye contact. "I think you're both incredibly strong." She smiled an encouraging smile. "I couldn't have done it."

Noah paused and huffed out a breath, "I think you could have, but I'm glad you don't ever have to find out."

Kobie held his look long enough he was almost squirming in his skin. Would he ever get used to a female making eye contact with him? He didn't think so. "You're right because we are ending this insanity that we're being forced to live with."

One of the women that had recently been rescued stood outside the door to the house, looking at them. She had a panicked look on her face.

"I think she needs you," Noah said and jerked his chin in that direction.

Kobie turned, "Alena has been having some problems with Indy since they got back." She said softly.

Noah felt his chest tighten, the female's nephew was around eight and if anyone knew the hell young shifter boys went through in Tomas' world, it was him. "It's going to take time, for-for the boys we brought back to remember it's okay." He couldn't say it out loud, so he nodded, hoping she would understand. "They just need to remember they're boys, and none of it is their fault." He nodded again.

Kobie put her hand on his arm, compassion bleeding from her all over him. "You should spend time with them, Noah, the boys, I think they would benefit from your knowledge of what it was like." She smiled again, "and hearing it from someone who survived it..."

"I think she's right."

Noah jolted and turned to see Emersyn standing a few feet away. He hadn't heard her come upon them, but if there was one thing imprisonment taught a body, it was to move without sound and blend into the background.

"They're so frightened, especially when they look at one of the girls or women." she glanced to Kobie, and then those emeralds locked on him, "I don't know what they tell the boys, but I know what they try to program the girls with and," she looked over at Alena, "and if anyone can get through to them, it would be you, Noah."

He swallowed, then tried to force air into his body in any way possible. "I, uh," both women standing so close to him had his cat freaking out. He stepped back, trying to make it look like he was considering what they said, "I-I could try." He jammed his hands into his pockets and balled them into fists, forcibly inhaling to oxygenate his lungs.

Kobie smiled up at him, "great." she looked over at Alena quickly, "are you good here?"

He glanced at Emersyn then to Kobie, "I—"

"Noah has some good news," Kobie said and looked at Emersyn.

The look on Emersyn's face grew to hope so fast, it was like she'd flipped a switch. His cat froze inside him, with the expression on her face anxiety poured from her.

"You have news of Aspyn?" Her eyes were wide with expectation.

He nodded, while he tried to get his brain to switch gears and produce the words she needed to hear. "We, uh," he turned to Kobie to see she was walking away. He was on his own, "they've figured out where Lindon's remaining clan is," he shrugged, "or close enough."

The anxiety changed into excitement. It was so fast it made him dizzy.

"And that's where Aspyn is?"

He opened his mouth to say he wasn't sure, but that's not what came out, "Yes." He frowned, "it makes sense he'd send her to his clan to look after." He added, even though he had no idea why the man had done anything he had.

She rushed at him, closing the space between them in a few steps, grasping his forearm in her warm hand. She looked up at him. "When are we going to get her?"

His cat crouched, not in an alert way, but in fear. She was touching him, voluntarily touching him, again. Then her words registered in his mind, "you're not going." It came out with a lot of hostility and a tone that he'd swore he'd never use toward a female again. It had been a command, not a reply.

She jerked her hand back so fast as if he'd hurt it. The excitement on her face sunk to a look that was sad and then to something else.

"We don't know what we're walking into." He said quickly. He could fix this. He had to fix it. "I don't want to take a chance that you'll be hurt or..."

"Thank you." She said stiffly, "but that is not your decision, is it?"

He opened his mouth but wasn't quite sure what he should say. Warnings were sounding inside his head.

"Aren't I free now?"

He nodded, "yes." He could *never* do something that would make her feel otherwise, not after what she'd lived through—what they'd lived through.

"Okay. Then I'm going, Noah, to get my daughter." Her stance changed, from the timid closed-off form to her hands on her hips and her chin raised.

Noah sucked in a breath, trying to find the words to speak. He wasn't an educated man, but he wasn't addled either, he thought. Right now, it was like he didn't know a single word.

Stepping close to him, she poked her finger into the center of his chest, her green eyes sparkling up at him and his mind screamed danger. "You know what got me through all these years?"

He started to shake his head, but she didn't give him a chance to.

"You." She jabbed him again and then dropped her hand away to rest back on her hip, "I didn't know you—-didn't think I'd *ever* see you again but knowing there was still someone out there to fight for me," she made a soft growl sound, and his cat was suddenly alert, looking for the threat, "it meant *everything*, Noah." She made a softer growl, "so I know that I will be safe when you're there and I *will* be going to get my daughter." She jerked her chin once and then turned and walked away from him quickly.

Noah, mouth hanging wide open, rubbed his hand over where she'd poked him. He didn't know what had just happened. He turned to see Blair and Calum standing across the yard, they'd seen the whole thing. Blair gave him a wide-eyed look and shifted his head to the side twice, telling him to go after her. Calum looked at Blair and then nodded to Noah. He scowled and turned to see she was almost to the trailer. Why was he going after her? His cat switched modes——again and concern flooded through his mind. Gritting his teeth, he started walking toward the trailer. What the hell was he supposed to say? He had no idea. He didn't even know why he was going after her. She'd said her piece and that was that, right? What more was there to say?

His hand was on the door, and he was about to rip it open when his cat made another emotion known. Caution. Noah exhaled a deep breath and rolled his shoulders, trying to ease the tension that seemed to be the only thing holding him together right now. He released the handle and knocked on the door lightly. "Emersyn," he looked at the ground, listening to hear inside, "I'd like to talk." He had to force his tone to be lighter than the emotions churning inside him.

The door swung open so fast it almost caught him in the face. She stood in it looking at him. "You can't tell me what to do, no one is going to ever again."

He swallowed; it wasn't the opening he had thought he'd get. "I'm not trying to."

"Fine." She stepped up the stairs, "you can come in then."

He stepped into the trailer and immediately regretted it when her scent assaulted him. Stopping on the step, he decided this was far enough inside. Maybe it was because his cat was so close to the surface, but it seemed like it was stronger than it had been. He released the door, so it wouldn't close, he needed the air to flow freely.

She moved as far from him as possible in the small space, her hip resting against the table at the front of the trailer. She watched him, without moving—was she even taking a breath? Emersyn may never have shifted, but her cat was close, controlling her whether she realized it or not. "I'm sorry," he didn't take her eyes off her, trying to gauge what she was thinking, "about out there, I didn't mean to…"

"Give me an order?"

He nodded. Noah tried to put his hands in his pockets, but his elbows hit the sides of the stairwell, so he crossed them over his chest and tried to appear like he was relaxed and okay being in a small space with her. "We don't know what we're walking into," he searched for the words to explain to her why he'd reacted the way he did, "I just—I don't—" he looked at the floor for a second, then took a deep breath and exhaled it to try again. "I failed you once." He blurted out and then looked at her. "I can't…"

Her expression changed from defensive to shock. "You didn't fail me." She made one of those sounds that women made when they were annoyed. "There were four of them, Noah, there's nothing you could have done."

He'd relived that moment a million times in his mind, and knew every second of it. "If I'd kept my mouth shut and…"

"Could you have? Just stood there silently and nodded your head, yes sir, no sir?" She crossed her arms over her waist and hugged herself.

He was stupid for bringing it up again. "I don't know."

"I don't think so," her voice was a whisper, emotion close to the surface, "the other woman, that older one that was there then," she frowned, "I don't remember her name," she gave her head a slight shake, "she told me only a male discovering his mate would react that way," she held his look, unwavering for a second, "I was so young, hardly understood that there was a cat inside me at that point, but I knew you, I felt like we weren't strangers," she blinked, "that doesn't make sense, but I was more concerned for you than myself…"

"You shouldn't have been." His heart was thrumming a fast beat inside his chest, "you should have kept quiet and just let it be."

Her brows creased, "I couldn't." Her eyes moved, as she examined his face, "even with age and your beard, I still knew it was you when you turned on that light." A slight smile moved her lips, then was gone again, "I can't explain how, but I did." A pained look filled her eyes.

His legs felt weak, he gripped the half wall beside the steps to steady himself. He shouldn't have come in here with her. Not alone. He squeezed the ledge in his hand, trying to focus on something else, "just make sure you follow instructions when we go—" he frowned, "there." He had almost said to get Aspyn, but he didn't want to fill her with too much hope. What if the child wasn't there, then what?

She nodded stiffly, "I will." It was a whisper, but he could still hear how upset she was getting.

Sucking in a breath, he closed his eyes for a second, another mistake, taking more of her scent inside him. His cat stirred and Noah couldn't think clearly enough to figure out what the animal was trying to tell him. Moving in slow motion, he stepped down the step backward.

"Noah." She lunged forward and grabbed his hand which still had a strained grip on the wall. "You're a good man." She said quickly and then nodded when he gave her a shocked look, "I know you are." The smile she gave him faltered, "Daisie told me all about the others you've helped." Still holding his hand, she wrapped her other one around her waist, "that you helped a girl escape, even after that day—"

The painful expression on her face, felt like a thousand knives were being jabbed into him at once. "I didn't care anymore what happened to me." He admitted and was stunned he'd said it out loud. He'd never told anyone how reckless he was after he found and lost his mate at the same moment.

Her face scrunched up, there was so much pain pouring from her that his cat went crazy inside him.

"Oh," she released his hand and pressed her hand to her stomach, "I don't feel good." she whispered, "I probably ate too much again."

It hit him all at once, it wasn't that her scent was stronger in the closed-in space, it was her cat. Her cat was very close to the surface. He panicked and turned to bolt out the door and run and get Kobie, or Shaelan, anyone. Emersyn grabbed his hand again; the grip was twice as hard as the last time.

"Noah." She said it with such pain, but also like a mantra and he didn't know why.

His cat more or less took a big paw and belted him in the head, he was sure he physically moved from the action. Noah dropped to a knee on the step so he could see her face. "Emersyn, your cat wants out." He said it softly, trying to use that soothing tone Blair always used.

Her eyes opened and she looked at him, fear was blazing from them. "I-I can't," her hand was shaking as she raised it to her throat.

He looked at the fading marks from where the collar had been. "You can now." He took her hand and held it gently, "no one is going to hurt you if you do." He stood up and backed down the step, "let's go outside and give her some room." He had no idea what he was doing, or how to talk someone through their first shift. He remembered what happened the first time he'd shifted after being free, his cat and he had freaked out. He thought for sure Gage was going to put him down that time. If it hadn't been for Kelsey— He helped her down the last step, "just take deep breaths, and uh, try to relax, don't fight it." He needed one of the women, anyone other than him.

He was sucking in breaths almost as uneven as she was as he backed them away from the trailer into a more open area. "You're doing great." Unlike me, he thought. She kept her eyes closed, focusing and he looked around, trying to see if there was anyone nearby that could help. Calum and Blair were still standing across the yard. Calum was on the phone and Blair turned to look his way. Noah sent him a 'help' look, at least he hoped that's what he conveyed. Blair looked confused and then his eyes widened, and he turned and ran toward the house.

Noah released a breath. He would get someone to help.

"Noah." It was more of a whine than spoken, the pain and panic pouring from her. "Don't leave me." She grabbed his wrist and he winced at how hard she was squeezing.

Something Cooper had told him popped into his head. Stay out of reach for first shifts, claws can come out faster than you can blink. He stopped walking and placed his hand over hers and gently pried her fingers off. "Take deep breaths," he glanced over her head to see Kobie and Nichelle running toward them fast. *Thank fuck.* That was the first thought he had. "The girls are coming, they'll help you."

"No." It was a yowl, not words. She stepped into him and grabbed his shirt, resting her head against his chest. "Stay." she panted.

"He's not going anywhere, Emersyn," Kobie said in a soft crooning voice. "But you need to let him go so he can strip down and shift," she moved closer, and Noah noticed her stance was cautious, "we need to get your clothes off, they must be hurting you."

Emersyn sucked in a breath and nodded her head against his chest.

"You've got this Emersyn," Nichelle said softly. "It's amazing once you let go and let it happen." She smiled at Noah as Emersyn released him.

"That's it." Kobie stepped closer, "let's get these clothes off." She gave Noah a pointed look. "Noah's going to shift so he can run with you."

Noah looked around, panic filling him. He remembered Kelsey's first run, he looked down at Nichelle as she pulled her shirt over her head, her first run she'd jumped in the river. Holy shit, he couldn't do this alone. He stumbled back a step and then looked over to see Blair and Calum stripping. He huffed out a breath of relief. He'd have backup. His cat was pacing inside him now, telling him to hurry up. Looking back down, he saw Emersyn was on her hands and knees now. She moaned and it spurred him into action. His clothes were off, and he shifted without thought.

Chapter Fifteen

Emersyn's legs gave out. She dropped to her hands and knees and tried to suck air into her body. Where did Noah go? She couldn't see him now. Kobie was on the ground in front of her, saying something, but she couldn't focus to hear her. The air on her skin burned. They said it would feel better, but it wasn't. She shouldn't be doing this. Shifting wasn't allowed.

Her whole body was shaking, making the panic more intense. Her skin felt like it was crawling with something. This was wrong. Something was wrong. Her breathing kept changing, it felt like it was out of control. She tried to slow it and breathe as they said, but her body wouldn't listen. She was panting—like a cat.

Opening her eyes wide, she managed to lift her head. In front of her was a huge deep orange tiger. She squeezed her eyes shut, trying to make her eyes adjust and focus. They were blurry for a second, and then it was as if a veil was lifted. The tiger in front of her was clearer, his coat a radiant orange now was so clear she could see the individual hairs in it. She looked into his eyes and knew it was Noah. Noah hadn't left her; he was right there in front of her. A soft coaxing sound came from deep in his chest and he moved closer, nudging her with his soft head.

Later she'd think about how she knew, but something inside her responded and told her that he wanted her to let go and let it happen. She trusted him. He was the only person on earth she had faith in.

Lowering her chin, she groaned through the startling feeling as bones popped. She felt removed from her body, not even sure if it was *her* body making those sounds. Her breathing felt steadier now, evenly flowing into her lungs. Opening her eyes, she looked down to see paws where her hands had rested on the cool grass. They were dark orange, almost close to brown. They were *her* paws.

She lifted her chin and then crouched low, so many scents were filling her, it startled her. She didn't know what most of them were. Plants, the dirt itself, bark, she didn't know how she knew it was tree bark, but it was.

With her legs shaking, she tried to stand taller. All four legs worked at once. She had four legs. Turning her head, she looked over her shoulder to see a tail swooshing back and forth slowly. She had a tail. A long-striped tail.

Her heartbeat felt like it had slowed and was less frantic as she looked to see how much clearer everything looked. Excitement filled her, she looked back to Noah to try to convey it when she noticed a young female standing beside him. *Mine* was the only thought she had. Curling her lip back, she snarled at her, a low growl coming from her throat.

"Nichelle." It was Kobie's voice, "move away from Noah."

The young cat listened and bound in the other direction.

Noah stood there, watching her, his eyes were gorgeous she thought. *He's ours.* Her cat's thoughts filled her head. Straightening, she took an unsteady step and then realized her body knew how to sync up the extra two legs and she moved closer to Noah. He stood completely still and let her move her face closer, inhaling his cat's scent.

When he made a sound that was similar to a low rumbling purr, her cat jumped back from him and stretched to her full length. Emersyn realized then she had shifted. There were no reprimands for doing it, no punishment. She was free.

Swinging her head, she looked to the trees and before she knew what she was doing, she was running full speed into them. It scared her but exhilarated her—she had no idea if she was in charge or her cat.

She could hear paws hitting the ground behind her and didn't care, she wasn't slowing down. She heard others sounds too, birds, and something smaller moving through the bush. She inhaled and found the scent and took off after it. She didn't want to catch it or kill it she realized, she just wanted to chase it. Run faster and chase it down. Running this speed was amazing. How were the others ever happy to on two after this?

Noah came up to run beside her and her cat had no desire to try to outrun him, but that didn't mean she was going to stay beside him either, she decided. It shocked her how easy it was to turn her entire body and go in another direction, and how she was able to navigate through the trees without fear of hitting one of them.

Lifting her chin, she scented around her again, there were more cats around her. She put on the brakes and came to an abrupt stop, sliding a few feet on the mucky ground. Her sides were heaving, but she still inhaled again, there was something not natural out here in the trees. Something man-made, she thought.

Crouching low, she turned her head and a sound she didn't know how she made came out of her throat. Her cat had conveyed something to Noah and a big white cat, she thought briefly might be Blair. They both lifted their heads and checked the scents around them. When both turned to look at her. They didn't look concerned. Didn't they smell it?

With a low growl, she took off in the direction it was coming from. A quick glance told her that Kobie was right there with her. Later she'd figure out how she knew the black tiger was in fact Kobie.

Kobie moved up beside her, and it thrilled Emersyn that she also picked up the scent the men hadn't. Emersyn didn't rush to move by her, she had no idea what she was doing, and her cat recognized the Alpha female beside her. Of course, it made sense and she felt stupid for not realizing it before, Blair and Kobie were Alphas.

Kobie slowed and lowered her body closer to the ground. Emersyn followed her, mimicking the careful steps the more experienced cat took. A movement to the left had both of them pause and turn to look. Emersyn was glad she was in cat form right now because the shock of seeing a huge black jaguar creeping through the brush would have made her unable to stay silent. She watched the male cat and knew after a few seconds that it had to be Calum. Even in the form of a man, he moved the same way, silent, cautious, and predatory.

Emersyn stopped and watched Kobie, and Calum moved closer to the thick grouping of trees, there were branches hanging low with vines wound around them. It was a perfect hiding spot, she thought if one wanted to hide something.

Noah moved up alongside Emersyn, his sides heaving from running, but his body was steady. She noticed he was slowly moving to put his body between her and the area in front of them. She realized she was sending out waves of anxiety and he had picked up on them. She stepped back, giving him the space to move if needed.

She dropped belly to the ground, her legs shaking as she watched Calum go into the growth until she couldn't see him. Kobie stood, like a statue watching where he'd gone in. Emersyn slowly took the air into her body, trying to figure out what was in there. How had she sensed it when the wet growth in the area was ripe with so many scents?

Calum came back out and was wearing jeans. She blinked, where had the jeans come from? She turned and looked at Blair to see a bag of some kind around his large body. They brought clothes with them. It made sense. She huffed out a breath, she had no clothes with her.

"Someone's been staying out here." Calum held up a worn backpack and a larger bag.

Kobie moved by him, still in cat form, and went into the bush. Emersyn wasn't sure what she was doing until she came back out, glanced once at her mate, and then started running in the opposite direction.

Calum set the items down and looked at Noah, "take Emersyn and Nichelle back up to the house—tell Cale what's happening."

Noah responded with a quick chuff sound. He turned to look at Nichelle, who needed no more than that to take off running back in the direction they'd come from.

Emersyn's cat didn't move, she couldn't focus to get her to. What if the person hiding here was here to take her back to that house? Lindon may be dead, but he had a lot of men that followed his orders. The panic became so real her muscles felt like they locked up.

Noah came closer and nudged her gently. A low yowl that echoed pain came out of her throat.

Noah looked at Calum.

"She's panicking," Calum told him.

Without hesitation, Noah turned back to her. He rubbed along her side while making soft chuffing noises. Emersyn may not speak cat yet, but her animal understood and overrode the fear that was paralyzing her limbs.

After a shaky start, she began to run back from the area she'd started in. She didn't have to slow down and look to see if Noah was with her, she could hear his paws landing in time with her own. It might have been the stress of the situation or even the exertion of the run, but when she saw the trailer, her legs felt numb. She stumbled twice and then decided for her own safety she should stop. She was shaking all over now. Would changing back be as scary as shifting into a fur-covered cat? Before she could think about it any further, her legs gave out and everything blurred. Her fur felt hard for a second then she realized fingers were dug into the dirt instead of claws.

"Just let it happen." She heard Shaelan say softly but couldn't focus to see her.

Closing her eyes, she forced herself to relax, and then her body shifted back into the two-legged form.

Someone covered her with a blanket. She turned to see Shaelan giving her a gentle look.

Noah, still a cat, came over and stood close to her. His cat eyes were reflecting his concern.

"I'm okay." She told him and reached a shaking hand up to touch the soft fur along his jaw.

"Nichelle told us what's going on," Shaelan told him. "Cale is on the roof and Jake and Gary are on the way over."

Noah chuffed and looked back to Emersyn.

"Go." Shaelan said, "I'll get her to the house and some food into her."

Noah looked only at her. "I'll be okay, just winded that was—" her voice was hoarse. She felt so weak. "Go make sure we're safe."

He puffed out a breath and then turned and ran into the trees.

Emersyn watched until he was gone. She looked up at Shaelan from where she still lay on the ground. "I'm not sure I can walk."

Shaelan smiled, "I figured as much." She glanced over her shoulder, "Franki and Mika are coming to help."

"Thank you." She struggled to sit up; her arms were so weak. "Is it always like this after?"

Shaelan bent down and put her hand under her arm. "No. The first shift is harder, but your health still isn't the best, so I knew it was going to be a rough landing."

Emersyn nodded, "it was like everything shut off all at once."

Shaelan looked over to see the other two women jogging toward them. "What was it like?"

Emersyn smiled, as she focused on keeping her knees locked so she wouldn't collapse. "It was amazing. I could see more, taste everything and smell the entire bush."

"Nichelle said you scented the location of the bags before Kobie," she smirked, "or Calum."

Emersyn was relieved when Franki took her other arm. "I think it was all of us at once or Kobie knew."

"Mmm," Shaelan held the blanket over her as the other two women helped her toward the house.

Emersyn felt, for a moment, like she wasn't even moving— she'd shifted for the first time in her life—became what she'd, what *they'd* been trying to suppress. Never again, she thought. She glanced back to the trees, hoping Noah was safe. He had to be all right. Her cat had confirmed what the woman had told her years ago. Noah was her mate. Is that why she felt safe around him?

She had a pretty good idea of what mates were and was also certain she couldn't be a true mate to anyone. Too much of her was broken. She had no idea what she was going to do about him just yet, but she trusted no one else to get her daughter back. Her world was a better place with him in it.

Noah had to be okay.

Chapter Sixteen

Noah pulled his jeans on and hurried toward the house. He motioned to Cale to come down from the roof. He'd rushed back ahead of the others so he could check on Emersyn, she'd looked so pale when she'd shifted back. Pulling the shirt over his head as he went, when he jerked it clear of his face, there she was sitting on the step looking at him. Her coloring looked better. "Are you okay?" He asked closing the distance between them quickly.

"A little shaky, but much better, thank you." She was holding a mug in her hands. "Did you find out who the bags belong to?"

Shaelan stepped outside. "Is everyone all right?"

He nodded and turned to look toward the tree line. "They'll be back shortly, they're on foot."

Cale jumped down from the ladder that led to the lower roof over the new backroom. "Did you find them?"

Noah nodded, and looked back at Emersyn, had she eaten? She needed to eat. "Uh, yeah."

"More spies for Tomas?" Cale swung the rifle over his shoulder.

"Uh," Noah rubbed his hand over his neck, not sure how to explain who they'd found, "not a spy. Definitely not working for Tomas."

Nichelle opened the door, "safe to come out?" She held a plate in her hand.

He nodded.

She came out and sat beside Emersyn, then held out the plate. "Eat." She smiled, "it helps a lot."

Shaelan looked at the trees again, making Noah turn. Calum was walking out, wearing his jeans and carrying the two bags they'd found. The expression on his face was serious, but he also looked like he wanted to smile. He walked over and dropped the bags on the ground and looked at Cale.

"We really need to go over this property." He looked Shaelan over as he spoke, no doubt checking that she was fine.

"How did they get on this time?" Cale sounded annoyed, "we've added cameras, and removed branches," Cale shook his head, "how the hell are they getting around it?"

Calum looked over his shoulder, "I guess we'll have to ask her and see."

"Her?" Cale turned to look where he was watching.

Kobie and Blair were coming out of the trees. He wore his jeans; she wore his t-shirt. Between them, a very dirty, angry teen walked with her arms crossed over her chest.

"She's a child." Cale hissed under his breath.

"It's more interesting than that." Calum mused quietly.

Shaelan didn't ask any questions, just rushed in their direction. Noah had no medical training, but it was clear she hadn't eaten a proper meal in a while, and her health, was questionable with how dirty she was. He thought maybe her hair was blonde, but with the dirt and other pieces of nature matted in it, he couldn't be sure.

When they reached them, she stopped and jammed her hands in her pockets, and glared at every adult that stood there. "I am *not* going back."

"We'll get to that part shortly," Calum said as he gave his mate a warning look to stay back, "what's your name?"

Her blue eyes flicked to Calum like he was a bug, if it weren't a serious moment, Noah would have laughed at that. She had guts, he had to give her that.

"Akira." She spat and then turned her focused gaze to Blair.

Blair stood there; arms crossed just looking at her.

"I wasn't hurting anything staying in your forest." She said, a slight whine to her voice now.

"How old are you?" Emersyn asked in a soft tone that Noah suspected was only one a mother would know how to use.

Akira glanced at her for a second, giving her a quick assessment, and then looked back to Blair. "Fifteen."

Blair flicked his gaze to Kobie and then back to her. He held her defiant look with ease.

Noah hadn't gotten close enough to her to know if she was a one-form or one of theirs. Angry defiant teen girls were something he had nightmares about and there was nothing on this earth that would make him move closer to find out.

Nichelle watched her for a moment and then looked at Blair, "is she..."

"She is." He answered quickly.

Nichelle relaxed and then looked at the girl, "I'm Nichelle. Would you like some juice or a sandwich?"

Noah blinked, it wasn't the first thing he would have done, but some of the anger seemed to drain away as she looked at Nichelle and then nodded without a word.

"I'll go get it."

A few of the adults exchanged a look, and Noah felt better in knowing they were just as surprised as he was.

"Akira," Emersyn moved over on the step, "why don't you sit down, you look exhausted." She looked at him for a second, "no one is going to make you do anything you don't want to do."

Noah frowned as he realized she expected him to make it so.

With a cautious look, the girl moved over and sat on the very edge of the step. "How did you find my stuff? I rolled it in that stinky plant."

Everyone looked right at Emersyn.

With her eyes wide, she looked from Kobie to Calum, "there's something metal, I think, in your bags and I could smell it."

Akira blew out a defeated breath. "I didn't think of that." She shook her head, "stupid."

"You did well, covering your scent." Calum's tone was more pleasant now.

"Gee *thanks*." She sent him a hostile look, "and here I thought rolling around in mud and yuck would be a great fashion statement."

Calum's mouth twitched like he wanted to smile but didn't.

Emersyn held out half the sandwich she hadn't touched yet, "you said you're not going back," Akira took it and the first bite vanished half of it, "back where?"

She looked at Emersyn as she chewed it and forced her throat to swallow.

Blair moved closer and crouched down, Noah only had to glance at him to know that he was over his shock of finding her and he was about to turn on that Blair power where he crooned and smoothed everything over to be peachy again.

Noah crossed his arms over his chest and watched the girl.

"Why don't you want to go back?" Blair said in that magic tone he used, "let's start with that."

Lowering the sandwich away from her mouth, she looked at him and Noah could feel the hostility return that fast. "I don't know *uncle,* you tell me."

Blair's expression switched to shock as fast as his color drained.

"You look just like him," she snarled at him, "except with fewer wrinkles, so I know you're related."

"He does." Emersyn agreed softly.

Akira jolted and looked at her. "You know my father?"

Emersyn just nodded, a haunted look appearing in her eyes.

"Hold on," Blair seemed to shake the stunned look off his face, "you made it here all the way from the Elden clan?"

Akira shrugged one shoulder, "I hitched a ride with those idiots he sent here." She looked at the sandwich, "they had no idea I was in the back. I figured you and he didn't get along, or else why was he going after you?" She took a bite and chewed it like she hadn't eaten in weeks.

"What were you planning on doing once you found Blair?"

Her shoulders dropped, and she heaved a sigh. "I don't know. I just," she looked at Kobie, "I just couldn't stay there and wait to be one of his breeders."

Emersyn made a sound of distress and put her arm around her shoulder. "You hated him."

Akira nodded, her head dropping into the crook of Emersyn's neck. "He's an awful man. He didn't even look at me until I started to grow boobs."

Alarms were going off in Noah's head, and his cat was furious. He had to cross his arms over his chest and focus hard to stand there and not move.

Blair dropped his head down; his sigh was audible. When he looked back up, his expression had changed to something softer, "where's your mother?" He barely whispered it.

Akira lifted her face away from Emersyn, "I don't know. I haven't seen her since I was little."

Noah's knees decided he didn't need to stand any longer. He dropped down into a very ungraceful squat. Her mother was from one of the houses. Emersyn's gaze connected with his own, she knew as well that this girl would never see her mother. She gave him a look, that made it feel like his chest was going to split wide open. It was like she believed in him, that he could fix this. When she looked away and leaned back so Akira would look at her, Noah almost slumped to the ground in relief.

"He's dead." Emersyn said in a flat tone, then looked at Blair, "Blair killed him." Her look softened, "you'll never have to see him again."

"For real?" She glared at Blair until he nodded. Just like that all the hostility and anger drained away and the girl collapsed in Emersyn's arms, sobbing.

Blair swore and stood up, pacing away. Kobie spun on her heel and went in the other direction.

Shaelan hurried over and knelt at the bottom step. "Let's go inside and you can take a hot shower and eat some more." She touched her back in a soothing stroke.

Noah could barely breathe. It was never going to end. The living nightmare of finding the victims that were a result of what Tomas had been allowed to get away with for too long. He stood up and moved in the first direction he could which took him away from the others. He couldn't be near anyone right now. It wasn't safe for him to be near anyone right now. How many children were out there being grown for this sick purpose? How many mothers had been taken from their children? He'd done nothing. He'd watched it happening for years and done *nothing* to stop it. He may as well have locked the doors himself. His stomach started rolling, he felt ill. Sweat soaked his shirt as he hunched over, leaning on his knees.

He could taste the bile in his throat and grit his teeth, sucking air in through his nose, trying not to throw up. Squeezing his eyes shut, he tried to think of something— anything other than the girls. So many of them, barely out of their teens, throwing their animal scents. If they'd just shifted earlier, just once it would have saved them. He could hear them crying, confused, not understanding what they did to end up in one of those houses. Through it all, he'd done nothing, turned a blind eye to their suffering, and watched that none got away. He was as bad as Tomas for doing that.

Opening his eyes, he gasped and then stood there hunched over breathing with his mouth wide open. He wasn't there now. He would never be there again. He stared into the field, he was outside, not back there. He was free now, free to find all of them and end it.

"Noah."

He straightened and turned ready to attack. Blair stood a few feet from him, his hands in the air. He hadn't even sensed him coming over.

"You good?"

Noah nodded, swallowing more bile down. He wiped his hand across his forehead which was streaked with sweat.

"Because you don't look good." Blair lowered his hands slowly.

"Shock." He tried to swallow, but his throat felt like it was closed off.

Blair gave him a wide-eyed look, "I'm feeling my own shock right now."

Noah looked at him, really looked at him, he wasn't lying. Akira was the second niece he'd found out about in a short time. "I wasn't there," he whispered and forced another swallow. "I never saw Lindon before-before you killed him."

"Hey," Blair tilted his head, a cautious look on his face, "you know I'm not blaming you, right?" His face scrunched up and Noah couldn't think past his body rebelling to figure out what it meant.

Noah knew he was panting now as if he'd just run a mile, but he had to let his body work through it. A process that felt so natural to him now, was the sweating, forcing air inside, trying to keep the contents of his stomach on the inside. "I didn't stop it."

"Fuck that." Blair glared at him, "like you had a choice." Blair's hand waved in the air, "you were in pieces when you came here, a fucking ghost." He made a low rumbling sound in his chest, "Jesse said the collar on your neck was practically embedded in your flesh when they found you," he gave him a hard look, "how the hell were you supposed to stop anything like that?"

Noah shook his head, anger coursing through him now, for Blair to forgive him so easily. "I didn't do anything."

"The hell you didn't." Blair grimaced, "you survived, and now—" he pointed a finger at him, "now you are. Your intel got us in the door, my friend and we're running with it," he nodded, "we'll find them all and end it."

Noah spun and paced away, then turned back and retraced his steps back to him, "I should have done *more*," the growl that came out with his words wasn't just determined enunciation, his cat was close. Too close. He stepped backward, trying to slow the adrenalin that he hadn't realized was bubbling through him.

"Noah."

He snapped his head to see Emersyn walking toward him. She was still wrapped in a blanket and looked too pale. He shook his head and wanted to tell her to get away from him, to run and lock herself in the house. His teeth were sharper, preventing him from speaking. She just kept moving toward him. He looked at Blair, hoping he was going to save her, would usher her away from him, but he just stood there watching her come closer.

"Noah."

The way she said his name made his cat pause, alert, scenting her to see if she was all right.

"I'm so scared," she whispered.

Of course, she was, he was scaring her. He sucked in a breath, *trying* to find the right thing to say.

He didn't care if he sliced his own tongue off when he spoke. He blinked; his vision kept shifting from his own to his animals. She was right in front of him now. Clenching his jaw, he held his arms at his side, his hands balled into a fist, he could feel the sting on his palms from sharp claws cutting into his flesh.

When she placed her hand on his chest, he held his breath. She shouldn't touch him. Shouldn't *want* to touch him.

"That poor child," she looked up at him, her eyes glistening with unshed tears, "it's awful." She sucked in a shaky breath, "what if—" a tear rolled down her cheek, "Aspyn..."

Noah wrapped his arms around her and pulled her against his chest. He growled low. Nothing would happen to her daughter. Nothing. He would make sure of it. Lifting his head, he saw Blair looking at them. Hugging her tight, probably too tight, he spun them both, so his back was to Blair, sheltering her in his arms.

She sobbed quietly, and it felt like he was being torn into shreds. Relaxing his hold on her, he rubbed his hand down her back, as gently as he could, at least he hoped it was gentle. His cat was giving him back some control, but he was so scared he would hurt her. His hand felt damp, and he realized his palms were bleeding and he was essentially wiping the blood off on the blanket. He wanted to step away from her, too many emotions were riding him right now. But he couldn't leave her.

Leaning down he rested his head on hers and took a deep breath, taking her scent inside him. His cat reacted immediately and backed off. She smelled of spices, making him think of someone baking in the kitchen. It was a ridiculous thought, what the hell did he know about baking? The pleasant scent was tinged with anguish, and he was sure it was that alone that had his cat settle down and behave. Now was not the time to lose control.

As she relaxed in his arms, he became aware of how it felt to hold her. Her soft body fit against his like she was the other half of his own. His gut tightened with need, and it startled him. He tensed and lifted his head from her. He'd never felt lust before but knew this was what it was. He'd seen too much in his life to ever want *that* part of a relationship.

Inhaling, he almost choked on the scent she was throwing now. He grasped her shoulders lightly and looked down at her. He had to be mistaken, she wouldn't want him, not after what she'd been through, not after what he'd done. "It's going to be okay." He told her, just needing to say something to hold her away from his body.

Emersyn took a ragged breath and nodded, "I'm sorry, I just..."

"I know. It all came back to me too."

"Are you okay?"

He stared into her eyes to see concern and worry. She was upset about him? That was ridiculous. "I'm good. Now." He tilted his head, trying to shrug it off. "I just need to eat after that run."

"Is that why?"

He knew she was asking if he was having issues with his cat because he needed to eat. He didn't want to lie to her, but his mouth did anyway. "Yeah. You have to eat regularly, or you'll struggle with control." It wasn't entirely a lie.

She gave him a quick assessing look. "Okay. I'll go make you a sandwich." She frowned, "I've never made one, but I'm sure it's not too difficult." She rubbed her hand over his chest.

He held his breath and realized she didn't care about the scars beneath her palm, in fact, there was no sign that she even noticed them. "I'll be right there." He stepped further back from her and dropped his hands away from her.

She gave him a soft smile and started toward the house.

Noah watched how uneven her steps were and felt worse knowing she'd expended energy she didn't have to comfort him. He looked down at the ground, assessing the state of his cat now. He was restless but was willing to work with him again. Blowing out a breath, he put his hands on his hips and stared at the ground in front of him.

"You good now?"

Lifting his head, he looked to see Blair had returned.

"Yeah." He rolled his eyes, "sorry about that," he tapped his head with one finger, "memories and shit flooded my head."

Blair gave him a surprised look. "That was something else." He motioned up and down his body.

Noah frowned, having no idea what he was saying.

"Your eyes, man, they were a cat." Blair snuffed out a breath, "and your muscles were doing this rolling thing like I've never seen, but you didn't shift."

Noah held out his arm and looked down at it. That hadn't happened in a long time, not since he'd been freed. "Oh, that." He looked back at him, and then touched his throat, "sometimes we forget there is no collar, so it's like he wants out but not completely."

Blair's expression was wide-eyed, "well it's freaky as shit, so let's not do that too often, okay?"

Noah had to grin at his expression. "I try not to."

"Well, good." Blair blew out a breath, "so you're good now?"

Noah looked over to see Calum and Cale standing by the house. "Yeah, well, I think so."

"That was convincing." Blair rubbed his hand over his hair and looked over his shoulder briefly, "it's weird, huh?" He waved his hand toward Noah, "how a mate can just settle shit down with a touch."

Noah did not feel settled down, not in the least, as far as Emersyn touching him went. "Uh," he glanced over to make sure no one was coming toward them, "not really."

"What do you mean, she settled your ass down pretty fast," Blair smirked.

Noah had no idea how to explain it. "It was intense for me." He spoke softly.

Blair gave him a puzzled look, "how do you mean? You looked pretty relaxed."

"Yeah," Noah lifted his hand then dropped it, "a bit arousing." He said the word slowly like it would explain everything to him.

Blair snorted, "*that's* normal." He smirked.

Noah shook his head, "maybe for you." He gave him an annoyed look, "I don't make females of all ages purr when I walk by."

Blair grinned, then sobered when he realized he was being serious. "But it's not like it was the first time you—" his jaw dropped, "*shit*, it was, wasn't it?"

Noah felt like having this conversation was the stupidest thing he'd ever done. The air was filled with awkward tension now.

"That's right," Blair continued, "your cat knew he had a mate all this time, so," he motioned to Noah's body, "so it wouldn't find others," he scoffed, "attractive." He crossed his arms over his chest and just looked at him. "I'm feeling a bit weird about this conversation now."

Noah gave him a hard look. "You think?"

Blair grinned, "so, ah, let's just end it with, if you need to talk to someone," he looked over his shoulder, then back to him, "about that then uh," he made a sour face, "Gage is probably the one that will understand the most."

Noah straightened, "probably, if it were a normal situation." Noah blew out a breath, "I don't think I can ever," he looked at the ground, trying to think how to word it, "after what I've heard and seen, I-I..."

"Hey."

He looked back to Blair to see him giving him a hard look, but he was moving his feet like he wanted to run the other way.

"One day at a time, my friend. Just take it one day at a time." He looked back to the house, "mates tend to figure it out."

Noah doubted that, but his face felt hot, and he just wanted to end this conversation. "Right." He agreed, even though he didn't. Clearing his throat, he motioned to the house, "Emersyn was making me a sandwich."

Blair nodded his head quickly, "yeah, go eat." He reached to pat him on the shoulder and then stopped, and gave him a thumbs-up, "I don't want to disturb your cat right now." He grinned, "scary, weird shit." He mumbled and spun on his heel and went the other way.

Chapter Seventeen

Noah looked out the window and watched the trees blur by them. If he had a list of things that should never be done, this would be one of them. Five adults piled into an SUV was not a good thing for him. He inhaled and then exhaled slowly, at least there were windows.

Calum was driving, and Blair was in the passenger seat. Emersyn and Kobie were sitting in the second seats, leaving Noah sitting sideways in the very back, trying not to bounce a shoulder or his head off things with every turn.

The women seemed content to just chat quietly, mostly things about Aspyn. It didn't take a genius to figure out that Kobie was distracting her with a conversation because Emersyn had been nervous about getting in another vehicle.

Calum glanced in the mirror every five minutes, he figured, checking on him, not the women. Add the constant looks over his shoulder that Blair was giving him had Noah wondering if Blair had shared their conversation with the other man.

He rolled his head side to side, or the looks could be because of the tense vibes he was throwing out there. Driving Noah didn't have a problem, but there was something about being a passenger that had his cat pacing inside him and his nerves on edge. Anything he had no control over tended to do this to him. It was surprising he did enjoy driving, when

Cooper had first insisted he get behind the wheel, Noah had almost had a complete breakdown. Now he had his official 'fake' license and enjoyed it. He didn't know how the Alliance pulled it off, but it wasn't like a man with no identification of any kind could ever have a real one. Noah was fine with playing the part of the man his new identification said he was, even if he knew the truth.

Taking a deep breath, he tried to settle down a bit. Instead of accomplishing that he'd just taken a huge whiff of Emersyn's spicy scent into his body. Now his cat paused, alert, watchful. Rubbing his hand over his face, he squeezed his eyes together for a second. If this dull thud in his temples would go away, he might be able to think his way out of the constant emotional baggage.

When he lifted his hand, he saw that Blair was looking at him again. Tilting his head, silently asking if he was okay. He was so far from okay, but he lifted one shoulder in a slight shrug leading him to believe he was just fine. The expression on his face told him that Blair hadn't shared the last part of their conversation and he was just worried that Noah's cat would freak him out again. Noah smirked at him, amused that he'd shaken Blair that much.

He crossed his arms over his chest so he wouldn't pull his phone out and look at the time *again*. The last check told him he'd been squished in this seat for three hours. He looked at the back of Calum's head, willing him to decide a stop would be a good idea. This was the first time he'd been away from Shaelan, and Noah couldn't tell how he was actually doing because he never really showed any emotion. The only sign the big man had given that it bothered him was when they were leaving, and he hesitated to get into the vehicle and looked back at Shaelan for a moment.

Calum tapped his phone screen, making a message leave the screen. "We'll stop before we cross the border and gas up and stretch our legs," Calum said as if he was reading Noah's mind. "Once we're up there, I want to keep moving." He made eye contact with him, "I know most of the clans, but if Lindon's been in the area, there could be surprises."

"When are we meeting up with the member of the special ops team?" Kobie sat forward.

"Just before we cross, she had to travel from Northwest Territories where the team was finishing a few things up." Calum glanced to Blair, then back to the road.

"Everything's all right?" Kobie asked.

Calum nodded but didn't speak again.

Noah's gut knotted. He was going to be trapped back here with another female. "Are we driving straight through or stopping?" He asked, hopeful for the first, "Blair and I could take turns driving."

Blair turned and smirked at him, "you think I'd let you drive with my mate in the vehicle?"

Noah shrugged, "Kobie could drive."

Blair frowned, "we're stopping closer to dark." He turned around and stared out the window again.

Noah could see the amused look on Calum's face in the mirror. He knew full well that when Blair had tried to show Kobie how to work some of the rigs, she almost tipped it over with them inside.

Kobie's soft laugh echoed through the interior. "I'm sure I'll be fine with a steering wheel." She offered.

Blair turned and looked at her. "Calum never gets tired, it's fine."

Kobie turned to Emersyn, "you should learn how to drive too."

Noah watched the reaction as she turned to answer her, "I've never thought of driving." Her voice was quiet, "I never thought…"

Kobie nodded, "there's lots of time."

Noah heaved a sigh of relief that she ended the conversation before Emersyn got upset. He knew he'd have to comfort her if she did and with his current state of being stuffed into too small of a space, he would have had to rip out a seat to do that.

After being stuck in the back for almost six hours, Noah stumbled from the vehicle with numb stiff legs and came close to eating dirt. Straightening, he stretched his arms above his head.

Blair grinned at him, "could be worse, could be Calum's car."

Calum gave him a warning look, "leave my car out of this." Clearing his throat, he motioned to the treed area, "you ladies can go for a run if you like."

Kobie looked at Blair, then to Emersyn, "are you up to it?"

Emersyn's expression changed to surprise, "I don't know."

Noah started to say he could go with them, to watch over Emersyn when a tall woman came out of the trees. Blair looked as surprised as he felt, but Calum wasn't even startled.

"It's safe." She said and kept moving toward them with long strides, "I just checked it out."

She had shoulder-length auburn hair and pale green eyes that Noah thought could maybe look right through him to his soul. His cat wasn't happy with the feeling either.

"Blaise," Calum said with a smile. "You got here before us."

She grinned at him, "when I heard I was meeting up with you, I knew it would be a short window, so I didn't dally."

Blair looked around. "Where's your car?"

"In a small-town North of here." She slung the bag from her shoulder and set it on the ground. "If you're going for a run, I'll come to watch over you." She looked from Kobie to Emersyn and then stopped and stared at her.

Emersyn frowned, "I feel like I know you."

Blaise's mouth quirked, she reached up and pulled her shirt down to reveal that half of her neck was dark with a scar, or birthmark, Noah couldn't be sure. She shoved up her right sleeve to show the dark pigmented skin on her arm.

Emersyn's eyes went wide. "Blaise." She said the name on a breath, then put her hand over her mouth. "You beat up my brother."

Blaise grinned, "I did, he deserved it."

"You two know each other?" Kobie glanced at Blair.

"We did when we were kids." Blaise said and then shook her head, "when I heard an Emersyn was going to be on this trip, I thought, what if it's her." She motioned to her, "then I saw those huge emerald eyes and knew it was you."

Emersyn put her hand over her mouth again and then nodded. "You work for the Alliance? Your family? Are they over here or still back there?"

"No, all of us are here now." She shrugged, "we've been trying to get your family to come over, but they still won't leave in case you came back. Maybe now they will."

Emersyn made a sound of distress.

Noah's cat didn't like this talk at all, it was upsetting her. He cleared his throat and looked around, "if you're going for a run, you should before it's dark."

Kobie nodded, "yeah, I don't want to be standing here when it is."

"We shouldn't stay here too long," Calum confirmed. He looked to Blaise, "you'll go with them?"

She nodded, "absolutely." She looked at Blair and then bowed her head to him briefly.

Noah breathed a quick sigh of relief; the upsetting talk of families was over for now. He watched the two women usher Emersyn toward the trees.

"Should I be bowing my head to you and Blair?" He heard her ask as they walked away.

Kobie's chuckle was the only reply he heard.

Turning back, he saw Calum dialing his phone.

"So why did you need to rid of the girls?" Blair gave him a curious look.

Noah looked from one to the other and then at the trees. He'd wondered why he was anxious to send the women off on their own. He clenched his jaw, that Blaise woman had better keep a good watch on them.

"Hold on, Dev, let me turn down the volume and put it on speaker." Calum's words had Noah focused on him again.

"Sorry about the mayday message," Devin said, "but I wasn't sure what time you left and wanted to give Noah a heads up."

Noah jerked back and looked at the phone. "Me?"

"Yeah, we've been stalling them for a long time, and they're done waiting."

Noah looked to see Blair had no idea what he was saying either. "Who?"

"Your family." Devin sounded exasperated, "your mother particularly," he cleared his throat, "she could rival my own on the scale of, you scare me."

Noah shook his head, he vaguely remembered her, but what he did recall he thought Devin's description was accurate.

"They're going to be at Ed's by the time you," he mumbled something, "shortly after you get back."

Noah's knees almost gave out. "What?" He'd heard, but needed to clarify what he'd heard, "my parents are going to Ed's? Now?" His heartbeat increased at the thought. How could he see them? How could he tell them about Carlene? He'd failed her and them.

"Noah?"

He blinked and looked at Blair, who made a point of looking at Noah's arm.

Shaking his head, Noah realized his cat was picking up on his distress and was trying to come out again. Noah had never had issues controlling his cat like he was the last few days. "I'm fine." He said in a quiet tone, "just…"

"Freaking out?" Blair crossed his arms and looked at him.

Noah nodded.

"They're not angry, Noah," Devin said, "just want to see you with their own eyes and want you to meet your siblings. The message says they're leaving at the start of next week."

Siblings? Noah's chin jerked to look back at the phone. "My what?"

"You have a brother and sister you've never met."

Noah's knees gave out then made him drop to squat. Blair came over and put his hand on his shoulder. Noah nodded his head, he was fine. All of them knew it was a lie.

"Sorry to dump this on you, but I figured you'd need a few days to process before you saw them."

"Understatement," Blair said and leaned down. "You good?"

Noah shook his head and stood up slowly, pausing to rest his hands on his knees. He didn't feel ill or the way he did normally, this was a genuine shock. "I have a brother and a sister." He whispered.

Blair grinned, "I have nieces."

Noah shrugged, yeah if anyone understood what he was feeling right now, it was Blair. "Uh, thanks, Devin." He looked at Calum and wasn't sure what he was thinking, "for the heads up."

"Any other bombs you'd like to drop on us?" Calum sounded amused now.

"No, I think that's it for now." Devin's tone was lighter as well, "I have more information about the ambassador issue, but it can wait until you guys get through this."

"Oh yeah," Blair put his hands on his hips and looked at the phone, "it's going to be all laughs and giggles here."

Devin did laugh at that, "I talked to Dad and Ed earlier about that clan," he cleared his throat, "I guess it's your clan…"

"I already have a clan," Blair said quickly.

"Well, you need to decide what you're doing with this one too, without an acting Alpha…"

"I know, they can't be under the Alliance's protection." Blair finished.

"Let's just get there and see what we're looking at first." Calum offered.

"Fuck," Blair paced a few feet away, "my property can't fit any more buildings without looking like a damn village."

Calum grinned, "clan village isn't just a coin phrase."

Blair looked back and gave him a hard look, "you know what I mean."

"Ed is looking into the land that runs to the East of it," Devin said.

"He's what?" Blair sighed, "shit." He stepped back, his hands clasped on his head, and closed his eyes.

Noah realized that he wasn't the only one facing hard times and trying circumstances. "Maybe they'll all be males and Ed is hoping to balance out the excess females in his clan."

Calum grinned when Blair opened his eyes and glared at him.

Devin chuckled. "Just get there safely and call me once you have things settled."

"We will." Calum glanced at the trees, "Blaise is already here."

"Did you know she knew Emersyn as a child?" Noah had to know.

"I had no idea," Devin said quietly.

"We're going to have to let you go, Devin," Calum was looking toward the trees.

Noah turned to see the women were coming back already. Emersyn was smiling and didn't look too unsteady with her steps, so he conveyed to his cat that she was well. He, however, was still numb at the idea he had siblings he'd never met and was going to have to face his parents.

Chapter Eighteen

"Why did we have to walk this far?"

Calum glanced back at Blair, "if the car isn't seen in the town, no one will know we're here."

Blair shrugged, "okay, but we could have parked at the top of the hill."

Emersyn smiled to see the look Kobie gave him. She didn't care if they had to climb twenty hills, she was close to finding her daughter and she'd do anything to get her back.

Glancing over her shoulder, she saw that Noah wasn't far behind her and Blaise behind him. She couldn't believe Blaise was here. She'd thought of her from time to time and wondered if she'd overcome the bullying she used to face. It wasn't her fault half of her upper body was covered in darker-colored skin. She smiled at her when their gazes met. Judging by the t-shirt she wore now, even in this cold, Blaise no longer cared what others thought of her. A woman as tall as Blaise carrying a gun, she was very comfortable holding would end any bullying for sure. She looked at the gun in her hand, or it could be that. She stumbled and turned to pay attention to where she was walking again.

Kobie stopped walking, so Emersyn paused as well. Calum was looking at his phone. He looked around slowly. She hoped they weren't lost.

"Some rough terrain coming up," he pointed, "but if we cut across here, we can avoid some of it."

"Done," Blair said quickly.

Kobie grinned, "I think we need to go for more walks."

Blair raised an eyebrow and looked at her, "and you'd like to fit that in when?"

She shrugged, "I'll figure it out." Kobie turned and looked around. "We need to go faster; I don't want to miss this woman when she checks for us."

"Would have been good if she'd mentioned a time," Blair mumbled but followed Calum.

Emersyn tripped over a small rock and came close to falling when a strong arm wrapped around her waist and prevented it.

"Careful," Noah said, his breath hitting the back of her neck.

A shiver went through her, and she was momentarily stunned to realize it wasn't a bad feeling, just one she never thought she'd feel. Her cheeks went hot as she turned and looked up at him. "Thank you. I'm not in the greatest shape." She rolled her eyes, "not much hiking in my life."

"I know, mine either until lately." He walked more beside her now, which made her feel better, less alone.

She didn't want to tell him that every little movement out there scared her. The closest she'd been to nature since that day she'd regret forever was when they allowed the windows to be open in the summer. Even after Aspyn was big enough to venture outside, she was not allowed to accompany her. It was too risky for a mother and child to go outside together.

"How are you doing?"

Startled out of her thoughts, she gave him a half-smile. "Anxious."

He nodded, his gaze moving over her face, almost as if he were caressing it with his eyes. "Everything will be fine." He told her, but she could see the doubt in his eyes.

His lying to her meant a lot at this point, he was still looking out for her, even in that small way, despite her being able to scent that he was having his own struggles. The car ride had been particularly hard, to sit there and feel the emotions coming off him and not be able to do anything about it. She wondered a few times on the trips if the others in the car were able to pick up on them, surely it wasn't just her.

Turning, she looked to see Blaise looking all around them, still holding the gun. She wondered what she did exactly, to be so versed with a weapon. Or weapons, as she'd spotted the knife handles sticking out of a strap on her leg. Whatever it was, she felt both intimidated and more assured that she was getting her child back, today.

"I'll be right back." Noah moved by her and walked quickly past Kobie until he reached Blair. He said something to him, making Blair pause in step and looked around. Nodding, they both moved to reach Calum, halting him and speaking to him. Calum looked down at the map in his hand.

"I'm going to check around that hill," Blaise said loud enough that both Kobie and Emersyn heard.

"I'm going to see what secrets they're keeping." Kobie gave her a forced smile, a lot of teeth showing, and went toward her mate.

Emersyn was happy for a minute to catch her breath. She really felt like she was slowing them all down. Resting her hands on her hips, she looked in the direction Blaise went, wondering what she was checking for exactly. Maybe she had to go to the bathroom, that thought occurred and she was happy she'd thought of that before they'd started out. She turned again and saw a single flower a few feet away, it was purple and stood out among the dying grass and weeds. It was juvenile and she knew it, but she still walked over to it, needing to touch the fragile-looking thing that was holding its own out here in the elements.

Smiling at the lonely bloom, she leaned down to touch it and the ground gave way under her feet. She tried to grab onto something, anything as her body fell. Her shoulder smacked a hard surface sending her spiraling in another direction. When she landed on her side, all she could do was gasp to find her breath again.

She didn't move for a moment, checking if the pain was from the fall or something serious.

Her face was covered in dirt, it was even in her mouth. The grit in her eyes made it impossible to open them without them burning. Sitting slowly, she groaned when she moved her arm, it was stinging. Panicking she brushed at her face trying to clear it.

"Emersyn."

She paused and blinked furiously as she lifted her chin to look up. It was so dark, the only thing she could see was the light above her where she'd come down.

"Stay back from the edge." Calum's deep voice echoed.

"Emersyn," Noah called again.

"I'm," she coughed clearing the dust from her throat, "here." She didn't know if she said it loud enough that they would hear her.

"No, I didn't bring a rope." Blair sounded annoyed.

"Emersyn, stay calm. I'm coming down."

"Noah, you can't…"

Debris started to fall on her head, she scrambled a few feet to her left and curled her arms over her head. A thud and quiet gasp told her that Noah had just jumped into the hole she was in.

He coughed, "Emersyn." She heard movement. "Are you all right?" He was right beside her now.

She reached out and then winced as the pain went through her shoulder. "I don't know." Opening her eyes wide, she tried to see again.

"Noah." Blair bellowed down the hole.

"I'm fine." He growled back at him. "Look for a way to get us up."

"Right, I'll just pop to the hardware store and grab a ladder," Blair called down.

"Noah, can you climb back up?" That was Calum.

"Give me a minute." He touched her side. "I can smell blood, she's hurt." His warm hands moved down over her leg before he switched to the other. "Can you move?" His breath brushed over her cheek.

"Yes." she leaned closer to him; thankful she wasn't alone. "It's my shoulder." Her breath hitched as she tried to see again. "It's so dark." It came out sounding like a whine.

"Hey," he touched her cheek gently, "close your eyes and slow your breathing down," his tone was so gentle, she didn't know how he stayed so calm. "Reach for your cat, she'll help you see in the dark."

"You can see?"

"Yes," he moved in front of her and lifted her arm, she sucked in a breath. "Close your eyes and focus."

She squeezed them shut and blew out a breath trying to focus on her animal. Normally they worked together, but with the panic filling her, she was having trouble. She heard ripping material.

"It's not too bad, I'm going to wrap this around and cover it, so it doesn't get any more dirt in it."

She hissed out a breath when he put something around her arm. It made it throb worse. She also was able to smell more than soil now, she could smell the blood. Giving her head a quick shake, she closed her eyes again and felt for her cat. She was there this time, shaken but alert.

"That's it. I'm going to look for a way back up. Don't move around, we don't know if this drops further."

Her eyes popped open when he said that, and she could actually see. Not as clear as she'd preferred, but she'd take it. "I can see now." She watched him move over a few feet, looking up in all directions.

"Noah," Calum called down.

"It looks like it's been dug up before..."

"Probably an old mining shaft or filled-in quarry." Calum's tone was even, with no panic or concern in it at all. "Is there anything to get a hold of to come back up?"

"I'm looking."

"Watch your head, I'm dropping some light sticks," Blaise shouted.

Emersyn watched them fall, the red looking so bright in the darkness. One hit the bottom and then another one followed.

"Thanks," Noah said as he knelt and looked over at her. "Stay near the side while I figure this out."

She bit her lip, it dawned on her that the man had jumped down here with her having no idea how they were getting out. She felt guilt fill her, he'd done that for her. At the same time, she was grateful he had. If she had been down here long alone, she would be freaking out. She watched him move to the middle and straighten to stand up. That made her look around, she was sitting on a little shelf with only a few inches of space above her head. Her chest tightened. All the earth above her could come down at any time. Her heartbeat stuttered in her chest. "Noah." She whispered, now afraid to talk.

"Hey," he was right there in front of her now, "it's okay, come on, come over here." He held her arm gently as she followed him back to the center and knelt beside her. He wrapped his arms around her and pulled her against his chest.

She closed her eyes and tried to slow her breathing. "I just wanted to look at a flower." It was her fault they were down her. If she'd just stood there and waited as he'd said...

She felt him suck in a breath, "this is not your fault." He squeezed her gently. "None of us could have known this would happen." He kissed the top of her head and then she felt him stiffen.

Reaching with the arm that wasn't throbbing, she wrapped it around his waist. "You are a stupid man for jumping down here." She rested her forehead against his chest, just near his heartbeat.

"Seemed like a good idea at that moment."

She smiled. "Do you have any good ideas to get us out?"

"Mmm, working on it," he sounded distracted, and she realized he was looking around trying to figure it out as he comforted her.

"Blair," he called out, "anything?"

"Not a fucking thing. We're in the middle of the emptiest field I've ever seen." Blair sounded angry now. "Not even a tree I can rip out of the ground."

"Can you climb up?" Calum called down to them.

"Even if I could, Emersyn's arm is hurt, and she can't." He rested his chin on her head briefly, "is there anything in the car?"

"Even if there was, we can't shift and take a chance of being seen out here in the open to run back," Calum answered.

"Right." He moved and released her, then touched her chin so she'd look up at him. "I need to go see how solid the walls are."

She looked into his eyes and saw the resolve there, that somehow, he'd get her out of there. "Okay." His face was so close, that she could taste his breath. Lifting her hand, she placed it on his cheek. "Thank you." She whispered, "again."

Something in his eyes changed and he released her chin and straightened up. "Stay here."

She felt chilled as he moved away and his body heat was gone. Pulling her legs up, she wrapped her uninjured arm around them and watched as he went over to the edge and ran his hand along the rough wall. he looked up to the top and then moved over to another place and did it again.

"Blair?"

"Yeah." His voice echoed down.

"I have a really stupid idea." His tone was without emotion.

"Those seem to be your thing today," Blair answered.

Emersyn focused on him and only him. If she started to look around again, she was going to panic and doing that just delayed him from getting them out.

Noah scoffed; he didn't disagree with Blair. "I'm going to have to bring her up with me, I don't want her to stress her arm until we check it over."

"Makes sense," Blair answered. His voice sounded muffled in some way, and it occurred to her that he must be lying on his stomach looking down into the hole. Were the others holding him, so he wouldn't fall in case more of the earth gave way?

"I don't think I can do it with my hands." Noah finally said.

"You're going to shift? Down there?" Blair sounded stunned, "Is there room?"

"Barely." She watched him move around the small space again while looking up, "there are some small ledges in a few places I think I can dig into."

"And if you fall?"

Emersyn cringed.

"Cats land on their feet, right?" Noah sounded distracted.

Blair snorted, "in theory. Climbing loose dirt isn't like climbing a tree, trust me, it's a full-body workout."

"Noah," Calum called down, he didn't sound as close to the hole as Blair did.

"Yeah?" He sat down and started to take off his boots. Emersyn's eyes widened; he was serious.

"Get mad," Calum told him.

"What?" Noah looked up at the hole, "I don't think—" he dropped his head down and huffed out a breath, "got it."

Emersyn looked up at the hole and then at the man taking off his boots and tying them together. She didn't see how getting mad was going to get them out of here. "Will your cat fit through the hole?" She looked up again.

"We're about to find out." He pulled the small pack off over his head and took off his shirt, then put it back on. As he stuffed his shirt into the pack, he looked over at her. "After I shift, you get on my back and hold on tight, keep your head down."

She nodded, too stunned to speak. He was going to carry her up on his back as he tried to climb out. She looked up and then down to where she sat. If they fell...

"Hey," he was right there beside her now, "I can do this," he whispered with his face level with hers.

She could see the determination in his eyes. She nodded, afraid to speak. He held her look for a moment.

"I'll get us out and then we'll go get your girl, okay?"

She nodded again.

"Put my boots over my neck after I shift, I'm not walking into that camp barefoot." He smirked fleetingly.

She took his boots and nodded again feeling like a mute, not being able to find her voice to speak.

"Okay move over a bit, I need a little room."

She looked and realized he was already naked. She blinked and jerked her eyes back to his face. He was risking so much to get her out of there and find Aspyn. She reached over and put her hand on his back and was shocked to feel the ridges under her hand. His back was as scared as his chest.

He watched her over his shoulder, a guarded expression on his face.

"I know you can do this." she finally managed to say. "If anyone can, it's you."

He searched her face for a second and then turned his head away and blew out a breath.

Emersyn moved away from him to give him enough room. She'd seen him as his cat, and she was having doubts there was room for both of them in this space. She heard the bones moving as his two-legged form shifted into his animal. As his skin disappeared, it was almost as if he blurred for a moment and then a large striped beast was a few inches away from her.

"You crazy son of a bitch, get your ass up here," Blair called down to him.

Noah lifted his big head and looked up; he made a soft chuff sound twice in reply. She wasn't sure what he'd said but could hear Blair chuckle. Crouching down, he turned and looked at her. She blinked, realizing he was waiting for her.

"Oh yes." She moved over so she was right up against him. Placing the boots over his large neck, she adjusted them, so they hung evenly, not even knowing if it was going to make a difference. She ran her hand down over his neck to his shoulders. "I can't believe we're doing this." She whispered and then moved slowly to lay over his back. She felt the leather strap from his pack and gripped it on either side of his body, ignoring the pain in her arm.

Noah shifted and made a soft sound. She didn't know how she understood him, but he was telling her that wasn't good enough.

"If I wrap my legs around you, can you still move?" She asked him as she did it. Wrapping her arms around his thick neck and chest and her legs until they were under his body. She blew out a breath and let her body settle. He was so big she felt tiny in comparison. She lowered her face into the fur, keeping her head out of the way, so he could move his freely. His fur was soft and thick. She realized as she adjusted her hands that the scars that were on his skin were beneath his fur as well. She squeezed her eyes shut, silently cursing the men that had marred his body with them. "I'm ready," she whispered into his fur. Her cat was closer to the surface now, giving her more strength to hold on with. His scent was dark and musky, and it somehow calmed her and the animal inside her, even though she could feel the tension in his body.

He moved his body up and down a few times, no doubt trying to adjust to the weight of a grown woman on his back, she imagined. She kept her eyes closed, not wanting to see anything from this point on. If she made the slightest sound, she could distract him from his task.

He made a low rumbling sound and she felt it vibrate through her whole body. She sucked in a breath and held it just as her whole body shifted to almost be upright on him. Biting her lip, she tried not to make a sound, but inside she was screaming in fright.

Noah growled out an eerie sound that gave her goosebumps. Her weight shifted and she squeezed harder with her legs trying to stay as still as she possibly could. The muscles under her hands flexed and hardened to the point it felt like steel was beneath the flesh and fur.

His sides sucked in for a brief second and when they expanded, she felt like she was dangling in the air. Clamping her teeth together she pushed her head into his shoulders, trying to hold on.

"A little more." Blair's voice sounded so much closer now.

Noah made that skin-tingling noise again and suddenly hands were grabbing her. She panicked for a second.

"Let go, Emersyn, we've got you."

She reluctantly let go of him and let her body be dragged in another direction. She hugged her arms to her chest and realized she gripped his boots in them.

"Get the rest of your ass up here," Blair grunted.

Emersyn opened her eyes to see she was laying several feet away and Blair and Calum were on opposite sides of the hole pulling on the pack strap around Noah. He had his head and both front legs out of the hole, sprawled wide in front of him.

She held her breath, scared he might fall back into it. Shifting, she went to get up, but a strong hand grabbed her arm. She looked to see a wide-eyed Kobie shake her head at her.

Blaise moved over to the men and dropped down onto her stomach. "Get a grip on this." She stretched her arms out, and what looked like a belt landed in front of Noah's one paw.

Noah growled a low sound and then shifted his paw and Blaise was dragged forward by the weight.

"Help them." Emersyn looked at Kobie.

Kobie scrambled over and dropped by Blaise's feet and grabbed her one leg and leaned back.

As more of Noah's body appeared out of the hole, Emersyn squeezed the boots tighter, holding her breath. When he lunged over Blair's body and landed behind him, she dropped back and panted trying to breathe like she'd been the one climbing.

Blair rolled away from the hole and lay on his back. "You are one insane son of a bitch." He started laughing quietly.

Noah stood up and gave his huge body and shake, sending dirt and debris all over Blair. Turning he looked over at her and walked with careful steps toward her. Once he reached her, he nudged her with his head until she sat up.

"I'm okay." She rubbed her hand over his face. Not even knowing the words to say. She looked down and then held out his boots. "I saved your boots."

"Let's get over to that hill people, carefully," Calum said.

Noah bumped his nose against her. She stood up with shaking legs and walked with her hip brushing along his side as he escorted her to where the others were going.

When they reached an area that mostly rocks, the others sat down and looked relieved. Noah pulled the boots from her hand and bound down the hill to a large rock formation.

Emersyn turned and looked to see the others eating and drinking.

"You bunch are my kind of crazy." Blaise grinned at Blair.

He blew out a breath, "Noah's trying out new levels of it lately.

"Let's look at your arm." Blaise stood up and brushed the dried grass off her black pants and then picked up her pack and came over to her.

Chapter Nineteen

"Do you think we missed her?" Kobie looked out around the tree.

"It's still early." Blair was on the other side of the tree.

Noah looked at them and wondered if they stopped to consider their light hair was going to stand out like a bright lamp in the trees now that the leaves were on the ground. He looked down, under the few inches of snow. The last part of the walk had been cold, wet, and had a lot of snowfall. He was glad it was after he'd gotten her out of the hole, or he might never have gotten his body out of there if the ground was slick with snowfall. Turning, he watched Emersyn play with her foot in it. Probably the first time since she was a child she'd been in snow. He frowned, or ever. He hadn't really asked a lot about where she was from. Did they get snow there? He'd have to talk to Calum when this was done.

Checking there was no one behind the building, he went over to her. "How's your arm?" He looked again to see Calum was still standing to the side of the building. "You should have shifted, it would heal."

She turned her head and gave him a look filled with annoyance, "I'd already cost us a lot of time."

He shrugged, "a few more minutes wouldn't have mattered."

"Someone's coming." Kobie hissed.

He turned back and leaned around the tree to watch. Calum stood in the shadows for a moment as a young woman walked behind the building. She stopped and looked around, disappointment was clear on her face, even from here. She wasn't very big, making Noah question how old she was.

"McKenna?" Calum stepped around the corner.

She spun around and looked at him, then looked around. Moving closer, with cautious steps, she didn't take her eyes off him. "Are you from the Alliance?"

Calum nodded.

"They sent one guy? That's it?" She swatted the strawberry blonde hair back out of her eyes.

Noah hadn't expected her to say that.

She put her hands on her hips and glared at him, "Took you long enough to get here."

Blaise moved out of the trees and started in their direction.

Noah looked down at Emersyn, "stay here until we're sure she's alone." She nodded. He looked over to see Blair give him a quick nod.

"I'll stay with Emersyn," Kobie whispered.

Noah moved around the tree at the same time Blair did. He checked over his shoulder to see if the women were visible where they stood. He didn't see them. When he turned back around McKenna was looking at Blair, her eyes were filled with fear.

She lowered her head. "Shit. I knew it was too good to be true."

Calum gave Blair an amused look.

Blair stopped and gave his head a shake. "I'm thinking I need to dye my hair blue or something."

Kobie was walking up behind him, "I think your man enough to pull off a faded pink at least," she glanced at Blaise as she walked over, and she nodded.

"I am not him." Blair sounded annoyed.

McKenna lifted her head and looked at him, a scowl on her face. "You could be his twin," she shrugged, "only younger."

"Lindon is dead," Emersyn said quietly as she came over and stood beside Noah.

The young woman's shoulders visibly dropped. "That explains why he hasn't been around." She nodded her head for a moment, "that makes it easier." Her hands were back on her hips as she looked around at them. "You guys are not what I expected. I took a big chance calling that number." She frowned, "but my gran said the story Lindon told was lies, so I'm trusting you." She scowled at Calum.

He looked completely unphased by her harsh scrutiny. "What did you expect." Calum scanned the area.

McKenna shrugged, "an army of big men."

Kobie grinned, "trust me, we're all you need."

Dark eyes turned to her and looked her up and down. "I didn't even know if that number was right."

"It hasn't been used in a while," Calum told her as he swung the backpack over his shoulder.

"We're looking for my daughter," Emersyn stepped forward, "Lindon took her."

McKenna raised an eyebrow, "that's kind of what he did. There are a few children there." She picked up the bag and slung it over her shoulder, "We should get moving. If I'm gone too long the big ugly one will come looking."

Noah glanced at Blair, he had the same expression on his face, what were they walking into?

"A girl named Akira showed up at our place," Kobie said.

"That's where she went?" McKenna frowned, "where is your place?"

"A few day's drive away from here," Blair told her.

"Good for her. I'd be gone too, but I don't want to leave my grandmother behind." She shrugged, "and she says she's too old to run now." She looked at Blair for a moment, Noah could still see the surprise in her eyes, "Kira got out at the right time." She smirked, "Lindon was furious when she wasn't there when he came back with some lame cat shifter." She turned and gave Noah a hard look. "If she'd been there…"

"We get it," Kobie said.

"How far is it? The camp?" Calum had his phone in his hand.

"Forty-five-minute walk." She pointed to a large hill, "that way."

Calum looked where she pointed and turned to Blaise, "you good to scout ahead?"

"I'm aces, boss." She grinned. "Still stoked that I'm helping you guys," she looked at Blair, "the man that took out the menace and," she turned back to Calum, "and Calum who cat eats wild bears for breakfast."

Calum blew out a breath and then shook his head. "I didn't eat it." He motioned to the direction McKenna had pointed.

Blaise shrugged and headed that way at a slow jog.

Noah chose to walk at the back where he could see everyone. His cat was still on edge after their mate fell into the earth. He would never be able to unsee the ground swallowing her. His heart he was sure stopped beating altogether until he heard her voice below. Emersyn slowed and looked over her shoulder at him.

Both seemed to be doing that now, constantly checking where the other was, not moving too far away. He wanted to lie to himself and tell him it was just from what they had gone through, but he knew the truth. He watched all the mated pairs doing it constantly. Kelsey and Gage were always pausing in what they were doing to check on the other one. Kobie and Blair seemed to sense the other one before they needed to look around. Calum and Shaelan even did it. He looked up at Calum, wondering how he was able to be here without losing his mind because he couldn't check on Shaelan.

Clenching his jaw, he looked behind them, making sure no one else was there. He didn't like the fact that they were just going to walk into the camp of this clan as if they belonged there. Shouldn't they observe it for a bit, know who was where, or if anyone else was watching?

He looked at Kobie, a step behind Blair, and wondered what the chances were he could suggest the women wait somewhere. His cat seemed surprised, confirming that there was no way Kobie would just stand back and watch the men walk in there alone.

Blaise came jogging back toward them. "All clear ahead."

Calum stopped and turned to McKenna, "how many are there that are loyal to Lindon?"

"There's four, he took the others with him last time he left," she shrugged, "none of them have come back."

"That's because they're locked in a cell at the Alliance," Blair said, crossing his arms over his chest.

"You got all of them?" Her eyes rounded. "You're about to make a lot of people happy." She looked him up and down again, "are you the baby brother that disappeared?"

Blair raised an eyebrow at that. "I guess I am."

She nodded her head slowly, "my granny told me about everything that went down." She gave him a hesitant look, "Lindon leaves your cousin in charge when he's gone." She scowled, "he's an asshole."

Blair looked at his mate slowly, then shrugged and turned back to her. "I'm pretty good at dealing with assholes."

Calum smirked. "Are there any that couldn't handle transportation somewhere else?"

Blair's head snapped back to Calum, a warning look in his eyes.

"Just covering all bases, Blair," Calum said calmly.

"No, everyone's in decent health." She said it in a way that made Noah feel like they weren't doing as well as she made out.

"How is it you're allowed to leave by yourself?" Noah watched her as she paused before answering.

McKenna scoffed, "oh, they think I'm an obedient girl." She bowed her head, "yes, sir, no, sir." She looked back at him, pinning him where he stood with a look of loathsome. "They don't even know I'm their worst nightmare. I sabotage just about everything they try to set up or do." She shrugged, "I even set fire to the supply shack to buy Akira more time."

Calum grinned and placed his hand on her shoulder, "glad you're on our side."

"I'm on *my* side, don't forget that." She shrugged off his hand, "I just want my clan safe and not terrorized and living in shacks with no heat or running water." She glanced at Blair, "you got that?"

Blair nodded, the muscle in his jaw was pulsing. "We want the same thing." He said quietly. Kobie moved over and put her arm around his waist and rubbed a hand over his chest.

Noah looked at Emersyn to see that she was looking up at him. For a moment, all he was aware of was her, the others faded into the background. If he were a normal man, he would lean down and kiss her mouth. He'd never kissed anyone before, but if he did, it would be her.

"Noah."

He jerked his head to look at Calum.

"We're going ahead with McKenna," he glanced at Blair, a slight smirk on his face, "Blair will come in after us, so everyone doesn't start bowing to him or he doesn't scare the hell out of them.

Blair sucked in a breath and stuck his chest out, "I'm a scary guy."

Kobie chuckled and started walking again.

"But I am." Blair hurried after her.

Noah glanced back to the woman beside him. "Stay back with Kobie, okay?"

She nodded, then put her hand on his arm, "be careful, please."

He looked at her mouth, the urge to kiss her popping into his head again. Turning on his heel he rushed after Calum.

Chapter Twenty

Noah didn't like the way he was feeling, the unknown had him tense and edgy. They were walking into this camp without a real plan in place. McKenna said she could walk them right to the door of the house that Lindon's followers stayed in. She said that no one else would look twice because the dead false alpha always walked strangers into the camp. Noah wanted to believe it was going to be that simple, but he didn't. Lindon had been missing for a while now and people would have noticed that.

He exchanged a quick glance with Blair, he wasn't feeling this simple plan either. Calum was too hard to read to know if he was buying they could just stroll in.

"Won't his men know?" Kobie whispered, breaking the silence in the group. "I mean, they must have tried to contact him, right?"

Blaise nodded, but the expression on her face said she didn't care one way or another.

Noah's cat was alert, poised for trouble and as hard as he tried to calm him, the animal wasn't falling for it. That was the last thing he needed, for him to lose control in an already tense situation.

McKenna pointed to a hill to their right. "You can sit up there and watch what's happening." She glanced at Emersyn and then Kobie.

"No one will notice us sitting there?" Kobie gave her mate a quick look.

"No," McKenna adjusted the pack on her back, "I could sit there for a month, and no one ever looks there." She turned completely and looked at Blaise, "if you're coming down with us, you're going to have to lose the weapons," she motioned to the gun strapped to Blaise's leg, "no female would ever have a weapon."

Blaise gave her a look as if she had just slapped her in the face. She turned to Calum.

"She's right, they won't look too hard at us, but an armed female," he shrugged.

Heaving out a sigh, Blaise unstrapped the gun and turned to hand it to Blair, "I want it back as soon as we're in."

He took it and tucked it into the pack and then put it on his back.

She scowled as she looked down the hill in the direction they'd go. "I'm keeping my knives." She undid the other strap on her hip and then lifted her shirt and then looped the leather around her waist. Yanking her shirt down, she adjusted her jacket so you couldn't tell they were there. "So, what's the plan? I'm being marched in as a new breeder?"

McKenna looked her up and down, "Lindon has brought other women in to help with the kids before."

Blaise smirked and looked down at herself, "do I look like a nanny?"

"No, but neither did they." McKenna turned and motioned, "we can see most of it from there, I'll point out where we're going," she paused and looked at Blair, "do you have a hat?"

He gave her a confused look.

"Your hair, it's bad enough you look like him," she glanced at Noah, "I just don't want the others panicking when they see you."

"Why would they panic?" Kobie looked from Blair back to her, "wasn't he the Alpha? They'd be used to him being there."

McKenna shook her head, "Him coming back was never for good reasons." She looked at Emersyn for a second, "he'd bring a child or take a girl, he never just visited without a reason." She sighed in an exasperated way, and swung the pack off her back, "I don't think you guys are getting it." Opening the bag, she pulled out a black toque and tossed it at Blair, "wear that, there will be less crying and freaking out."

Blair looked at it, his expression hard as he jammed it on his head.

Noah's heart felt like it was in his throat now. They were walking into a version of the hell he'd been freed from. Turning, he went over to Emersyn. "You stay up there," he pointed to the hill McKenna had pointed out, "and don't come down until I signal you."

She looked up at him, the fear in her eyes wasn't hard to see, he was feeling it too. She nodded. "Aspyn..."

"Don't worry, I'll get your little girl, Em," Blaise said in a tone that sent a shiver down Noah's spine.

"Okay." Emersyn nodded again. "Be safe." She held his look for a few seconds, before turning to the others, "all of you."

Kobie came over and stood beside her, "we'll be fine." She put her hand on Emersyn's shoulder all while giving her mate a pointed look.

"Let's do this." Calum motioned for McKenna to lead the way.

The camp turned out to be a grouping of sheds, the kind you would buy and assemble in your backyard to store garden tools. The only real building was a large cabin, that Noah guessed had already been here when Lindon had brought his clan to this new location.

Noah turned to see Blair and was just as appalled by the idea that they had been forced to live in these conditions. He couldn't guess what was going through his head, but from what he knew about Blair, there was no question that his plan of just introducing himself and leaving was no longer happening. Noah knew nothing about leadership or would ever have to know, but he decided he wasn't leaving these people here either. He was never leaving mistreated people behind again.

Calum looked angry and that was a first. Focused, determined, or annoyed he'd seen on the man's face before, but never angry. It made him feel better, slightly, if a man like Calum was going in with that kind of determination, then Lindon's followers didn't stand a chance.

In the center of the camp, a fire was going, a woman sat beside a pot cutting something up and putting it in it. Noah tensed when she turned and saw them walking in. McKenna raised her finger to her lip to tell her to stay quiet. The woman looked each of them over and then turned back to do what she had been. Noah was surprised it was that easy.

There were no guards, no one keeping watch anywhere he looked. How were these people kept here? The woman at the fire didn't have a collar on, and neither did McKenna. What had Lindon done to keep them in line? There had to be something. His cat nudged him to focus, now was not the time for the endless circle of thoughts in his head.

As they slipped between two of the sheds, an older woman opened the door and looked relieved to see McKenna. The expression in her eyes told him this was her grandmother.

McKenna went over to her quickly, "stay inside." She whispered. The woman looked at Calum and then at him and Blaise and nodded her head quickly. When she shut the door, McKenna started walking again. "Bedrooms are at the back." She whispered and motioned to the cabin, "there's a door off the deck."

Blair exchanged a look with Blaise, and both veered toward the back of the house. Noah reached under his jacket and put his hand on the butt of the dart gun. His cat was pissed that they weren't using a real one, but Devin's orders had been to bring them out alive. Noah sucked a deep breath through his nose and conveyed to his animal that there were children there and darts were safer. His cat's reaction still wasn't favorable, but he settled enough to let Noah do the driving of his body without the distraction.

"Do you want me to knock?" McKenna whispered to Calum, "no one would ever just walk in."

"Okay, knock, and then as soon as you go inside, you get out of the way." Calum looked over her head at Noah as he spoke.

Noah knew he was asking if he was ready and nodded his head, gripping the gun under his jacket. He didn't like that McKenna would be in there, he couldn't add another female to his conscience. He leaned down and looked her in the eye, "you get behind me as soon as I'm inside." She nodded, a nervous look in her eye like it was just dawning on her what was happening. She had guts, that he knew. For her to even reach out to the Alliance was risking her life. He decided then, that he would make sure she and her grandmother found somewhere good to settle. Somewhere that they would never feel suffering again. He didn't know what Blair planned to do, short of building a town on his property, but this girl deserved some peace.

Out of the corner of his eye, he saw movement and turned, ready to fight. Two boys stood there, their clothes were too small and dirty, and neither had a jacket on. Noah had no idea how old they were, but the bigger one was close to a teen, he looked from him to Calum and then grabbed the little one's arm and ushered him in the other direction. *Shit.* He was going to have to make sure all the children had a good place to live too. He knew what it was like to be afraid to do *anything.* Children needed to run, play and feel safe. He thought of Daisie, she'd been through a lot, but the good space she was in with the clan around her made all the difference.

With his jaw clenched, he turned back to see McKenna watching Calum.

Calum glanced at his phone. "Blair's ready, they can see inside." He looked at McKenna, "let's go." He tapped the screen and then put it in his pocket.

McKenna raised her hand and knocked on the door a few times.

Noah heard a muffled, "it's open," from the other side of it.

Later, he'd figure out what had come over him as they went through the door. Noah grabbed McKenna's arm and had her behind his body before she could say a word. The man on the other side of the room stood there with his mouth hanging open. Noah had the gun aimed at his face. He wasn't about to tell him it wasn't filled with bullets. "Sit." He growled, "arms above your head." The man dropped to his knees and raised his hands. Calum moved by him and went toward the door at the back of the room. He checked to make sure McKenna was okay, he shouldn't have grabbed her like that.

Blaise came through a window—literally, leaped through it. Noah blinked and then she was standing beside the man on the floor. "You watch him, I'm going hunting." She tossed something to McKenna. "Tie his hands behind his back. *Tight.*" Turning, she went to the door that Calum hadn't.

Noah took the ties out of her hand and went over to the man. He wasn't nice about it when he grabbed one wrist and pulled his hand behind his back. The ties were looped, so it was easy to figure out how to put them on. The man, no longer stunned, tried to jerk his hand free and get up.

When McKenna jumped back, a look of fear on her face, Noah, cranked his arm around his back and pushed him face-first on the floor. He jerked his other arm down and put the ties around his wrists and pulled them tight. Getting up, he left the man there on his face. "Go to your grandmother." He said in a gruffer voice than he intended.

"Gather everyone," Blair said as he came in dragging another man along with him. "I'll be out shortly to meet them." He shoved the man to the floor, "right after I have a chat with my cousin." The shock on the man's face was evident. "That's right, the vanishing baby has returned." Blair grinned and it wasn't even close to friendly.

Calum shoved another man out the door, his hands were already bound. With a firm grip, he guided him to the floor beside the guy that still lay on it.

The fourth man came through the door, not of his own free will. Blaise came along behind him, she looked quite happy. Noah looked to see blood on his face. She smirked and gave a little shrug, "he got a little too up in my space." She shoved him again, "go join your pals."

Noah turned to see Mckenna standing at the door, a stunned look on her face. "Are there any others out there that are with them?" He glanced at the men.

She shook her head, "no."

"Okay, go gather them up." He took the backpack off his back and held it out, "there are some bars in here and drinks."

Blair glanced to Calum and then pointed to the door he'd come in through. "My packs out there, grab the bars from it too."

"Once we've looked around in here, anyone that needs to warm up can come inside," Calum said as he looked with just his eyes around the room. "How many are here?"

"Uh, nineteen." She didn't pause to chat, McKenna took his bag and went out the door.

Calum nodded and pulled out his phone, "I need to call Devin," he looked at Blaise, "are some of your team nearby?"

She grinned, "they're probably bored by now."

He smirked, "call them and tell them to come to collect these four."

She smiled, "with pleasure." She heaved a big sigh, "I was hoping for more action."

Calum chortled, "there's going to be a lot in the next while, you'll get your action."

"Aces." She grinned and went out the door.

"I'll go tell the girls to come down." Noah went out the door and hurried along the edge of the cabin to the back where they'd been able to see when they'd looked down at the sad example of a clan's camp.

Chapter Twenty-One

Emersyn had to force herself to go down the hill slowly. The second Noah walked into her sight and motioned for them to come down, her heart started racing. "Does he look upset?" She couldn't tell from this far away.

Kobie went down the slope and put her hand out to help her follow, "I'm not sure, Noah doesn't express much as far as expressions go."

Sliding a few feet, Emersyn paused and looked back down at him, "his eyes, they tell you everything."

Kobie kept going, carefully placing her feet, "maybe I don't speak the same language as his then."

Emersyn wanted to watch him as she went down, but she needed to pay attention. Falling down the hill and injuring herself was not what she needed when she was moments away from seeing Aspyn again. She winced when she put her arms out to balance herself, yes, she didn't need another injury.

The last ten feet or so, she no longer cared if she fell, she went by Kobie and ran down them. The momentum almost landed her on her face, but Noah was there and caught her before it happened. She grasped his jacket and looked up at him, "did you see her? Is she here?"

"I'm not sure. There are a few little girls that look like Blair here," he glanced over his shoulder, "there are nineteen people here, Emersyn."

She nodded, of course, they had other things to do.

"We're going to move them into the cabin so they can warm up and get some food," his brow creased, "maybe wash up a bit."

Emersyn clung to his arm as he spoke, her knees felt like they were going to give out. She nodded again, "but everyone is all right?"

He turned and started walking, she was so glad he didn't move his arm from her grip, she wasn't sure she could walk on her own right now. If Aspyn wasn't here…

"They're dirty, cold, underfed, but otherwise okay." His tone was barely more than a whisper.

"Oh my god." Kobie stopped and looked at the sheds, "I thought maybe they just looked small from up there."

"It's bad." He glanced at her and then motioned with his head to keep walking. "Blair's close to losing his—" he cleared his throat, "losing it."

Kobie blew out a breath, "I figured it would sink in soon." She navigated around the last shed and then stopped, "has he talked to them yet?"

"No. He and Calum want to talk to the men in the cabin and then we'll go through it." He looked down at Emersyn's hand and then placed his over top of hers. "I think he's waiting for you to be here to talk to them."

Kobie nodded and walked quickly toward the cabin.

Noah walked slowly, looking down at her every few seconds like he was waiting for her to have a breakdown. Honestly, she was close to it. She wanted to know if Aspyn was here, but what if she wasn't?

"They're all by the fire," he pointed, "once Calum brings Lindon's followers out of the back of the cabin, we'll move them inside."

She nodded; not sure she had a voice to speak. Her heart was beating erratically. Her cat was close but watchful. A little body with snowy blonde hair ran out from between two of the sheds and right by them. Emersyn held her breath. Her hair was the same color as Aspyn's. "Are there a lot of Lindon's children here?"

Noah gave her a careful look, "I'm not sure, a few with that hair color."

The hand on his arm started to shake, and she blew out a breath, trying to prevent the overload she knew was coming.

"Emersyn," his tone was hard, but gentle at the same time.

She lifted her chin, swatting at the tears on her cheek. He gave her a quick smile.

"Look."

She followed where he pointed. There was a woman sitting on the cold damp ground, in her lap was a little girl, her blonde hair the same as the last. When she turned her head, Emersyn put her hand over her mouth to stop the sob. It was her baby. "Aspyn." She whispered and then started running, "Aspyn." She called louder.

Aspyn looked around and then saw her. She could see the excitement on her face.

"Mommy."

She'd been so afraid her own daughter wouldn't recognize her. The woman nodded to her, and those short legs started running toward her.

Emersyn dropped to her knees when she was close and held open her arms. Aspyn launched herself into them. "Oh, baby, I'm so happy to see you." She hugged her and closed her eyes, not caring that the tears were rolling down her cheeks. "Are you all right?" She leaned back and looked at her. The silky hair was matted, and her face was filthy, but those blue eyes were so bright and happy—she was the most beautiful thing she'd ever seen.

"Penny watched me." Aspyn dropped down to sit on one of Emersyn's legs. "She kept me warm too."

Emersyn looked back to the woman she'd been sitting with. She smiled at her, making the tears flow freely. "That's good, baby." She hugged her again, "I'm sorry I wasn't here." She felt someone walk up behind her and somehow knew it was Noah. She looked up at him through the tears in her eyes. "This is Noah, baby, he came and got me and brought me here."

Noah gave her a quick look and then smiled down at her daughter.

'Thank you', she mouthed to him. When he looked away, she glanced to see why. Calum was coming out of the cabin with a man, his hands were tied behind his back. Blaise met him at the steps and grabbed the man's arm and dragged him along to the closest shed, she opened the door and shoved him in.

Emersyn hugged Aspyn to her, angling her body so she wouldn't see the men coming out like that. She was no stranger to others being handled roughly, but this time she could control if she had to see it or not.

Calum came out the door with two more men this time, they seemed to be walking along on their own.

She looked around at the others standing near the fire, no one moved or spoke, they just stood there holding the children close and watched these men being marched by them. Emersyn didn't need to ask if there were any softer feelings toward any of these men. There wasn't, it was plain in their expressions how these men had treated them wrong. The men were clean and clearly well-fed, unlike everybody standing in soiled, ill-fitting clothing.

Aspyn turned and gripped her neck, squeezing it. She placed a hard childlike kiss on her cheek and Emersyn had never felt anything more right in her life than the love of her child. Her gaze flicked to the door when Calum came through it again. Her heart jumped up to lodge in her throat. It was him, the one that always came with Lindon. She scrambled up and stepped back, clutching Aspyn tight in her arms.

She turned to see Noah watching her, a questioning look on his face. She opened her mouth, but then couldn't speak the words, terror had paralyzed it.

"Stay. Right. Here." Noah said, in a low rumbling voice.

Emersyn watched with her eyes wide as he made fast work reaching the steps. At first, she thought he was going to grab the man and toss him in the shed, but he didn't. Calum gave him a confused look and then his expression changed to surprise as Noah grabbed the man around the throat and lifted him right off the ground.

He stepped with a few long strides, carrying the man along with him until he was pressed up against the wall of the house.

There were gasps among the group, but no one, not one, moved to assist the man as he dangled there, struggling without the use of his hands to free himself. He tried to kick out at Noah, but the hold he had was too tight.

"Noah. Shit. Blair." Calum jumped over the small deck and went over to him.

Emersyn heard the door slam, but couldn't look away as Noah just stood there, like a giant statue holding the man that was struggling as the air was cut off from his lungs.

Calum grabbed his arm and was saying something Emersyn couldn't hear. Blair appeared beside him on the other side, trying to put himself between Noah and the man.

Emersyn looked to see both Kobie and Blaise just standing there watching, not moving to help. Blaise looked amused. She spotted the woman, Penny, and moved over to her quickly. She trusted her to keep her daughter for a few more moments. "Can you watch her, please?" She nodded and put her arms out to take her.

Emersyn moved quickly over toward the men. She put her hand on Blair's arm to move him out of the way. He did but kept his hand on the man's leg trying to keep him up in the air. "Noah." She stood beside him, making sure to keep clear of the man's leg as he kicked out at him.

"Noah, let him go." Calum's voice was strained.

Emersyn placed her hand on Noah's chest, she could feel his heart beating beneath it. He looked down at her, shock on his face that she was there. "He doesn't deserve a quick release." She said it softly and knew she was going to hell for saying such a thing, but it's what she felt. "Release him to face his full due."

The anger in his eyes changed that fast. He stepped back, pulling her along with him. Emersyn put her arms around her waist and hugged him as she glanced over her to see Blair and Calum picking the man up off the ground.

Blair looked over to Kobie, "grab him some water."

She didn't look to see if Kobie did or not, she lifted her chin and looked up to see Noah wasn't taking his eyes off the man. "Thank you." She said softly, "but he's not worth changing you into what they are."

He looked down at her now. Giving his head a slight shake, "there is no punishment that could be done to them that would come close to equaling all the lives they've ruined."

A low rumble came from his chest and her cat was right there, alert, waiting. She swallowed to find her voice. "I know, but you're better than that."

"Am I?" His brows creased.

"You good now?" Blair came over to them.

Noah sucked in a breath and then looked down to see she was still against him, he stepped back and then turned to Blair.

"You have to stop losing it, bud, and scaring the crap out of me," Blair smirked.

Calum came over and gave him a wary look. "I don't know what you eat for your strength, but text it to me later." He shook his head and then looked at Blair, "ready?"

A woman wearing nothing more than a t-shirt came over to Calum, she was holding a boy that couldn't be more than two years old. Emersyn could see she was shivering. She grabbed Calum's arm, "please don't leave us here." Her voice was shaking.

Emersyn smiled at her. "You look cold," she undid her coat and took it off, "here." She held it out to her. Taking it with a grateful look in her eyes, she slipped it over her son's body. Before Emersyn could turn, Noah was holding his jacket out to her. Taking it, she smiled up at him and received an awkward smile back. Slipping her arms into it, she inhaled and was pleasantly surprised she could smell nothing but his scent.

Noah looked at Blair. "Let's get this going."

Blair blew out a breath and nodded, even though his expression said otherwise.

Noah turned back to her and touched her arm. "Go over with Aspyn," he glanced in that direction, "we don't know how well this is going to go over."

Emersyn nodded.

Blair put his hand up before she could move. "Thanks again," he turned his head and gave Noah a hard, but playful look, "for disarming the beast of fury once more."

Emersyn smiled at that. She nodded and then turned and walked quickly back over to the woman. Aspyn leaned over into her arms as she reached them.

"Who are they?" Penny whispered.

"They're with the Alliance," Emersyn said softly and then pressed her nose into Aspyn's neck and inhaled her scent. It was like a needed medicine to her.

"The Alliance," Penny said and then moved closer to her. "Are they taking over the clan?"

Emersyn frowned and looked to see the horror on her face. "No, they're here to free you from," she motioned to the shed Blaise stood in front of, "them."

"Really?"

Emersyn nodded, and then looked to the cabin to see Calum and Noah standing on the bottom step, Blair on the top. "Listen."

Chapter Twenty-Two

Noah looked over at Emersyn while Blair dug deep for the courage to speak. He didn't envy him. Kobie was in front of him right now, hand on his chest and talking softly. He put his hand on his chest, realizing that it was what Emersyn had done to him, again. As she watched him, her expression changed, and then she shifted her daughter and placed her hand on her chest, near her heart. Noah almost shook his head telling her she misunderstood, but then he saw the darkness in her eyes lighten for a moment. He dropped his hand and looked back at Blair, almost blurting out to get on with it. The sooner they got this over with, the faster he could be back in the shop breaking shit.

Blair inhaled a deep breath and then nodded to his mate. He stepped to the edge of the top step and pulled off the hat McKenna had given him.

Noah looked to see McKenna and her grandmother were the only two in the group that didn't look shocked. Some of them looked frightened as well.

"My name is Blair Elden," Blair said in a clear loud voice. "Many of you won't remember me or even know I existed," he paused and looked to see the only other elder in the group step closer to McKenna's grandmother and take her hand. She was smiling. "I was sent away to live somewhere safely," Blair continued, then gave his head a quick shake, "I didn't even know I had a brother until recently—" He blew out an exasperated breath, "I'm sorry, I had no way of knowing what you were going through." He put his hand on his chest and looked around at them, "Lindon is dead and my mate," he glanced at Kobie, "and I would like to help all of you."

"What about the Alliance?" One of the few adult men shouted at him.

Blair gave Calum a quick look before answering him, "we work with the Alliance."

"The Alliance kicked us out because of something our old Alpha did." Another of the men announced.

Pieces clicked in Noah's mind. That's why they stayed with Lindon, to be caught away from an unregistered clan, meant death. He'd recently learned that when Ed and Gage had been talking about Deacon's new status. It explained it. He looked around at the sheds, he'd probably have risked death to live like this. Turning, he looked back to Blair.

Blair raised an eyebrow and looked at him for a moment. "You've been lied to. The old Alpha, my father, was fighting with Lindon because he didn't want to help another organization," he glanced at Kobie, "an organization that sells and trades shifters."

Noah had to hand it to him, he didn't sugar-coat it. The gasps in the crowd confirmed most had no idea.

"Did you bring my Mommy too?" A little girl came running toward the steps. She looked at Emersyn, "you brought Aspyn's."

Kobie put her hand on Blair's arm, telling him she had this one. She went down the stairs and squatted down in front of her. "What's your name?"

"Wren."

Noah noticed she stayed out of Kobie's reach.

"Well Wren, we didn't bring your mom today, but we're going to look for her."

Wren turned those blue eyes on Blair, and Noah was struck by how alike they were. She had to be related. She turned around and looked at one of the other women, then back to Blair, "are you my uncle?"

Blair's look softened, "I am." He came down the steps and put his hand on Kobie's shoulder, "and this is your aunt Kobie."

The little one gave Kobie a long assessing look before the hard look changed, "I'm coming to live with you?"

Kobie looked up, amusement in her eyes, as Blair's expression changed to shock, "if you'd like that, then yes."

"I don't have details right now," Blair smiled down at Wren, then looked around the group again, "I won't make false promises, but you will be warm, dry, and fed."

Noah watched him look his way, his expression said he really had no clue.

"We have a few things to do inside and then all of you can come in the cabin, get washed off, and warm and we'll get some food going." Blair stepped back from the steps.

Noah noticed he hadn't said where they would be warm, dry, and fed. He looked around at the group, there had to be nine or ten children. He rubbed the back of his neck and tried to figure out how the hell they were going to get this many out of here. Was there a road nearby? There had to be a path or something.

"Noah."

He turned to see Calum looking at him. "I'm going to field a few questions with Kobie," he turned and smirked at Blair, "you go in with Blair and dig around and see if there's any paperwork inside."

Noah nodded his head, that was much better than being out here in the emotional river from all the shifters projecting every possible feeling under the sun right now. "On it." He jogged up the steps and into the cabin before anyone could say a word to him.

The door slammed behind him, and he tensed and turned around. Blair stood there with his eyes closed leaning against the closed door.

"Thank fuck." Blair hissed out a breath. Opening his eyes, he pushed away from the door. "Did you see the look on Kobie's face?" He shook his head and kept going, not giving Noah a chance to answer. "I'm so screwed." He pointed to the kitchen area, "I'll start there."

They were both in here hiding, he knew that, but it still had to be done. Blair was overwhelmed by the discovery of more nieces and an entire clan that was his and Noah just needed to distance himself from all those faces. He didn't know any of them, none had ever been in a house he guarded, but they were all victims and he felt like they knew what he'd done when they looked at him.

Blair slammed a cupboard closed. "Once we're done in here, they can come in and eat some real food." He sounded disgusted and Noah didn't blame him, they were half-starved and yet the cupboards and fridge were full in the cabin.

He opened one of the drawers of the cabinet on the far wall and pulled out a book. Noah didn't read very well, but even he could tell this was important. "Blair." He turned to him and held up the book.

Brows furrowed, Blair came over and took it from him, and opened it. He flipped a few pages skimming it quickly. Noah wished for a moment he could read that fast. Maybe once things settled down, he could talk to Beth about a bit of schooling.

"Holy shit, dates, names, locations." Blair gave him a wide-eyed look, "jackpot." he frowned and looked back at it. "This is a record of who Lindon moved, traded, picked up," he glanced at him again, "I don't know if him doing this is seriously stupid or," he looked back at the book, "a brilliant way to cover his ass." Holding the book out, he pointed to something, "he has names of who he contacted."

Noah didn't bother looking at it, knowing he wouldn't be able to read the scribble, "we can find the people running these trades," he waved his hand, "or whatever."

Blair's grin was slow. "Yeah." Grasping the book in his hand, he turned back to the drawer, "let's see if there's more treasure in here."

Noah gladly moved away from the unit to look elsewhere; Blair could read what he found. Going over he opened the closet door. Blair made a loud groan noise. "Are you okay?" He glanced over at him.

Blair stopped and looked at him, "no. I am not okay." He waved a hand in the air, the pages flapping with the movement, "did you see how they were living? My brother did that."

"He didn't do it alone." Noah thought of the Tomas family.

Blair snorted and yanked open the other drawer, "No, but he took over, and then he-he..."

"Are they coming home with us?" He needed to know that every one of them would be somewhere with people that wouldn't abuse them anymore. He looked at the floor, he'd never had anywhere to reference as home before, and just realized it.

Blair stuffed some papers in a plastic bag, "of course they're coming home with us. What the fuck am I doing with them?" He waved the arm around that bag was in, "winter is right on our ass and the house is already full." He looked at the bag in his hand and then set it down in slow motion, so he wouldn't jerk it around with movement again, "It was just me; you know and the guys," he shrugged, "and Kelsey," he rubbed his hand over his hair, "then I picked up nine females, whatever," he shrugged, "nine seems like nothing right now," the arms flew up from his body again, "then—fuck. There are twenty-seven of us now. *Twenty. Seven.* Ten are children or teens." He blew out a breath, "now we find nineteen more..."

"Twenty." He scowled at him, "I'm pretty sure Emersyn is staying with them," Noah's chest hurt just thinking about it, "they all understand what she's been through."

Blair nodded his head slowly, at least he had some understanding of what suffering clans felt like. Kobie's had been through a lot.

"What the hell am I doing with forty-seven people, Noah?" His tone was filled with worry, "I mean, go, team tiger and all that. Our kind is strong now on the numbers side but——I'm just—I have *four* nieces and who knows how many more relatives out there."

Four? He thought of the light blondes he'd seen, it made sense. Noah closed the closet, "I get it. My parents had two more kids after Carlene and I were taken..." he didn't know why he was bringing that up.

"That's right. It's ah, gotta be weird."

Noah exhaled slowly, "yeah. I mean I get it, but it's just a surprise..."

"That life went on without you."

Noah could only nod to that. His words hit hard. His parents had just continued while he and Carlene...

"Shit." Blair groaned and dropped to squat on the floor. He held his head between his hands. "What the hell am I doing with all those people?"

Noah watched Calum come into the cabin.

"Sorry to interrupt your breakdown..."

Blair's head popped up and he glared at him, "Bite me, Bagheera." He stood up and waved a hand at him, "why don't you go find Baloo and eat him."

Noah smirked, normally he didn't get the movie references the guys made, but that one he understood.

Calum wiped his hand over his mouth, a smirk under it. "To clarify," he gave Blair a blank look, "he was actually a leopard, not a jaguar, and," he shook his head, "I didn't eat the bear. I fought with a bear."

Blair snorted, "asshole." He smiled at him. "Really he was a leopard?"

Calum leveled him with an unamused look, "we have other problems right now."

Blair looked narrowed, "what now?" it came out as a whine.

"Devin's on route."

Noah's head snapped back to Calum.

"What?" Blair shook his head, "here? Now?"

"That's generally what on route means," Calum said, a scowl on his face.

"Why? We have no way to keep watch here, and he doesn't exactly sneak in places in stealth mode..."

"He's flying in."

"See." Blair turned and lifted the bag up.

"Rayne is sending enough warm jackets and clothes to support an army," Calum said.

"Fuck me." Blair whispered and then held up the bag, "Lindon kept records of everything he did. Names, places, clan..."

Calum came across the floor and took the bag, he looked in it. "Recent?"

Blair leaned back against the wall like he needed it to hold him up, "from when I was about," he squeezed his eyes shut for a second, "five until a month ago."

Calum reached into the bag and pulled out the book. Opening it, he skimmed it fast, as Blair had done. "Son of a bitch." He whispered it, a note of disbelief in his voice. "Your brother was a sick asshole," he glanced at him fleetingly, "but he just handed us the key to ending this shit."

Blair nodded and looked over at him.

Noah sucked in a deep breath, and held it, almost afraid to ask. Blowing it out, he motioned to the book, "end *all* of it?"

Calum kept turning the pages slowly, "different contacts from different countries," he said quietly and then looked at Noah, "I'd say it gives us a good shot of finding all the traitors out there peddling their own kind."

Noah felt lightheaded, he put his hands on top of his head and stood there looking from one to the other. "Seriously?"

Calum nodded. "Yeah." He held the book up, "I'm going to hold onto this and put it right into Devin's hands."

Noah dropped his hands; his whole body was vibrating. They could end it. For good.

"Hey."

Noah looked back over to Blair, "don't lose it right now, bud, I'm like—dangling by a very thin thread right now and I don't think I could pry you off another asshole today."

Noah snorted, "it's just," he shook his head, "I never thought there would be a way."

"Don't go celebrating yet." Calum turned back to the door, "we have a long way to go to stop them."

Noah sucked in a breath, reigning in his emotions, "yeah. Of course."

"We'll leave picking through here to the clean-up team, let's get everyone in here where it's warm." Calum opened the door and went out.

Noah turned to Blair, momentarily both forgetting the past and uncertain future. Aiden Tomas and his empire were going to fall.

Chapter Twenty-Three

Noah stared into the flames, it was oddly peaceful, almost hypnotizing, that something so dangerous appeared to be controlled. The irony of his thought wasn't lost on him. He'd proven earlier that he was just as unpredictable as the fire.

Blaise's team had been in and out with the four men and he'd noticed how everyone seemed more at ease after they were gone, then again it could have been from full bellies too. How long had it been since they ate a real meal? He'd dumped whatever the woman had been cooking, the smell made him nauseous.

Devin had flown in, and his helicopter was parked at the top of the hill where the girls had waited. The security that traveled with him was scattered around the perimeter of the camp and Noah was glad for it. He was too tired to stand watch. Not tired enough to sleep though, not in that cabin. He'd had to get out of there, it was like a sea of bodies on the floor and furniture. He hadn't even managed to lie down and attempt it before the walls started to close in on him.

Calum was standing, leaning against one of the sheds talking on the phone. He kept smiling, so Noah knew Shaelan had to be on the other end of it. Devin was on the opposite side of the camp talking on his phone. It was hard to tell who he was talking to because his expression didn't seem to change much, but if he had to ponder a guess, he'd say it was Rayne. She had wanted to come with him, but he'd made her stay behind and rest. Noah had overheard a brief conversation between Calum and Devin that she had just gone through her first cycle. Bad images flooded his brain anytime *that* word was used or implied.

Picking up the stick, he poked at the fire, making it spit sparks and grow angry. How sick was it that he felt a connection to a damn fire? It was ridiculous, but so were half the things he thought, so it wasn't surprising.

Blair and Kobie came out of the trees, walking hand in hand and talking quietly. Noah blew out a breath, a twinge of jealousy going through him. What was it like to have that kind of connection, to not feel panic and terror when you were that close to someone? He'd never know that, and for the most part, he accepted it. Dropping his head down, he concentrated on breathing and staying calm. His cat had been on edge since they'd walked into this pathetic excuse of a camp, and he wasn't going to settle until all of these people were out of here and somewhere safe. It was things like this that fueled his anger and resentment for the Tomas organization.

"You're throwing some tense emotions around."

He looked up to see Calum sitting down across from him. "Couldn't sleep?"

Noah shrugged, "too many bodies in there for me."

Calum smirked, "it is a bit crowded."

Noah didn't want to talk about his issues with sleep. "How's Shaelan?"

"In her happy place, reading, researching, testing," he shook his head, "probably won't sleep until I'm back and force her to stop."

"She's pretty amazing." Noah offered.

"Yes, she is." Calum watched Devin walk toward him. "Wonder if he came up with any answers."

"Answers?" Noah tried to read Devin's body language as he came their way, but all he could pick up on was irritation.

Then again, the prince always seemed irritated with something.

"On where we're taking these people." Calum got up and picked up another piece of wood and tossed it into the fire. "Transport is on the way to get them out, we just need a direction to go."

Noah bit his lip so he wouldn't blurt out that he was accompanying them to wherever they were going. He'd at least figured out that his cat and conscience weren't going to give him a moment of peace unless he saw with his own eyes that they were okay.

"Midnight meeting?" Devin stepped over the log and sat down.

"How's our princess?" Calum asked him.

Devin rolled his eyes, "shopping for supplies, clothes, and every other possible thing."

Noah glanced at the house, "she should add toys to the list." Both men looked at him, he shrugged, "I went through the sheds, there's not a single toy in them. Children should have toys." Noah remembered the ones from the houses, there were never any toys.

Devin sighed, "I'll let her know."

Calum turned to watch Blair and Kobie come over. "Feel better?"

Blair gave him a blank look, "not really." They sat down beside each other, Kobie leaning into him.

Noah didn't know how he looked so calm when he knew from his earlier rant he wasn't. If he weren't waging his own furious battle inside, maybe he'd be able to pick up on his emotions and get a sense of how Blair was doing it, but all he could feel was his own anger bubbling just under the surface.

"You good?"

He turned to see Blair watching him and nodded. He was not going to lie to him.

"Okay, I'm just not up for any more beast of fury moments tonight."

Noah smirked. "I think we're safe just sitting here." Again, another lie.

"Do you need to go for a run?" Kobie asked, all while giving him one of her assessing looks.

"No," he sighed, "just worrying about them," he motioned to the cabin.

"That brings me to the next part of this evening's entertainment." Devin said in a quiet tone, "I talked to dad."

All eyes looked at him.

"He agrees we can't send anymore to Blair's, at least not with winter so close."

Blair heaved a loud sigh.

"We can't separate them," Kobie said quickly.

"No, we agreed on that too." Devin leaned on his knees and stared at the fire. "He has Ed and Bruce both trying to find a location, somewhere between them." He looked at Blair, "are you claiming them as your clan or are we starting a third tiger clan in the province."

Kobie leaned closer to Blair when he shook his head. "I don't know," rolled his head from side to side, "I mean they are my blood," he looked at the cabin, "some of them, so I can't just send them off on their own," he looked back at Devin, "right?"

Devin nodded his head slowly, "I get that, so the men left," he straightened up, "are any of them able to watch over the clan," he glanced briefly at Noah, "as Bruce does for Ed?"

Blair lifted his hand and then dropped it, "I don't know. All three of the adult men..."

"Weston, Arlo, and Harrison," Kobie said softly.

"Right." Blair exhaled, "I don't sense a lot of strength in any of them."

"They're down right now." Noah said before he could continue, "they've had to watch and accept what's been happening all these years." He looked from Blair to Devin, "they didn't give in and help Lindon, but they stayed to try to watch over them." He wasn't sure what he was trying to say, just knew that he had to stand up for them.

"What about you?"

Noah frowned, "me?"

Devin nodded, "what about you staying with them and keeping things together, for the winter at least until we can figure out the land next to Blair's."

Noah knew his mouth was hanging open, but he couldn't process enough to close it. He turned to see Blair and Kobie were both looking at him too waiting for him to answer. "I," he looked back to Devin, "I can barely keep myself together most days," he motioned between Calum and Blair, "as they found out earlier today." He snapped his mouth shut and shook his head, "I don't know anything about running a clan." He started to stand up, then changed his mind, if he got up, his cat would take that as a signal "I hadn't even been around a clan until I went to Ed's," he snapped his head back to look at the prince, "you were there at the camp, you know how bad I was..."

"I think you're perfect for the job," Kobie said softly.

Noah turned to her, and she nodded.

"You, better than anyone else will understand what they've been through, what they're going to go through." She gave him one of those soft 'females' looks, the ones he didn't quite understand, but usually meant he was going to be talked into something. "I know you struggle with it every day, but you're coping and overcoming," she tilted her head to the side, "I think they need someone like you to learn how to live again."

Learn how to live? When had he done that? He walked around each day in a fog of fury and guilt, trying to keep it together. He looked at the cabin, inside were so many people that needed someone that would watch out for them, guide them, and defend them if necessary. He wasn't that someone. "I," he turned to Blair, hoping he at least would get where he was coming from, "know nothing about *that*." He shook his head, "there's a bunch of kids in there..."

"Nine children," Kobie said.

He gave her a blank look for a moment. "There are nine kids in there," Noah gave Devin a wide-eyed look, "what do I know about looking after children?"

"You're great with Daisie," Kobie said before either of the other men could speak. "She thinks you're amazing."

Noah frowned; he'd never done anything with her really, just talked to her when she wasn't busy with schoolwork. He turned back to Blair, "there's a lot of work at the shop."

Blair shrugged, "we have all winter to get everything caught up."

"Why don't you think it over for a few days?" Calum stood up, "we still have to find a place to take them." He looked at Blair, "without turning your place into a trailer park."

Blair groaned.

Noah needed to get out of there, he was afraid to let his cat out to run, but right now he was more scared of trying to keep his animal on the inside. He couldn't be responsible for nineteen people, he just couldn't. A sound came from the cabin, he turned to see Emersyn standing there hugging a blanket around her shoulders. Cocking his head, he watched for a second, before getting up. He knew what brought her outside and away from her child, the nightmares. He didn't excuse himself, just got up and went over to her.

"Trouble sleeping?" It was a dumb, obvious question, but it was all he had.

She nodded.

"Is Aspyn sleeping okay?" He rubbed his hand over his chest, hoping to keep his cat under control.

"She's curled up with that little girl, Wren," some of the tension faded from her face, "it's pretty cute seeing them sleeping like that."

He nodded. "She seems to be doing okay." He hadn't spoken more than three words to her, but he'd watched her for most of the day. He'd been looking for those telltale signs he'd seen too many times, the rounded eyes, startling at every sound or when anyone moved, the quiet observing that children did when they had been through more than their body could handle or worse shutting down completely, mentally checking out and sitting alone, unmoving as if paralyzed He'd seen all of that with Leah long ago.

Emersyn blew out a breath, "yes. I'm so glad." She sighed again, "I can't explain how worried I've been that-that…"

Noah moved fast and was right in front of her before she could continue, "they looked out for her here, didn't let anything happen to her." One of the women, Nora, he thought was her name, had watched over Aspyn along with her four-year-old son, Mason.

"I owe them for that." She looked over her shoulder at the door, "I'd like to stay with them." She said it softly as if the idea had just formed in her head. Turning back, she gave him a long appraising look, "I don't think I can just go back to my family as if I've been on a very long vacation, Noah."

"I understand." He confessed, "I haven't seen my family since they got me out."

"How long is that?"

Taking a deep breath, he tried to figure out how long he'd been 'free', in the body at least. "Uh, I think maybe a year now." He nodded his head slowly, "I was at a facility for a while and then to the prince's camp before I came to Ed's," he was surprised by how long it had been, "then I started helping the Alliance and it's been," he exhaled, "a bit busy." He left out the part of the facility being the refuge center they took all the males rescued to until they were sure they weren't helping the organization they were shutting down.

"Does it ever get better?"

Her anxious tone made him look back down at her. Something deep inside him knew what she was asking, even if he couldn't put it into words. "Not really, but you learn how to function despite it." Should he have lied to her? No, she deserved to know the truth, to be in control of her own world now.

"You seem to be doing good."

Her emerald eyes were wide, looking at him full of hope. "I have good days." He shrugged, figuring it was better than saying bad days.

"I'm better now that I have Aspyn, but still when I close my eyes…"

Noah didn't know what possessed him to do it, but her reached out and gently, carefully, not wanting to startle her, pulled her into his arms. "I know." He leaned down and rested his head on top of her head, moving his hand up and down her back, trying to coax the tension to leave her body. She held herself still but didn't freeze up or shove him away. "It's going to be better," he lifted his head and leaned back so he could see her face, "you'll see, once you realize you get to decide what you do and don't want to do." He tried for an encouraging smile but fell it fell short and probably looked more like a cringe. "We'll get through it." His mouth said before the words registered in his brain.

"You're coming with us?"

He stood there, feeling like he wasn't in his own body. Her eyes were filled with so much hope it caused his chest to ache. He nodded, not having any words that could explain how much that was a bad idea.

Emersyn leaned into him and wrapped her arms around his waist. "That makes me feel better." She sighed, "I know you won't let anything happen to Aspyn." Her arms were around him, but not relaxed. She was as at odds with a hug as he was.

Noah frowned, she hadn't said herself, just her daughter. He needed to move, he couldn't stand her and hold her like this. It started with his chest feeling tight and then his gut. This wasn't right. None of it was right. "Listen, we're going to need a list of what everyone needs," he shrugged, not even sure, "clothes and stuff." He cringed, he was not good at this sort of thing, "maybe you could do that in the morning?"

She looked up at him, "I don't write very well." She whispered like it was her own fault.

"Me either," He glanced at the cabin, "get one of the elders to do that part, you just do the leg work." He swallowed trying to create some salvia in his mouth that had gone so dry it felt like it was cracking.

She smiled slowly, "I can do that." She nodded.

Noah let out a slow shaky breath and glanced away from her to see Blair standing at the bottom of the steps, he jerked his head to the side. "I'm needed right now," he tried to lick his lips with a dry tongue, "you go back inside and hug that baby girl of yours."

Emersyn nodded; a lot of the strain was gone from her expression now. She stretched up and placed her lips against his cheek. Noah stiffened, even with the growth of his beard he felt like it seared him all the way to his soul. "Thank you, Noah." She stepped back and then put her hand over her mouth. "I don't know why I did that." She turned and quickly went inside.

Noah gasped out the breath he'd been unintentionally holding. With stiff steps, he went down to Blair.

"We're going to do a quick check of the area," he looked over his shoulder, "Devin's guards will keep an eye on the cabin." He lifted his eyebrows in question, "you in?"

Noah nodded. Five minutes ago, he was afraid to let his animal out, now if he didn't, he was going to lose what was left of his sanity.

Blair grinned, "ah, the mind fuck that goes with finding a mate." He chuckled and started walking over to Devin and Calum.

Noah scowled at his back as he followed. What did that even mean? It's not like his mind was ever clear at any other time. He took off his jacket and clenched it in his fist. He would go for a run and then get some sleep. The trip back to— wherever they were going was bound to be long and trying. Noah stomped right past where Blair and Kobie stood, going further into the trees. He hadn't asked about transport, hopefully, they sent enough vehicles that they weren't squished in them with no room to move or breathe. He needed to do something about his mouth too, he thought as he tossed his jacket over a tree branch. Every time he opened it around

Emersyn, he was making promises he knew he couldn't keep. He could barely navigate an entire day without some misstep or serious fuck up—how was he going to look out for her and her little girl?

"A little less inner turmoil and more shifting," Blair gave him a wary glance as they walked by him.

Chapter Twenty-Four

Emersyn looked at the driver again. She was so nervous around males she didn't know. Noah seemed comfortable enough with him though, so she wondered if they worked together freeing others. What was his name again? Ash? Ashton, or something like that.

When she turned her head back, Wren was smiling at her. Her unofficial guardian, Penny was drifting off to sleep beside her. Emersyn raised her finger to her mouth so the girl would stay quiet. She nodded and looked down at the fastener on the seat she was in, her inquisitive mind distracted by it.

They'd been in this van since early this morning. After only two short stops, her legs were cramping and she could no longer feel her bottom, but she wasn't going to complain. Aspyn was beside her and they were both free and safe.

The driver tapped his phone that sat in a holder beside the steering wheel, he turned and looked at Noah. "We're stopping at a secure location for the night."

"Before we cross?"

The man shook his head, "right after." She saw him glance in the mirror and then she turned to look at the back of the van. There was no window, so she wasn't sure what he could see in it.

Noah shifted in his seat and turned to look at everyone. His gaze stopped on the only other male aside from him and the one driving. Liam, she guessed was ten or eleven and he'd been very quiet the entire trip. "Can you give us a hand with the bags when we stop?"

The boy's eyebrows went up, erasing the solemn look on his face. He nodded.

"Thanks." Noah glanced at her for a moment, then looked at Aspyn as she slept. He seemed like he was checking that she was okay. His eyes flicked back to her for a second and then his expression blanked again just as he turned back around. "How long?"

"Half hour."

Neither of them had spoken much on the whole drive. She knew Noah's ghosts, or as close as anyone would ever know, but she wondered what haunted the driver. His eyes had that look in them, the one that said he'd known suffering. Was that why Noah accepted him? She opened her mouth to ask, then closed it again. Shaking her head, she reminded herself she was free now and allowed to talk when she wanted to. Swallowing the fear down, she sat forward slightly so they could hear her without her waking the others. "Do you work together for the Alliance?" Her voice shook, but she felt proud of herself for doing it anyway.

Noah glanced over his shoulder and looked at her, "different teams, but we've worked together a few times."

The driver nodded, "from what I hear we'll be spending a lot of quality time together in the very immediate future."

Noah searched her face for a moment before he turned back to the driver. "I can't express how much I'm looking forward to that, Asher."

Asher, she thought, his name is Asher.

"Calum said you and Blair found some sort of journal with a lot of names and locations."

She watched Noah nod. Emersyn thought of all the women that had come and gone in the houses she'd been forced to stay in. She closed her eyes for a moment and wished for them to all be found and freed. Opening them she watched Noah, she could only see the side of his face as he looked at Asher.

"Yeah, he said it went back to when he was around five."

Asher jerked his head and looked at him briefly before turning back to watch where he was driving. "Holy shit." He whispered.

"Yeah." Noah nodded his head and then looked back out the window.

"Jesse said we're going to get some of Konner's clan next week."

Noah's head snapped to look at him, "they found more?"

Asher nodded, "it will be a joint effort again, there's more than one location."

Noah blew out an audible breath, "he's got to be juiced about that, after this long."

Asher rolled his head from one side to the other, his muscles must be sore from driving this long, she thought. "I haven't talked to him, but I imagine after there only being a dozen of his kind this long that he's stoked about it."

Emersyn looked from one to the other. She had no idea what juiced and stoked meant, but she had to assume it meant excitement. It hit her then that Noah wasn't going to be staying with them. She looked at her hands in the low light, she knew he had to go and help others, but had never thought about what it meant for him to do it. Her stomach tightened, panic filling her. She knew it was ridiculous, but since he'd found her, she felt like nothing bad was going to happen to her from now on. It was silly, to have a feeling like this about a man she didn't know. About any man. She blinked when she thought that. She trusted a man. That was something she never thought would happen.

"How's your nephew doing?" Noah shifted in his seat as if he were trying to get comfortable. That made her feel better, that it wasn't just her suffering on this car ride.

"He's recovering." Asher made a low-sounding noise, "it's really hard to watch," he glanced at Noah, "if he could shift, it would be faster, but until his ribs heal more he can't."

Emersyn watched Noah tense. She knew he had scars and understood what Asher was saying.

"He's a tough kid." Noah finally said, his tone had more tension to it than it had moments before.

"Yeah, he's a good kid." Asher's voice was quieter now. "There's the crossing."

"One of ours on?"

Asher nodded.

That was the end of the talking. Now there was just tense air inside the vehicle as they came to a stop. Emersyn sat back and watched between Asher's head and the side of the van to see out the front window.

The vehicle in front of them had Calum driving, she had to assume the other van was behind them. All she could make out was a man standing beside the truck Calum drove, then he stepped back, and Calum pulled away. He motioned for Asher to go through, which he did with a quick nod to him as they went past.

"Ever have to get through without one of ours?" Noah asked softly.

Asher shook his head, "no, Zain is brilliant about getting our kind on duty and being there when we have to bounce over a border."

"Let's hope that never changes."

Asher turned to look at him, "don't even think such things. We would be sunk so fast."

Noah blew out a breath and just nodded in reply.

"Mommy."

Emersyn turned to see Aspyn rubbing her eyes. "I'm right here, baby."

"I have to pee." She said in a sleepy voice.

Turning she saw Noah looking at her, "five minutes?" He kept his voice soft.

Emersyn turned back to her, "we're going to stop in just a minute, okay?"

She nodded and rubbed her eyes again. Emersyn brushed her hair back from her face. The very first thing she was doing when they got where they were going was bathing her child, even if it was in a sink. Feeling her hair this filthy and seeing the grime on her clothes made her feel like she had failed her on so many levels, it made her gut ache.

"This must be the place."

She turned to look again. They were pulling up to a large gate. A woman ran out and opened it and they drove through. She tensed, not knowing what to expect from now.

"Hey."

She glanced to see Noah looking at her. His look told her everything was fine.

"You're safe here." He said quietly.

Chapter Twenty-Five

It felt like his heart was lodged in his throat, making each breath harder to take. Being trapped in a vehicle for the last few days hadn't done him any good. He felt like he was suffocating. If he could just put the window down and breathe fresh air it would be better, but with children behind him, he didn't want them to be cold.

Movement beside him, had him jerk his head to see Asher giving him a strange look. He shook his head, telling him it was nothing. Of course, Asher and the other shifters behind him would be picking up the emotional storm he was weathering, but he seemed to accept the lie without comment.

"You're going to be shoveling snow a lot sooner than you want to be."

Noah looked back out the windshield to see there was snow on the ground, he hadn't even noticed it. When was the last time he'd experienced a winter, one with snow? He couldn't remember. The last house he'd been at hadn't been in a state that saw any significant snowfall. Swallowing, trying to clear the obstruction in his throat, he glanced back over to Asher, "Ed has plows, I don't think they do a lot of shoveling by hand."

Asher smirked, "that sounds like fun."

Noah shrugged; he had no idea. He needed to keep talking to distract his mind from smothering him. "You don't get snow where your clan is?"

Asher looked back out the windshield. "We do. A ton of it." He gripped the steering wheel harder, and his knuckles went white, "I'm not there much."

There was a note in his voice that resonated with Noah, but he couldn't be certain why. "Do you think things will slow down for the winter," he looked back out the window, and he recognized where they were now, "with the teams?"

Asher snorted, "with some of the information Calum was relaying from our prince, I don't think so. We're hot on their as..." he glanced over his shoulder, "tails now."

Noah smirked at the fact that he'd caught himself before swearing in front of the kids. He frowned; he was going to have to remember that.

"I am so thankful you found us when you did."

Noah turned to see Emma talking. She was the only other elder in the clan aside from McKenna's grandmother.

"The prospect of living in that shack in the middle of winter," she made a face, "my bones weren't looking forward to it."

Delilah caught his eye before he could turn back around, "is it a big house or a smaller one?"

Noah looked to see the others were watching him now, "I'm not sure. I've driven by it many times, but it's far back from the road, so I couldn't see the layout."

"Blair said it used to be an old children's camp." Penny glanced at Wren for a second, "what kind of camp?" He could hear the fear in her voice.

He didn't blame them for being hesitant, not after what they'd been through. "I don't know." He motioned to the windshield, "there's a lot of abandoned places around here." He cleared his throat, "people think living up here will be fun until they realize how remote it is then they run back to the city."

"I'm okay with remote." Delilah nodded, "as long as it has heat and water."

Noah shifted, wanting nothing more than to turn around and go back to his private torment, but he didn't want to have a vehicle packed with women and children panicking. "Ed, that's my Alpha," it wasn't a lie, he didn't know his own clan at all or the Alpha there, "I talked to him this morning and he said the guys—the men I work with," he tried to offer her a friendly smile, but wasn't feeling it, "were working on that." He glanced at Emersyn to see she was solely focused on him, he forgot what he was going to say.

"Are we close to your clan?"

Her voice seemed to bring him back to the conversation. "Uh, I think Blair said fifteen, twenty minutes from his and Ed's clan."

"I just want a bed to sleep in." Liam, who hadn't said three words the whole trip said.

Noah did grin this time, "if I know Beth, my Alpha's mate, there will be a steady stream of trucks hauling in furniture and everything else."

Penny closed her eyes and smiled slowly, "I can't wait to cook again," she opened them, "real meals."

Several of the others nodded. He honestly had no idea what they were going to see when they got there and he didn't want to get their hopes up, "there's probably going to be a lot of work to be done before winter is here."

"We'll get it done." Emma said as she nodded her head slowly, "if we get to stay in one place, we will work around the clock."

"You guys moved a lot?" Asher asked and Noah was grateful it took him out of the conversation. Speaking to one female was hard for him to do, having the whole group of them looking at him had him sweating.

"Lindon moved us a lot." Emma said, "I'm guessing so he and his pack of rats couldn't be found." Noah watched her smile wide, "the best thing I've ever heard was Blair telling us he was gone. Good riddance. I hope they torture him in hell."

She clamped her mouth closed and nodded. "Next to Noah dangling his sidekick by the neck that is, that's my top favorite memory now."

Noah turned to look at Asher, he had one eyebrow raised and the expression said there would be questions later.

"This must be the place." Asher slowed the van. "You weren't kidding about it being back off the road."

Noah watched out the windshield to see the drive was long and winding. He watched Calum navigate it slowly. He wondered if Ed had a spare plow he could leave here. One of the men would probably be able to use it with a bit of practice. As they crested the small hill, the drive led through some trees, he could see a privacy fence ahead. The paint was faded, but things like that would have to wait until spring now.

The gate was open, so they pulled in. Noah spotted Cooper's truck right away. Something inside him settled just knowing that he was here. There was another black truck parked there, one he didn't recognize.

When Asher parked the van, Noah had the door open before he could put it into park. He breathed in the fresh air and closed his eyes. The familiar scents of this area calmed his cat almost immediately. When he heard one of the other doors on the van open, he turned around to see the others climbing out.

Calum came over toward him. "That fence will come in handy." He glanced over his shoulder at the kids that were joining the adults as they all grouped together. "A lot of small people to keep track of." He smirked.

Noah nodded and then turned and looked at the house. It was one level and spread out to cover a large chunk of the fenced-in area.

Blair looked exasperated as he walked over to them, "that little Crystal could give Daisie a run for her money with chatter."

Kobie leaned into him and nudged him. "She's adorable."

Blair rolled his eyes, "she kept me awake at least."

The front door opened, and Cooper stood in it, leaning on a cane. Noah hoped that meant his leg was getting closer to healing. The last time he'd seen him it was a crutch.

He looked at Blair, "you might want to call home." He smirked, "somethings going on over there, Jake and Gary lit out of here to lend a hand."

Blair swore and pulled his phone out. He dialed it quickly, then frowned, "Daisie, why are you answering this phone?"

Noah didn't know who he'd tried calling, but he stood watching, hoping that everything was all right.

"What? Okay, okay," he lifted his hand like she could see him, "slow down. Who did?" Blair's eyes widened as he turned to look at Kobie, "are they back yet?" He nodded, "okay who went with them?" He nodded again and Noah was about ready to yell and ask what was happening. "Ah, yeah, Kobie and I will pop home in a bit, tell her I'll see her soon when she's back." He hung up the phone and looked at Kobie. "Annamarie's first shift."

Kobie put her hand over her mouth, an excited look on her face, "did it go well?"

Blair shrugged, "Mika, Nichelle, Jake, and Gary were trying to corral her back to the house Daisie said."

Noah grinned, "Jake's going to love helping with that again."

Blair laughed, "yeah." He inhaled and looked around, "we'll head over in a few minutes." He looked back to Cooper. "What's the status here?"

Cooper gave him a blank look, "we've only had time enough to clear out the rubbish, aired it out, and give a good sweep." He turned and moved back out of the door, "water's on, all three bathrooms are cleaned, and the furnace smelled like something died in it, but we aired out the rooms, so it smells a lot better now."

Noah rubbed his hand over his jaw, a lot of work ahead of them.

"Beth will be descending upon us in about an hour with supplies and things." Cooper winced, "you going to bring everyone in or make them stand out there until they're frozen?" He went back inside.

Blair jolted and turned to look at Noah, "we'll bring the gear in later."

Noah nodded and turned around to see Emersyn standing behind him, holding Aspyn. He stepped back and motioned to the open door.

She gave him a long look and then started to walk with hesitant steps into the house.

"It's a big house," Emma said as she went by him.

Noah glanced over to see Kobie was talking to Blair quietly. He had that look on his face again, the one that went with him saying 'what the fuck do I do now?'. Noah blew out a breath and looked over to see Calum was on his phone. He imagined he'd be heading to Shaelan as soon as possible.

"It feels safe here," Judah said as she took McKenna's arm and went toward the door. McKenna just smiled at her grandmother.

Noah looked around slowly, what did safe feel like? How could she tell that just by standing in the yard for two minutes? Noah waited and went in last. Cooper stood by the door.

"Want the tour?" He motioned to the hall to the left, "the others are gathering in the main room," he started walking slowly, "figured you could use a minute to catch your breath."

That's why Noah liked Cooper, he seemed to know without him having to explain anything. The hall they were going down had a door on either side.

Cooper stopped beside the first one. "This place is set up like a big square, you can get anywhere down any hall."

Noah leaned in and looked to see it was a bedroom with beds built into the wall. He glanced at Cooper.

He shrugged, "Beth said those beds would likely be replaced with ones you could move," he motioned to one of them, "but some of the boys could stay here." He frowned, "I forget the numbers Ed told us."

Noah sucked in a breath, "nine children, only four with parents."

"Saw some teen boys, or close to it." Cooper turned back to the hall, "that room might be good for them."

Noah nodded, "I'll leave that up to the women, they'd know better than I."

Cooper nodded, "there are two rooms in the back," he looked over his shoulder at him, "thought maybe I'd take one of them for a bit." He motioned to the next room, "help get things sorted here."

Noah blew out a breath, "that's a good idea."

Blair came around the corner, "he just wants an out, so he doesn't have to paint the equipment at the shop."

Cooper grinned at Noah, "I hate painting."

Noah smiled back at him, "there's going to be a lot to do here."

"See, that's my figuring too." Cooper nodded and then motioned to the room again. "This here could be an adults' room.

Noah leaned and looked into the room. It wasn't too big.

"We're going to run back and see if they caught up to Annamarie," Blair said, "we'll be back here shortly with some food."

Noah nodded, "I'll uh…"

"Just let everyone wander around and pick a room for now." Kobie offered. "There are snacks and drinks in the vans, that should tie the kids over until we're back."

He straightened and nodded. "Yeah, okay."

Cooper waited until they went out the door and then started walking again. "There's another room in the back, thought you could use." He paused and looked back at him, "you're staying over here, right?"

Noah hadn't decided until right then, "I probably should, to help them get settled."

"I thought as much."

The hall they were in now had six doors in it.

"I rounded up some of your stuff, which was next to nothing."

Noah looked in the first door to see two beds built into the wall. He paused when he saw the lock on the outside of the door. That would be coming off A.S.A.P. "I don't need much."

"You need new shoes." Cooper said and continued down the hall, "I tossed those ones you had." He made a face at him, "smelled like something crawled in them and died."

Noah grinned, "blame Jake for that one, he got stuck at a site that was that slushy grey muck."

Cooper pulled his phone out and looked at it, he answered it, "yeah." He nodded, "they're all here now." He nodded again, "will do, Beth." He tucked the phone back into his pocket. "Incoming in twenty minutes."

Noah looked into a room that was a clone of the last two. "What's she bringing?"

Cooper chuckled, "everything."

Noah raised his eyebrows. He knew enough about Beth that she'd probably rented a fleet of trucks to bring everything in one go. "Okay," he turned and looked down the hall, "I'll go tell everyone to move the vehicles out of the way." He paused in step, "the black truck, who's driving it?"

Cooper leaned on the cane and looked at him for a moment. "That's yours from Ed." He nodded his head once and then turned to go back down the hall. "Keys are in it." He called over his shoulder.

Noah stood there watching him walk away. He blinked and then smiled slowly, no more chasing the guys around to get keys and borrow one of the trucks. He had his own truck? He frowned and headed toward the door fast. He had his own truck.

Chapter Twenty-Six

Three hours later, Noah opened a door he hoped would lead outside. His heart was racing, and he was one step from hyperventilating. There was too much going on inside. Not only had Blair and Kobie returned, but they'd brought others with them to help. Beth had called Gage and Kelsey, also—which brought the total of bodies inside to way too many.

He was thankful for all everyone was doing to help set this place up, but with so many women discussing ideas and things being moved, boxes unpacked, and children screeching around in all the excitement, his head felt like it was going to explode. Beth had come through with the toys, so much so that they were going to have to make one of the rooms into a toy room.

Blair had brought Akira back with him and it had been a loud reunion when the rest of the clan saw that she was alive and well.

He leaned back against the door and took a deep breath.

"I couldn't deal with it either."

Noah turned to see Emersyn sitting on a bench. Out in the yard, Aspyn and Wren ran around chasing each other.

"It's so busy in there, I couldn't breathe." Her voice shook when she said it.

Blowing out a breath, he went over and sat on the bench across from her. "It's ah," he looked at the house, "a bit crazy in there."

"I'm so used to it," she touched the side of her head.

"Being alone and having just your thoughts?"

"Or torments." She nodded, "but yes." Turning, she watched the girls for a moment, "I thought I'd keep a few of the kids out of the way."

Noah looked at them, the yard was empty, nothing for them to do but run around. "We'll have to see about getting a slide or something."

"Maybe some swings?"

He nodded, "Did you claim a room?"

She looked at him for a moment before answering. "I'm going to be sharing one with Penny and Wren. The girls are quite attached to each other."

Noah watched Wren help Aspyn up. The image of him doing the same for Carlene when they were little came to mind. He cleared his throat, "that's good. That they have each other." When he turned back to her, she had that look in her eyes, the one that made him feel like she was seeing inside of him.

She blinked and looked down at her hands, "Noah, there are locks on the doors." She whispered it.

Straightening, he shook his head, "not now. I had Cooper go around and take them all off."

When she closed her eyes, he took that opportunity to admire how lovely she was. He was glad at that moment that all her scars were on the inside, and she was left to appear perfect on the outside.

Lifting her lashes, she gave him a small grateful smile. "Thank you. I should have known you would notice that and do something about it."

The way she said it made him wonder if she had some sort of misplaced belief that he always did the right thing. He wished that were true.

"Emersyn?"

They both turned to see McKenna standing at another door. Noah wasn't even sure where that one was located inside.

"Beth is going over the online school options." She gave Noah a quick glance, "if you wanted to join, for you or Aspyn." McKenna turned back to her, "I don't know about you, but I'm tired of reading at a beginner level."

Noah clenched his jaw. He needed to speak to Beth, or maybe Cooper, about his own education or lack of one.

Emersyn stood up, "I would love that." She smiled at Noah, a real smile—it made him feel like some of the weight sitting on his chest lifted, if only for that moment.

He watched them round up the girls and go back inside. When the door closed, he just sat there for a moment and looked around the yard. He still couldn't believe this place had been sitting here empty. Later when everything was organized and the excitement settled down, he'd have to ask Ed what sort of camp it was meant to be. The locks on the outside of doors really hit him in the gut, setting off all sorts of alarms—and bad memories. Taking a deep breath, he exhaled it like he was expelling the bad images in his head.

He jumped up off the bench, needing to move. It was a good thing this place was here though. He moved toward the back fence, noticing that some boards had recently been replaced. He wondered who he had to thank for that. The yard was almost the size of Ed's equipment yard. More than enough space for kids, of all sizes, to burn off energy.

Nodding as he went, he'd help them get settled, then go back to Ed's to work. Turning he spotted Cooper walking along the side of the building, he stopped and pointed in the direction he'd come from.

Curious, Noah started toward him. "Did you need me?"

Cooper took off his hat and gave his nearly bald head a brisk rub. "I wanted to show you something." Putting his hat back on, he grinned, "they're moving the appliances in."

Noah looked at the house, "maybe I should go give them a hand." Doing something physical right now would help keep him out of his head.

"Jake and Gary will try to outperform Blair and Gage; you'll just get stepped on."

Noah grinned, "it might be fun to watch."

Cooper shook his head, "then you and Calum would end up involved and that's more testosterone than should ever be in one space." He motioned along the house, "come on."

Noah walked slowly so Cooper wouldn't have to try to walk faster on his leg. He wanted to ask how it was feeling, but also didn't want to get that look from Cooper. "Do you have a clan? I mean, one before Ed's." He had no idea where that had come from.

Cooper glanced at him but kept walking. "Yeah. I keep in touch a bit. My sister is there."

Noah waited to see if there was more.

"I have a niece too," he scoffed, "she lives in the city," he glanced up at him, a look of annoyance on his face, "she refuses to acknowledge what she is—I don't know how a body can do that." He shook his head, "once you know, it's hard to unknow something like that."

Noah was surprised, by all of it. "She's safe in the city?" He didn't feel like anyone could be safe in a place where there were *that* many people.

"I have to believe she is." He stopped and looked at him, "if she's never taken a chance of being what she is, then I guess she's found a way to pretend she's one of them." He nodded and then pointed.

Noah turned to look and saw a small building on the corner of the property.

"Gage wanted to set it up as a guardhouse, but I told him with the fence you wouldn't need cameras every two feet like Blair has." He shrugged, "there are a few men in this clan and there are the boys, they'll be shifting soon."

Noah nodded and went toward the house to look inside. Why was Cooper talking to him about all of this when he should be talking it over with Blair? He walked through it, noting it hadn't been cleaned at all. There were two small bedrooms and a bigger one. The kitchen was basic, but the house was only thirty seconds away. There was a small sitting area. His brain automatically checked the doors, for locks. There weren't any.

"I guess whoever was going to be running this camp was planning on staying here."

"What kind of camp was it?" Noah looked in the last door to see it was a bathroom.

"I think Ed said it was supposed to be a reform camp for boys that got into trouble."

Noah rubbed his hand over his jaw, which would explain the tall fence and the locks on the doors.

Cooper chuckled, "guess they realized if one of them got out, they'd never find them in all this land around it."

Noah nodded, "yeah if they did survive the animals, they'd be lost in the trees forever."

Cooper grinned. "That's for sure." He looked around. "What do you think?"

Noah looked around again, "I agree, I don't think a guardhouse is needed."

Cooper gave him a blank look, "not about that. About this little house is perfect for a young family starting out." He held his look, "maybe a family that's been through a lot more than the rest and needs space and quiet." He nodded.

Noah frowned, "sure," he shrugged, "it's only steps from the rest of the house."

Cooper glared at him, "I meant for you, dummy." He jerked his chin toward the door, "and your girl in there." He grinned, "her little one looks like an angel."

Noah was sure his facial expression changed five times before he could form a word. "I—uh..."

"Blair told me he asked you to oversee this branch of his clan. I think it's a great idea." Cooper took off his hat and scratched his head, then put it back on and adjusted it, "these people have been through a lot, and you understand."

Noah walked to the other side of the room and looked out the window, "I know nothing about clan life, Coop." He watched a small orange domestic cat move cautiously over to the shrubs heading toward the back. His first thought was every child here would want it as a pet. He'd never had a pet, most shifters didn't. He smirked and thought of Leah's Thera, did she count as a pet? She was more of a guardian than anything.

"From what I've heard, neither do they. Not a proper clan."

He heard Cooper moving around but didn't turn to see what he was doing. "I won't be around much. The teams are going to be busy."

"That's what I'm here for."

He turned and looked to see him sitting on a dusty chair that looked like it might collapse at any moment. "You're staying here? What about the shop..."

Cooper shrugged, "I'll still go over and lend a hand when needed, but," he placed the cane in front of him and leaned on it, "Kelsey's got Gage now, and the boys are all on the right path," he lifted one shoulder, "I like to go where I'm needed." He looked at the door they'd left open, "a lot of young boys over here that will need direction with no father in their life."

Noah opened his mouth and then snapped it shut. He'd never realized it before. Jake, Gary, and Blair, they'd all been with Ed for most of their life and he'd never thought once about where their families were. Did they have family left? "I, uh think those kids would be lucky to have you around."

"Of course, they would." He grinned, "and with you and your girl running the show here, Blair won't freak out nearly as much."

He was talking about Emersyn and him being mated and running this part of the clan for Blair. He blinked, trying to sort through all the thoughts rushing into his head. Emersyn couldn't handle that many bodies around her any more than he could.

"Before you get lost in that empty head of yours, I know it's not picture-perfect and easy, never said it was." He stood up, "but things have happened in this clan's life that isn't right and it's gonna take someone that knows where they're coming from to help them heal."

Noah gave him a quick look, "heal?" He wanted to laugh, but didn't, "there are some things that you can't heal from, Cooper, they're just always there waiting—" He waved his hand around, "I tried to tell Blair that when he asked me to stay here…"

"Might want to refresh those excuses in your brain, because it looks like time is up."

Noah looked to see him motioning to the door. He went over and looked out and saw Calum, Blair, and Gage walking toward the house. Panic hit him, he needed to be outside, needed air. He went out and then stood there like his feet had forgotten how to move. Closing his eyes, he forced air into his body for a few breaths and then opened his eyes to see the three men watching him as they approached him. He heard Cooper's cane on the floor behind him and knew he was flanking him from behind.

Calum stopped a few feet before the others, his eyes assessing him like he knew not to crowd him. "I'll be heading out in a few minutes."

Noah nodded, "say hi to Shaelan for me."

Calum gave him an abrupt nod.

Blair glanced at the house then back to him, "it's coming together good in there."

Noah nodded.

Gage gave him a careful once-over. "Blair told me you were considering staying over here and overseeing this branch of the Elden-Sorum clan." He nodded his head, "it's a good idea, Noah."

"I was going to stay for a bit until they get settled." That part was true, he wanted to make sure they understood they weren't prisoners now, that they could go outside or go for a run without having to fear for their lives.

"Is Emersyn staying?" Blair pinned him in place with a look.

"Yeah, she uh, Aspyn is really attached to Wren, so she wants to keep them together." The sweat started to roll down the back of his neck.

"That's good." Blair grinned, "Daisie is pretty excited about having girls to play with."

Noah frowned, realizing it was all young boys over at Blair's. "I'm sure she'll take them all under her wing and set them right." He grinned.

Blair rolled his eyes, "that's what we need a whole group of Daisie-level energy." he cleared his throat, "look I'll lay it out for you." He motioned to the house, "four of those in there are my blood," he shook his head, "doesn't matter that I didn't know they didn't exist until this week, but, I'd sleep better at night knowing you're here to watch out for them."

Noah's chest tightened and his throat felt like it was being squeezed, he sucked in a breath and tried to search for the words to explain it to them, again.

"Noah, you're going to be here while they settle," Gage looked around, "and there's a lot of work to do before winter," he turned back to him, "just try it on, see how it fits."

He frowned, Gage was talking like he was trying on a shirt, not taking on the responsibility of a clan. A squeal from behind him had him jump and turn, ready to take on whatever was behind him.

"There he is, Mommy." Aspyn was running toward him. Her little legs were going so fast he was sure she was going to fall forward and land on her face.

He squatted down as she got closer, ready to catch her if she fell. She landed in his arms with such momentum he had to brace so he wouldn't fall back and land on his ass.

"I got you this." She held up a little stuffed tiger. "I have this one to sleep with me so I'm not alone." The stuffed cat she'd been carrying around was shoved close to his face. "I told Mommy you need one too." With an expectant look filled with excitement, she pushed the tiger against his chest.

Noah kept his arm around her so she wouldn't fall back and took the stuffed animal from her. "Thank you." He held it out like he was looking at it, but he wasn't really seeing it. His throat was so tight with emotion that he wasn't sure he could speak. "He can stand guard while I sleep." he managed to whisper.

She grabbed his face, almost taking out his eye with the other stuffed animal, and kissed him in a hard, awkward kiss. Before he could react, she turned and started running back to her mother.

"Sorry if we interrupted," Emersyn said in a small voice.

Noah stood up and shook his head. "It's fine." He looked down at the little girl hugging her mother's leg. "Calum was just saying goodbye."

Emersyn looked behind him. "You're leaving?"

Noah couldn't look at any of the men right now, he glanced down at the orange-striped tiger in his hand.

"I'll be back, with Shaelan," Calum told her. "She will want to check everyone over."

He turned to see the hesitant look gone from her face.

"That's a good idea. The kids," she looked down at her daughter, "just to make sure they're all fine." She smiled at him, but Noah noticed it was a carefully guarded smile. "I should get back inside and see about helping with some snacks for the kids."

He watched her pick up Aspyn and walk away. The little girl watched him over her mother's shoulder until they went around the corner. He couldn't look at the men right now. His vision was blurring and for once it wasn't from the fury he fought to keep inside him. "I'll stay and see how it goes." He said and hoped they heard because he wasn't repeating it.

Chapter Twenty-Seven

Bolting upright, Noah swung his legs over the side of the bed. With a shaking hand, he wiped the sweat and hair back off his forehead. Running his hand over his chest he felt the welts beneath his fingertips and then he was able to drag air into his body to try to slow his breathing. It was a cue that usually dragged him out of the nightmare to the present. They were scars, not scabbed over gashes in his flesh.

His cat was right there with him now, ready to spring into action. Neither of them would ever allow something like that to happen to them again. Not ever. Taking a deep breath, he blew it out slowly. That would be it for sleep, it always was.

He got up and grabbed his jeans and pulled them on. He hoped the kitchen was far enough from the sleeping areas of the house that he could go and get a drink. Picking up his phone, he checked the time. Four in the morning.

Shrugging, he grabbed his shirt and slung it over his shoulder, it was later than he normally woke up. Going out into the hall, he looked to see Cooper's door was closed and no light on. He wasn't worried about his steps making noise, moving without sound was something he had learned how to do a long time ago. If you were silent, you didn't bring attention to yourself.

Going down the hall, he glanced around the main area, and it hit him that it looked like a home. Furniture, a few throw blankets, and a couple of toys sitting on the coffee table. He rubbed his hand over his chest. Had he ever felt like somewhere was home? He wasn't sure.

He went into the kitchen and stopped to listen. Not a sound, well, except that someone snored quite loudly. Moving in almost slow motion, he located the cupboard with the coffee and set up the brewer. When it made the first gurgle sound, he sucked in a breath and held it. Sending the machine a hard look, he headed to the other side of the house, maybe he'd go see how far that noise was traveling in the silence. The last thing he needed was all the little children being woken up by a coffee brewer. Then he wouldn't be anyone's favorite.

Slowly, he walked down the halls, a few doors were closed, but most of them were left open. He understood why, they'd been closed in windowless sheds for who knows how long. He'd overheard a few of the men telling Gage about some of the other locations Lindon had dragged them to and the sheds sounded like the better of the lot.

He paused outside one door and looked in. Someone in one of the beds moved, it was the oldest boy, Julian, he thought his name was. Even in the low light, Noah could see he was startled to see him standing there. He wondered if he'd woke him or if nightmares had. He raised his finger to his mouth and then gave him a little nod. The boy sucked in a breath and then dropped back onto the bed in relief. Noah waited until he was sure he was staying there before he continued down the hall.

He moved by the next door and then stepped back and looked inside. Emersyn was in this room, and Aspyn slept with her. He glanced at the little bed to see the blankets hadn't been disturbed at all. The girl stirred and looked over her mother at him. He put his finger to his mouth again. She nodded and lay back down, snuggling into her mother. His chest tightened with emotions he wasn't sure he'd ever felt before.

Spinning on his heel, he moved with long strides back to the kitchen. Pouring a cup of coffee, he had to focus to not spill it, and his hand shook. He turned and headed for the first door that led to the outside. He shoved the door hard and then winced when it swung around and hit the wall behind. Closing it slowly, he checked to make sure he didn't break it.

"Probably should get a stopper for that."

Noah jumped and slopped hot coffee on his hand. He turned to see one of the men standing a few feet away. He couldn't think of his name, Harrison or Weston?

"I did the same thing," he shrugged, "and I wasn't trying to run through it like you were."

Noah blew out a breath, then switched his cup to the other hand and wiped it on his jeans. When he looked back up, he saw that the man was looking at the scars on his chest.

"I hope whoever did that is dead."

Noah inhaled through his nose, "not yet."

He nodded, "hope you find him." He smirked, then held out his hand to him, "Harrison. I don't think we've met officially."

Noah wiped his hand again and then shook it briefly. "Noah."

He smirked at him, "pretty sure we *all* know *your* name."

Noah took a sip of the coffee and then glanced at the door. "I made coffee if you want it."

"I might get a cup in a minute." He looked at the fence. "I was trying to work up the courage to go for a run."

The chill in the air registered as he stood there. Setting the cup down on the damp ground, he pulled his shirt over his head. Harrison was looking at his bare feet when he looked at him again. "You're free to run here, just take a running partner. No one runs alone."

Harrison nodded, "it's just getting past the last twenty years to go do it."

"They didn't let you shift?" he took another sip.

"Oh, they did, but it was only when it was convenient for them and there were armed men waiting if we went too far." He blew out a breath.

Noah nodded. "I understand."

Harrison glanced at his chest, "I know you do." He looked to the fence again. "What you did," he turned back to him, "to Peter back at the camp," he paused and watched Noah's face, "we were all cheering you on silently."

Noah looked at the ground for a moment, "I shouldn't have lost control like that."

"Was there a connection between the two of you somehow?"

Noah took another sip, trying to figure out how to explain it without explaining all of it. "Emersyn." He said it like her name would explain all of it, Harrison continued to look at him. "She ah, was frightened of him."

He nodded slowly, "I get it." He brushed his messy black hair back from his face, "Lindon's men were bastards." He gave him a hard look, "they rose through the ranks overnight just for following him."

Noah didn't understand the ranks in a clan, aside from Alpha and second, that was it. "Before all this happened, who," he frowned, "which families worked with the Elden's?"

"Judah's family were the second family." He turned back to look into the yard, "there's just her and McKenna left now."

Noah drew in a deep breath, and exhaled it slowly, "if it weren't for McKenna, we wouldn't have found you."

"We all figured as much. She may not have been raised with the clan functioning as it should be, but she got this strength built-in, the kind you can't teach." Harrison blew out a breath. "I'm going to go grab some coffee and see if I can work up the balls to go for a run."

Noah nodded and stepped back from the door. He frowned, "uh, are any of the younger ones shifting yet?"

"You mean the ones your age or younger?" He grinned at him.

Noah opened his mouth, then smirked, "okay, who doesn't shift?" He was surprised that he looked his age to this man, most couldn't see past the weight of his life that he carried on his back.

"Other than the little ones, Liam and Everett haven't yet." He thought for a minute, "Julian has only once."

Noah nodded, "thanks. We'll have to let everyone know about taking a partner with them when they go for a run."

Harrison looked at him for a moment, an unreadable expression on his face. "I hope you're sticking around for a while." He shrugged, "Blair seems likable and nothing like his brother, but you're a better fit for us."

Before Noah could say anything, he went back inside. He stared at the door for a moment and then turned away and took another drink. He should have talked to him about helping keep things in order around here. He opened the door and went in before he could change his mind. Yes, he'd said he would stay for now, but he had to go help the teams. That wasn't optional for him.

He made it to the kitchen and then Aspyn came around the corner. Putting the cup on the counter, he picked her up. "You shouldn't be up wandering around by yourself." She wrapped her arms around his neck and rested her head on his shoulder. He should ask Beth about gates or something for the doors with the kids in them. Then the door could still be open, but the children wouldn't be running around alone.

Harrison stood by the counter smirking at him.

"I have to pee, but I don't remember where the bathroom is." She leaned back and looked at him, her blue eyes wide.

"Oh. Okay. I'll show you." He moved down along the tables and headed down the hall, trying to remember where the closest bathroom was. He almost walked by it. The door was closed. Tapping on the door lightly, he listened and then opened the door. Setting her back on her feet, he nodded down at her. "There you go." He hesitated and then stepped back, hoping she didn't need help. He knew nothing about any of *that*.

"Noah?"

He spun around to see a sleepy but concerned Emersyn standing in the hall.

"Is Aspyn with you?"

He nodded and pointed to the door.

Her shoulders sagged, then she started toward him. "I almost had a heart attack." She put her hand on her chest and huffed out a breath.

Her hair was a mess, her eyes barely open and the clothes she was wearing were wrinkled and skewed on her body, but she was absolutely gorgeous. When he realized she was standing there looking at him, he spurred his brain to work. "We should, uh, find some kind of gates for the door with little ones." He shrugged, "so the door can be open, but the kids can't wander around alone."

She smiled and then nodded, "that's a good idea." Her voice was soft and rasping with sleep.

Noah inhaled a deep breath, and his cat was right there as his system filled with her scent. The toilet flushed and the door was opened wider.

"Mommy." Aspyn went over and hugged her.

"Hi, baby." She touched her head and smiled down at her, "think you can sleep a bit longer?"

As if the word cued the reaction, Aspyn yawned and nodded against her mother's hip. "Okay." Emersyn leaned down and picked up. "Thank you." She gave him a soft look and he once again forgot how to speak and instead nodded his head like he was one of those bobble things that Jake had on the dash of his truck.

He waited until they went back into the room before he stepped back a few steps and then spun around to go back to his coffee. He wanted to go for a run now. Needed to. Unfortunately, he'd just finished telling Harrison that no one ran alone. He kept his eyes on the floor in front of him as he went. Pulling his phone out he looked at the time. If he called Jake at this time of the morning, he'd be incoherent and useless. Reaching the counter, he picked up his cup and then spotted some boxes stacked in the corner. He had no idea what was in them, but it would give him something to do until he could do what he wanted. As soon as Cooper was up, they'd have to go over when was the best time to go for a run. Did any of the others have the same issue that Harrison did? He set the cup down and went over and opened the first box. His gut told them all of them had the same fears as he did about running freely. He pulled out a smaller box and looked in it. Glasses. He shrugged; he could do this quietly. Turning around he saw Harrison open the dishwasher and look at him.

"They washed everything." He said quietly.

"Even if it's new?"

Harrison nodded.

"Okay." Setting the box back in the larger one, he picked the whole thing up and took it to the counter. He was missing the shop already. At least over there he could go beat on something to give his head something to do other than replay that same old loop.

Chapter Twenty-Eight

Noah held the four-by-four above his head so Blair could bolt it at the top. He hadn't needed to talk to Beth about swings or a slide. A truck pulled in after breakfast with delivery and now they were trying to assemble the monstrosity that she had purchased.

"She sent one to your place too?" He looked up to see Blair balancing on the top beam of the 'jungle set'.

Blair didn't look at him, just nodded his head. "Yeah, Franki is over there with a couple of the men putting it together."

Noah watched the snowfall on the ground. "It could have waited until spring."

Blair paused and looked down at him, "explain that to Beth." He turned so he was sitting on the support beam, "just hold it there until I get the bottom ones lined up." He jumped down to the ground.

After unpacking the boxes of dishes, Noah put up curtain rods, assembled shelves, discussed carpeting for the kid's area, and discussed colors of paint. It wasn't even lunchtime yet. He realized Blair was talking to him and turned to see he was holding the two-end post up in the air watching him. "What?"

Blair smirked, "I said the outer walls are up on the buildings, so now the interior could be done."

Noah bobbed his head, "that's good."

"That's fucking great." Blair looked up at where the beams connected, "it means it's going to look less like a huge slumber party in the house."

They both realized at the same time that there was no way for either of them to let go and go up to bolt them together.

"Shit." Blair looked at him and smiled, "I'm much better as a mechanic than construction."

Noah looked up, "If you slide that over so the notches line up, I can hold one side."

Blair looked at him, then moved just his eyes as if to say look.

Noah turned his head to see Cooper standing by the house with that grin on his face, the one he got when one of them did something stupid and he was going to spell out how stupid to them. "How does he always know?"

They both watched Cooper go over to the oldest boy, Julian, who was breaking down boxes, and said something to him. Julian looked over at them and then nodded.

"I should have followed the instructions," Blair mumbled.

Noah gave him a side glance and then watched Julian jog toward them. He'd suggested that, but Blair had said it was a simple setup.

He stopped a few feet from them. "He said you could use a hand."

Blair snorted, "of course he did." He looked at the other end of the swing part, "think you can climb up there and shimmy across to here?"

Julian looked to the other end and then up at the support above them. He shrugged one shoulder, "yeah."

"Okay," Blair pointed to the box on the ground, "grab two of those bolts and," he reached into his back pocket and held out the wrenches, "these. We'll hold it steady."

Noah watched him go down to the other end and climb up the cross support then right up to the top like it was nothing. He was a tall boy, making him wonder how old he was exactly and how much more growing he had to do.

As he slid across toward the end they were holding upright, he glanced down at Noah, "we're staying here, right?"

Noah nodded, "yeah."

"Good." He pulled one of the bolts out of his pocket and started to unthread the nut. "It was weird, sleeping in a bed last night."

"It was comfortable though?"

Noah watched him as he paused but didn't look down at Blair to answer him.

"It was a real bed inside a warm house, so yeah."

The places Lindon had dragged them to keep the clan hidden and off the radar had been anything but comfortable. The sheds were probably preferred to shipping containers, tents, caves, and just a bush with no shelter. Noah thought as he watched him frown at the parts in his hand.

"What do I do with these things?" Julian held out the washers.

"One goes at the top before you put it through and the other on the bottom before you put the nut on."

Julian looked at the pieces in his hand and nodded. "I've never done something like this," he confessed as he leaned slowly toward the end.

"You're doing great," Blair told him. "Later I'll take you over to check out the equipment Noah and I get to play on."

Noah smirked, some days there was a lot of play between the work parts.

"Just don't agree to game with him," Noah said with a smile.

"Game?"

Blair gasped, "oh you wait, my young friend until the internet is hooked up and we get the consoles set up."

Noah gave Blair a surprised look.

Blair grinned, "of course, Beth got gaming consoles." Blair jerked his head toward the house, "with so many boys in there, it's the only thing that soothes them."

Noah snorted, "it doesn't sound very soothing when you and Jake are swearing at each other."

Blair shrugged one shoulder, "not my fault he's jelly that I'm better than him at every game."

"You guys are weird." Julian smiled down at them, "in a good way."

Noah smiled back up at him, "just get that done before one of the women comes out and yells at us for you being up there."

"Good point." Blair nodded.

He was silent as he concentrated on getting the first bolt in place. "You guys are afraid of the women?" He paused and looked down at Blair and then at him.

Blair nodded his head, "if the women aren't happy, then it's not a good time, my friend."

Julian's expression was focused as he thought that through and tightened the second bolt. "Everything's different now."

"But good, right?" Blair asked him.

Julian sat up and balanced on the beam and looked down at the ground, "I think so." He jumped down to the ground. Noah noticed the way he landed and there was no mistaking the young shifter was in contact with his animal. His landing was graceful and precise.

Noah released the board and backed away from it as it might fall. He turned to Julian, "Blair and I were going to go for a run soon and check the area, did you want to come?"

The first thing Noah noticed was the surprise on his face, and then it changed to fear.

"I, uh," Julian swatted his long black hair out of his face, "I have only done that once." He shook his head, "it wasn't what I thought it would be like."

"This time no one will be standing over you with a gun," Noah told him.

Blair's head jerked to look at him, a shocked expression on his face. He recovered quickly, "that's right." He motioned to Noah, "we're going to need help with patrols and keeping an eye on things here, so it would be great if you'd help us."

Julian frowned, "I don't know anything about stuff like that."

Blair shrugged it off, "your cat will help."

"My cat?" He rubbed his hand over his chest, a confused look on his face.

"That's right." Blair looked around, "take a deep breath and tell me what you smell right now."

Noah watched as the boy did.

"What did you smell?"

Julian grinned, "lunch cooking."

Blair looked at the house and inhaled, he turned to Noah and grinned, "he's right. Guess we're going for a run after lunch." His phone ringing had him pause to pull his phone out of his pocket. "It's Devin." He looked at Noah, the playfulness gone.

Julian watched him walk away with the phone to his ear. "I still can't believe you guys got us out of there."

Noah jammed his hands in his pockets, "you aren't the first and won't be the last we help." It was the only thing he could think of to say.

"This morning," Julian looked at the front of Noah's shirt, "those scars, who did that?"

Noah exhaled slowly, trying to keep his cat from reacting as he thought of how to explain it. Then it dawned on him, "do you have scars, Julian."

Julian looked at the ground, making his hair fall over his face so Noah couldn't see his expression. "Some. N-not like yours."

He wanted to reach out and touch his shoulder, offer some sort of contact to let him know he wasn't alone, but he knew better. If the boy had scars on his body, even the friendliest touch could spook him. "The men that Lindon worked with did it." Noah watched for a reaction. "No one will ever do it again. Not to me or you."

Julian raised his chin and looked at him, he searched his face, looking to see if he was telling him the truth. "Is it normal to be afraid of everything?"

Noah held his look, even though he wanted to turn around and smash the playset they had just put up. He nodded, "it's hard, I know," he blew out a breath, wishing Cooper were here to talk to him, "but you get through it." He nodded, "you have a lot of others around you now that will help." Cooper wouldn't mind if he used one of his lines, he was sure.

He could see the jerky breaths the boy took and then he nodded. "Okay."

"What about the other two older boys?"

"Liam and Everett?" He shook his head, "they uh, haven't changed yet, so they didn't get an example of what happens if they don't follow the rules."

Noah clamped his jaw shut for a moment, while he processed what he was saying. Lindon beat them after they shifted so they'd always toe the line. It had been the same for him. He didn't know what to say to distract from it, he didn't want him to think he didn't care that it had happened to him. "They're lucky they have you to help them through when it's their first shift." he nodded.

"Yeah, I'll help them." He turned and looked at the fence, "I'd like to try," he motioned to it, "go out with you and Blair maybe after lunch."

Noah grinned, "great, it's pretty amazing when you're not afraid." He glanced over to Blair, "I should warn you though, Blair is this really pretty white cat."

Julian grinned and looked over at him, "Is that like an Elden thing?"

Noah motioned for them to head toward the house, "I'm not sure. His mate is a black one."

"Black? Really?" He gave him a wide-eyed look, "I feel plain now. I'm just orange."

Noah nodded, "me too." He watched Emersyn open the door and look out at them, "Emersyn is almost a chocolate color."

"Damn," Julian mumbled, "I didn't know there were that many different kinds." His eyes widened, "sorry I swore."

Noah shrugged, "just don't do it in front of the women or kids." He paused and gave him a pointed look.

"Yeah. Got it." Julian looked over at Emersyn, "Is she your mate?"

Noah cleared his throat, "she is." He watched her as she stood there, watching him, "it's complicated for us."

"I just noticed the way you two look at each other," he shrugged, "it's the same with Kobie and Blair." He paused and looked over at his Alpha, "he's pretty cool for being related to Lindon."

"He killed Lindon to save you and a lot of others." Noah wasn't sure if he should have said that, but there was something about Julian that made him feel closer to him than the other children. He'd known the cruelty that others could never dream of existing.

"I'm glad." He started walking again, "I hope it was a painful bloody fight."

That surprised Noah. "It was over quick. Lindon wasn't as good as he thought he was."

Julian snorted but made no comment.

"Lunch is ready," Emersyn said as they reached the house. She looked at the playset. "Will it be done soon? Aspyn has been staring out the window since you started."

Noah glanced back at it. "Just have to put the swings and slides on." He glanced to see Julian roll his eyes at him as he looked back and forth between them.

"Go get cleaned up for lunch." He told him in a tone that was anything but authoritative.

"We're going for a run after lunch if you wanted to come."

Her eyes widened and then she smiled, "I've been wanting to, but didn't want to bother anyone."

"It's never a bother." He rubbed the back of his neck, trying to keep his hands busy so he wouldn't reach over and brush the hair back from her face. "We need everyone to know the area well."

"Okay." She nodded, "I'll see if someone will watch Aspyn so I can go for a run."

Noah glanced over her shoulder to see Julian backing away from them as he fluttered his eyes at him. Noah scowled at him but didn't mean it. Julian was acting like a teen boy and that meant it wasn't too late for him to find a normal life. Noah looked over at Blair, "I'll be there in a second. I just want to see what Blair found out."

She smiled up at him and his heart started skipping around in his chest like he was some carefree child.

When the door closed, he spun around and closed the distance between him and Blair. Blair was just tucking the phone into his pocket. "Lindon beat them," he growled between clenched teeth, "after their first shift so they'd stay in line."

Blair squeezed his eyes shut and stood that way for a minute.

Noah remembered that it was his own brother that had done these things. When he opened them again, Noah could see the rage in his eyes.

"How many?"

Noah glanced back at the house, "Just Julian, the other boys haven't changed yet," he looked back at him, "but I don't know about the women." He shook his head, "it's not something you can just go around and ask them."

Blair nodded, "Shaelan will be back soon, I'll talk to her."

Noah nodded, "she wanted to check everyone."

"Yeah, we'll get her to record scaring or something." Blair blew out a breath. "If it were possible, I'd kill him a second time."

Noah rolled his shoulders and tried to shake the tension that was back tenfold. "Emersyn and Julian are going for a run with us after lunch."

"Good. Running, as you know, is a great way to exorcise a lot of ghosts."

"It's a temporary fix." Noah couldn't argue that.

"You have to stick with me here, Noah," he motioned to the house, "I'm barely holding my own against the kids at home," he waved his hand around, "I know nothing about trauma and the shit they've been through."

Noah turned and looked at the house, "I haven't even figured out how to deal with it."

"I know, but I don't even know what I should or shouldn't do." He started walking, "I don't want to freak anyone out."

"Well," Noah caught up to him, "for starters, don't touch any of them unexpectedly."

Blair looked at him, "see, you do know." Blair stopped suddenly and gave him a wide-eyed look; he placed his hands beside his head like he was trying to squeeze it. "Between here and home," he dropped his hands, "that's what, nineteen kids?" He rubbed his hand over his head, "what the hell are we going to do when they all start shifting, Noah, or worse their hormones kick in."

Noah looked at the house, then back at him, he opened his mouth and then snapped it shut again. "I don't..."

"Shit." Blair swore softly, "I don't even know how to deal with all that." Blair shook his head, "I can't even think about it anymore right now, there's too much shit going on."

"What shit?"

Blair stopped with his hand on the door handle, "Devin said our team is on hold again."

"Why?" The only thing that prevented Noah from sitting in a corner rocking himself into a frenzy was the idea that he would be back out with the team in a few days.

"Tomas is panicking, he's moving damn near every location we knew about."

Noah frowned, "are they able to keep track of them and follow them."

"They're trying, the incursion team, special ops, and a few other teams are all on it now, tracking movement."

Noah clenched his jaw and squeezed his eyes shut, they couldn't lose them, not when they just found them all. He opened his eyes and then inhaled slowly through his nose.

Blair patted him on the shoulder, "we'll find them. All of them."

"I just hope that book we found is still useful."

"I said the same thing to Devin, and he said that so far it's only the local locations that seem to be on the move."

Noah shifted his head from side to side trying to loosen the tense muscles, "so Tomas is only thinking about himself."

"Seems like." Blair grinned, "which is good for us."

Noah nodded, "and Konner, the locations that had some of his?"

"They're still where they were." Blair pulled the door open, "guess they think their security will save them."

Noah went in the door after him, "nothing is going to save them."

Chapter Twenty-Nine

He pulled his shirt back on quickly. If it were just the guys from the shop around, it didn't bother him as much, but with so many around here, he didn't need to see those looks on their faces. The ones that bled pity when they saw his scars.

As he stepped out through the gate to the yard, Julian came running toward him, shirt and shoes in his hands. Noah paused to tell him to put his shoes on because it was snowing, then he saw tears on his face and froze. He'd had to persuade him to shift, promised him it would be different from before. He frowned, Julian had run like the wind and jumped any obstacle out there, he thought he'd enjoyed it. He prepared to apologize when Julian threw himself at him and hugged him tightly. Noah sucked in a breath and held it, trying not to panic but wanting to console him at the same time. When his grip loosened, he looked down to see Julian smiling.

"*That* was amazing."

The tears weren't from fear or trauma. Noah was slow to smile, as he stepped back to put space between them. "You have quite the speed." He tilted his head to the side, "maybe just try not to jump so far until you have more control."

Julian grinned and bobbed his head up and down, "I just— I can't believe how awesome that was."

Noah smiled, a real one this time. "It's pretty cool." He glanced over to see Kobie and Blair coming back into the yard, "Kobie will work with you on tracking and hunting."

"Really?" Julian looked from her back to him, and Noah noticed the guarded look in his eyes was gone. Julian spun on his heel and rushed toward them.

Noah blew out a breath and then looked around for Emersyn. He turned to see if she was back in the yard already. She'd seemed like she enjoyed the run, her cat was less hesitant this time. Scowling at the ground, he moved back to the gate to look for her.

She stood in the opening of the trees, near to where they had shifted. She had her back to him, so he couldn't see her face. He could smell the saltiness of tears and hurried toward her.

She turned her head and glanced at him as he got closer. "I feel so silly." Her voice shook with emotion.

Noah's throat tightened; his cat was still, wary. "What's wrong? Your cat looked like she was having fun."

Emersyn nodded, "she did, we did."

He stepped closer so he could see her face. It was stained with tears. He didn't understand.

"Look." She turned her head.

Noah jerked his chin and looked in the direction she was. There was nothing there, just open land. They were on a hill, so the view stretched out for many miles.

"It's beautiful." She whispered.

He nodded; he couldn't deny that. When she looked up at him, he forgot what he was going to say. Her eyes were drowning in unshed tears, and it made them sparkle as gems would.

"I want to stay here, Noah." She smiled at him, "with this clan," she looked back out from the trees, "with this endless wilderness." She wiped at one eye, "I want Aspyn to grow up in the open, not locked in a house or surrounded by cement and buildings."

He blew out a breath, "you don't have to go anywhere if you don't want to." It wasn't what he wanted to say, but those words he couldn't speak out loud.

She smiled up at him again, and he could see there was a tinge of happiness in her eyes. It made his heart swell seeing it. "And you? Are you going to stay?"

He frowned, "I said I'd help Blair..."

"No, I mean are you going to stay here at this house, with this clan, after they're on their feet again."

He nodded slowly, "I don't have plans to leave," he shrugged, "I might go help Ed from time to time and I do have to go out with the teams..."

"This will be home for you though?"

Maybe it was the way her scent was wrapping around his insides or the fact that his cat felt like he was rolling around inside him, but he couldn't quite focus to understand what she wanted him to say. "This area is my home now." He hoped that was the right answer, "I'm not going back to my family's clan." He hadn't decided that in such a definite term until his mouth just said it.

"Good." She smiled again and then placed her hand on his chest and rubbed it gently.

It was such a small movement, but he felt it through his whole body. It relaxed him but tensed his cat. Being in conflict internally wasn't a new thing for him.

"I want to run every day." She looked at him through her long dark lashes, and he was rendered mute.

He nodded.

"And when you're here, I want to run with you."

Noah looked at her, really looked at her. The sprinkle of freckles across her nose and cheeks was wet and shining from the tears. He reached before he realized it to wipe her cheek dry and then froze when she lifted her face to him and didn't shrink from his touch. His heart felt like it was beating so fast it was closing off his throat as he fought to draw air into his lungs. Everything moved in slow motion but seemed lightning fast as he leaned down and placed his mouth gently against hers.

When she didn't pull away, he did it again. He felt her hand move up to his neck and the warmth of her palm against his skin sent a shiver through his whole body. Touching her hip, he kissed her again. It was awkward and needy when he knew she deserved so much more.

Jerking his head up, he gave her a cautious look. "I shouldn't have done that." He blurted out.

Her hand moved down his shoulder, then the length of his arm. "I didn't mind, Noah."

His cat was frozen inside him. Offended beyond any measure that he'd taken such a liberty with her. "We should get inside now." He stepped back and held his hand out in the direction of the gate.

She nodded, "yes, we're deciding on paint today." She smiled up at him once more before she started for the gate.

Paint? She was thinking about painting? She should have smacked him, or-or he didn't know but she should have done something.

The afternoon was busy with more tasks of setting things up, and moving things that had been moved ten times now already, there was always a better location. When it was suggested to go outside and put new weather stripping on the many windows and doors, Noah raced outside with Blair. Emersyn kept giving him looks, ones he understood but didn't understand at the same time. He'd seen them before, just never directed at him. Why she was, he didn't know.

"Does that work for you?"

Noah blinked to see Blair looking at him, with a strange look on his face. He looked to see he was still holding the window that was already back in place. He had no idea what Blair had said, so he nodded, "looks good."

Blair grinned then shook his head. "Are you even in there?"

Noah frowned, "what?"

"That's what I thought." Blair motioned to move to the next window. "I *said*," he shook his head again, "that Beth is taking Kobie and a few of the women from here to get more clothes now that we know sizes, and I have to be at my place to give a hand with the interior of the buildings, Jake and Gary are going to be helping me, so," he paused as he slid the window up, "can you run over and give Gage and Kelsey a hand in the shop?"

Noah jolted; he hadn't heard a word he'd said. "Uh, yeah." He took the window to hold while Blair put the strip on the bottom of it. "Gates. They need gates."

"Gates?"

He looked at the house, "for the bedroom doors so they can stay open, but the little ones don't wander at night."

Blair blinked and then nodded, "I'll tell Kobie, but back to a second ago—where is your head at?" Blair smirked, "I mean, I know you're usually stuck in it, but today it's like you're an empty shell."

Noah scowled at the window he held, thinking they came out way too easy, from the outside. He'd have to ask Cooper about locks for them. Although, if someone was in the yard to get to them, they'd already be dead. "I kissed Emersyn." He mumbled, hoping that answered the question.

"Okay." Blair shrugged as he worked, "I guess that's distracting." He smirked at him over his shoulder, "in a good way."

Noah shook his head, "it's not a good way."

Blair turned and tugged the window out of his hand. "She didn't like it?"

Noah opened his mouth and then closed it. "I don't know." How was he supposed to know something like that?

Sliding the window back in place, Blair turned around and put his hands on his hips, and looked at him. "You don't know?" He rubbed his hand over his hair, "well, did she kiss you back? Or did she stiffen like you tasted like her least favorite food?" Picking up the box, he started walking to the door that was next.

Noah stumbled after him, "I think she kissed me back." Had she?

"You think?" Blair stopped so suddenly, that Noah almost walked into him.

"I've never kissed anyone before," Noah confessed.

Blair looked at him, his mouth gaping open. "Okay, wait." He set the box down, "I know you lived in some sick ass version of hell," he lifted his hand in the air, "for years, but," he huffed out a breath and put his hands on his hips again, "weren't you surrounded by women? Didn't you ever sneak a kiss?"

Noah shook his head, realizing he had never fully described what he'd gone through. "None of us were there by choice." He said in a low tone.

Blair blinked, "right. Fuck. I'm sorry, I just—" he lifted his hand and then dropped, "you've never kissed anyone before? I know you said," he wiggled his hand in his direction, "never done that before, but I thought," he blew out a breath and then frowned, "why do you keep telling me this shit?" He smirked, "I mean, yeah you were there for me when my head," he tapped his hand on the side of his head, "was a mess, but you could share this with someone else."

Noah raised one eyebrow, "with who?"

Blair held his look for a second. "Right. Jake would broadcast it; Gary would blush and be less than helpful." He nodded and picked up the box, "okay, so," he started walking again, "she didn't freak out, that's good." He went over to the door and set the box down again, "what did she do?"

Noah reached up and held the trim in place while Blair cut it. "She uh, smiled at me." He frowned, "and rubbed her hand up and down my arm."

Blair paused and glanced at him, "so she was okay with it."

Noah glared at him.

"What? You didn't want her to like it?" He shook his head and then jerked the piece of striping from his hand to put up.

"I am not good for her." Noah swung the door back further out of the way, "she deserves so much after what she's been through."

Blair gave him a strange look, "I'm confused." He leaned closer, "bud, she's your mate, you're it." He nodded.

"I can't *be* that." He gave his head a brisk shake. "I..."

Blair grinned at him, "dote on her, understand her, know what she needs..."

Noah chuffed, "no."

Blair nodded his head in an exaggerated way, "yes you do. You jumped in a hole after her," he chuckled, "without knowing what was at the bottom." He pulled the strip out to measure the next part, "you were ready to crush that guy's windpipe," he shrugged, "and had the strength of Thor because we couldn't get you to let go." He gave him a quick look, "you put things in the trailer that you knew she'd never had..."

"That doesn't mean I'm good for her." Noah scowled at the side of his head.

"Would you ever hurt her?"

"No." That was a dumb thing to ask.

"Will you protect her and Aspyn from anything?" Blair cut the strip and tossed the rest of the roll at him.

He caught the roll and gave him a blank look. "If I can, yeah, of course."

Blair nodded his head as he put the strip along the side of the door, "then I'd say you are good for her and exactly what she needs." Blair squatted down, "we need a plastic strip for here, this one is garbage." He stood up and jerked the door out of his grip and started to close it when Emersyn appeared in it. She gave Blair a brief smile and then looked at him.

"I made coffee, Noah, if you wanted some."

Noah swallowed and nodded his head quickly. "I can come in and get some."

Emersyn smiled, a soft look in her eyes, "I'll get it. I know how you like it." She turned to Blair, "um, would you like some?"

"I'm heading out in a minute, but thanks."

When she closed the door, Blair swung his head to look at him. "She didn't mind the kiss at all, my friend, in fact," he shrugged, "she wouldn't mind another one."

Noah looked from him to the door, "what do you mean?"

Blair threw his head back and laughed, "oh, we have a lot to teach you." He sobered and then patted him on the shoulder, "just trust me, she didn't mind at all, and you have nothing to worry about."

Noah watched him pick up the box and walk away. He glared at his back, he had everything to worry about. The thought of touching a woman made him want to throw up. She had been abused by Lindon, there was no way she welcomed his touch. He put his fingers over his mouth. He still didn't know why he kissed her like that. The sooner he got to the shop, the better. He needed to think about all of this and try to figure it all out.

Chapter Thirty

Emersyn watched Aspyn come down the slide. She squealed with delight and landed on her bottom on the ground. Each time she heard her laugh, or saw her smile, she wanted to cry. Not out of sadness, but with relief. Her daughter was free. She would never know the horror that her mother had lived through. She hoped she was young enough that she'd forget all of it. Lindon, hearing her mother cry, seeing the other women bruised and void of any spark for life. All of it, that's what she wanted for her.

"Be careful." She held her breath as she went up the ladder again. Wren was right behind her. She owed so much to that child. Wren had been by her side when she couldn't be there. While she was only six, she acted much older. For such a young one, she had seen too much. Crossing her arms over her stomach, she wondered if they would be able to find her mother.

Penny had told her that Wren's mother was one of the clan Lindon had taken away and no one knew where. How could he do that to his own clan members? A chill went through her, and it had nothing to do with the cold outside. He had killed, maimed, and sold his own clan members. She would have to ask Noah if they had any ideas where she might be.

She watched as the girls took to running around the yard. She was never going to tell her daughter about her father. Never. Aspyn was full of joy, and she intended to keep it that way as long as she was able.

Penny came over, zipping her jacket up. She gave her a brief smile. "It's strange." She said as she pulled up her auburn hair. "To come outside whenever we want."

Emersyn nodded. She had spent her life looking out a window wishing to feel the air on her skin. It was cold today, but she didn't care. Cold air on her face was better than wishing to feel it.

"Are you planning to stay?" She motioned to the house, "with us?"

Emersyn pulled the collar of her jacket up and checked on the girls. They didn't seem to even notice the drop in temperature. "Yes."

Penny looked relieved, "oh good." She looked over at the girls, "they're so attached to each other." Tucking her hands in her pockets, she kicked at the thin layer of snow on the ground. "Wren was so withdrawn until Aspyn arrived." She blew out a breath that was visible in the cool air.

"I have no wish to go back to my clan." Emersyn pulled her hand through her hair to move it from her face and paused to feel it was damp from the snowflakes. That was something she'd wished for when she was trapped inside. "Half of them are here, half are still in another country." She glanced at Penny wondering if she would judge her for having no desire to see her family. "I will talk to them when I'm ready."

Penny nodded, there was no judgment in her eyes. "I'm glad you're staying." She turned and smiled at the girls. "I'm going to get in on this chase." She turned and ran toward the girls.

Emersyn blew out a breath and marveled that she could see it in front of her face. Movement caught her attention and she turned to see Cooper walking back along the side of the house. She hadn't spoken to him other than a hello when their paths crossed, but he seemed like a nice man. She wondered what had happened that he walked with a cane, and hoped it wasn't permanent. She understood what it was like to not have free movement. He knew Noah, she'd heard them speak a few times. Noah seemed to listen intently when he spoke, so she knew there was respect there.

He paused and turned around like he had sensed she was watching him. She froze, panic filling her. With a jerk of his head, he called her over.

It took a few deep breaths for her to build up the courage to do that. She just had to remind herself that she was safe. The males here were not part of the world she'd escaped. Noah trusted him, so she should too. All of that only half worked, but she was going to go speak to him despite it. She didn't want to be rude.

He gave her a pleasant smile when she was closer. "I guess the cold doesn't bother them." He motioned to the girls.

"I don't think they've even noticed." She clasped her hands in front of her.

"It's nice, hearing children play." He nodded his head and then turned to look at the little house at the far end, "I need a woman's opinion." He jerked his chin toward it and started walking.

She looked back to see Penny was still playing with the girls and decided she could help him for a few minutes. She walked behind him, head down, hands clasped together out of habit. It was safer that way. Silent and docile.

When he reached the little house, he opened the door and went in.

Her nerves were getting the better of her and she was only able to step into the door frame and stand there. She looked around. It was a small home, as far as she could figure. A very dirty, dingy one.

"I don't know where to start." He stopped in the middle of the room and stood there. "Do I toss it all outside and go from there or clean it up piece by piece?" He made a sound that was similar to a growl, but not at the same time. With his cane clunking against the floor, he went over and sat down on a dirty wooden chair. "This cold makes it ache something crazy." He leaned down and rubbed his hand down his leg. "I can't wait to shift and heal it all up once and for all."

"You were injured?" She stepped inside a few more feet.

He took off his hat and rubbed his hand over his head. She was able to see his brown eyes better now, they were hard but filled with compassion at the same time. "I was in the shop alone and a jack stand gave out and the rig fell on my leg a while back." His tone told her he was very annoyed with this. "It should be safe to shift soon. I plan on haranguing Shaelan when she comes back to check on it and give me a thumbs up."

She put her hand over her heart which had accelerated as he spoke. The work they did sounded dangerous.

He put his hat back on, "don't worry, Noah is safe. We're just doing clean-up at this time of year." He grinned, "tune-ups and painting. We all hate it."

She nodded and stood where she was.

"What do you think?" He looked around the room.

Emersyn blew out a breath and looked around. "Well, first I-I would open a window and let some air in here." She had no idea what the smell was, but it bothered her nose. A lot.

"There's a bit of mildew in here." Leaning on his cane, a soft look on his face, "go on, have a look around."

She took a few hesitant steps and then went down the short hallway. The doors were all open, which she was thankful for. A closed door would always haunt her, and she knew that. It had been hard enough to bring herself to close the bathroom door when she had a shower in the house. The first room was small, empty, and very dusty. She looked down to see boot prints on the carpet. Backing out of the room, she went to look in the next door. It was about the same size. In the next, there was a dresser and bedframe, nothing more. Wrapping her arms around her waist, she went over and pulled the curtain aside. Dust billowed out from it. The light from outside made the room look much better. It also allowed her to see the grime on everything. How long had this place sat empty?

She stepped out of the room. "Was the house this dirty?"

Cooper chuckled, "worse. We cleaned things out of there that I'm still not sure I want to know what they were."

She smiled and looked through the last doorway. It was a bathroom. There was no curtain on the window in here, but the glass was thick with a pattern on it, so no one could see in. Leaning around the door, she looked in the tub and cringed. The smell that offended her system was definitely coming from this room.

She went back out to see he was still sitting leaning on his cane. She felt bad for him, his leg must really hurt in this dampness. Going over to the kitchen area, she opened a few cupboards and looked inside. They were probably the cleanest spots in the whole house. She turned and looked at the big window that overlooked the yard. It would be peaceful to sit there in the morning and wake up, she thought.

"It's pretty bad," Cooper said.

Nodding, she turned back to look at him. "There is a lot of cleaning required."

"Yeah. Think we can salvage the furniture that's here."

She looked at the table and chairs, they were wood, so she imagined they'd clean up nicely. The bed had no mattress, so that also would be okay. She nodded. "I think the carpet and curtains should go."

"I was thinking that too. A lot of the smell might go with them."

She hugged her waist. It was such a small thing, for someone to ask her opinion, but it made her feel useful and that was rare. At the same time, she felt like she was waiting for the catch. It was nothing against him, it was just what her circumstance had programmed her for.

"So, do you want to give me a hand cleaning up this place?" He leaned back in the dirty chair and looked at her.

She wondered if he wanted it so he could move in here. It made sense. Blair had told them he was going to stay over here and lend a hand, but he was probably used to fewer bodies and less commotion. "I could give you a hand."

He tapped his cane on the floor. "Great." His smile was genuine. "I'll get some of the boys to pull up the carpet, then we can see what we're dealing with underneath." He nodded as he looked around, "there's no rush," he looked at the door, "but with the painting and non-stop action in the house, this might be a nice quiet place to work too."

Emersyn nodded. She didn't blame him for wanting to seek somewhere quiet.

He stood up slowly, making her wonder how the rest of his health was. "I was thinking we'll put a couple of those motion sensors outside, so no one can sneak up on the house." He moved over to the door and flicked the lock a few times. "This is a good sturdy lock, should keep anyone out."

All she could do was nod in agreement. Maybe it wasn't just her that needed to feel safe. "I can go get some of the supplies from the house and start," she turned and looked at the kitchen and then to the hallway, "removing some of that smell." She smirked at him.

"It is awful isn't it." He grinned, "you go check on your girl and grab some cleaners, I'm going to open a window or two and try to blow that stink out." He turned and flicked the switch beside the door. The light came on and then a bulb popped, putting the room in darkness. "I'll go see if I have more lightbulbs too." He stepped back from the door.

Emersyn breathed a quick sigh of relief. She'd been trying to build up the courage to walk by him to the door. "I'll be back shortly." She gave him a quick polite smile.

"No rush at all, Emersyn, it's not like we're going anywhere."

She hurried toward the house, feeling an odd sense of serenity inside of her. They weren't going anywhere. This was home from now on. No more being moved from one house of confinement to another of the same.

Smiling, she opened the front door and went inside. Kicking off her shoes, she moved with purpose to the supply closet in the kitchen. Once she got some of the immediate grime out of there, she could bring a few toys and Aspyn could play while she cleaned. She'd never painted before but hoped that Cooper would get her some paint so she could fix up his house for him. He was a nice man and deserved that much.

She wiped the fog from the mirror and stood there clinging to the towel wrapped around her. Turning her head from side to side, she checked again for the mark from the collar. It wasn't there, yet she would always feel it around her throat. It had been there to control her, control her animal, and now that it was gone, she should feel free. Her memories were never going to let her be completely free.

Her face looked more filled out. She tilted her jaw up and looked at one side, then the other. Had she ever had this much weight on her body? Aside from carrying Aspyn, she had never seen her bones covered in enough tissue to hide them from sight. It made her feel healthy, to look at anyway. The internal damage was always going to remain.

Opening the towel, she looked down at her body. She had curves. Feeling good, she looked back to the mirror and then lifted her right arm and turned. The scar was there. Shaelan said it always would be. Dropping the towel, she touched it. The welt ran from under her arm down her ribs and stopped at the back of her hip.

She drew in a slow breath and tried not to remember, but how could she not when she wore the proof that it had happened. The scar would remind her how she got it every day for the rest of her life. She felt the pain like it was yesterday and not years ago. After they'd dragged her up those stairs, when Noah was trying to stop them—they'd taken her back down hours later and shoved her downstairs. At the bottom lay a bloodied, almost unrecognizable man. It had been Noah. He was to be her example of what happens if you don't listen. She could still see the man lifting his arm with the leather strap in hand, she'd broken free of their hold and rushed to cover his body with her own. She felt no life within him at that moment and thought they had killed him. The accidental strike on her body had angered the man in charge and for a short while she was treated fairly. The guilt smothered her each day after that. She'd gotten a decent man killed. For years she watched and hoped he'd be one of the men that were assigned to whichever house she was moved to, but she never saw him again and truly believed him to be dead. Noah had been beaten because of her and it wasn't until she saw him in that basement years later that she found out he was alive.

A tear rolled down her cheek. She wore one scar for him. It was nothing in comparison to those on his body. The marks that she couldn't look at without seeing blood smeared over them. Her cat moved inside her in a motion of comfort. She sucked in a breath and nodded to herself in the mirror. She was okay. She was free. Her daughter was free. Noah was alive. Those were enough to keep her steady and strong to carry her into the next phase of her life. She'd never thought she'd have a life, so she wasn't going to waste it.

Picking up the towel, she wrapped it around herself again and went over to the sink to brush her teeth. She'd been in here long enough; she didn't want to leave Penny with both girls too often. More guilt hit her. Before Aspyn was taken from her, she would never let her out of her sight. Now, she had to force herself to let her move around and have freedom. Eventually, she would run out of things that would distract her from sheltering her constantly again.

As she changed, she realized she felt useful tonight. Helping Cooper with his house had done her more good than she realized. She smiled at the woman in the mirror, the one with rosy cheeks instead of hollow shadows. She looked at her mouth and puckered her lips out. Noah had kissed her. She had never been kissed before. In fact, that's the only thing she'd been able to fight against with Lindon, keeping his mouth off hers. She wanted to kiss Noah again but had no idea how to go about making that happen. Grabbing the pajamas, she was going to sleep in, she jerked the pants on and kept glancing back in the mirror. The woman in that mirror was not the girl she remembered. Pulling the shirt over her head, she made a face at her, now all she had to do was figure out how to be a free woman. Instead of a scared girl.

Chapter Thirty-One

Noah slammed the truck into park and hopped out of it. He hadn't meant to be gone this long but had gotten lost in working. The familiar rhythm of the shop had been what he needed to settle down. He was halfway to the door when he saw the lights were on in the little house. He hadn't even realized the power was hooked up for it.

Going over, he opened the door and then blinked. The carpet was gone, and the place smelled of a lot of different cleaners. "Hello?" He waited. No one answered. Looking beside the door, he found the switch and turned it off. Had they run out of areas of the main house to clean? He didn't think that would ever be possible, not with all the kids.

He took one step inside and then stopped and looked down at his boots. He cringed, too many months in the bunkhouse. Bending down, he took them off and then looked for a space on the mats beside the door. So many shoes in many sizes were lined up on them. Seeing them all together reminded him how many were living here. Shifting a few pairs of small child-sized shoes, he set his on the matt and then looked down at them. It was an odd thing to see his boots sitting beside such small ones. It was something he'd never thought he'd experience again—living with children. These ones though, he was going to make sure they were allowed to be children and not timid shadows of children.

Shaking his head, he scowled at the floor and headed down the hall. What did he know about children? Nothing. He paused when he heard voices. Someone was in the kitchen. Going around the corner, he saw Emersyn and Julian sitting at the end of the long table, their heads close together, talking softly.

Emersyn sat up and looked at him. Her hair was wet and smoothed back from her face.

Julian turned in the chair and it was the only explanation he needed when he saw the pained expression on his face. Nightmares had woken him. Noah knew the symptoms that went along with that. Without a word, he went over to the fridge and opened it. The sandwiches Kelsey had brought him in the shop he'd burned off hours ago.

He felt her come up beside him and turned to look at her.

"I can make you something if you're hungry." She whispered. She gave him a steady look, and then glanced at Julian briefly.

Noah looked to see he was leaning over the table, his head in his hands. He turned back to her, and she nodded at him. She wanted him to go speak with the boy. He started to object and then ended up nodding. He knew about nightmares, but it's not like he could give him the secret to ending them. They never ended. Blowing out a breath, he released the fridge door and moved over to the chair she'd been sitting in.

When he sat down, Julian lifted his head and looked at him. Noah could see the pain reflected in his eyes. He lived with that pain every day, asleep and awake. "Some nights are bad." He said softly.

Julian nodded, "I thought now that we're here it would get better." He scrunched up his face, "but it's like when I know it's okay to relax it's worse."

Noah rubbed the back of his neck; the ever-present knots were bad tonight. "I won't lie to you, there is no secret to making them go away." He shrugged one shoulder, "you just have to remember that you got through it, and it will never happen again." He leaned on the table, closer to him, "I won't let it happen again."

"My whole family is gone." Julian's voice cracked with emotion, "and I'm not."

Noah inhaled through his nose slowly, trying to keep his cat calm. He didn't handle others' emotions well. He barely dealt with his own most times. "I know." He finally said. He tried to remember his age but wasn't entirely sure. "I was taken when I was six by the people that Lindon worked for." Would telling him make a difference? He didn't usually share. "I was there for fifteen years," Julian's eyebrows went up, "*every* moment I spent there haunts me, awake or asleep," he lifted one shoulder and let it drop, "when I can sleep."

"But you seem okay."

Noah snorted softly, "not really." He glanced over to see Emersyn look at him, understanding in her eyes, he looked back to the young body in front of him, "I just have to keep trying, one day at a time." He exhaled, "some days are bad," he glanced down at his dirty hands, "really bad, but," he looked up and held the look in Julian's young eyes, "everyone around me helps. It may not look like it, but I see the guys at the shop, each with their own story," that he still didn't know really, "and now there's everyone here," he watched Emersyn turn around and lean back against the counter and look at him, "we're all survivors and will continue to be."

Julian sat there, his expression changing for a few seconds as he processed it. Noah's chest felt tight to see the doubt and pain on his face. "Can I go with you tomorrow?" He blurted out, "when you go to work?"

Noah couldn't mask the surprise on his face, "uh, sure." He grimaced, "it's not very exciting right now, we're doing maintenance and painting," he held up his hand to show the yellow paint on it.

"That's okay, I just," Julian looked around, "I'm not used to being inside so much."

Noah nodded slowly, "we can find something for you to help with." He smirked, "Kelsey is a great teacher when it comes to operating the rigs."

"Kelsey? But she's a..."

He stopped when Noah raised an eyebrow at him, "don't ever say anything like that in front of her or Beth," he frowned, "or Kobie," he grinned, "just strike that whole belief right from your head," he lifted his arms to motion around them, "here everyone is equal." Noah watched the conflict on the young man's face, "got it."

Julian blew out a breath and then tapped the side of his head, "it's so hard to get his voice out of my head."

He didn't need to ask whose voice he meant. Lindon had left a wake of damage behind him. "Well, if you're ever unsure, just ask, okay?"

Julian nodded and then leaned back in the chair. "I'm going to try to sleep again." He pushed his chair back. "Thanks, Noah." when he stood up, he turned around to look at Emersyn and nodded to her.

She came over and set a plate on the table in front of him and then sat down.

Noah looked to see there were biscuits and cheese on the plate.

"It's better than one of those bars." She scrunched up her nose.

Noah grinned, "Yeah, not my favorite either."

"You helped," she looked in the direction Julian had gone, "when he came out, he was in tears and sweating." she gave him a soft look, "well, you know."

Noah nodded his head slowly. "Yeah, I guess we both do."

"I feel guilt more than anything most times." She confessed.

Noah opened one of the biscuits and busied himself by putting the cheese in it. Talking about this with her was going to bring out things he wasn't sure he could contain.

"Aspyn," she said in a breathless whisper, "I wouldn't have her." He glanced briefly to see the pain on her face, "I wake up soaked in sweat, screaming in my head because of," she clasped her hands on the table and squeezed them together, "everything, but then I look at her and think if I hadn't gone through that, she wouldn't exist, and *that*," she cleared her throat softly, "is worse."

When he heard her exhale a shaky breath, he looked at her completely. Not knowing what else to do, he reached over and put his hand over hers and held them. He had no words for her. How could he tell a mother anything that would make it better? He couldn't. There were no words he could say to express how it haunted him, what she'd been through that wouldn't have made it sound like he regretted her having her child. He clenched his teeth together and held her look.

"You know it's not your fault, what happened," her emotional look changed into something serious, "you are not responsible for them taking me or anything that happened after that."

Noah swallowed the lump in his throat and nodded. Those were words he'd never say out loud. He knew she was right, that part wasn't on him, but there were so many he hadn't helped. There was too much suffering that he could have stopped and didn't.

Shifting their hands, she put one of hers over his. "I should get to bed before Aspyn wakes and finds me missing." She stood up and then leaned down and placed her lips against his cheek. "You're a good man, Noah."

He watched her walk away. Lifting his hand, he touched where her lips had. He blinked and realized tears were filling his eyes. Wiping them away, he looked down at the plate but didn't really see it. He wasn't a good man. He chuffed out loud and shoved the plate away. He was a shell walking around in a body, that was it. His every moment was filled with more emotions than he could process, to the point it probably appeared he was void of all feeling. Standing up, he turned to leave and then looked down at the plate and sneered at it. If he didn't eat now, his cat would be too hard to contain. Grabbing the food off the plate in his hand, he spun around and headed for his room. Good man. It was ridiculous.

Chapter Thirty-Two

Emersyn watched Noah and Julian get in his truck. The teen looked so excited; it made her smile to see that emotion on his face. She wished for something to take the pain out of Noah's eyes but knew it wasn't going to be as simple as taking a ride to a shop.

"He'll help him through it."

She was startled and turned to see Cooper standing behind her.

"Sorry, I didn't mean to give you a fright." His expression was apologetic and concerned.

She blew out a quick breath, "it's not your fault. I just startle easy."

He nodded his head slowly for a second, then motioned to the small house, "I had the guys put the paint and supplies inside for you. We left the heat on too, so it wouldn't be so damp in there."

"Oh," she looked at the house, "you want me to paint it?" She bit her lip; she'd never done something like that.

"It's your vision with the colors, so I thought you would." He smirked, "the floor is going to be redone after the painting."

That was a relief, if she was bad at painting, the mess would be hidden. "Okay, I'll try."

"There's nothing to it, you watched Jake yesterday paint the hallway." He motioned his arm up and down, "pretty simple."

She smiled, "there won't be children running around."

Cooper grinned, much like he did the whole time Jake had tried to keep the kids from using the hall he was working in. "Your little one joining the schooling today?"

Nodding, she glanced back to the gate Noah had gone out. "Yes, um, Nichelle?" she glanced back to him for confirmation she had the right name, "is coming over to help get the youngest ones started." She didn't say that it bothered her that she wasn't able to help because she could barely read herself. A grade two education wasn't much help.

"Kelsey will be here this afternoon; she's going to help bring the adults back up to the right level." He smirked, "it should be colorful with her helping."

Emersyn had only met her for a few seconds the first time she had come over. "She seems nice."

"She can be, but don't let her looks fool you, she works in the shop right alongside the guys and makes them look bad on a daily basis."

That surprised her, that a woman was on the same level as the men.

Cooper watched her, "I have a feeling once you settle into living, you'll be one to reckon with as well."

Emersyn laughed softly, "I don't know about that." She glanced a last time at the gate and then started walking toward the small building. "Is Noah going away soon?"

Cooper walked alongside her, barely using the cane, she noted and hoped that meant his leg was feeling better today. "I'm not sure when, but he likely will be." He opened the door for her, "they don't want to give them too much time between to reorganize."

Emersyn went in and looked around, she loved seeing this place cleaned up. Sheets had been put over the furniture piled in the middle of the room. "I suppose it is good that they go out quickly then."

"Each time he comes back he seems a little calmer." Cooper went over and tapped his cane against the cans on the floor. "You need to start with the primer, get a good base coat so your colored paint looks even."

She frowned and went over and bent down to look at the cans. She focused on the words on them and sounded the one out inside her head. Touching the top of one she turned to look at him, He nodded that she'd picked the right one.

"Grab that tray and rollers and bring them over to the counter, I'll show you how to get it done without a mess."

Emersyn picked up the things he pointed out. "What do you mean he seems calmer?"

He came over and set his cane on the counter and picked up the black tray. "Noah feels like he needs to atone for his sins and until that ghost is done haunting him, he's going to be on the move a lot." He gave her a steady look, "it could take years until he runs it out of his system."

"Sins?" She watched him put the fuzzy roller on the handle, so she would know how to do it herself.

"He blames himself for—everything that happened when he was taken and after." He glanced at her, then picked up a screwdriver and hammer, "we put holes in the can, so the paint doesn't run over the lip of the can when you pour it."

She watched him open it and puncture the edge of the can. "He's not to blame, for any of it." How could he think that? She knew he felt guilt, but it was completely misplaced. She'd been taken and she sure as hell knew it wasn't her fault or anything that had happened. She watched him stir the paint with a flat piece of wood. Some things may have been her own doing when her mouth spoke words she should have kept in her head, but the actual reason she was there, was not her fault.

Cooper pulled the black tray over, then looked at her for a second before he started to pour the paint into it. "That's not how he sees it." He watched what he was doing, "he blames himself for you being there. Blair told me he tried to get you out."

Emersyn watched as he took a brush out of a package. "I know. I was there that night," she said softly, "the night they put all those scars on him."

Cooper paused and turned to look at her. "They did that in front of you?"

She shook her head, "no, just brought me down after to see him." She didn't mention her scar.

"Sick bastards." He muttered and picked up the tray, "grab the brush and roller." He started down the hall.

She picked them up and followed him. "He was unconscious at that point," she frowned, "or I guess he was." When he set the tray on the floor, she looked around, not sure where to start. "I thought he was dead."

Cooper nodded his head slowly, "something inside him died that night, you can be sure of that."

She sucked in a shaky breath and motioned to the tray, "where do I start?"

Cooper held out his hand, "good place would be to cut in the corners." He pulled the brush from her hand, "you do the areas the roller won't reach without rubbing the other wall."

She watched him do the one corner and then looked around. "I'm going to need something to stand on."

"I'll get a step stool brought over." He turned around and held the brush out to her. "Having a project is very calming, helps you think things through while you work."

She looked at the brush and went over to the tray and dipped it in. "Is that why Noah never stops moving?" She looked at him as she moved to the corner he'd been in, "he came back late last night and was gone right after breakfast today."

He nodded when she looked back at him for approval of what she'd done, "he thinks too much if he's standing still."

Frowning, she went back over to the tray and picked it up, and moved it closer to the corner. "I understand that." She dipped the brush in the tray and then turned to the wall, "it's the dark that gets me."

"I figured you would understand more than most."

His voice was quiet, and she could tell he was staying by the door and not coming up behind her. She appreciated his efforts to make her more comfortable. It was a habit she'd developed for her own survival, to always be aware of where others were.

"I think you're what he needs to start healing," he made a soft sound, "as much as he'll ever be able to."

She paused and looked over at him, "me?"

Cooper took off his hat and gave his head a brisk rub, before putting it back on and giving her a steady look. "You are his mate," the expression in his eyes softened, "there's already a connection no one else will ever have with him."

Emersyn turned back to the wall, not wanting him to see what she knew would be in her eyes, fear. The fear of being touched was real and was something she could probably never get over completely. She thought of when he'd kissed her, that had been nice. She wanted to kiss him again but didn't think she'd ever be comfortable with a touch beyond that. "I don't know if I can help him." She meant it and it caused her sadness she couldn't describe.

"I think over time it will come together for both of you." His movement on the floor echoed in the empty room. "Take your time, I'm going to get some more coffee, then I think I'll tinker with the intercom out here."

She glanced to see he was leaving the room, "the intercom?"

He paused, "that little box by the door, it's so you can talk to the main house."

She smirked, "Is that what it is?"

Cooper nodded, "I'm going to see if I can get it working." He glanced around the room, "I figure by lunch you'll be making this place look like a million bucks."

She watched him walk out. "A million bucks?" That was an odd saying. Cooper had a lot of those, but he was a nice man, so she knew none of them was a bad reference.

Turning back to the wall, she looked to see what she had done, then to the roller on the floor. She should have asked him how she used that exactly. She'd watched Jake use it but hadn't paid that close attention because she never imagined she'd be asked to do something like this. She bit her lip, maybe standing too much bothered his leg. It made sense that he'd ask her and not any of the men. They had enough to do.

She looked out the window to see the snow falling in slow motion. It was pretty to watch. Peacefully falling from the sky. She knew it wasn't always that way, from staring out windows for much of her life. When the winds picked up they would whip it around and make it nearly impossible to see. Bending down, she wet the brush again with more paint. Part of her wished the storm days in her life were over, but she couldn't afford unrealistic expectations. She might want it, but there were never going to be 'pretty' days for her.

Chapter Thirty-Three

She worked through most of the day, taking a short break for lunch and spending time with Aspyn. Her daughter was running around singing ABCs, or three or four random letters from the alphabet. It did her good to know her child was going to learn and be filled with knowledge.

Kelsey had brought Julian back over for the older kids' lessons, but Noah hadn't returned. The more she thought about him, and the things Cooper had said, the further she pushed herself to get this done. As she saw the grimy stained walls gradually become white, and smooth, the better she felt. Her mind would never shut off to the point she didn't think about it but keeping physically busy was helping.

Now, at the end of the day, she had two walls left to do in the main area of the little house. It was so bright in here. She was excited to see what it was going to look like when the colors she'd chosen were on them. It was odd that Cooper had just nodded to her selections. It was as if he had no real opinion of the way he wanted it to look in here. She bit her lip and turned to look at the cans, hoping his trust in her judgment wasn't going to lead to disappointment. Emersyn had never gotten to choose anything in her life, so it was going to be interesting to see the result.

He'd worked on the intercom and only disturbed her progress once to look at flooring and carpets. Again, he'd accepted the ones she had pointed to and said those would work. She hoped they did.

Setting the brush down, she went over and got the newly opened can of primer. Her arms were aching, her back was stiff, and she'd never felt this good in her life. She'd done this, on her own, and was even more surprised at her own pace. No one had told her to do it or watched over her.

"Emersyn."

She spun around and looked at the box beside the door.

"Aspyn is all tucked in and asleep." It was Penny.

She went over to the box and pushed the button like Cooper had shown her, "thank you, I shouldn't be much longer." She released the button and started at it.

"No rush, I'm going to bed now too, so the girls won't be in the room alone."

She felt a small twinge of guilt. "Thank you, Penny." She backed away from it and watched it in case she spoke again. Was it bad she wasn't in there with her? After all the time she'd needed to hold her again, here she was working and not spending time with her. Aspyn's excited face flashed in her mind, she seemed happy enough and had only been clingy when she was tired this afternoon.

Turning around she looked at the unfinished walls. It would be silly to stop here. Another hour and she will have finished the base coat, as Cooper called it. Pouring the paint into the tray, she balanced it carefully and placed it on top of the step ladder. She wasn't nervous going up it now, she'd done it at least a hundred times today. She smirked as her legs confirmed that count when she went up it one more time.

She was pleased with herself as she ran the brush along the top of the wall. Her control of where the paint went was much better. The first few rooms hadn't been so. Cooper had shrugged it off and said he'd get the guys to do the ceiling with ceiling paint and no one would be any wiser to her brush slips. Ceiling paint, primer, bathroom paint. She'd never imagined so many kinds before. Cooper complimented her work and told her she had a knack for this sort of thing. It may have been a small thing on the large scale of everything, but to her it meant a lot, to be good at something.

As she moved to the length of her reach, she hummed softly. She didn't know any songs, so she just made it up as she went. She was free, she could, sing, hum, or even dance if she wanted to. If she knew how she may have done that too.

"Emersyn?"

She jumped and then grabbed the top of the ladder when it wobbled. With her heartbeat in her throat, she glanced behind her to see Noah standing in the doorway, filling close to every inch of it and his expression wasn't a good one. Blowing out a breath, she looked down to see she'd put her hand in the paint tray. Setting the brush down on the edge of it, she lifted her hand and watched the paint drip from it.

"Shit. Sorry." His tone was softer now. She heard his boots echo on the floor and turned to go down the ladder. He held up a rag to her. "I was just surprised to see you in here."

She took the rag and he backed away from her in a not-so-subtle way. Wiping at the paint on her hand, she leaned back against the ladder and looked at him. "I'm helping Cooper fix this up." She stepped down carefully, not wanting to touch anything with her white hand. "It's a lot of standing and up and down," she glanced to see his expression was completely closed off now, "I don't think he could do it with his leg."

He made no motion to let her know that he agreed or understood anything. Finally, after several seconds of silence, he looked around, "you've done the whole place today?"

Happy enough that she'd managed to get most of the paint off, she nodded, "yes. I didn't think I would be able to, but once I got going on it," she looked around and smiled, "I surprised myself."

"It's going to be a surprise when you look in the mirror." He said in a light tone, but without a smile or even a smirk.

She cringed, "how bad?" Checking her other hand to make sure it wasn't covered, she reached up and touch her hair.

She'd gotten paint in her hair. "Oh. I guess a shower is in order." She motioned to the wall she'd been working on. "I just have to finish these and then I'm done for the night." Going over to the counter, she picked up her bottle of water, briefly wondering if the taste of paint would wash away eventually too.

"I can finish it for you."

She looked over to see he was scowling and couldn't figure out why he would be. Didn't he want Cooper to have a quiet place of his own? "I started it," she shrugged a shoulder and tried not to wince at the sore muscle, "I can finish it." Even from here, she could see the muscle in his jaw pulsing as he continued to look at her. "How was your day?"

He blinked and then looked at her like he hadn't even seen her even though his eyes had been locked on her. "Good." He cleared his throat, "got a lot done."

She made a point to let him see she was looking at the state of his clothes. "I can see that." She smirked, "were you painting too?"

Noah looked down and then wiped at the yellow streaks on his jeans. "Yeah," he moved his hand back and forth, "with a sprayer." He smirked so quickly and then sobered again just as fast, "it's challenging."

Capping the water, she placed it back on the counter. "I'm barely able to use a brush and roller, I don't think using a sprayer would end well for me."

A hard expression was in his eyes now, "you should be resting, not," he motioned to the wall, "doing all this."

That surprised her. "Resting from what?" She stepped around the small island counter and went to the paint can. If they were going to be chatting, she should at least put the lid on it.

"Just resting," he frowned, "building up your strength," he said it slowly like he wasn't sure of the words until he said them.

Squatting down, she put the lid on the can and then dropped the cloth over it to tap it back on, having learned without it paint splattered everywhere—like on her face. "I feel fine." She smirked, "well my arms might feel different tomorrow, but I feel good." She tapped the top of the lid like Cooper had shown her and then set the rubber hammer on top of it and stood up. "I've spent years doing nothing, Noah," she looked at the finished wall, "I want to help."

He looked like a giant statue standing there, his arms folded over his chest, his face hardened by whatever it was he was thinking. "I just think," she watched his chest rise and fall, "there's no rush to get this house finished." The words came out in a hurried way.

That surprised her, that he would say that. "You don't want Cooper to have his own place? Somewhere quiet he can escape all the kids and commotion in the house?" She hoped she had enough paint in the tray to finish. Not waiting for his reply, she went over and carefully moved the ladder over so she could finish the top. Then all she had to do was fill it in with the roller.

"Cooper?" he snorted, "you think Coop wants this for himself?"

She looked over her shoulder at him and then adjusted the tray on the top, so she wouldn't wear it when she went back up. "He asked me to help him with it."

Noah grinned, and it wasn't necessarily a happy one, "did he actually say he was moving in here? Did he say it was for him?"

Emersyn paused her foot on the first step and looked at him. "I don't remember his every word, but he asked for my opinions and help."

"Uh-huh," he shook his head, "did he pick the colors," he waved a hand around, "or anything?"

Stepping on the ladder, she stood there. The emotions pouring off him were all over the place. Her cat was awake and telling her he needed her, and she wanted to be there for him but didn't know if she could do that. "We picked things out together?"

Noah snorted loudly, "did he at any point say I want that?"

Frowning, she forced her legs to move, to go over to him, she made it to a few feet from him and couldn't take that last step. "I-I don't know." She didn't remember the words exchanged when they'd been going over paint colors or any of it, but Cooper had been happy with the result and that was all that mattered.

"I can't believe he did this." He muttered.

"Did what?" She could feel his pain now and even her cat was wary, not knowing what had happened.

Noah looked up from the floor, "this," he swung his arm out away from his body.

It felt like it was in slow motion, a gut reflex that she'd depended on to survive this long. She put her arms beside her head and cringed from him. As soon as she'd done it, she knew she shouldn't have.

Noah stood there with terror in his eyes, his skin blanched so whitely he looked like a ghost.

She dropped her arms and straightened slowly. "Um," she shook her head, trying to force her breathing to return to normal.

Noah dropped down onto both knees and looked at her with unshed tears in his eyes. "I would *never* hurt you." He said it with such pain that her chest tightened with emotion.

She hadn't been raised in a clan, but she knew he was offering her the most subservient gesture he could. She raised a shaking hand to her throat, needing the physical reminder that there was no collar there. "I-I don't know why I did that." She shook her head, "I startle too easily and you," she motioned to him, "you swung your arm out…"

"I shouldn't have," he whispered it, "I know better."

"It-it's late," she nodded and took a small step, no more than an inch toward him, "we're both tired."

Noah dropped back on his heels and looked at her, his shoulders were slumped, hands lose in his lap. "That's no excuse." He closed his eyes and when he opened them, she saw the raw pain inside them, "I told them I wasn't the right one to be here," she watched a tear fall from his eyes and roll slowly down his cheek, and at that moment her heart felt like it broke apart, "I shouldn't..."

She rushed to him, knowing full well that the sudden movement could have her swatted across the room and didn't care. Wrapping her arms around his head, she hugged it against her chest, much like she would if Aspyn was upset. "Shh," he leaned down and placed her cheek against the top of his head, "you are the *only* one that could help any of us, Noah." She kissed the top of his head and didn't care if tears were running down her face.

"I'm not." He said in a rough voice. She felt him suck in a breath and then he touched her hips hesitantly. She was sure he was going to push her away but then he wrapped his arms around her and squeezed her, holding her close to him.

Emersyn's breath caught in her throat, she expected the panic to hit her but instead of the tension and muscles freezing she felt something that she could only label as serenity. A small peace she'd only ever felt when she held her child, only this was different in many ways.

She loosened her grip on his head and looked down at him. When he lifted his chin, she brushed the hair back from his face. She wanted to offer him words that would ease his pain, say something that would make it be better, but there were no words in existence that could offer that, not after what they'd been through. Her hands shook as she held his head between them and leaned down and placed a kiss over one of his tear-filled eyes. The shaking was less when she repeated it with his other eye.

Noah's grip loosened on her and then his hands clenched on her hips. His breathing was uneven when he opened his eyes and looked up at her. He searched her face, and she didn't know what he was looking for. She could see fear in his eyes, and the pain, that was always there, but there was something else, something she didn't recognize—

He rose until their faces were level and then he put his hand lightly on the back of her head.

She held her breath waiting for the panic to come. Her cat was right there, watchful and waiting with her. When his lips touched hers, she gripped his shoulders and closed her eyes. His lips were soft, and she could feel he was shaking as much as she was. She sucked in a breath when he lifted his mouth away. Opening her eyes, she looked to see him watching her, a careful assessment of what his actions had done. She didn't want him to know that she was unsure, that she didn't know what she was feeling. Putting her hand against his soft beard, she leaned back down and pressed her mouth against his. She didn't know how to do this, but even her cat was okay with it. The gentle touch of their lips changed, it wasn't slow or hesitant, but felt natural, like it was supposed to happen that way.

Noah released her head and placed his hand in the middle of her back, his other hand moved from her hip to rest on her waist. His touch sent heat through her, but the rise in temperature she usually felt was a warning. He tilted his head to the side, increasing the pressure of his kiss and it made her heart accelerate and a shiver moved through her. She felt lightheaded and almost dizzy but didn't want to stop.

Without notice, he jerked his head back and looked at her. She swayed from the sudden movement and gripped his shoulders tight so she wouldn't collapse on the floor. Her knees felt weak. He didn't speak, he didn't make a move to kiss her again, he just knelt there, a soft look in his eyes. It was the most intimate thing she'd ever experienced. His grip on her shifted until he was running his hands lightly up and down the side of her ribs, she could see the indecision in his eyes. Did he want to kiss her again? She couldn't be sure, but as this was the only time in her life, she'd felt a gentle, welcome touch and closeness, she was willing to stand her just like this all night if he wanted to.

His brows creased, a confused look appearing in his eyes. She swallowed, trying to figure out what had just happened. Noah leaned back away from her and then in slow motion, he lifted the side of her shirt up. Her scar. She sucked in a breath and tried to jerk the material out of his hand. His gaze flicked to hers, something soft and asking was in his eyes. She released his hand and let him lift the shirt up a little higher.

She watched his face when his hand stopped moving. He winced, pain on his face, then it changed to anger. When he looked up at her, she could see the hurt in his eyes. He touched the scar with a shaking hand. Without looking away from it, he spoke, barely loud enough for her to hear him.

"Who did it?" His breath was erratic as if he was barely holding onto his composure.

Emersyn grasped his hand in hers and pulled it from the scar. She held it and looked down at him. "The one that put the scars on you." She said softly, knowing she didn't have to describe the man to her. They would both see him when they closed their eyes, she knew this. "That night," she swallowed, trying to force the words from her throat, "when-when," she made herself hold his look as she said it, "that night," his eyes narrowed, "after," she huffed out a breath and tried to think of how to say it, "they brought me down to you," his eyes widened, "you were on the floor, not moving, covered in—" she couldn't say it, "they used you as an example so I," she sucked in another breath and breathed it out fast when his eyes filled with tears, "I threw myself over you when they were going to—going to..."

Noah dropped his head down and pressed it against her chest. "I'm so sorry." His voice was shaking, "I didn't know."

She shook her head and hugged him again, "I thought you were dead." Her voice gave out on the last word, it was barely audible.

"It's my fault." He leaned back from her, jerking his head out of her hold. "I didn't—," he shook his head, scowling, "my cat, when we saw you come in," he winced, then squeezed his eyes shut, "I didn't know why but I had to protect you—" he looked up at her, the hard, unreachable look was back in his eyes, "I didn't know."

Emersyn huffed, "neither of us could know." She shook her head, "I didn't know about mates or any of—" she touched his face, her hand vibrating, "it's not your fault."

He pulled back from her and stood up so quickly, she teetered.

She knew where his actions were coming from, she'd lived it too, but that moment a few seconds before had meant something, and she wasn't going to let him brush it away like it hadn't happened. She stepped over to him, right in front of him, with hardly enough space between them for air. Looking up at him, she placed her hand on his chest and forced him to hold her glare. "It's not your fault, it's not my fault." She used a hard tone, keeping his interest in what she was saying. "I know," she nodded, "I know you will find him," she corrected herself, "them," he was looking down at her, a watchful expression on his face, "and you will stop them from *ever* hurting anyone again." She held her breath, masking the shock from her own words. It hadn't been where she was going with it, but on some level, her cat and his had connected a few moments ago and she'd spoken what both needed to hear to get through this moment.

He was motionless for so long that she wasn't sure what he could be thinking. Finally, he let out a long-held breath and placed his hand over hers. "I will. I swear I won't stop until I do."

A tear rolled down her cheek. In all the years of captivity, she had never dared to imagine such a thing, but now, that was what she needed. Not for herself, not even for him, but to stop them from repeating it over and over again and ruining the lives of others.

He squeezed her hand like he was going to let her go.

"Noah." She said it quickly. He looked back down at her, his movement stopping, "don't take this away from me," she looked at the wall beside them, "it makes me feel useful." She whispered.

Some of the tension drained from his face, just enough that she knew he was seeing her and wasn't blinded by the fury inside him. "Emersyn," he touched her cheek with his other hand, "I would fight gods to give you the stars if that's what you needed." He winced. "That was a corny line, I don't know where it came from."

Emersyn smiled up at him, feeling like some sort of bridge had just been constructed between them. "I think it was lovely." She swiped at the tear on her cheek.

"You," he said softly, "are lovely," his gaze moved over her, "paint and all." He smirked so briefly that she almost missed it.

She leaned forward and rested her forehead against his chest. When he rested his hands on her hips, she decided that to them, this was the equivalent of hugging. They both knew what the other could or couldn't handle. "Do you think we'll ever be normal, Noah?"

She felt him rest his cheek against her head, "I don't know." She could feel his breath on her head as he spoke.

"Noah are you out there?"

They jumped apart and Noah braced for a fight.

"It's an intercom." Emersyn pointed to the box by the door.

He relaxed and went over to it and pushed the button. "I'm here." He scowled at the speaker like he wanted to smash it.

"Uh, we need you in here, or-or the backyard."

Emersyn glanced at the tray of paint and decided whatever was happening, it would have to wait for the panic in Julian's voice had her cat on full alert.

"What's going on?" Noah now watched the speaker intently.

"It's Everett, his cat wants out, like now, *right* now."

Noah swore softly, then pushed the button, "get him outside." He squeezed his eyes shut, "get uh, Harrison and McKenna up."

"Yeah."

He turned and looked at me. "How old is Everett?" He bent down and undid a boot.

Emersyn opened her mouth and then stuttered, "uh, twelve, I think." She kicked off her shoe and when he paused to look at her foot she shook her head, "I'm coming." She left no room for any other comments.

He opened the door and then paused to take off his boots and jacket. "Okay, hopefully, five of us will be enough to keep him from running too far."

Emersyn's heart was beating rapidly as she tossed her other shoe to the floor and followed him. She was a tiger shifter. This was her clan, and she would do anything to ensure they were all safe. She jogged behind him, watching as he tossed his shirt to the ground, and so would the man in front of her, even if he thought he wouldn't.

Chapter Thirty-Four

Noah walked out into the kitchen to see half the clan was already there. He paused, debating ongoing right outside. Changing his mind, he forced his feet to continue. The late-night vigorous run had allowed him to get some actual sleep but had charged the others if the chatting and smiles were any indications.

He went over to the counter and opened the cupboard to look for a cup when Emersyn came over and poured coffee into the one beside the pot. She put a teaspoon of sugar in it and then held it out to him.

As he lifted the cup to his mouth, he caught the 'see' look Cooper was giving him and scowled back. It was a cup of coffee for crying out loud it didn't mean they were a perfect couple and ready to mate.

Everett shook the long hair back from his face and grinned at Noah. "Sorry about last night." He didn't look sorry at all.

Noah shrugged, "it was a good run." He leaned on the long island, not feeling like he could go sit at the table with the others. The distance was better for him. "Once you get used to it, you're going to give everyone a good race."

"Even Calum?" He looked to Cooper, then back to him, "I heard he's fast."

Noah smirked over at Cooper, "if you can beat Jesse or Evanna, then you'll be the fastest."

"Are they jaguars too?" Julian stopped eating and looked at him.

"Leopards." Noah took a sip of his coffee.

"I think the one to beat is Thera," Cooper said quietly.

"Whose she?" Everett glanced between them.

Noah straightened up and grinned, "she's a real leopard."

"Like real, real?" Everett's eyes were huge.

Noah nodded. He watched Emersyn go over and lean down and kiss the top of Aspyn's head and then set a cup of juice on the table for her.

"That's the darndest thing I've heard yet." Harrison said softly, "I can't wait to see her."

"You should get Kobie to work with the boys," Cooper looked over at McKenna, "and girls, bring them up to speed on tracking and hunting."

Noah dragged his gaze from Emersyn and then nodded, "it's a good idea. I can ask her when I go over there today." He shrugged, "unless she comes here first."

Cooper leaned back in his chair, "can you give Emersyn a hand before you go?"

He paused his cup halfway to his mouth.

"Show her how to tape off the trim and windows before she paints." Cooper made a face, "my leg is aching something fierce today."

Noah set the cup down on the counter and looked at him, he knew exactly what he was trying to do. Aching, his butt. He'd watched him hop in and out of rigs when he was supposed to still be in a wheelchair. "I can."

Cooper nodded, then smiled at Emersyn, "he can't hurt anything with a roll of tape."

Noah gave him a blank look and hoped the older man got the hint of what he was really thinking. When he put his hand over his mouth, he knew there was a smirk behind it because Cooper's eyes were crinkled at the edge and sparkling with humor.

"You can show me after you have some breakfast," Emersyn said and turned back from the counter and set a plate in front of him.

Noah looked down to see eggs, toast, potatoes, and bacon on his plate. He hadn't even registered the smell of any cooking. His stomach rolled, reminding him that the light snack after the run last night was long gone. Nodding, he leaned over and opened the drawer, and grabbed a fork. He looked at the long table, there were few seats with empty chairs. Looking back down at the food, he picked up a piece of the bacon and popped it into his mouth. It was hard enough to stand in a room with so many bodies, sitting among them was something he wasn't sure he would ever do. As he dipped his toast into his egg, he looked up to see Emersyn standing at the other end of the counter eating hers. No one was behind her either, she had her back to a wall so it would stay that way. The similarity had him glaring down at the plate, but he wasn't ready to admit it.

"When the thing gets hooked up today, will you show us how to play those games?"

Noah looked over to see Liam was looking at him. "The internet is being done today?" He nodded. He set his fork down and picked up the cup, "I'm not exactly the best gamer, guys," he glanced at Cooper briefly, "but if Jake or Blair isn't around, I can show you how to play," he toasted his cup in the air, "badly." The boys grinned; they didn't care how he played.

"I can show them."

Noah jumped and turned to see Gage and Kelsey standing in the entrance hallway. Noah shook his head, "crushing the controller because you lost isn't really the way they need to learn how to play."

Gage waved him off, "it wasn't on purpose."

Kelsey smiled up at him, then patted him on the chest. "You shouldn't play competitive games and you know it."

Gage frowned down at her, then smirked and leaned down and hugged her briefly. When he straightened, he jerked his hand behind him. "Shouldn't you at least keep the door locked if you're not going to keep the gate closed?"

"We don't need to lock the door." Harrison stood up and motioned to the chair he got out of in case one of them wanted to sit down, "we have Noah, he'll keep us safe."

Noah couldn't mask the surprise on his face, so he turned his back to all of them and went over to the coffee pot.

"No one knows their clan was even in existence," Cooper said quietly, "so chances of them being…"

Noah turned around, "Gage is right. We're relaxing too much." He gripped the mug tight in his hand, the heat of the cup gave him something to focus on so he wouldn't panic and do something stupid like telling these people he was the last thing he needed. He looked at Cooper, "see if you can fix the wiring on it today and we'll get Blair over here to wire a new box."

Cooper nodded and stood up slowly. "Probably best," he reached over and ruffled Everett's hair, "with the poor direction this one has, he's liable to run right out the gate next time."

"You had your first shift?" Kelsey moved away from Gage and went over to sit in the chair that Cooper had been in, "what was it like?"

"Scary at first," Everett shook the hair back from his eyes, "then Noah talked me through it, and it was," he looked over at Noah, "a little crazy for a while."

Gage came over and opened a cupboard for a cup, "crazy how?"

Julian started laughing, "his front and back weren't communicating very well."

Gage glanced at Noah, "sounds like he has a lot in common with Gary—I think he backed up for half a mile his first shift."

Noah almost choked on his coffee. "Really?" He coughed.

Gage nodded, "there's a reason we don't get him to drive the rigs that twist or have too many levers." He winked over at Everett, "I'm sure you'll be able to outrun us in no time."

"How old are you?" Kelsey leaned on the table.

"Twelve," Everett said with pride, even though his face was red with embarrassment from all the attention.

Kelsey spun in the chair and looked at her mate, "how is that even fair?" She scowled at him, "boys shift *that* early, and we," she waved at Emersyn and then McKenna, "have to wait until we're in our twenties."

Gage toasted her with his cup, "because we need years of practice to keep up with you ladies."

Even Noah smirked at that one. He was smooth, not Blair-style smooth, but he knew how to smooth the ruffles. He lowered his head to look at his plate. He had no idea what to do with ruffles, hell he couldn't even handle a slight wrinkle. Taking a big bite, he forced himself to chew it, even though his appetite was gone.

"I'm going to go through the house with the ladies and see if there's anything else that's needed." Kelsey said then leaned down and smiled at Aspyn, "or the kids require more."

Aspyn put her cup down, "I want a real tiger." She said in a serious tone.

Kelsey grinned and then glanced at her mother, "I don't know if I can get one of those today, but I will keep an eye out."

Aspyn nodded and then picked up her toast. "Okay."

Noah shoved the plate away and picked up his cup, "any word from Devin?" He looked at Gage. He needed to know he was going to be going back out soon.

Gage nodded, "I don't have details, but Calum and Shaelan will be back tonight, I'm sure he knows more."

Noah nodded his head. That was good. Something was happening. He glanced at Emersyn, "I'll show you how to do that now." He turned from the counter and headed to the door with fast steps. Jamming his feet into his boots, he was out the door and sucking in the cool air like he'd been starving for it.

He heard the door close again and just stood there holding his coffee in a shaking hand.

Gage stepped around him, giving him plenty of space. "I'd ask how you're doing, but the expression on your face says a lot."

Noah blew out a breath, then gave him a quick side glance, "I'm trying."

"You're doing pretty damn good." Gage lifted the cup and blew on the liquid inside it. "I've never seen you stand in a room with people for longer than three minutes before." He glanced at the house, "never mind stay long enough to eat."

Noah looked down at the laces hanging out of his boots and decided he didn't care. He started walking toward the little house. "I'm trying," he looked to see Gage was following, "but honestly, I'm getting edgy and need to go back out with the team." He opened the door and then froze when he stepped in. The night before came back all at once. Holding Emersyn, kissing her—the scar on her side.

"This place is coming along fast."

He went over to the ladder and set his cup down and bent down to do up his boots. "Emersyn's been doing it."

"She must be doing it fast; I was standing in it three days ago and it was a god-awful mess."

Noah kept his head down and switched boots. "Cooper dragged her into it."

"Into what?"

He stood up and looked to see Gage going over to look out the window. "She thinks she's doing it for *him* to live in." Noah scoffed, "she thinks she's doing it because it's too hard with his leg," Gage grinned wide, "right. He could probably run ten miles and outdo us all, leg or not."

"If she likes doing it, what's the problem?" He touched the wall to see if it was dry before he leaned his shoulder against it and took a drink.

Noah blew out a deep breath and dropped his hands to his hips, "Cooper thinks this would be a great little place for a new couple to live."

Gage started to nod his head and then stopped, "you?"

Noah nodded, "I tried to explain—" he waved his hand around, "everything to him but it's like he's deaf when I'm speaking."

Gage chuckled, "not deaf, just sees different things than you do."

Noah picked up his cup and walked to the hall to look at the other rooms, "pretty sure when he looks at me, there's no mistaking that I'm messed up." He could tell she'd started in the small room, there was more paint on the floor and the ceiling line.

Gage was still where he had left him after he looked in the other two rooms. "She's been through a lot…"

Noah glared at him, "I *know* what she's been through." He snapped back at him.

Gage lifted one brow at him. Noah recognized it as a warning and clamped down on his emotions. "As I was saying, she's been through a lot, and you understand things no one else is going to." He paused and held his look, "that's probably what he's seeing that you can't."

Noah looked down at the dark liquid in his cup to give himself a moment to filter through his words before he said them. Gage wasn't his Alpha, but he was Alpha family and he and Calum both refused to put up with any sort of disrespect. "I can't be…"

"You don't know that, Noah," Gage's tone was softer now, "not for sure."

"And I'm supposed to, what? Bumble it and do more damage to both of us when I fail?" He huffed out a breath and shook his head, "there's—it's," he closed his eyes for a second and then opened them and gave him a level look, "she was there that night," he motioned up and down his chest, "when I got these."

Gage looked at him for a moment, his expression was unclear, then he nodded his head slowly and Noah thought, finally, someone gets it. "Seems she may be the only one that understands what you've been through too." Gage moved away from the wall and went over to the ladder and took the tray down and looked in it. "We've all tried to help you and we just don't have the knowledge to do much."

Noah frowned, "I don't expect you to."

"I know." He pulled the stuck brush from the tray, "but we want to." Setting the brush back in the tray, he held his look with steady patience. "Or is it you don't want to be helped?" He set the tray on the floor and then picked up his cup, "are you afraid you might let some of it go, Noah? Afraid that you don't know who you'll be without carrying all of that with you."

Noah scowled at him, "what do you mean?" He thought of his words again, and then his eyes widened, "you think I want to be this way?" Is that what he was saying? "You think I don't want to feel normal? Not freak out all the time?" Noah shook his head, "I'd just like to experience a full night's sleep, just once…"

"That's not what I meant." Gage rubbed his hand over his face, "I understand being afraid of things changing, Noah…"

"Changing? This would have to be a complete overhaul, Gage," he tapped the side of his head, "it's so fucked in here—" he blew out a breath and then shook his head, he couldn't get worked up right now, he just couldn't, Emersyn would be walking in the door at any second. "I don't know." He whispered, "I don't know what I want right now." He gave him a steady look, "I just know I need to go back out with the team and help."

Gage looked at him for a long silent moment and then nodded his head, "I can't disagree with that. Devin said without you they wouldn't have found half the places."

Noah shrugged it off and went over to the stack of paint cans and bent down to look at the color samples on the lids. They weren't bad choices. "I just wished I could do more." He glanced over at him, "there's so many missing." He stood up, not wanting to get into it right now. He was trying to keep his mood light, or as light, as it ever got, so he could show Emersyn how to tape off the windows and things and then go over and help Blair. "Listen," he looked down at the cane then back to Gage, "when Blair and I are gone, could you…"

"You know we'll help over here as much as we do Blair's."

Noah nodded, "I figured." He wiped his hand over his damp forehead. "Thanks."

The door opened and Emersyn stepped inside. She unzipped her jacket. "Sorry it took me so long," she pulled it off, "Aspyn was determined she needed a real tiger until Kelsey told her how much they ate." She grinned, "now she's decided that's gross and her stuffed one is fine." She looked from one to the other and then took her jacket off.

Gage bent down and picked up the tray, "I'll go clean this for you."

She cringed when she looked at it, "Everett's shift distracted me from cleaning up."

He shrugged, "It's fine." With a smile, he took the tray and his coffee and went out the door.

She hugged her jacket to her and looked over at him, "I'm sorry if I interrupted…"

Noah shook his head, "we were just talking about him helping Cooper over here when Blair and I go back out."

"Do you know when you are?" He watched her squeeze her eyes shut and then open them again quickly, "sorry." She huffed out a breath like she was annoyed with herself. "How long are you usually gone?" She clutched the jacket to her like it was her lifeline.

"Two or three days," he shrugged, "we get there, go in and then keep moving so they can't track us or follow us." He regretted the words as soon as they were out of his mouth.

She stiffened, her eyes filling with fear, "they do that?"

He nodded, not quite sure how to back out of the hole he'd just dug.

"It makes sense now, what was said in the house about the gate."

Noah went over to the counter and picked up the tape. "Cooper will get it fixed. You'll be safe." He was saying every curse word he knew inside his head. Turning around, he tried to look calmer than he felt, "No one knew where Lindon had the clan, so they're all safe," He moved closer, trying to sense the emotions that went with the thoughts flashing through her eyes. "No one followed us from that house, or the one we stopped at. Calum would have known. You're safe—Aspyn is safe."

She moved her head slightly and he thought maybe it was a nod. "I know. I just *feel* safer when you're around," she looked down at her hands gripping the jacket tightly, "and when you go with Blair and Calum—"

She sucked in a shaky breath that he felt it all the way to his guts. The fear was crippling when it played with your head, he knew that better than anyone. He put his hand over his stomach like it was his own pain. Cursing some more at himself, he went over to her. Noah wanted to make her feel at ease, even though he doubted that was ever something that could happen to her, or him. He wanted to gloss over it in Blair style but didn't have the arsenal of words and soft tones the other man had. What he couldn't do was lie to her and tell her everything was going to be fucking peachy fine, when he knew there was no way to guarantee that. So, he started with that and silently prayed the rest would just come outright. "I won't lie to you, ever." He stopped close enough that he could pick up her scent without having to inhale to do it, her scent was both his glory and his failures. "I don't know how much I'll be here." When had it changed from, he was only here temporarily? He focused on her eyes, trying to keep from looking at her mouth and that lip she was murdered with her teeth. "I have to," he gave his head a slight shake and then put his hand over his heart, "I *need* to help free others," he leaned down so their faces were closer to the same height, so he could see she was understanding what he was saying. "I need to stop those people, Emersyn, do you understand?" His cat was moving around in him, restless, just at the mention of them. "I know I'm never going to find peace, but there's a small part inside me that lives on the hope that if I stop them, if I end their torment of our kind, then someday, I might be able to breathe just a little easier." His vision started to blur slightly, and he had to look away from her until he got it under control again.

"I understand, Noah, I do."

When he looked back at her, she was nodding her head.

"I just can't bear that you are putting all of this on yourself." She sniffled like her emotions were riding her too, "you're only one man and when they took you," she tilted her head and gave him a soft look, "you were just a child."

He clenched his jaw, so he wouldn't blurt out his first thoughts on what she was saying. She deserved more than him going off on her. "I just," he clamped his mouth shut and breathed out slowly through his nose. He didn't know how to word this, "I have to keep moving." He watched her hoping she got it because that was all he had. "When I stop, bad things happen." Noah held his breath watching for a reaction, he couldn't explain what things. There was no way he could ever put it into words. How did you describe to someone that your own mind worked against you often, that the rest of your body rebelled with it?

"I understand—some," she said the words slowly while giving him a steady look, "just know that I think you're a good man and nothing could ever change my mind on that." She nodded her head and gave him a small stiff smile.

Noah wanted to reach out and touch her hair, brush it back from her cheeks so he could see all the freckles that decorated her skin. Gripping the tape roll tight in his hand, he jammed the other one in his pocket. She licked her lips, and his eyes were drawn to that. Even his cat was paying close attention to her scent now. He wanted to kiss her. Not an 'it just happened' kind of kiss like the last two times, but one that he was thinking about right now. He told his body to step back, but his feet weren't moving.

Chapter Thirty-Five

The door flew open, and Penny rushed in, "are the girls here with you?" She waved a hat around, "I just ran in to grab Wren a hat."

Emersyn shook her head, already heading out the door. "They're probably hiding." She glanced over to see the main gate was closed and felt relief.

Noah moved by her and started for the small bush beside the fence. When he reached it and turned to say something, he froze as he looked to the other side of the yard.

She went around the corner of the house. The gate leading outback was open. Her breath caught in her throat.

"They can't have gone far." He started running for it. "Stay here." He called over his shoulder.

Her legs felt like they were weighted down as she followed him. She should listen, she should stay here, he wouldn't tell her if there wasn't a reason to. She watched him pause by the open gate and take a deep breath, he was scenting the air. When he leaned down and took off his boots quickly, her heart began pounding faster.

Blowing out a breath to calm her breathing, she inhaled slowly and tried to process what she could smell. She clutched her jacket to her chest and squeezed her eyes shut. She could smell the girls and knew their scents well, but there was something else she didn't know.

"What happened?"

Opening her eyes, she saw Gage standing beside her.

"The girls." Penny pointed to the gate, "I was only gone a minute."

Gage looked at Emersyn, "did Noah go?"

Emersyn nodded. "There's something out there."

Gage's brows furrowed as he started walking toward the fence, he shook his head and then took off his jacket and dropped it on the ground as he went through it.

Emersyn sucked in a breath; she should go help them. Her baby was out there.

"What's going on?" Kelsey came running across the yard.

"The gate was open."

She heard Penny say but couldn't take her eyes off it.

Kelsey went by her toward the gate. She bent down and picked up Noah's boot and then went over to the other one and tossed them both to land beside Gage's jacket. She stood in the open gate and Emersyn could see her take a slow breath in.

Emersyn lurched and took fast steps over to her like her feet were finally freed. "What is it?" She motioned, "out there?"

"Coyote," Kelsey whispered and then turned to look back through the gate.

Emersyn put her hand over her mouth so she wouldn't make a sound.

Kelsey turned around and gave her a steady look, "don't worry, the guys can handle a mangy coyote." She nodded, "I don't smell blood. The girls are fine."

She nodded, even though she wasn't feeling assured at all. Instead of looking for them, she watched the redheaded woman turn around the reach up to jiggle the latch on the gate.

"It's loose, probably didn't latch right after the last person came in." She turned back and looked over her shoulder.

Emersyn dropped the coat and went over to look out the gate. A large male tiger was trotting toward them. He was huge and mostly white with brown and orange coloring. On his back hugging him was Wren.

"Wren." Penny ran out the gate. She rushed toward him and scooped the child off his back.

Gage stopped and turned to watch behind him.

Emersyn held her breath. She didn't have to hold it long, Noah appeared out of the trees running slowly. Aspyn was on his back with her arms hugged around his neck, her smile so big that pain went through her chest. She was all right. When he was closer, she darted toward him and grabbed her baby girl off his back. She hugged her tight. Aspyn pushed against her chest and looked up at her.

"Mommy, Noah is a *real* tiger." Her eyes were huge with excitement.

Emersyn dropped to her knees, hugging her into her chest. "You shouldn't have gone out here alone."

"I wasn't alone, Mommy, Wren was with me."

Emersyn hugged her again and turned her head to look at Noah. His sides were heaving. Even in this form, she could see the torment in his eyes. "Thank you." She whispered, knowing he would hear her. He looked at her, his eyes totally focused on her. As she started to get up, he swung his big head around and then took off back into the trees. She watched him until she couldn't see him and then turned to see Gage coming out of the trees with just his jeans on.

Kelsey went over and hugged him.

Gage glanced in the direction Noah had gone. "He's tracking the coyote down."

Emersyn shifted Aspyn so she could see both. "Alone?"

Gage looked like he wanted to smirk but didn't. "He'll be fine. He needs to run it off." He dropped his boots to the ground and then pulled his shirt over his head.

"The latch is worn," Kelsey said softly.

Gage looked at the gate. "Let me go dry off my feet and I'll take a look at it."

Emersyn could hear Penny giving Wren hell, without sounding angry, and turned around to go back through the gate. She set Aspyn on the ground and then squatted in front of her. "You never go outside the fence without one of the big people." She watched the happy look fade from her daughter's face and then she nodded.

"We wanted to see out there."

Emersyn inhaled a deep breath, to try to stay calm. Kelsey and Gage were walking across the yard. She looked back at the open gate; her chest felt tight. They weren't concerned Noah was out there alone, but she couldn't bring herself to walk away. She looked back at Aspyn. "Go inside with Penny. I'll be there in a minute."

Penny came over and took her hand. "I think that's enough outside time for now." She gave Emersyn a relieved look.

"They'll fix the latch." Emersyn tried to convey calm, but she was feeling anything but inside. Standing up, she went back over to the gate and stood in it, watching the trees. She heard someone come up behind her and turned to see Cooper heading her way.

"He won't be long."

His tone was so matter of fact that it irked her. "What's he going to do, kill everything out there?"

Cooper shrugged, "if he has to." He leaned on his cane and looked at the gate. "Most of the wildlife avoid the areas we run," he looked back to her, "they're just not used to us being on this land yet."

Emersyn held his look for a second and then turned back to the trees. She'd never thought of it before. What their kind meant to the wild creatures. She hugged her waist trying to warm the chill that went through her. They were predators.

"Put this on." Cooper held her jacket out to her. She didn't even know where she'd left it.

Stabbing her arms in the sleeves, she pulled it together and held it like that. All these years she thought the people that held her were the predators because they were in control. Now, she was seeing that in normal circumstances her kind were. They walked on legs like one-forms, but when they turned into their true forms, they were more dangerous than the real wild animals—in the body of an animal, but with the intelligence and knowledge of man. Right now, she couldn't think past the worrying about Noah to figure out if that realization made her feel better or worse.

She was sure she'd carved a rut in the five-foot area she paced around while she watched for Noah to return. Gage was working on the gate behind her and would try every few minutes to engage her in conversation, but she couldn't think past the fact that Noah was out there still. If she knew it was one coyote, she might feel better, but she thought maybe they traveled in packs or whatever they were called. He could be out there in trouble fighting a whole group of animals.

Gage paused and looked down at her. "He's on the way back."

She tilted her head and gave him a look, not even sure how he'd know this.

"Listen," he said softly.

Emersyn turned away from him and closed her eyes. She slowed her breathing and concentrated on the sounds around them. She could hear birds and something skittering quickly through some brush somewhere close by. When she heard the steady pattern of something larger connecting with the earth, she opened her eyes. He was running back this way.

"He's going to be broody," Gage stood beside her now, "blaming himself for a rusted, worn latch."

Emersyn glanced up at him and nodded, "I know." She looked back at the trees and noticed just then that the snow was falling. Reaching up she touched her hair to feel it was quite wet. How long had it been snowing?

"He found the girls before I could catch up to him," Gage admitted quietly. "He would have carried them both back if I hadn't been there."

Emersyn barely glanced at him, "did seeing him scare them?"

"Your little one knew it was him. I don't know how, but she did."

Emersyn blew out a breath, "I guess the explanation I planned to give her is happening a few years early."

"She probably knows, Wren was telling her all about it when I got there." He turned so she could see him looking down at her, "it's better if they know it from the start." He nodded, "ask Kelsey what it's like if it's hidden from you."

She glanced up at him, "is that even possible? To hide for long?"

Gage smirked, "her parents managed it and if they were alive, I'd be the first one to give them hell for it."

She wasn't sure what he was talking about, but curiosity would have her asking Kelsey at some point. Right now, she looked to see Noah coming out of the trees. He carried his jacket and boots but had already gotten dressed. Who had put his boots there? She missed that completely when she was lost in her head. His head was down, so she couldn't see the expression on his face. His stance and stride told her that Gage was right, and he was internally chastising himself for an old piece of metal not working the way it was meant to.

"Find them?" Gage asked as he got closer.

Noah's head popped up and he paused in step, his eyes moving over her then he looked at Gage and nodded. "The rest of the pack won't be back."

Gage made a grunting sound. "Good."

The rest of the pack? So, he had killed at least one and she had been right, about there being more than one? She moved her eyes over him slowly and couldn't see any injury of any kind. When she inhaled subtly, she didn't pick up and blood scent either. She gave him a look of inquiry.

He ignored it completely. "Girl's okay?" He stopped at least five feet from them, his gaze locked on her.

She nodded and hugged her waist. "Yes. Thanks to you."

Noah scoffed at that, "I should have checked the gate latch before now."

"Wouldn't have done any good. It broke off, you couldn't have predicted that." Gage said in a low tone as he moved back over to the gate.

Noah watched him for a second and then waved his hand, "I'll go dry off a bit, and then I'll show you how to tape off the windows."

Emersyn raised an eyebrow at him. Just like that, it was the end of the discussion about what had happened. She narrowed her eyes and looked at him for a second and then spun on her heel and went through the gate with stiff movement. She would check on the girls and then go back to the small house.

She watched him through the window as he spoke to Gage in the yard. His posture was stiff, almost to the point of looking hostile. Emersyn didn't have to be outside to know what they were talking about, Gage looked patient as he spoke, and Noah closed off completely. He was still blaming himself for the latch. Crossing her arms over her chest she watched him, practically studied him. This was the man that kept her from going insane or giving up. She knew nothing about him all these years, only that he had fought for her. He had risked his life for her. She didn't need to close her eyes to remember how he looked when she saw him that night, it was burned into her memory forever. She had honestly thought she was hallucinating when he came down into that basement—it wouldn't have been the first time she'd imagined him during a low moment. He'd never spoken in them though, so that should have been her first clue it was real. He was nothing like she'd imagined he would be like. He was so fierce and strong, even if he didn't think he was.

Whooshing out a breath, she watched him walk toward the little house she was waiting in. His expression told her that he was completely shut down, lost in his head. She chortled to herself, if anyone understood getting trapped in your head, it was her.

He came in and closed the door and then stood there, looking her over from head to toe, completely avoiding eye contact. She bit her lip and forced herself to stand there and suffer his scrutiny for about ten seconds longer than she ever thought possible. "It wasn't your fault." She said softly.

His tortured gaze connected with hers. "I should have checked everything."

"Why was that your responsibility?" She mentally cheered for her quick reply without vibrating like she was going to crumble to the floor. "There are many people living here," she waved a hand in the air, "many come and go from the other two homes," she sucked in a quick breath and hoped she didn't look as nervous as she felt, "why did that fall to you to do?" She had been conditioned to never challenge a male.

His expression changed slowly, as did his breathing. He was fighting the second nature that had been beaten into him too, she thought with satisfaction. "I should have thought of it." He shook his head, "I told you that you and your child would be safe here…"

"And we are." She compelled her feet to move her toward the counter so she could pick up the tape. "You found them; the gate is fixed." She couldn't look at him for a few seconds while she gathered more courage to hold his stare. "Everything is fine now." She blew out a breath and then turned and looked at him. He hadn't moved. She held up the tape, "how do I do this?" Without waiting for a reply, she went over to the window. Could he tell she was holding her breath now? She wasn't sure, but she did until she heard his boots on the floor.

He stopped a foot from her and reached and gently took the roll from her hand. Pulling out a foot of it, he held it along the wood that lined the window. She watched him, his hands were steady, his breathing wasn't erratic. She wanted to ask him how he was able to control himself when her cat could sense the anger and anguish rolling through him.

"Are you going to work in here all day?" His voice was soft, and he still wasn't looking at her.

"As long as I can." She watched how he lined the tape up with the wall so she would be able to paint right to the edge of it without hitting the trim. "I'd like to get it finished before Cooper wants to put the flooring in."

Noah's hands paused, and he cocked his head to the side for a moment, his face hidden from her view. "Just take breaks and don't forget to eat." He finally said.

"Once I get out here done, I was going to bring Aspyn in with some toys and give Penny a break." She clasped her hands in front of her.

"I don't think Penny minds." He ripped off the tape and then reached up to the top. She would have to use a ladder to do the rest.

"I just want to get this done for Cooper."

He huffed out a breath and then lowered his arm, leaving the tape roll dangling from the wall. "Cooper doesn't want to live in here." He said it, sounding exasperated and slightly angry at the same time.

"What do you mean?" She looked around the room, "he doesn't like it, does he?" She closed her eyes and sighed, "he barely said a thing about the choices I made," she opened her eyes and looked to see he was standing there, his hands on his hips shaking his head.

"I should have told you. *He* should have told you." He was looking at the floor, so she wasn't sure what was happening.

"Told me what?"

"He wasn't asking you to clean this place up for him to live here," he looked directly at her, "he wanted it done for us to live here."

"Us?" She blinked wondering if she'd misunderstood somehow. Her eyes widened, "us," she motioned between them, "you and me?"

He jerked his head to the side, "and Aspyn."

Emersyn opened her mouth, then snapped it shut. The three of them living here. "Is it because we're not actually part of this clan?"

Noah looked surprised, "no. I don't think any of those others care about that."

She shrugged, "I don't know much about clan life or rules."

"That's not why." He inhaled a deep breath and then blew it out, "because we're mates." He blurted it out, then looked at her to the floor, then back to her again.

"Oh." She hugged her arms around his waist, feeling a little awkward now. "Why didn't he tell me that?"

Noah snorted, "I don't know," he rolled his eyes, "he thinks we'll fix each other," he lifted his hand and then dropped it again, "that we'll find happily ever after or whatever."

She almost smirked at his description. "I, uh, don't think such a thing really exists."

He nodded and looked at the window, "would you have still done it if he'd told you why?"

She watched him look all around her, but not directly at her. Would she? "I think I would have, yes."

He didn't mask the surprise from his face before she saw it.

"I've never felt useful," she stared at him, hoping his gaze would eventually connect with hers again, "I enjoy doing it."

"Keeping busy helps with," he wiggled his fingers beside his head. With slow, hesitant movement, he lifted his eyes to look at her, "I'm surprised you're not upset."

"Because he wants us to live here?"

"No, because we didn't tell you."

She had to move, "Is that why you looked so annoyed when you came in here last night." She opened the cupboard; she already knew was empty and looked in it.

"Yeah, but not that you were doing it, just-just..."

"That Cooper didn't tell me why?"

He started to nod, then scowled and pulled his phone out. His expression lightened quickly, as he raised it to his ear. "Ed? Do you need me over..." his coloring paled and he looked at the floor, "when?" His eyebrows went up, "now?" He nodded, a vacant look on his face. "Okay." He slid his finger over the screen and looked down at the phone.

"Is everything all right?"

Chapter Thirty-Six

Noah watched the car come through the gate. Right behind it was Blair's truck. It was good he would be here too—he trusted him to keep things under control if it got messy. His heart was racing so fast in his chest that he could barely breathe. Spinning on his heel, he walked to the side of the house and stood there looking at the ground. For years all he wanted was to see his parents again and now they were here— a decade too late. How could he face them? They were going to ask about Carlene and to even think her name rendered him incapacitated, never mind explaining what happened to her. Movement beside him had him turn, ready to take down whatever was too close to him. Blair and Emersyn stood there.

Blair tilted his head, his open hands at his side like he was bracing himself. "Thought you could use a bit of support." He said in a quiet tone.

Noah felt his animal roll through him, more annoyed by it being Blair and not something he could jump. He could feel the animal staying close to the surface, waiting.

"I'd ask if you're good, but I can see you are not even close to it." Blair looked over to where Emersyn was standing and motioned for her to stay there.

Noah scowled at him, "I wouldn't hurt her." It came in a guttural tone, closer to a beast than a human.

Blair gave him a shocked look, "I know. I just asked her to let me talk to you for a minute." He stood straighter and put his hands on his hips, but Noah could still see that watchful look in his eye.

Noah nodded, afraid to speak again.

"I know circumstances are beyond anything I could understand," Blair paused and watched him for a second, "but I would give anything just to see my parents one time." He nodded his head and then looked over to the corner of the house. "Just one time."

Noah hesitated, processed that. He'd forgotten what happened to Blair's parents. Was he being rash about how he was feeling? It was his fault they were taken, he hadn't listened and stayed within the boundaries set by his father. He swallowed down the bile rising in his throat. The least he could do was tell them what happened. He turned to see Ed and Gage standing there with four others. His family. He snapped his head back to look at Blair.

Blair may have looked like he was relaxed and all good with everything, but Noah's cat could taste the Alpha vibes pouring off him. Did he even know he did such a thing? Could others sense it as he did?

"Just give them a few minutes," Blair nodded, "and keep the scary one on the inside, that's all I'm asking."

Noah flicked his gaze from him to Emersyn and then back to him again.

"She wanted to be here with you." Blair stepped back so she could come over.

Noah cleared his throat, trying to find his voice. His tongue felt like it was paralyzed. He was glad Blair knew enough to move away from her. Noah's cat was feeling very proprietary right at this moment—because he needed to be dealing with *that* shit too right now.

Her steps were slow and hesitant. He inhaled and could smell the fear and anxiety pouring off her. Yet she was still coming toward him. "I would never hurt you." He said in a low voice when she was in front of him.

"I know." She reached slowly and put her hand on his clenched fist, "I'm not afraid of you," she coaxed his fingers to open, actually pried them apart, "I'm afraid *for* you."

Noah's sight was bouncing back and forth between normal and cat vision, but he could still see her eyes clearly. In them, he saw fear, worry, and anxiety. She squeezed his hand and continued to look up at him. The muscles in Noah's jaw pulsed with tension. "You don't have to…"

"I want to." She took a deep breath and then nodded. "I can't even imagine what it will be like to see my family again."

Noah swallowed and closed his eyes. He took a deep breath, communicating with his cat that Emersyn was right beside them and he had to keep it under control. He focused on the warmth of her hand against his. He could feel it vibrating, but she still held it tight. Opening his eyes, he looked down at her and nodded. Inside his head, he was telling her thank you, but he couldn't find the words. It was going to take a lot to get his legs to move, but he would try, for her.

When he turned to walk over, a young girl was walking toward him. The air exited his lungs all at once. She was around fourteen years old and was exactly how he'd pictured Carlene would look at that age. Her hair was the same strawberry blonde with those out-of-control waves in it. As she got closer, he saw Carlene's eyes looking at him with much scrutiny.

"Steady." He heard Blair say in a hushed voice.

He felt Emersyn lean closer to him and hug his arm while still holding his hand, but couldn't look down at her—the ghost of his sister was walking across the lawn toward him. He saw Jake coming, running over behind her. Noah tensed, not wanting Jake to walk in front of her. He gasped and then remembered to take a breath.

"We were, ah," Jake stopped beside Blair and didn't move to come closer, "giving you a few minutes," he looked at the girl, "but someone is in a hurry."

Noah watched her stop and look at him, he expected to see the pain in her eyes, the look of betrayal because he let her be taken…

"So, you're him, huh?" She said and then put her hands on her hips.

Noah blinked; it wasn't Carlene.

"This is your sister, Tiana," Jake said quickly.

"Tia," she spat, giving him a side glance.

Noah's knees felt weak. He had to focus on staying standing here. Emersyn moved her hand up and down his arm, drawing his attention to her for a second. She was looking up at him, her eyes reflecting encouragement and confidence. He couldn't understand why she felt that toward him right now.

"Your Alpha, Ed, has been telling Mom and Dad all about how you're some kind of vigilante hero now," she crossed her arms over her chest and looked him up and down, "or some shit." She cringed and looked over her shoulder to where the others still stood. "Don't tell Mom I said shit—she has a fucking fit when I swear."

Noah heard someone chuckle and knew it would be Jake without looking. This girl was the image of Carlene, but there was nothing sweet or innocent about her. "I didn't know you even existed until recently." He said and was surprised his voice sounded normal.

She snorted, "lucky you. We've lived every day knowing about you and our dying sister—Mom drags us to the doctor three times a year to get jabbed."

Noah lowered his head, thinking maybe he hadn't heard her right.

"So, is this your *mate*?"

She said it with such disdain his head popped back up to glare at her. His cat rolled under his skin. She wasn't looking at her with a judgmental look though, so he was able to settle him down.

"Did you bite her?" She snarled, "that caveman crap." She muttered, "I can tell you if some guy tries to put his teeth in me, I'll be ripping them from his jaw and wearing them for a necklace." She huffed out a breath.

Noah blinked and then looked to see Blair holding his hand over his mouth and Jake grinning.

"Uh, Tia," Jake stepped closer, "I think you'd get along with Akira, *really* well." He motioned to the backyard, "let's go see what's going on in the house and I'll introduce you."

Tia looked away from him and then to Jake, she lifted one shoulder. "Whatever." She started walking toward the backyard.

Noah watched her walk away.

"I like her attitude," Jake said quickly and jogged away.

His mind looped back to what she said. *Our dying sister…*

"Noah."

He blinked and looked down at Emersyn. Her eyes were asking if he was okay. He nodded, even though he was so far from okay or any semblance of it.

"Do you need a minute?" Blair stepped in front of him.

Noah sucked in a breath, he squeezed Emersyn's hand. Only she could understand what he was going through.

Blair looked over his shoulder. "The rest are coming over." He said when he turned back.

Noah exhaled, then forced his body to work properly to inhale again. His back was soaked in sweat. He wanted to take his jacket off but didn't want to let go of Emersyn's hand to do it. The connection to her was the only thing keeping him standing here. If it weren't for her, his cat would have won the tug of war to get out and he'd be running as fast as his paws could move right now.

Emersyn rubbed her hand up and down his arm, then flexed her hand in his.

He wanted to look down at her, but he couldn't look away from the three people walking toward him. The boy was probably twelve, maybe a bit older, it was hard to tell. He reminded Noah of how he used to see himself before… he shook his head; he couldn't think of *that* right now. The boy had fear in his eyes and Noah found himself inhaling, trying to find the threat that was scaring the child. He watched the eyes so similar to his own look him up and down and it dawned on him that it was him scaring the boy. Sucking in a breath, he blew it out and clenched his jaw to focus on calming down.

Emersyn shifted to stand closer to him and he drew on her closeness to stay calm. His cat seemed to agree with that.

It took persuasion to look from the boy to the woman standing there with her arm around him. It was his mother, older, but it was her. He remembered needing to see her for so long, then her image faded from his mind, and in its place was a dark blank space that should have been filled with her and loving motherly memories. He noticed she was shaking and cocked his head, trying to figure out why.

Our dying sister... "What was wrong with Carlene?" He growled it. For years he'd pictured seeing them and saying how sorry he was that he failed them, but now those feelings of guilt and sorrow were gone, in their place was anger. They'd kept something from him.

His mother gave his father a hesitant look. He stiffened and then turned to look at the man he could barely remember a thing about. He had a hard look on his face. Noah remembered that look, it used to go with the fear and respect he felt for his father. Now, an older man stood before him, looking him eye to eye and he felt no fear by his presence. In fact, he realized, he felt nothing for him. Noah turned back to his mother. "Was she sick?"

She nodded, a pain in her eyes. "It's a very rare disorder that our kind has." Her voice shook with emotion. "We didn't tell you because we didn't want—want..." She put her hand over her mouth.

"She wouldn't have lived to her tenth birthday, Noah."

Noah's head snapped back to look at the man in front of him. The way he'd said it, so cavalier, made him tense, "she was fifteen when she died." It was the first time he said it out loud and admitted that it had happened. "She lived through hell that long." His voice shook.

"Noah."

He flinched and looked to see Everett and Julian running toward him. Emersyn squeezed his arm tighter.

Everett slid to a stop, "is it okay if we go for a run with McKenna, Harrison..."

"And Kelsey," Julian said in a high-pitched voice. "We'll be careful."

Noah blew out a breath and looked at how excited they were.

"Kelsey said we had to ask you first." Everett looked over toward the backyard.

Noah glanced to see Kelsey standing there beside McKenna. He nodded and turned back to the boys, "you make sure you *follow* them." He looked directly at Everett.

Placing his hand over his heart, Everett nodded, "promise."

Noah nodded again. "You have to do your schoolwork as soon as you come back."

Julian nodded, "absolutely."

They both grinned at him.

Noah watched them take off running back to Kelsey, he caught the look Blair was giving him and scowled. "They need run packs."

Blair nodded. "Beth is picking up several today." He smirked, "new tigers left and right lately."

Noah felt some of the pressure ease inside him. The air was easier to pull into his lungs until he turned back to his *family*. He looked at his brother, whose name he didn't even know, "have you shifted yet?" His attempt of using a friendly tone failed.

He shook his head, a nervous look on his face.

"Ollie just turned twelve." His mother said quietly.

Ollie? What kind of name was that? Noah glanced down at Emersyn so he wouldn't blurt it out and embarrass the kid. He cleared his throat and turned back to the boy, "Everett is twelve, his first shift was yesterday."

Ollie jerked his head to look in the direction they had gone, "I'm kind of scared to, but really excited at the same time." When he looked back at Noah, his eyes were filled with that child excitement that was seriously lacking with the clan here. Their life had prematurely drained all childish feelings from their young bodies.

Noah gave Blair another quick look, "you could, uh, come to stay here sometime if you want," he motioned to the fence, "there's a lot of lands to run."

Ollie gave him a surprised look and then turned to his mother, "that would be cool." He bobbed his head a few times, "it's different having a big brother." He shrugged, "but after Tia, anything would be better."

Blair chuckled quietly.

Noah found if he focused on his brother, he was able to keep his cat calmer. He was still there, right under the surface, but under control—so far.

"Mommy."

Emersyn's grip loosened as she turned to see Aspyn running toward them. Nora, he thought her name was, stood by the corner holding her son, Mason's hand. Aspyn slammed into her mother and clung to her leg, then looked up at her.

"Nora is going to go look at wild—" she frowned the turned to look at her.

"Herbs." Nora called out, "we're going to look for wild herbs to see if any are still good to pick." She motioned to the big gate, "Weston is coming with us."

"Can I go, Mommy? Please?"

Noah looked down at the way she was looking up at her mother. Every time he looked at her, he searched for signs of trauma and abuse in her eyes, but he never saw any. Emersyn glanced up at him as if asking his opinion. "They should go out back and not along the road." He flicked his gaze to see Blair's opinion. He gave him a slight nod.

"I'll go tell them," Blair said and backed up a few steps before turning to walk.

Emersyn put her hand on Aspyn's head, "you listen and do as you're told."

Aspyn nodded, then squeezed her leg in a hug. She looked up at him and smiled, then turned around and looked at his parents. "Noah is a *real* tiger."

His mother smiled down at her. "That's exciting."

"Can I ride on your back again?" He looked down to see she was looking up at him, her blue eyes huge.

"He's not a pony," Emersyn said in a light tone.

"No, he's a tiger." Aspyn nodded and then took off running back toward Nora.

"She's adorable." His mother said to Emersyn.

Emersyn smiled but continued to hug his arm.

Blair came back over, "There's tea and coffee inside, why don't we head in?"

Noah looked to see he had his charming smile beaming at them. He was having a hard enough time just remembering how to breathe evenly, but Blair would charm the hell out of them with his magic skill and that would give him the space to adjust to this.

Emersyn didn't move from his side as they walked back to the front of the house with Blair. Blair paused at the corner and looked back at him, his expression asked if he was doing okay. Noah lifted one eyebrow at him and then blanked all expression from his face again.

He closed his eyes and took a deep breath and then let it out slowly. When he opened them again, he was looking into those brilliant emeralds of Emersyn's. "My sister was dying." He whispered it.

"I heard." Her expression was pained but compassionate.

Noah could have stood here and looked at her face for the rest of the day—if his cat wasn't pacing inside him. "I didn't know what I'd feel when I saw them." He gave his head a small shake, "I didn't feel much, they're strangers."

"Your brother seems nice." She smirked, "and your sister has some spunk to her."

He grinned, "what kind of name is Ollie?" He shook his head, "poor kid will probably be teased for the rest of this life."

Emersyn gave his hand a gentle squeeze, "I think he'll be fine."

He nodded and hoped she was right. "I do want to get to know them, I think."

"Take some time, there's no rush."

The patience in her tone was soothing and guilt went through him, she deserved so much more for a mate than he could ever be.

"Noah."

He blinked, forcing his thoughts to stop and not suck him into that darker place.

"Go for a run, check on the boys and keep an eye on Aspyn."

Inhaling a deep breath, he nodded. That idea sounded much better than going into the house and drinking coffee with strangers. "Thank you." He mumbled. "I don't think I could have stood here if you hadn't held me here."

She smirked, and then released him like she just realized she was still holding onto his arm. "I expect you to hold me up if I ever have to re-meet my family."

Noah looked at her mouth and thought of bending down to kiss it lightly. His cat rolled through him again. "Deal." He stepped back before he did something like grab her and freak her right out.

"Go run." She whispered as she backed toward the front of the house.

He watched until she disappeared around the corner and then turned and headed with long strides to the side gate. A tear rolled down his cheek. It was like they hadn't even cared that Carlene was dead. He growled a low noise. Although they'd known she was going to die, had known before they were taken. He'd get to know his brother and sister, if only to protect them from the horrors of this world—beyond that, he didn't feel he was the child of Elona and Vinson Reyes anymore.

Chapter Thirty-Seven

Emersyn stayed on the far side of the counter. She looked down at it, this seemed to be her favorite way to be among the others without having to be close to any of them. It was odd, she'd spent years wishing for some company, and someone to talk to—now she had a house full of them and couldn't bring herself to be near them. If anyone walked up behind her or touched her in passing, she have a full-on panic attack. She leaned on the countertop and looked around at the others that were inside. The kids were all excited about the boxes on the one end of the table, computers that Kobie had brought for school. Emersyn couldn't decide if she was excited about it, but the chance to learn more than basic words would be good.

Noah's mother did seem nice, but there was something hidden in her eyes. She watched his father sitting at the table talking to Cooper and Ed. There was something about him that just froze her blood in her veins, then again for most males, she was like that.

She looked at the window and wondered how much longer Aspyn was going to be out with Nora. It was good that she had so many around her to look after her, but each time she was out of her sight for too long that fear set in. The fear that something had happened.

Going around the counter, she went over to sit near the sitting area. She smirked as she did, once the internet was going, she doubted this would be a quiet corner. The entertainment center was loaded with screens and more electronics than she'd ever seen in her life. She was sure the children, and adults would make good use of all of it.

Sitting down, she turned so she could glance out the window from time to time. The side gate was visible from here. She watched Noah's mother come over and sit in the chair across from her. She was trying not to judge her by Noah's feelings.

"I don't think we were introduced." She smiled, being pleasant enough. "I'm Elona."

"Emersyn." Noah looked a lot like his mother, she decided, with the same-colored eyes and hair. She couldn't guess her age but was sure the stress of losing two children was a factor.

Elona turned and looked out the window, she glanced briefly over at her mate before turning back to Emersyn. "I lost my little boy and now he's returned a giant of a man." She smiled fleetingly. "I'm still processing what the prince and Ed told us." She looked down at her clasped hands. "It's almost too much to handle."

Watching out the window for a moment, she tried to decide what she could or should say to that. "The little boy," Emersyn paused when Noah's mother looked back to her, "he died a long time ago." She could have worded it differently, but the truth was sometimes needed. "In his place is who Noah needed to be to survive." She raised her cup and took a small sip while she measured what the other woman thought of that.

Elona closed her eyes for a second and then looked back at her, a steady assessing look on her face. "You were taken too, weren't you?"

Emersyn sucked in a few short breaths and then nodded. "When I was eight." She watched her lift her hand to cover her mouth for a moment, she tried not to judge her by the fast recovery. This woman knew heartache too well to do that.

"Was your girl born there?"

Emersyn nodded, then looked out the window. She needed to see her now, answering questions about it had her stomach churning.

"I'm sorry, that wasn't a very nice way to ask."

She looked back at her. "It's fine." She blew it out, "I haven't been free for very long, so it's still affecting me quickly." She tried to hold her look, but the pity on the woman's face made her want to grind her teeth.

"You're mates?" Emersyn lifted her lashes and looked at her. "Noah and you?" The look of pity was gone, "you're good for him." She nodded, "I could see how hard it was for him—seeing us and you seemed to calm him."

Emersyn licked her lips and then decided a drink was better. If she had any idea how close he'd been to losing control of his cat, she wouldn't be sitting there so calmly. Lowering the cup, she nodded. She didn't want to paint an ugly picture, but she also needed to tell this woman the truth, it's what she would have wanted if it were Aspyn. "We are." She lifted her brows and then blew out a quick breath, "I don't know if we'll ever *be* what mates are though."

She watched the confused look slide over to replace the pleasant smile on Elona's face. Turning back to look out the window, she couldn't even begin to explain how complicated it was. All of it faded to nothing when Noah came running through the gate with both Aspyn and Mason on his back. The children were laughing so hard, she had no idea how they were staying on his back. "She's going to treat him like a pony." She said with a grin on her face.

Elona turned and looked. "That's Noah?" Her voice was breathless.

Emersyn nodded. Noah made a big production of lowering his long body to the ground. When his belly was on the ground, Mason slid off and landed on his bottom on the ground, he was laughing so hard. Aspyn was hugging Noah's neck and talking to him. Noah stood up and shook his large body, leaving her daughter laughing. Crouching down, he waited for

Nora to pull her off and then leaned forward and licked her face. Aspyn collapsed laughing again.

When he lifted his head and looked right at the window, she knew he could see her watching him. Turning, he bound back through the gate. She watched that Aspyn and Mason didn't give Nora issues about going to the front door before turning back to Elona.

His mother glanced over at Ollie and then smiled at her, "children heal everything eventually." She whispered it.

Emersyn turned to look at the little brother that Noah already liked. "I guess we'll find out." She whispered more to herself than as a reply.

When the other woman gasped, Emersyn turned quickly to see why. She was looking out the window with her hand over her mouth. Almost afraid to see why she looked anyway. Noah was walking back in now, with just his jeans on and boots were undone. He ruffled Everett's hair and smiled down at him. His shirt was in his hand. She turned to look at his mother, knowing the scars on his body are what had her reacting. Had he done it on purpose? "His back is worse." She said softly and then stood up. Just the fact that Noah was standing there with the others without his shirt on was a big deal for him. "Excuse me." She went over and picked up the shoes she'd left by the back door and slipped them on.

Going out the door, she headed straight for him, not even feeling the hesitation she normally did. Everett and Julian were still laughing at something he said. Noah was smiling back at them, a real smile. In the time since he'd stepped into that basement, she couldn't remember that she'd seen him smile that way.

He snapped his head around when she was almost to them and looked at her. In the few steps before she reached them, he had checked her from shoes to her hair and was now giving her a cautious look, as if to ask if everything was all right. She smiled at him, hoping it reassured him that everything was fine.

Kelsey and Harrison came through the gate. She pointed at him. "You cheated."

Noah smirked at her then shrugged, "you should check the terrain before attempting to win a race."

Kelsey scowled at him and then smiled slowly, "next time you're at the shop we're having a rematch."

Noah pulled his shirt over his head. "Okay." He told her as he put his arms into it. He glanced down at her. "You should have your jacket on." His tone was soft and not void like it normally was.

She shrugged, "I saw you with the girls and," she glanced toward the house, "needed some air."

He nodded but didn't look at the house.

"Is your cat as fast too?" Harrison asked her. "I feel like I'm a hundred next to these ones." He motioned to Noah and then the boys.

Emersyn gave him a wide-eyed look, "I'm not sure how fast I am."

Noah stiffened and then spun to face the house.

"Noah?" She looked in the direction he was.

"Stay here." He started to run down the side of the house.

"Oh," Kelsey looked at Julian, "go get Blair out to the front." She started to jog after Noah.

Emersyn didn't know what was happening, but she ran after her. She tried to take in the scents around them into her system, but her adrenalin had kicked up several notches and she couldn't pick out anything. So much for being in tune with her cat. She thought as she rounded the corner and almost slid into Kelsey. Moving around her, she froze. Noah had a man pinned against the doorframe—by the throat. Kelsey put out her hand to stop her, but she shook it off and went toward him.

The door opened and Blair swore. "Noah. He's supposed to be here, he's hooking up the internet." Blair pointed to the truck that clearly stated what he was doing.

Noah released him and stepped back.

Emersyn rushed over and stood in front of him. She put her hand on his chest, making him look down at her. His eyes were close to his cats again. She could tell just by how hard his chest was that he was really fighting his cat right now. "Noah." She took a deep breath as he looked down at her, "breathe."

He inhaled a slow breath and then released it and looked nowhere but into her eyes. Her own cat was close, not on the verge of coming out, but she knew that their mate was distressed and wasn't doing a very good job of helping her right now. She rubbed her hand against his chest again. Lifting his hand, he put it over hers, holding it there. She felt his chest rise and fall again.

"That's my fucking brother right there."

Emersyn turned to see Tia and Akira standing by the corner of the house.

"Tia," Elona said with a stern mother tone.

Tia lifted her hands in the air, "what? Seriously? That was some impressive rage right there." She smiled at him, "now I *know* we're related."

Noah squeezed her hand, keeping it against his chest. He gave her what could have been a smile, but it was hard to be sure what it looked like. He blew out a breath and then turned to look at the man he'd attacked. "Sorry."

The guy shook his head, "hey," he held his hands up, "it was my bad for not calling Blair like I was supposed to. He told me not to barge in here unannounced." He rubbed his throat, "now I know why."

Noah looked at Blair.

Blair shook his head, "it's a good thing he's an ally or we'd be in some deep shit right now." He grinned at him, then pointed to the little house, "go walk it off or something." He shook his head and then held the door open, "it's safer in here." He told the man with a grin.

Noah looked down at her, "seems like this is becoming a full-time job for you."

Emersyn smiled up at him, "I have a lot of free time." She looked over at the little house, "think you could show me how to do that taping thing now?"

Noah nodded and lowered their hands. He glanced at the window of the house, and she didn't need to look to see his mother was still standing there. When he released her hand, he looked over at Tia, "know anything about painting?" She shook her head, "Me either, come help us make a mess."

She grinned and grabbed Akira's hand and ran toward the small house.

Emersyn knew his bad moments far outweighed his good ones but seeing him without the dark shadows in the recess of his eyes made her feel better than she had in a long time.

"I'll watch Aspyn for you while we do the lessons," Kelsey told her, a smile on her face. She jerked her chin telling her to follow Noah.

Inclining her head to her, she turned around and started after them.

Chapter Thirty-Eight

She should have listened to Kobie's suggestion and gone for a run before bed. The ache in her back and arms wouldn't allow her to sleep comfortably. Sitting up, she looked over to see Aspyn sleeping sideways in her own bed. Emersyn was torn between a mother's pride that she slept in her own bed but had also had a few melancholy moments because she missed her beside her. Getting up, she stretched slowly and tried to relieve the tight feeling in her back.

The floor was cool on her feet, but she didn't want to move around too much in the room to find socks and take a chance on waking the others. She didn't know what time it was but knew that it was either too late or too early for children to be up and charging through the halls.

She opened the gate in slow motion, afraid it would make a noise and disturb Penny. With a grin, she closed it just as slowly—she felt like a burglar sneaking out of her own room. As she went down the hall, she remembered that Tia was sleeping on the couch in the sitting room. The rest of Noah's family had gone back to Ed's, but Tia had insisted on staying to help paint. Emersyn wondered how it was going to look in the daylight. Things had gotten a little messy as they got tired.

She walked silently to the other end of the kitchen where she could see her asleep on the couch. She really liked her. Sure, she was a little liberal with her language and opinions, but Emersyn knew one thing for certain, no one would ever force her to do something she didn't want to do. She envied her being like that.

When she opened the fridge, she winced and paused, the light it threw into the dark area was so bright. Cocking her head, she listened to see if it disturbed Noah's sister. When she heard no movement, she carefully took out the milk and set it on the counter. Her hope was a snack and something to drink would have her feel fuller and maybe allow for some sleep. Pausing, she looked at the cupboard and wondered what she could make for a snack. The fewer drawers and things she used, the less noise she'd make.

Carefully setting a glass on the counter, she thought about Noah as she poured the milk. His light mood, well, after he tried to strangle the workman, hadn't lasted long. They'd gotten everything taped off and he seemed to be okay with the girls helping and then he suddenly withdrew back inside himself. Shortly after that, he said he had to go help with ceilings at Blair's and left. He didn't return until after everyone had gone to bed. If she'd been sleeping, she wouldn't have heard him come in. Somehow, she sensed him, more than she heard him going through the house. She was glad at that moment that she hadn't been, or she wouldn't have heard him walk through and pause outside the doors to check on everyone. She wondered if he did that every night.

Setting the box of biscuits beside the glass of milk, she decided she'd just stand here and eat them, rather than slide a chair across the floor. Before she could take the first bite, she heard a muffled sound and paused to listen. The cry of anguish echoed in the silence. Later she'd wonder how she knew who it was, but she set the biscuit down and headed down the hall where Noah and Cooper's rooms were.

As she reached the doors, Cooper stepped out into the hall. He didn't move to open Noah's door, so she did quickly and went inside. Noah was struggling in the bed, keening heart-breaking sounds, and mumbling incoherently. She went over and looked down at him, not even sure if she should try to touch him. He'd never consciously hurt her, she knew that, but he was lost in his own version of hell at this moment.

She leaned down as close as she dared, "Noah," he didn't even pause in his battle. She glanced over her shoulder to see Cooper was at the door, he nodded to her letting her know that he was there if she ran into any problems. Putting one knee on the bed, she caught one of his flailing arms and stopped it from striking her. The tortured look on his face almost broke her.

Lowering her face close to his, she touched his cheek, "Noah, wake up." She whispered close to his ear and winced as his other arm hit her in the shoulder. "Shh," she placed her mouth close to his ear again, "you're okay, it's just a nightmare." She stroked his jaw softly and kept whispering to him, "you're not there, it's not happening." She swallowed the lump in her throat, "I've got you."

His face contorted with anguish and then the tension in his body stopped. His quiet sob filled the silence. She started to sit up when he shifted to his side and pulled her to sit on the bed. Curling around her body in a fetal position, he rested his head in her lap as his body shook with silent cries.

Emersyn put her hand on his head and brushed the damp hair back from his face. She was relieved she'd managed to pull him out of the terrifying cycle of his past, but he was so vulnerable right now, that it was hard to stop the tears that fell from her eyes. His arms tightened around her, and she didn't care if he squeezed the breath from her body, she would stay here as long as was needed.

Turning her head, she looked to see Tia standing beside Cooper now. She had her hand over her mouth and tears in her eyes. Cooper was talking softly to her, and she nodded and then looked at her brother once more before turning to go back down the hall.

"She'll keep an eye on Aspyn for you."

Emersyn nodded, not able to speak right now with her own emotions so close to bursting free.

Copper looked at Noah again and pulled the door, so it was almost closed, but not latched.

She looked down at Noah and knew he was wide awake now by the way he held his body, but he made no move to release her. Leaning down, she pressed her cheek against his shoulder and stayed like that, just holding him. She knew the nightmares you relived were worse than the ones that paralyzed you. Those you could will yourself out of if you fought hard enough. The ones that felt so real that your body believed it was happening again, those ones, like now, opened all the doors and broke down all the walls you worked hard to build.

He took a deep ragged breath, and she expected him to pull away from her then, but he didn't. He was focusing on his breathing, trying to convince his body that none of it was real, but she knew the truth. You could tell your mind a thousand times that it wasn't real, yet at some point, it had been, and some things could never be erased.

Lifting her head, she smoothed the wet hair back from his face, "do you want to talk about it?" She knew the answer before he gave it.

"No." His voice was hoarse from the strain caused by his screams. His arm flexed around her as if he was checking that she was really there. His grip relaxed, but the tension in his muscles remained.

She sat up a little further so she could look at him. She would stay here as long as he allowed her to. Placing her hand on his back, she gently ran it back and forth in a soothing motion. She could feel the scars beneath her touch and didn't feel hesitant at all. They were a part of him and there would never be a moment in his life that he could forget about them. She knew this and she understood it because her mind and memories were as warped as his.

The low light didn't affect her ability to see him clearly and she was pleased to realize that her cat was in fact helping her without barging into the moment. She blinked and tears fell down her cheek. Her heart felt like it swelled in her chest when she watched him, as his facial expressions relaxed just slightly, just enough to tell her that he was pulling out of the numb state finally. Would he allow her to stay when he did? She needed to stay.

Her breath caught in her throat as it dawned on her that she'd felt this overwhelming sensation inside her once before. The one that made her chest feel too full. She'd had this unbearable feeling when she'd looked at her daughter for the first time. It wasn't the exact same, she knew that nothing could ever compare to the love one felt for their child, but she did love this man that was holding her. She sniffled, trying to prevent the dam from opening and the water to pour from her eyes. Blinking she looked away from him trying to process her discovery. She could have brushed it aside and given the credit to it having some connection to him being her mate, but this went so deep, there were no other feelings attached to it, just love. The kind of feeling that told her she would do *anything* for this man to protect and care for him. *Anything.*

The stuffed tiger that Aspyn had given him sat on the little table looking at the bed. She swallowed the lump in her throat and whispered, "Aspyn would be so disappointed in her gift not doing its job."

Noah's arm around her relaxed and he rolled his head to look at it. "Pretty big job for a small piece of stuffing." His voice cracked as he spoke. He wasn't nearly as settled as she had thought.

Emersyn grinned, "we could look for a six-foot one."

Noah turned his head in her lap and looked up at her, "I don't think the guys would ever let me live that down." His face reflected that his thoughts weren't as light as his words, but she understood that the little things you did to lie to others to cover up the truth were okay.

He closed his eyes and blew out a deep breath, "did I wake anyone else?"

She licked her lips and decided small lies worked for other reasons too. "Cooper. I was in the kitchen."

His eyes popped open and just like that his torment was brushed aside, "Is everything all right? Are you okay?" He shifted and lifted his head away from her to prop himself up on his elbow.

She wanted to hug his head and tell him not to, but she just let her hand fall to her lap instead, "I needed a snack."

"Did you go for a run and not eat after?" The concern on his face almost made her cry again.

She shook her head, "no. Burned a lot of energy working on the house I guess." She wanted to squirm as he studied her face, it felt like he was looking inside her and seeing all the ugliness that she hid in the dark corners inside her.

When his gaze shifted, he looked at how he was still curled around her and how close they were. She watched the emotions change on his face and then felt the way his body stiffened, but he didn't move away from her. Eyes with the nightmares in them cleared from his vision as he looked back to hers. "I'll be okay now." His voice didn't shake as it had.

She wiped the wet from her cheek and gave him a quick look. Just like that he'd stuffed the horror back into the box and the man that didn't think he deserved to show vulnerability was back. "Well, I'm not so don't move." She said in a gruff voice.

His surprise was quickly masked with concern as he huffed out a breath and fell back onto the bed. "I shouldn't stay here," he flicked his gaze to the ceiling, "every damn time you look at me, I drag it all back for you." He moved his head slowly from side to side.

Emersyn sat straighter and looked down at him. The urge to smack him startled her and made her pause to see if it was her feeling or her animal's opinion. She was even more shocked to find it was her own. "That's ridiculous." She said it louder than she had intended. "You think with you out of sight it's going to magically be all better?" She glared at him and then placed her hand in the center of his chest as if she needed to hold him down so he would have to hear what she had to say. "It's always there." Her voice cracked. "Always, Noah, whether I see you or not." Her eyes filled with angry tears which annoyed her more that she couldn't say her piece without it affecting her. She swatted at her eye to stop them. He was looking up at her now, pain evident on his face. Pain for her, not himself. "You have no idea how much better you make it," she snorted softly, "if it can even *be* better."

He shifted but didn't try to displace her hand from his chest. Concern creased his brow; confusion clouded his eyes. "How could I possibly make it better."

"You just do—and you don't even see it." She was annoyed that the words in her mind weren't coming out as she thought them. "You're so strong, yet I know deep inside you doubt everything about yourself, about others," she shook her head and then took a quick breath, "I look at you and I see an incredibly strong man that keeps going despite weaknesses or his own fears." She swatted at her cheek with a shaking hand, "And—and you're so stupid sometimes I just want to smack you." More tears fell, from frustration with herself for being unable to explain it to him with any sort of clarity.

He shifted on the bed and then reached to tenderly brush the tears from her face. His eyes were bleeding with compassion and concern.

"And I'm ridiculous." She whispered, "I come in here to comfort you and end up blubbering like a baby instead."

He didn't smile or even acknowledge that she'd spoken. Raising up, he placed a quaking hand gently against the side of her face. His hand was so large she realized that it reached so his fingers thread through her hair to hold her head too. She held her breath as he leaned closer and then placed a feather-light kiss over her eye before shifting to do the same to the other one.

When she opened her eyes, he was watching her, with such a tender look on his face, and she wanted to cry again. Had anyone ever looked at her with that look before?

"You make me want to be a whole man inside." He said it so softly that she wasn't sure he'd spoken the words. "To be a normal man." He added. She licked her lips, and his eyes followed the movement. "You deserve someone that will treat you like the treasure you are," his look connected with hers again, "not someone like me that can't go a single day without some sort of breakdown."

She put her hand against the side of his face. "You understand me, Noah, there's no one else on this earth that ever could." She meant it. "That means more to me than anything else." She knew there would never be a happily ever after for her. As long as he was present, she wouldn't need to seek that unobtainable fantasy.

He took a ragged breath but didn't release her. She wasn't sure if she leaned toward him or he toward her, but somehow, they were now only a breath apart now. She could taste his fear and anticipation and knew that she was projecting the very same to him. She wanted to tell him it was okay, that it was going to work out, but she couldn't find the words to say what they both knew was a lie. Life had done that to them, taken all illusions and shown them the dark truths and there was no going back from it.

His lips touched hers and were shaking from a nervous hesitation, or it was hers vibrating, she couldn't be sure. No other part of their bodies touched now, just their lips and one hand on the others' faces. She didn't know how to kiss him the way she wished, how to express how just this slight thing felt like everything.

He tilted his head and brushed his lips over hers again and it robbed her of her breath. Her cat was close and content to just stay there and observe what this connection was doing to them.

Noah's fingers tensed against the back of her head, but not to push her away, he tilted his own further and kissed her again, a little longer this time. Each time their lips broke away from the others, their breathing grew more erratic, it was terrifying, and she didn't want it to stop. She gasped softly when his lips moved over to touch her mouth. She had never been touched before in a way that she welcomed, but his touch was like no other had been. There was caring, in his touch, there was love in it. He may not say it, but she felt it.

With each movement, he would pause and check for her reaction like he was waiting for her to pull away from him. She closed her eyes and moved her hand to gently hold the back of his head, silently asking him not to stop. His breath was hot against her jaw, and it only added to the effect his touch was having. She lifted her chin, encouraging him to continue.

She heard him take a deep breath and draw her scent into his body, it felt intimate and for the first time in her life, something made her feel sexy. She couldn't prevent the shaky gasp when his mouth moved to her throat. The warmth of his lips on her skin sent shivers through her and something deep inside her she had never felt flamed to life. She had to force herself to remember to breathe and it came out in an uneven panting.

A low rumble came from Noah, and he shifted slightly closer, so his chest brushed up against hers. Emersyn clutched his head and he stopped moving. Her cat nudged her inside as if to say fix it. She couldn't find the words to speak and was afraid to break the magic of this moment, so she turned her body to allow their chests to press up against each other.

Noah hissed out a breath like he'd just been burned but still didn't move away from her. With a hesitant move, she reached to touch his back as his arm threaded under hers and tentatively rested against hers. At no point did he close his eyes, they watched her, caressed her even when his lips weren't. He exhaled, with his mouth close to her neck again and she felt like his mouth was somehow draining the tension and fear from her muscles as she fell against his chest with more weight.

Her cat was acting like the proverbial one and rubbing against her insides as if she could feel him. Emersyn closed her eyes and felt her mouth move to smile as he continued to do magical things against her throat and shoulder.

When he released her head and pulled her into his body, she didn't even panic. The contact felt natural and despite the hesitation from both after, they both relaxed into it. Noah made another low animalistic growl, and it sent shivers of heat and awareness through her. He lifted his head and held her look. For that moment all that could be heard was their own breathing. Her cat stilled inside her and she thought it was to allow her to feel this on her own.

Noah's mouth closed over hers again and when she felt his tongue dip inside and touch her own, she moaned no louder than a whisper from the feeling it caused. He paused, seeing if that had been a sound of panic or not. When she moved to make their mouths touch again, he continued with more vigor than before. She was dizzy, her body hot and she would never forget this moment ever.

Feeling spurred on by his reactions, she moved to taste his mouth and stabbed her tongue off sharp teeth. Horrified, she jerked back and put her hand over her mouth.

Noah stiffened and moved back from her; she could see the apology on his face before he opened his mouth. "I'm…"

Shaking her head, she put her hand over his mouth and then opened her own to feel the sharp feline teeth filling her mouth.

Noah's eyes rounded as he watched her actions.

Emersyn covered her mouth again and then shook her hand. "My cat," she mumbled around the foreign teeth in her mouth, "wants to bite you." She blurted it out without even realizing that was what was happening.

Noah gave her a wary look. "Bite?" He said it slowly, his voice still deep from the emotions their kisses had stirred in him. "Mate bite or…"

Emersyn nodded, hoping that was the only reason her unpredictable creature would want to bite this man.

Noah opened his mouth to say something and then closed it and looked down at the bed for a moment. He shifted and was sitting on the edge of it now, nowhere near as close to her as he had been. "I don't—" he lifted his hand and then looked at her, "I didn't expect that kind of reaction." He blew out a breath, "I actually didn't know what to expect."

She felt awful and later when she was alone, she would be having some harsh words with her animal, in or outside of her head. "I've never kissed anyone before." She said it so fast that she had no idea why she had.

He looked at her, surprise on his face.

Now she felt like she needed to explain. "I never *let* anyone kiss me before." She knew he wouldn't ask for details, because he understood what she'd been through.

He reached toward her, then hesitated. She watched the internal debate he was having go through his facial expression. When he gently took her hand in his, she hoped that meant he'd won. "I've never kissed anyone either." His hand flexed around hers, "after hearing—knowing what," he shook his head and then huffed out a breath.

"I understand." She nodded. It had crossed her mind once or twice since he'd rescued her, wondering if he had been like some of the other guards, but her heart had told her no and now it was confirmed for her mind too. She ran her tongue over her teeth and was happy to feel they were her own and not partially her cats. She smirked, "we're quite the pair." She whispered it.

Noah tilted his head and then nodded, "if it wasn't so fucked up it would be funny."

They sat there, the silence growing longer, and just held each other's gaze. It wasn't how she would have liked to end such an intimate moment between them, but she had to go check on Aspyn and at some point, at least lay down and attempt sleep. "I should," she looked at the door, "Aspyn." She turned back to him.

He cleared his throat and slowly released her hand.

She stood up and then he grabbed her hand again, only to wince that he'd done such a thing. She squeezed it gently, "It's okay, Noah."

He stood slowly, so many emotions were going through his eyes that she wasn't sure what to expect. She could feel the tension rising in him again. "I'm uh," he looked down at her, that pain was back in his eyes again, but there was something new there too, "I'll be going back out with Blair and Calum in two days." He watched her as he spoke. "Calum and Shaelan are back at Blair's they'll be here in the morning." He rubbed his hand over his jaw but still held her hand, "that's why I didn't get back earlier, we were talking to some of the other teams and planning—things." He took a deep breath.

She didn't want him to leave but didn't want him not to either because she knew what he was doing. "Just make sure you come back." She said hesitantly, suddenly wanting to tell him how she felt about him. "I don't care how often you leave or for how long, Noah, just *always*—come back."

The pain in his expression changed to something lighter for a few seconds, and he nodded. "Always."

She felt, more than heard his conviction in that one word. Nodding her head slowly, she suddenly needed to get out of the room and breathe. "I should…"

"You should finish the house and decorate it however you want." The words were hurried as they fell from his mouth.

She blinked up at him.

"So-so you and Aspyn have a quiet place," he nodded, "I know all the commotion of so many get to you," he lifted one shoulder and let it drop, "the same as me."

Emersyn opened her mouth to ask if he was planning to join them in that house or if he was just telling her this so she would have something to do and somewhere to go when he wasn't here. Blowing out a short breath, she closed it and nodded. "I'll think about it."

He looked relieved by her answer, making her question what he meant more. Leaning down, he kissed her cheek softly and then released her hand as he straightened up. "I'll see you, ah, later." He looked nervous and filled with doubts again.

She smiled at him, "I'm hoping for five minutes of sleep before Aspyn is jumping on the bed."

He smiled, "I'll take her for a run later or something to give you a break."

"Okay, but if she asks for a saddle for you, it's your fault." She took a step back toward the door. "Try to rest, Noah." She whispered it and then went out the door before she started spewing all the questions his words had filled her head with.

Moving down the hall, she kept going right past the kitchen. A snack was not on her needs list now. She felt emotionally wrought, but giddy and puzzled all at the same time. When she turned the corner, she saw that Tia was sitting outside her door. She took up quietly.

"She hasn't even moved." She whispered.

"Thank you." She reached over to open the gate, wishing she were tall enough to step over it. When she glanced back at Tia, she saw that look that she hated seeing on faces. Pity, only this one was blended with worry. "Don't ever let him see you look at him with that look on your face." She said quietly. "Ever."

Tia nodded, then licked her lips and blew out a breath. "Got it." She turned and went down the hall without another word.

Chapter Thirty-Nine

Calum handed Blair the window. "I feel like one of us is the topic of conversation." He said it quietly and looked past Noah to the backyard.

Noah was standing outside the window as they replaced the weather strips in the small house and worked inside. He glanced over his shoulder to see Shaelan, Kobie, and Emersyn with a bunch of the little ones on the slide and swings. When he looked over, Emersyn turned and looked right at him, she smiled and then turned back to the women and put her hand over her mouth. Was she smiling at him or something they said?

"Pretty sure it's the scary one they're discussing," Blair said.

Noah turned to ask why when he closed the window. With a smirk on his face, Blair flipped the lock on top of it. Scowling at him through the glass, he turned and went to the next window.

Both men stood on the other side of it grinning at him, taking their time unlocking it and opening it. As soon as the wood cleared the bottom, he helped to shove it up to the top. "What do you mean?"

Blair smirked and glanced at Calum as he pulled the window out. "We're old news now, no need for the girl huddle over there."

Noah unrolled some of the strips and glanced over his shoulder again before running it along the edge as Blair peeled off the old. "I, uh," he scowled when it started to stick to itself, "told her to move in here last night."

"Alone?" Blair looked at him as he pulled the last side off.

Noah shook his head, "no, Aspyn too."

"Wait," Calum looked from Blair and then at him, "you told her to move out here with her little girl? What about you?"

"I'm going with you guys in two days." He made sure the last piece was good and stuck.

Calum lined the window back up and started to slide it in place.

"But you're moving in too, right?"

Calum closed the window and locked it before Noah could answer. Glaring at their grins, he turned around to go to the other side of the house. He paused at the corner and glanced over at the women. Shaelan was telling Emersyn something, and he didn't know what was being said, but even Kobie was laughing. He cocked one eyebrow at them and then stomped to the other side.

He waited until the window was opened to look at Calum, "I'm not sure what she's telling them, but your mate has the other women almost doubled over laughing."

Calum swore under his breath and then shook his head. "I'm sure there are chains somewhere in the story."

"Chains?" He watched to see if he was being serious.

Calum sighed and then nodded. "No one told you I was chained to a wall when I met her?"

Noah shook his head; still not completely sure he was telling the truth.

"I'll tell you on the long drive when we head out." He pulled the window out and stepped out of Blair's way.

"So," Blair gave him a quick glance, "are you?"

Noah fumbled the roll and almost dropped it on the wet ground, he focused on getting the strip started and then flicked his eyes toward him, without really looking at him, "I thought

I could take one of the little rooms," he shrugged a shoulder, "or something."

"Or something?" Blair stopped and leaned on the window ledge. "I thought with the looks you two have been giving each other something had changed," he lifted one eyebrow, "between you?"

Noah opened his mouth and then snapped it shut. He didn't know what to say, or how to ask what he thought he wanted to say—or some shit. "She wanted to bite me—her-her cat."

Blair cocked his head to the side, then glanced behind him to Calum, "that's a bad thing?" He said it slowly like he was trying to figure out where Noah's head was.

Noah stabbed his fingers into the strip to make sure it was secured. He really wanted to stab them into Blair's eyes right now. "I just—we haven't," he shook his head, "I don't know if we will ever…"

"Can we finish this intellectual conversation when I'm not standing here holding a window that I can't lean against the wet paint—that you *are* leaning in, Blair." Calum grinned.

Blair jumped back and whacked his head on the upper window as he pulled it inside. "Shit." He looked at the wall below the window, "just place a chair here." He glanced at Noah and nodded. "Get in here." He swatted at his pant leg.

Noah heaved a sigh and then turned around to go inside. He ran through what was said last night and in his mind it all made sense. Emersyn hadn't said otherwise either. Opening the door, he was met by the other two giving him one of those looks. The look that said, 'you did what?'

He closed the door and stood there.

Blair lifted his hand, "so you told her to move in, without saying you were going to as well, but not as a couple?"

"We both have trouble being in the house with so many people."

Calum nodded and glanced at Blair. "That part makes sense."

Blair shrugged, but turned back to Noah, "did you tell her you were moving in too?"

Noah opened his mouth, then winced, "it was implied—I think?"

He blinked, in slow motion at him and then gave him one of those 'you fucked up, buddy' smiles, that really wasn't a smile. "Okay, first, you need to clarify that with her—before we head out with the team."

Noah put his hands in his pockets and then pulled them out again and crossed his arms over his chest. "I can do that."

Blair went over to the window and looked out in the direction the women would be. "When did she want to bite you?"

He asked it like he was asking if Noah liked the paint job, just matter of fact. "Last night." He uncrossed his arms and needed to move. He went over to the counter and turned on the tap, then turned it off. "I had a bad night," he glanced at him, then turned back and opened a cupboard, "a really bad one, she heard me." He shouldn't have to say more than that to Blair, they'd shared a bunkhouse, and he knew how bad it could get. "After—" he shut the door a little too hard, "we were talking and," he waved his hand around in the air and then leaned down and opened the oven and looked in it, "we kissed a few times."

Blair snorted, "that's it?"

Noah turned and looked at him, not sure why he's said it that way.

Blair grinned at him, "I wished Kobie's cat had been that easy to get through to."

"Pretty sure it was the woman and not that cat that time, Blair," Calum said in his usual level tone.

Blair shrugged, "whatever, but still," he turned back to Noah, "how do you feel about that?"

Noah leaned back against the counter and looked at the floor.

"Your cat?" Blair asked with a more serious tone, "how does your cat feel?"

Noah scoffed, "you've seen how well my cat and I communicate." He looked over at him.

"You have more control than you think," Calum offered, "or you'd change fully without warning."

Noah shook his head, "that will never happen. It's a lot of work to get him to come out at all," both men looked surprised at that, "for years if he did, I paid the price, so," he lifted his hands and decided nothing else was needed to be said.

Blair moved away from the window and then glanced at Calum, "how does that work? If they claim each other without," he waved his hand around, "more between them?"

Calum lifted one brow at him, "do I look like an elder?"

Blair sputtered for a few seconds.

"I'm kidding." Calum braced his legs further apart and crossed his arms over his chest, he was looking at Noah when he started talking, "it's happened before, due to injury, pregnancy," he nodded, "other reasons. The marking is for your cat, not you. Some cats are out of control when it comes to their mates."

Noah nodded to let him know he was following him, hoping he'd continue.

"The," he turned his head slowly and gave Blair a blank look, "*other* part of the relationship is for you and her and," he turned back to him, "there's no set of rules that say how that works, it's entirely up to the two of you."

Blair huffed out a breath. "I thought my life was complicated." He gave Noah a slight nod, "I think you just need to sit down and talk to her, both of you figure it out."

"Is that what you did with Kobie?" Noah had never really asked; they were just one day 'mated'.

Blair grimaced and then rolled his eyes, "it was a complete shit show, I spent a lot of time chasing her," he snorted, "literally a few times," he sobered, "but as you know her whole world had—" He trailed off and then held his look, "okay, I get it now." He blew out a breath, "I didn't see it when you were talking about it before, but both you and Emersyn—" he waved his hand around.

Calum grinned, "you used to be smarter."

Blair glared at him, "there used to just be me to worry about now there's," he flung his hand in the air, "forty-seven or eight, I don't know—*too* many people I have to think about and so much shit I have to remember." He sighed.

Calum watched him for a minute with a smirk on his face, if Noah wasn't mistaken, he only brought it up to wind Blair up again. He watched Blair pace around in a circle with his hands on his head for a moment, "are you done, or do you need a few more minutes?"

Blair held up his hand and then paced three feet to his left and then nodded, "done now." He gave Calum the middle finger and then smiled at him.

"I told Tia and Ollie," Noah paused after he said that name, "that they could come here any time they wanted."

Blair blinked and looked at him, "what's two more, right?" He grinned, "I'm kidding, that's fine. Your brother is quiet, I like him." He glanced out the window, "your sister, she's uh, blunt to put it mildly."

Noah grinned, "she knows what she likes or doesn't, there's nothing wrong with that."

"Your folks are going back tomorrow," Calum said quietly.

Noah inhaled slowly, "I feel no connection to them at all."

"That's not unusual in circumstances like this. You've been through a lot and their lives are basically the life you no longer know."

Noah turned to Calum to see a sincere look in his eyes, "yeah, I'll still go say bye to them before they head back when I take Tia over to Ed's."

"Times up," Blair said making both of them look at him. "Here come the ladies and they look like they have a purpose to all be heading this way."

Calum went over and looked, "shit." He scowled at the floor, "I haven't done anything wrong recently."

Blair shrugged, "I've been too busy to screw up." He looked over at him and Noah's heart started beating faster, "it's got to be directed at you, bud."

Noah's eyes felt like they bulged out of his head, he gave it a quick shake. Then he saw the smirk on Calum's face as Blair looked at him. "You guys suck, you know that?" He moved over to the window to look for himself. They just looked like they were walking this way, not like they were on a mission. "Asshole." He looked at Blair, "I could have lost it."

Blair shrugged, "the beast tamer is walking this way, we're good."

Noah looked back out the window, Emersyn was talking to Shaelan, and she looked—happy. It was nice to see her not look like she wanted to bolt for the first door. He knew there were going to be bad moments, that was just part of it, he almost laughed out loud at that, his *moments* far outweighed hers.

All three of them jolted and moved from the window when the door opened. Noah glanced briefly at the other two women's faces and then looked at Emersyn, she stepped further from the others than Kobie and Shaelan, but that look of suffocating wasn't on her face, so she was okay.

Kobie smiled at Blair, "we're going to take your niece home with us for the night," she nodded, "give you a chance to get to know her."

Blair cocked his head to the side, "Which one?"

Kobie smiled, "Aspyn."

Blair looked from her to Emersyn, "she'll be okay with it?"

Emersyn nodded, "Kobie told her that you're a big white tiger," she smiled, but didn't look directly at Noah, "so now she has to see that for herself."

Blair rubbed his hand across his chest, "sure, I guess if she's okay with it."

Noah smiled and then looked at him, "at least then she'll be asking to ride on your back."

"Ride on my back," he looked from him back to Kobie, who smiled sweetly at him making him snap his mouth shut and shrug, but his expression said there would be a discussion about it.

During the whole exchange, it wasn't lost on Noah that Emersyn wasn't looking at him at all. The look on her face wasn't bad, but it made him nervous, and he didn't know why. He glanced at Calum to see he was watching Shaelan, with a questioning look on his face.

The silence started to feel heavy, and Noah couldn't handle it. "You did a great job in here." He blurted out and turned to look at the kitchen area. "Do you want to keep those cupboards or-or would you like something different."

Blair cleared his throat, "we have new ones coming for the houses if you want us to add to the order."

Noah turned his head to send him a quick thankful look and was only met with a big grin.

"I like them," Emersyn said as she moved to go stand in front of them. "Kobie is going to help me with the fixtures," she looked at the window, "curtains and things."

Noah nodded, all while looking at her, trying to figure out why she was looking everywhere but directly at him. He was used to women not making eye contact with him, but she always looked him directly in the eye. "Okay, just let me know if you need a hand." He turned and looked at the door, "I'm going to go see if Cooper needs help." Head down, he went to the door and out it. He didn't even know where Cooper was or what he was doing, he could be taking a nap for all he knew. He paused in step and shook his head; he'd never known him to have a nap.

He walked to the other side of the house and looked around, no one was there. Which worked for him, he stopped and looked at the snow on the ground. Something had changed with Emersyn. Things weren't the same. He clenched his teeth together. Last night. He somehow fucked it up.

"Do you always mumble to your boots?"

He jerked his head around to see Tia standing there. Each time he looked at her, he saw Carlene—and then she spoke, and it was like Carlene evaporated and in her place was this course, but extremely cute girl. "Uh, just thinking."

"Is that what it looks like?" She smirked at him.

He couldn't help but smirk back. He waved his hand around by his head, "shit going on."

"I believe that's called life," she shrugged, "but what do I know, I'm just a kid."

He did grin to that, "a kid with the mouth of a thirty-year-old man."

"I don't believe in double standards, equality all the way for me."

Noah nodded, "I've noticed." He watched her to see if she was offended by his tone, "I think it's great."

"But you don't agree?"

He opened his mouth to answer, and she shook her head. "Sorry, couldn't help razzing you." She heaved a dramatic sigh and lifted her phone, "I've been summoned to go back over to Ed's" she rolled her eyes, "Dad's orders." She tucked it into her jacket, "they'll ask me ten thousand questions about you like I'm their little spy or some shit," she shrugged, "what happens at Noah's casa stays at Noah's casa." She looked him up and down, "listen, I'm surprised, but I really like you. I didn't want to because you were like," she held her arm in the air, "on some pedestal, but seems you jumped off it without their permission, so we're good."

"I never wanted to be on a pedestal." He told her truthfully. "Once, a long time ago I would have loved to know they thought of me, but…"

"I get it, life moves on," she shrugged, "they'll get over it." She rolled her eyes, "they're trying to pre-program Ollie to be their precious one," she snorted, "they really don't know him at all." She blew out a breath and kicked at the ground, "but if you were serious about me coming here, then, yeah, I will be back as soon as I can swindle them into wanting a break from me." She looked up at him, with a look of vulnerability in her eyes.

"Any time you want."

She nodded and then launched herself at him and hugged him tightly.

Noah tensed and then managed to recover and give her a slight squeeze.

"I'm glad you came back, brother." She said with a shaky voice.

Noah blinked and then nodded but couldn't speak.

She released him and then looked concerned, "I probably shouldn't have grabbed you, sorry, I'm just not a touchy-feely person so it was," she lifted her shoulders, "go for it before I change my mind kind of thing." She dropped them and looked at him.

"It's fine." He motioned to the front of the house, "do you need a ride back over?"

She shook her head, "no, Blair and Kobie are going to drop me off on his way home. That way you don't have to see Mom and Dad before tomorrow when she'll get all sappy on you."

Noah nodded, "appreciate that." He sucked in a quick breath, "it's not that I don't like them, I just—they're strangers now and I'm not the little kid that disappeared anymore." He wanted her to understand.

"I get it. Dad's not easy to get close to either," she gave him a hesitant look, "was he always like that?"

Noah scowled, not at her, but trying to think back, "I think," he nodded, "I think he was," he shrugged, "he wasn't around much then. He worked a lot."

"Now with having to stay close together, and no," she made quotes in the air, "pretending to blend in with the ones' we get lots of quality family time." She groaned, and then blew out a nervous breath and looked at him. "I heard you're going back out there to rescue more of our kind."

Noah nodded.

"I'd ask if it's dangerous, but just breathing for us is now, so," she motioned to him, "be careful, kick some evil ass, and set our people free." She winced, "that sounded less corny in my head."

Noah never talked about the ops, but now, suddenly he wanted to tell her everything. "This trip is, uh, to get some of Konner Flores' clan back." He tucked his hands in his pockets so he wouldn't wave them around like an idiot, "the water clan," her eyes widened.

"I thought they were all gone."

He shook his head, "no, we actually found his mate and now we know where there's more."

"You guys seem to be bringing mates home." She smirked, "I like yours. Emersyn, she seems like she's all skittish, but there's this strength in her, you know?"

Noah nodded and hoped this wasn't going to turn into a conversation about mates, he could barely talk to the men about that, never mind a teenage girl.

She pointed to the side of the door, "I'm going to go before this gets awkward," she winced, "or I cry or some shit." She turned and then paused, "can I get your number? You know we could text or something?"

Noah jolted and then nodded and pulled out his phone, he frowned at it, and then held it out to her, "I don't even know it, so-so put yours in mine too." He handed it to her.

She took it and swiped the screen, "normally I'd chirp you and say old people and technology or some shit," she looked over and grinned at him, "but you get a pass because you were seriously oppressed and it's not your fault your knowledge is stuck back in the dark ages."

He watched her put the numbers in both phones. He really liked her, and it had nothing to do with the fact that she looked like Carlene, it was because he knew she would always give it to him straight and he needed that in his life. He scowled at the ground, the guys did too, but they were dicks about it. He looked up at her again and wanted to ask her things that she was probably too young to know, but he needed…

"You okay? You look like you're having some kind of seizure."

He blinked and then blew out a breath and pointed to his head, "constantly. My-my mind—I want to do or say something, but then I sometimes forget that I'm allowed to…"

"Hey—I get it," she nodded, "not what it's like, but what you're trying to say."

He looked to see Blair standing at the corner of the house and felt saddened to know that she was leaving. "So, when you come back, I'll take you over and show you how to drive some of the rigs." He only knew a few, but he wanted to do something with her.

She grinned, "really? That would be epic." She held out his phone.

He took it and jammed it in his pocket, then motioned to Blair, "better not keep him waiting, he's got a lot going on."

She glanced at him and nodded, "he's pretty cool, for a pretty boy." She shrugged.

Noah snorted. Damn, he really liked his little sister. "Try to stay out of trouble and keep an eye on your—our little brother."

"Full-time job." She lifted her hand and let it drop. "I'll talk to you soon, Noah." She looked like she wanted to say something else, but then spun on her heel and headed over to Blair.

Blair looked at him and gave him a quick salute. His expression said he was trying to convey something to him, but Noah had no clue what this time. Drawing in some air deep into his body, he turned and decided he should at least go find Cooper now and see what he was up to now.

Chapter Forty

Noah hung his head down and let the water run over him. The rest of the day had gone better than he could have anticipated. When he'd finally tracked down Cooper, he'd been outside the fence with a chainsaw. After the problems at Blair's, he'd decided it was a good idea to cut back any branches or trees that were too close to the fence. Noah hadn't thought of that, and he was glad that Cooper had. He had been worrying over leaving here to go out with the team, but Cooper had thought of everything, so his cat and he was more settled about going.

Cooper enlisted the help of the three boys, Julian, Everett, and Liam to drag the brush out of the way. Then there was talk of a fire pit being put in the backyard for gatherings. Noah was all for the firepit, it was a great place to sit and forget things or overthink them—the gathering part he wasn't too keen on.

He glanced down at his arms, very proud of the fact that once Cooper had let him take over the saw, he hadn't cut anything off or injured anyone. He couldn't be held responsible for Liam being clumsy and tripping over things, that was all thanks to a growing body and learning how to navigate it. None of the boys had complained, not once, and they even smiled while working. It was good to see them settling into life here. By the time they were finishing up, Akira and a few of the women, whose names he still couldn't keep straight had come out to haul the blocked-up wood inside the fence.

Overall, it was a good day for the clan. He flipped off the water and grabbed the towel. He hadn't seen Emersyn once since they stood in the little house and his cat was not happy with that. If he couldn't go one day without seeing her, what was he going to do when he went away? He wondered if Cooper would keep him up-to-date or would her just harass him. He frowned; he already knew the answer.

He rubbed his hair with the towel and then started on his body. It wasn't just his cat that wasn't happy right now, he still couldn't figure out what he'd done to make her not look at him. He paused and stood there half bent over when he realized it was the first time in over a decade he wished for a female to look him in the eye.

Tossing the towel at the hamper, he grabbed his clean jeans and yanked them on over still wet legs. He winced as they tried to rip all the hair off his legs. Closing his eyes, he took a deep breath and then exhaled it slowly before opening them. Tomorrow couldn't get here soon enough. He needed to get back out there where he knew what was what. Go in, get people out, move on to the next.

Picking up his shirt, he turned it around pulled it on, and then caught sight of himself in the mirror. The scruffy beard he was growing changed his face enough that he didn't look like that man—the one that had worn a collar. He leaned closer and glared at his own reflection. He could grow a body covered in fur in seconds, but the hair on his face looked so sparse and patchy. How did that even work?

He stepped back and tried hard not to look as he raised the shirt, but he always did. The crisscross white welts over his chest always drew his attention. He knew his back was worse, he remembered when he broke free of their hold and was able to cover his face and throat from the lashes. Pulling his arm from the shirt, he ran his hand over the scars that rose above the rest of his skin. Emersyn had no problem touching them, which he knew of, but he couldn't even look at them without feeling the pain and fury that he'd felt at the time. His cat had even tried to break free, and Noah had to turn his attention to keeping him contained before it happened. If that had, they would have likely just shot him then and there. Had his cat saved him by distracting him or made it worse? He couldn't be sure, all he clearly remembered other than the sting on his flesh as he was prepared to do anything to get away from them and go set that girl with the emerald eyes-free.

Blinking, he sucked in a breath and then yanked the shirt over his head. Gathering up his dirty clothes quickly, he opened the bathroom door and almost leaped through it. He just needed to get away from the mirror. Away from the memories that followed him with every step he took. He was almost to the hall to his room when movement from the kitchen caught his attention. Emersyn stood by the counter. She motioned to the plate sitting on it.

"I warmed it up for you."

He paused in step and looked at the plate then back to her. He'd forgotten to eat. Again. He nodded, "thanks," he looked at the clothes bunched up in his arms, "I'll just drop this off in my room." He took long strides to his room and basically tossed them in the door and then closed it. She'd made eye contact with him, and he couldn't get back fast enough to see if she did it again. As he reached the kitchen, the image of Julian teasing him popped into his head. He wasn't like that, he'd never been like that, distracted by relationship—things.

He was both pleased and shocked that she was still in the kitchen when he walked in. She'd sat at the table and put his plate on it as well. His cat was alert now. Were they the only ones up?

"You disappeared when dinner was ready." She said quietly.

Noah took the long way around the counter to get to that end of the table. "Yeah, I, uh, went over to Blair's to ask about bricks to make a firepit."

Her expression didn't change one way or the other. "Did he have any?"

Noah sat down in the chair across from her and slid his plate closer. "Yeah, he had some, then we got distracted doing things in the new houses."

"Everyone must be excited about them."

He nodded, even though he had no idea. He knew Blair was thrilled to get some of the people out of the house. He focused on his plate for a second. *House.* He had to talk to her about the house. Set that straight. He took a bite and then chewed it fast because it burned his tongue. Pushing back from the table, "listen, I wanted to talk to you," he went to the fridge.

"I need to speak to you too."

He grabbed a bottle of water and then closed the door. "Okay." He took the cap off and had a big enough drink that it stopped the pain on his tongue. What could she need to speak with him about? He tried to read her thoughts from her expression and couldn't. Why he'd suddenly think he could figure out what a woman was thinking, he had no idea. Going back to the table he sat down.

"You go first." She said and then clasped her hands on the table and looked at him.

Noah picked up his fork and then looked at her, she didn't look mad or upset. Turning his attention to the plate, he stabbed the closest thing on the plate. She wasn't mad or upset, so that was good, right? He chewed and then swallowed it before he looked back at her. "When, uh, when I said you and Aspyn should move into the little house," she held his look with a patient expression on her face, which made him nervous all over again, "I didn't—well, I meant that-that I was thinking I would too." He sucked in a breath and continued before he changed his mind, "I mean I could stay in one of the little rooms, you and Aspyn can have the big one," he shrugged, "I don't-don't need a lot of space really—" She smiled at him and then nodded, and he just stopped talking. What did that mean?

"That's part of what I wanted to talk to you about," she motioned to the plate, "please finish your meal and then we'll talk about it."

Noah nodded, even though inside his head he was screaming. How was he supposed to eat when he had no idea what she wanted to say? Part of what she wanted to talk about? Like what part? What else did she want to talk about? He stabbed something with his fork. And why was she sitting there looking so calm? What had she talked about with Kobie and Shaelan? What did they tell her? As he chewed, he glanced her way and then looked away again. She was sitting there looking so patient and-and calm. He'd already thought calm, but it was true.

She laughed softly and he jerked his chin up to look at her, "I can almost see the monologue scrolling across your forehead, Noah."

He almost reached to touch his forehead like it was happening. "Just thinking." He mumbled and then took another bite.

"I can see that, and you can stop panicking, nothing bad is going on." Emersyn put her elbows on the table and leaned her chin on her hands. "Promise."

He noticed she said it the way she did when she told her daughter the same thing, but just nodded and took another bite. When he first sat down, he wanted to eat slowly and spend a few minutes with her before attempting to sleep—now he wanted to hurry so he could find out what she wanted to talk about.

"Did you," he almost choked as he swallowed and had to take a drink to recover, "did you have a good day?"

"I did." She glanced around the room, "it was odd not having to chase Aspyn down for bed though."

"She's probably being spoiled over there." Was that an encouraging thing to say?

"I'm sure she is."

He looked at her for a second and then nodded. What made him think he could stay in a house with her? He couldn't even come up with enough conversation while he ate.

"I could make you something else if you're still hungry."

He blinked, he'd been sitting here staring at her and not even realizing it. Looking down he saw his plate was empty and didn't remember eating most of it. "Um, no. I'm good." He stood up and picked up the plate. Going over to the sink, he rinsed it off and then went to open the dishwasher when her hand touched his to stop him.

"They're clean, just leave it in the sink."

He almost dropped it in the sink and winced at how loud it sounded. She was slow to move her hand from his and he had to fight the urge to grab her hand and put it back. Being touched freaked him out, but with her, he found he wanted to feel the warmth of her touch.

"I was going to go out and get some fresh air," she looked up at him, "I'm getting better about being inside, but just knowing I can go out—" she shrugged.

He nodded, then stopped because he just kept doing it like an idiot. "It's cool out there, you should grab your jacket."

Her smile was slow as she looked up at him. "I wanted you to come with me."

Again, the only response he could navigate was to nod. He motioned to the door off the kitchen. Fresh air might help to restore his brain to fully functioning again.

"I'll get my jacket." She looked down at his feet, "you should get your boots at least."

Noah looked down at his bare feet and frowned. "I'll be right back."

Chapter Forty-One

She almost put her shoes on the wrong feet. This was a lot harder than she thought it would be. Emersyn was trying to do what Kobie and Shaelan told her to do. Project calm, because Noah picked up on every other emotion too easily. They were right, the last thing she needed was for him to panic and his animal to go into protection mode, then she'd never get him to hear what she needed to say. He was already close to panic, or that could be nerves.

Putting her jacket on, she did it up quickly and then went back to the kitchen. To wait for him. She had no idea how she was going to say what she wanted to, none at all. The advice given was just to tell him the truth. She cringed, the truth was ugly, and speaking it out loud would end with her being too upset to tell him. She heard him coming back and took a deep breath before she turned around to smile at him. Did her smile hide the truth of how nervous she was? They were real smiles. It was easy for her to smile at him.

"Is everything all right?" He made a jerky movement with his hand, "with you?"

She didn't want to verbally lie to him, so she just smiled again and nodded her head. Opening the door, she stepped out and took a deep breath. The cool air was nice. All scents changed in the cool air, she noticed and was pleased by her little discovery. With slow steps, she walked toward the playset, having no idea what she was going to do once she was there. "So, we are going to have a firepit?"

Noah walked beside her, his hands jammed into his pocket, his head down. "Yeah. I thought it was a good idea." He paused and then pointed to the other side of the yard, "I thought we could put it there with some benches or chairs or something around it."

He sounded unsure of his idea. "That's a good idea." She went over to one of the swings and sat down. She felt a little giddy inside, she hadn't been on one since she was a girl. Pushing it back she let it rock her back and forth in a slow easy motion, dragging her feet lightly along the ground.

Noah stood there beside the swing, his hands still in his pockets. He had his head down, causing his hair to fall over his eyes, so she couldn't see his expression.

Inhaling subtly, she took his scent into her body, he was so nervous and tense she didn't know how he was just standing there. Closing her eyes, she lifted her feet, so it felt like she was floating with the motion of the swing. She knew exactly how he was standing there so still when so many emotions were going through him. It was something you learned to survive. Reacting to anything could land a backhand across your face or worse. She opened her eyes and looked at him, he'd lived through the worst part. "Do you ever think of how it was amazing that it was you that was with that team when you came to the house and found me?" She watched him watching her. "I mean what are the odds that it would be you and not one of the others?" After he searched her face for a long silent moment, he shook his head. "I do. Think about it." She kicked her feet so the swing would move again. "I don't believe in fate and all that," she shrugged, "stuff." She was trying to find a way to lead into what she wanted to talk about, hopefully, she managed it before he had one of his episodes where his mind got the better of him. "If it hadn't been you to find me, I could have ended up anywhere," she saw him take a deep breath, "I wouldn't have Aspyn back and," she stopped the swing and stood up, "I wouldn't know you." His breathing was growing to be more erratic, and she knew she needed to talk faster before he froze up or worse. "I'm sorry, I'm trying to figure out how to say what I want to say."

"It's okay if you don't want to move into the other house or-or if you don't want me to," he nodded, "I get it."

"That's not it, Noah." She stepped closer to him and then paused to see if her cat was still with her, she needed her with her right now. "I do want to move into the other house—with you." Her cat was quiet, but very much aware of every word, every breath they each took, and how his cat was starting to stir. She put her hand on his chest and was glad he had left his jacket open, so she could feel the heat of his body beneath his shirt. It calmed her almost as much as she knew it did him. "Last night," she blew out a nervous breath, "was," she licked her lips trying to find the word to describe it, "unexpected," his eyes flicked to connect with hers and she saw the guarded look in them, "not the kiss, that was," she felt her cheeks heat and could only smile, "I was talking about the part with my cat and wanting to bite you." Confusion went through his eyes, and she sucked in a breath, "this was much easier to talk about with the women." She gave him a hesitant smile, "I don't know how to say this." She started to move her hand when he grabbed it lightly and held it there.

"Just say it." His voice shook, "I'm going to lose my mind if you don't get to the point." He grimaced, "you know what I mean?"

She nodded and bit her lip. Did she just blurt it out? Blowing out a breath, she forced herself to raise her chin and meet his look and hold it. "We're mates," she cringed, bad start, "I mean we've proven that it's true." She watched him hoping for some kind of reaction.

"Yeah," he said it breathlessly, "it's strange, but-but not in a bad way." He spoke slowly like he was afraid to say it. "I can feel when you're close and," his muscles tightened under her hand, "when I think I'm going to lose it, you can just," he patted her hand on hers, "and it calms both of us."

She smiled, hearing him say it meant more than just knowing it. "I talked to the women about my cat ruining our moment last night and wanting to bite you," she tried to gauge his thoughts about sharing something like that with others, he didn't look upset by her confession, "they both think if I did, if-if," she swallowed quickly, "if I did, that our cats would feel more connected and stable." She shook her head, "that's not the word they used, but what they meant was it would help you keep yours calmer and-and mine would stop being so afraid of everything."

His brows furrowed, "your cat is afraid of everything?" The concern in his eyes was intense, "you should have said something, I could have helped."

Her eyes filled with unshed tears, and this was exactly what she was hoping to avoid. "You already help me and everyone so much, I didn't want to bother you."

His eyes searched her face, "when you're out running, you didn't look afraid."

She shook her head quickly, "not then. Then, well, once she's out she's fine, I'm talking about all of the rest of the time."

He reached and caught a tear with his thumb before it had a chance to fall from her lashes. "You should have told me."

"You have enough to focus on—"

His expression softened, "focusing on you helps me not focus," he tapped his head, "on all this." He stood there, looking down at her, "they said marking me was a good idea?"

She could hear the doubt in his voice. "I'd like to know what you think about that."

His brows furrowed, then lifted as he thought about it.

"I've seen you watch the mated couples." His expression was panic. "No one else notices. I don't think anyone watches you the way I do." She grimaced, "that sounded creepy."

His lips twitched like he wanted to smirk, but the serious question she'd asked was weighing him down. "I never thought," he released her hand and took a deep breath as he thought. When he stepped back, her hand dropped away. "I don't know—you want to?"

She could hear the surprise in his voice. "You're a good man, Noah, I've told you that and you understand me and my," she took a deep breath, "limitations."

A look of understanding appeared in his eyes. "I'm not exactly a catch." He frowned and looked at the ground for a moment, "I don't know if I can do this—" he motioned between them, "I don't know if I can be a mate, the way other men can be—"

"That kind of fits in an odd way," she hugged her arms around her waist and wished for a moment this wasn't as difficult as it was. "I don't know if I will ever be able to," she closed her eyes and tried to think of how to say it, "I know you're nothing like," she opened her eyes, she couldn't say his name "*them*, and would never…"

"No." He stepped closer and then stopped before he reached her, "I would never hurt you."

"I know." She swatted her cheek to try to erase the tear on it. "I don't know if I will ever…"

Noah nodded and closed the distance quickly. He touched just her cheek, with the back of his fingers, but it felt like the most loving touch she'd ever felt. "You know I don't care about that, right?" He lifted one shoulder and then let it drop, "I'm not saying I'm not attracted to you," he sucked in a breath, then blew it out, "but I don't," he shook his head and then clamped his jaw shut.

It was sad and emotional, but she couldn't help a brief smile, "we're a perfectly broken couple."

His nostrils flared, "couple." He whispered it, tasting the word on his tongue. "Are we?"

"I believe that's what I've been trying to talk to you about and find out." Her nerves were back again, the careful composure she'd spent all day working on was gone. She needed to know now if she waited any longer, she was going to end up having one of her panic attacks and then that would be the end of this discussion. "Do you want to mark me,

Noah?" His eyes rounded and looked huge for a second and then his whole expression and aura changed. Noah opened his mouth, then he shut it and squinted for about ten seconds before he finally closed his eyes and took a deep breath. When he finally opened them again, she could see how uneasy he was talking about this. She stood there patiently, giving him the time, he needed, despite how anxious she was feeling.

"I do—" he stretched the word out slowly, "I just don't know if I can." He put his hand over his heart, "I mean, I would be honored, even though I'm not deserving of a mate," he motioned to her, "especially you, but I have problems with my cat too." He rolled his eyes, "as you know."

It looked like he was squirming just saying that much to her, she moved closer again and wanted to touch him, but didn't want to spook him as her cat confirmed that was a possibility. "Well, that's a start, right? That we both want to?"

He looked at her for a moment, and then seemed to relax. "Yes." His voice was deeper, and she wasn't sure if that was a good thing or a bad thing.

She hugged herself and just looked at him. He was much stronger than he thought he was. She hated that he doubted himself so much.

His eyes narrowed and then he glanced to the side a few times. "We should talk about the house." He blurted out and then nodded.

Emersyn had to fight not to smile, he was just as out of place in this conversation as she was, and the house was a neutral topic for them. Although if she gave him too long to think about that he'd realize it was another important step for both of them. "Let's go look at it. I want your input on what to get." She clasped her hands in front of her to walk over. "Cooper told me that we didn't have to worry about the cost of anything."

Noah made a sound of exasperation and reached over and pulled one of her hands to hold in his. "Every time you do that it takes me back there." She walked along with him, "you don't have to walk with your head down and hands clasped in front of you anymore." He glanced down at her, and she could see the haunted look was back in his eyes again.

"I forget sometimes." She whispered it.

"I know." His tone had softened. "So do I, a hundred times a day."

Chapter Forty-Two

Noah had never seen her this excited about anything, not since she'd seen her daughter at that pathetic cabin site. Emersyn trailed off in what she was saying and looked back at him, she had a smirk on her face.

"If either of us could write properly it would have been good to make a list of everything we just decided." She huffed out a breath and put her hands on her hips.

He couldn't help the grin on his face as he held up his phone. He stopped the recording. "Voice recording. I use it a lot, so I don't forget instructions," he cocked his head to the side, "but don't tell the guys, they have no idea."

Emersyn opened her mouth and then closed it and came over to him, "show me." She listened to them talking on the recording until he paused it. She grinned at him, and his breath was stuck in his chest, she was so pretty when she did that, "I need one of those."

"A phone?"

She nodded, "yes, I want to be able to talk to you when you're not here or for you to call me—if you want?"

The skittish look on her face felt like a punch in the gut. He hadn't thought of that, but the idea he liked. Every op had everyone on their phones, and he had no one to talk to except the people that were already there, and Cooper, but those conversations were short and sweet, to say the least. He tucked the phone into his pocket, "Beth probably has one, we can check in the morning before we head out." He blew out a breath, "I have to say goodbye to my parents too." He wasn't looking forward to that.

"Really?" She put her hand over her mouth her eyes bright. "Thank you." She stretched up and kissed him right on the mouth. He knew it was just from her being excited, but his cat was right there with him for once.

Reaching out, he touched her hips, softly, a careful action so he didn't startle her. The excitement on her face faded to something serious and expectant. Just holding her like this was hard for him to keep other images out of his head, but he pushed through them and leaned down to brush his mouth over hers lightly. He paused and just looked down into her eyes, he liked that she looked at him anytime they were this close, it was like the power of her look was enough to bat the demons away in his mind. "I never thought I'd want to kiss someone." He whispered, "but your taste is the most perfect thing I've ever experienced."

Her response to his words was reaching up and gently pulling his head toward her face. He almost grinned as their mouths touched again. Then the feelings started inside him, the ones only she could ever stir inside him. He feared them, loved them, and never wanted to not feel them again. His hand shook as he gripped her hips and pulled her body close enough that he could feel the heat from her body. His insides felt like they were ignited now. Taking a chance that he wouldn't offend her; he deepened the kiss. She made a soft moaning noise, and he was ready to pull away, afraid he was scaring her or hurting her, she grasped the back of his hair and pulled his head down further. Noah thought his heart might explode inside his chest, and another body part he was trying not to think about because he didn't want to stop kissing her.

When they finally separated it was because neither of them could breathe. He rested his forehead on hers and relished that he was breathing her breath inside him. It felt natural and right and so few things he did ever felt like that to him. "Did you," he swallowed trying to settle his breathing so he could speak, "do you know how the marking works?"

Hearing her accelerated breathing was doing strange things to him, and it took him a moment to check on his cat that it wasn't a bad thing. She nodded, then grinned at him as she continued to struggle with her breathing.

"The woman," she drew in another breath, "the woman has to mark the man first." Her eyes widened, "it's a consent thing."

Noah lifted his head and looked down at her. Her eyes were heavy from the feelings they had been stirring in each other and to him, it was the most beautiful sight he'd ever seen. The idea of carrying her mark and scent mixed with his own made him feel a small measure of peace inside. His cat was very enthused by the idea and other than killing that was the only time Noah could remember his cat being that way. "It should be a consent thing. Always." He was talking about more than just the marking and he knew that she would know that without him having to spell it out. "Do it." He leaned down and kissed her mouth softly.

Emersyn's eyes widened slightly, then she nodded slowly. She touched her mouth, "do you think my cat will know? My teeth are normal right now."

Noah had no idea; he knew nothing about this. He'd actually walked away a few times when the guys were talking about things like this. "I think she will." He hoped. He kissed her again, without warning, without slow cautious movements, and feeling her respond to him made his cat move even closer to the surface. It wasn't a cautious thing, or to protect him, but to observe. If he were anything but a shifter, he would find that creepy as hell. He started to think of her teeth piercing his flesh and expected nausea to kick in, but instead, he realized it would be the only welcomed scar on his body.

Dragging his mouth from hers, he lightly held her hips and then dropped down to his knees so she could reach his neck easily. Releasing her, he pulled his jacket off and then his shirt quickly. He'd seen the marks on the others and knew where he would be. His mate's mark. A dizzying feeling went through him, he froze thinking it was the ill feeling coming out of nowhere as usual, but then realized it was anticipation and nothing bad.

Emersyn ripped the zipper down on her jacket and brushed it from her arms. She placed her hands on either side of his face and looked down at him. Noah's hands clenched in a nervous move on her hips. He wanted her to hurry, if not he might lose his mind. He could count on one hand the number of times he'd looked forward to something and still have a finger or two left, but this, *this* made up for all of it. Having her as his mate made up for the years of wrong in his world.

She lowered her mouth to his and kissed him, taking control of the kiss and he was completely shocked by his own reaction to it—his cat felt like he was doing flips inside him, which made the frenzy of the moment even more intense.

Noah stabbed his tongue into her mouth and groaned when it met sharp teeth. He could taste blood and knew it was theirs mixed, his cat froze when he sensed her blood mixed with her taste and scent. It was intoxicating and both were almost to their limit by the time she lifted her head and tilted his chin up.

Noah's chest shook with each breath he took, and a low animalistic sound came from his throat when he felt her breath on his skin. It was right below where his collar would have rested and his only thought at that moment was the collar would never leave its mark on him again, but he would be wearing hers. It was complete gibberish, and he knew it and for once didn't give a damn what was going through his broken mind.

When her teeth pierced his flesh, his grip tightened on her hips. He hissed out a breath, his animal did much the same. He could feel the change running through him as their scents mixed and thought he might drop to the floor in ecstasy when she released him.

As soon as she removed her feline teeth from his flesh, she licked over it and then grasped his hair and kissed him with such passion he could barely catch up to her. He wanted to and there was never a time he thought he would want to kiss someone this way.

Emersyn tore her mouth from his and held his face between her hands, "mark me, Noah," her breathless voice sent a shiver through him.

If he thought about it, he knew something would go wrong and he'd overthink himself right out of doing it, so he didn't give himself or his cat the chance. Running his hands down the side of her legs, he cupped her behind the knees, so she would drop onto his lap. He wanted to hold her while he did this, show her that touch could be with love. And he did, he realized, he did love her. She was his strength when he thought it was lost forever.

When she moved to take off her shirt, he shook his head, he didn't want her to feel exposed or vulnerable, not with him, not ever again. He brushed the hair back from her neck and leaned down to kiss the soft skin. A light tug on the sleeve revealed the spot he needed access to. When he kissed her throat again, she moaned softly and his whole body sang in a reply to her. His cat was getting impatient now and he really couldn't blame him, she was theirs and they needed everyone to know it, to step cautiously when near her.

Pressing his nose into her skin, he inhaled her scent inside of him and he felt his teeth change against his tongue. His cat was always that close. He closed his eyes and touched the back of her head with care as he bit into her flesh. The taste of her blood hit him and then his cat—everything changed without warning. A feeling of panic and vileness flooded into him so suddenly, he pulled back from her and licked over the mark, and then set her gently from him.

He scrambled to his feet and darted for the door, ripping it open. He didn't make it two steps before his stomach started to lurch inside him. He leaned on his knees and bent over, trying to breathe through his nose and stop the terror that was flashing every bad thing he'd seen through his mind.

"Noah." She was right beside him.

Panting for air, hoping to be able to speak, he reached his hand toward her, "It's not you." He clamped his mouth closed through the next wave. "It's not you." He said again because he wasn't sure if he'd spoken the words out loud the first time.

She placed her hand on his back near his shoulder blades and rubbed it gently. "I know." She leaned over and rested her cheek against his shoulder, and he stayed hunched over. "Slow your breathing, through your nose." She said softly.

Noah nodded and reached back with his hand again and held what he thought maybe her thigh. He tried to draw in a slow breath as she said but his stomach lurched again.

"You're not there anymore, Noah."

It sounded like she was whispering it right in his ear, he couldn't be sure, but her voice, her nearness seemed to be helping him fight his way back out of the dark place.

"You're here with me now." She continued, "we're going to start a new life together that will be what we want." Her tone sent a shiver down his spine, and he realized she was talking his cat down with each word.

He nodded his head but was afraid if he tried to talk, he would throw up. He'd been fooled too many times into thinking his body was settling only to have it flare up again.

"I'm getting cold," she said softly, "we can go inside and open a window and sit beside it."

He drew a deep breath through his nose again and then nodded. Very slowly, he straightened all while measuring what his body's reaction was to the movement. It seemed to be subsiding. If he moved slowly, he could get her back in the house where she'd be warm.

Noah didn't see a thing as she guided him into the house again and to the wall. He lowered himself and sat down resting his arms on his raised knees and blew out long breathes, trying to get it under control.

He felt her wrap his jacket over his shoulders and his chest contracted with the emotion of her genuine show of concern for him. He knew the others worried about him all the time, but none of it compared to this. He heard her open the window a bit and then she sat down beside him. When she rested her head on his shoulder, he lifted his head and looked at her. Just that fast, his cat was calmed and settling down. His gaze landed on the bite on her neck and that was it, his cat realized that the blood was from that.

"It wasn't you." He said softly. Closing his eyes, he took a few relaxed breaths and then looked at her again. "I can't—any time I think of touching a female," he watched to see she was completely focused on him, her eyes showing patience and understanding, "even the slightest touch," he bounced his fingertips off the side of his head, "it takes me back there." Why were her eyes filling with tears? "It had nothing to do with you." He reached over and moved her jacket aside so he could see the full bite, his mark on her. "It's nothing to do with that." He flicked his eyes to see hers were still sparkling with unfallen tears. "I'm sorry if I ruined it."

She shook her head and wiped her hand over her eyes. "You didn't ruin it." She leaned around and moved his jacket to see his, "I was actually panicking about what came next."

He snorted, "we are so broken we're fucking perfect." He mumbled it, but she still smiled.

"I agree. To the perfect part." She tilted her head to the side and searched his face, he didn't know what she was looking for, but her posture relaxed so it must have been there. "We should go inside soon." Her eyes momentarily rounded, "Aspyn will be a ball of energy tomorrow and talk non-stop about her sleepover."

Noah pretended to wince, "maybe it's good I won't be here."

She smirked, but then her look changed. "I will miss you."

"I know this is going to be," he shook his head, "nothing like what a normal mated relationship is like, but I have to do this, you understand that right?"

She nodded. "I know and I don't begrudge that you are, not at all." She reached over and touched his cheek softly, "you'll find them all and free them to discover their new lives, Noah, I know you will."

He leaned closer and pulled her head toward his. Resting his forehead on hers, he closed his eyes and just wanted to sit there like that forever. Close, their breathing in sync with the others, peaceful. Before he moved away, he kissed her forehead and then took her hand. "Let's go in the house and chase some sleep."

She laughed softly, "that's the best description of it I've ever heard."

He pulled her to her feet, and she placed her hand on his bare chest and looked up at him.

"You're not sleeping in a different room when you come back."

He watched the look in her eyes and wondered where she was going with it.

"We can chase sleep together in the same bed." Her face flushed slightly, "it might be hit-and-miss for a while, but I just want you close to me when you are home, is that okay?"

Noah rubbed his hand over his beard briskly. "I'd like to try." He leaned down and kissed her mouth, "my demons seem to be afraid of you, so maybe the nightmares will stop." He knew that would never happen, but he also hoped what he said was true or at least possible.

"Okay." She yawned, then covered her mouth.

Noah went over and picked up his shirt, "if you want, we can try tonight." The idea of feeling her close to him through the terror of the night, when he was at his absolute weakest was very appealing to him. He hadn't been making it up when he said his demons were afraid of her.

"I'll go change and come to your room." Her face was flushed, a nervous look in her eyes.

Noah just nodded, because if he tried to speak right now, he was afraid he might swallow his tongue. He had found and lost his mate, then found her again and now she wore his mark for all their kind to see. He watched her go to the door and hoped this wasn't some sort of dream that would turn into a nightmare like all the rest.

Chapter Forty-Three

Noah quickly picked up the clothes he tripped over and tossed them in the direction of the basket in the corner. He paused to see it was full. When had he had time to do laundry? Going over, he yanked open the dresser drawer and was relieved to see he had another pair of jeans left to pack for tomorrow.

Closing it, he turned in a circle and looked around the room. Emersyn was sleeping in here tonight. Why had he thought that was a good idea? Putting his hands on his hips, he tried to settle his breathing so he wouldn't freak out. He looked down at the jeans he wore, and his eyes rounded, he couldn't sleep naked, not with her in the bed.

After tearing through two drawers, he finally found the track pants Beth had bought him. Pulling them out he looked at them. They reminded him of the loose pants they made him wear all those years. It was these or naked.

Stripping off his jeans he stabbed his legs into the soft material and pulled them up. Looking down at them, he sneered, he hated the feeling of them brushing against his legs.

Shaking his head, he turned around and looked at the bed. There was only one pillow. Lunging for the bed, he crawled across the mattress. Where was his other pillow? He couldn't' share one pillow with her. He looked between the wall and the mattress, and it wasn't there. Checking the top of the bed, he got off and looked underneath. It was a pillow; how hard would it be to see? Grabbing the blankets that were balled up, like they usually were after a night of wrestling in his sleep, he was relieved when the pillow fell out of them.

He placed it at the head of the bed and brushed it off like it was dusty or some shit. This was not going well. He was out of breath like he'd just run ten miles. He untangled the sheet from the blanket and shook it out, trying to get it to land on the bed neatly. He'd watched Kelsey do it and she had some kind of magic that made it float onto the bed like a feather. His landed in a twisted strip in the middle of the bed. Dropping it, he rushed around the bed to fix it and almost took his ankle off on the bedframe. Cursing, he dropped down to rub the bone as pain shot up his leg.

A light tap on the door had him freeze, panic paralyzing him for a few seconds. Jumping up, he opened the door and the breath whooshed out of his lungs when he saw her. Had she gotten more beautiful in the last five minutes? He was sure she had. When he realized he was staring at her, he shuffled out of the way so she could come in.

He closed the door and then the room felt like it shrunk. His eyes flicked to the window, did it even open?

"Have you talked yourself out of it yet?" She gave him a tender look.

Hissing out a breath, he shook his head, "not yet, but my head is working on it." He would always tell her the truth, even if she didn't like it.

Nodding her head slowly, she turned and looked at the bed and tilted her head to the side. Without a word, she went over and took a hold of the sheet and lifted it in the air and did this motion with her wrists and the sheet landed across the bed like ripples in the water. Apparently, it was female magic to work a bedsheet properly.

"I changed twice." She said in a soft nervous way, "which is silly because they're basically the same outfit, just different patterns." She walked to the end of the bed and picked up the heavy blanket.

Noah stood there unable to move. He watched her work the blanket with the same ease as she had the sheet. She moved silently, with grace and he was awestruck by it. He blinked and looked at what she was wearing. The bottoms were loose and seemed to flow around her. Pattern, what had she said about the pattern? It looked like paint splotches on the material to him. When she finished adjusting the blanket, she turned around and he looked at the rest of her outfit. The top hugged tight to her skin and his mouth dried up. Her arms were bare, and a small portion of her waist too, the rest of the material outlined her form beneath it. She looked so fragile and lovely; it made his chest tighten. When he realized he was ogling her, he jerked his gaze up to look at her face but was distracted along the way by the very clear bite mark on her throat. His bite mark. *Mine*. His cat interjected into his thoughts. Clearing his throat, he finally took a step toward her. "You look lovely." His voice cracked with the strain of forcing the words to leave his mouth.

Her cheeks flushed and she lowered her eyes for a moment. "You make me feel that way when you look at me." She smoothed her hand over her stomach and took a shaky breath. "Do you mind if I sleep next to the wall?" She lifted her lashes and looked back at him, "it's-it's I always put my back to the wall."

Noah nodded, he had *no* problem with that, he needed to be near the edge in case he had to get up fast. He frowned, what if the dreams were bad and he started flinging his arms around? He could hit her. This was such a bad idea.

"I can see you working on talking yourself right out of it." She gave him a patient look.

"I-I don't want to accidentally hit you in my…"

"I sleep with a four-year-old, Noah, trust me, no one can compete with how much they flip around." She leaned over the bed and pulled the bedding back. "I get elbowed, kicked, head-butted," she glanced over her shoulder at him, "we'll be fine."

He blew out a shaky breath and nodded again. "Okay." He took a step toward the bed, then stopped and motioned to it.

Her smile was slow, but it was breathtaking once she did. Her eyes flicked to the bed then back to him, "this is so silly."

Noah was thinking more terrifying than silly.

"How hard can it be, right? Couples do it every day."

She was talking softly, and he wasn't sure if it was to him or herself, so he kept his mouth closed. He watched her crawl across the bed and for the first time he was glad they hadn't listened to him and had gotten him a full-size bed. If they'd gotten the single, he suggested they would have had to sleep so close—he shook his head, he couldn't take that further or this would be over before it began.

"Noah?"

Blinking, he looked to see her on the other side of the bed, her legs under the cover, sitting there looking at him.

"Are you going to get in the bed or stand there all night?" She smirked.

He lunged for the bed and got in it fast before he changed his mind. He sat there, his legs under the covers, and looked down. He should have put a shirt on, but when he started sweating, it clung to him, and his unconscious mind thought of bloodied material sticking to him. "I can't sleep with a shirt on." He mumbled, keeping his eyes on the blanket.

Emersyn reached over and touched his shoulder; her hand was warm. "That's fine." She lay down, pulling on his arm lightly as she did it.

Noah coughed out a deep breath and lay back until his head was on the pillow. He held his body stiff and looked up at the ceiling. That's when he realized the light was on. Flipping the covers back, he got up and flipped the switch off.

Getting back in the bed, he yanked the covers and lay there, breathing shallowly.

He heard Emersyn laugh quietly. "I'm thinking, now what?"

"Yeah." He squeezed his eyes shut. "The others are so lucky they know how to do this together stuff."

"Maybe."

The bed shifted as she moved around, and he wanted to turn to see what she was doing but didn't want to know at the same time.

"Why don't we start with something simple and easy?"

He did turn to see her lying on her side looking at him.

Her hand moved down his arm to his hand. "Just hold hands."

Noah forced his clenched fist to open, so she could thread her fingers through his. He could do this, hold her hand. He'd kissed her and put his mark on her, holding her hand was easy. He continued to talk to himself, to keep his thoughts focused on simple things so he wouldn't do something to make her regret putting her trust in him.

He had no idea how long he'd done that, but he'd covered quite a few moments in his head that he'd had with her, when her hand relaxed in his, he turned and saw that she was relaxed. She was sleeping. He shifted carefully, almost in slow motion, so he wouldn't disturb her and could still hold her hand.

When he finally managed to get completely on his side, he lay there and look at her. He had a mate, and she was right here in front of him, prettier than any woman he'd ever seen. His cat rolled through him and for once it wasn't in panic or survival mode, it was just because they were here with her.

He was still afraid to fall asleep, in case he hit her when he was flailing around. That happened every night, so why he had thought this would be the exception, he didn't know. This was fine, he could stay up all night and then just nap on the ride tomorrow.

Noah's eyes popped open. Disoriented, he tried to remember if the nightmare had awakened him. When he went to roll over, he couldn't move his arm. Lifting his head, he saw the reason was about five foot five with her back pressed against his front. She was on his arm, but what made him tense was the fact that he had his wrapped around her and she was hugging it to her chest. He was afraid to breathe and didn't want to move and disturb her. Lowering his head, he tried to figure out when he had fallen asleep. He couldn't remember. His cat nudged him, telling him to stop thinking and go back to sleep. Taking a deep breath to try to relax again, he closed his eyes, her scent was everywhere. Moving his head closer, he pushed his nose into her hair and inhaled again. Her scent was different now, still hers, but not at the same time. He wondered if he carried hers like that too.

She sighed in her sleep and moved to press back into him. Noah lay there, waiting to see if she was awake. He needed to focus and stop the brain banter before tension and other bad things started pouring from him and disturbing her. Inhaling through his nose, he breathed it out slowly, forcing his body to relax. Never in all of his life had he ever thought he could lay and hold a woman like this. He smirked and pushed his nose into her hair again, not a woman, Emersyn. Only her.

Chapter Forty-Four

Noah watched the car pull out of Ed's lane and then looked down at Emersyn. She smiled up at him.

"I do like your sister." She said softly.

He squeezed her hand and nodded, "so do I, she's going to be a handful once she shifts."

Emersyn laughed, "if anyone can catch up to her."

Noah turned to see Gage coming out of the house, he saw him note they were holding hands and didn't care one bit what anyone's thoughts or opinions were. Last night, through the night, and this morning, being with her—no one could take that from him.

He walked over and stopped a good distance and then held out a phone. "Mom put the numbers in."

Noah reached over and took it and then handed it to Emersyn. She looked at him with huge eyes. He grinned, "you said you wanted to call." She nodded and looked down at it like he'd just handed her the most amazing thing ever. He paused and realized it was probably the first thing she had ever been given. "Cooper will show you how to use it." She nodded and hugged it to her chest.

The sound of a truck coming in the drive had them turn to see Blair driving and even from here that there were four people in it. He glanced over at the van and knew they'd be leaving in a few minutes.

Kelsey came out and down the porch steps, she smiled at Emersyn with a genuine smile and then held her hand out to him. Noah frowned at it.

"Do you want me to put her number in your phone or were you going to try to guess it later?" She smirked at him.

He shook his head and then took out his phone and handed it to her.

At the sound of the truck door closing, Noah turned to see Blair coming over. "Your little one is a *bundle* of energy." He smiled at Emersyn. "Kels can take you over to pick her up if you want, she was busy with Daisie watching the TV when we left."

Emersyn smiled, "Was she good?"

"She was fine." Kobie came around the truck and Noah didn't miss the look that passed between the two women.

Blair stopped and cocked his head to the side, an odd smirk on his face, but didn't say anything.

"All your gear in the van?" Calum walked around with his arm around Shaelan.

Noah nodded, "Yeah, filled it up too, so we didn't have to stop for a while."

Calum turned back to the truck. "I'll just get Shae's gear stowed."

Shaelan came over and looked from him to Emersyn, a knowing look on her face.

Noah had to wonder if they could smell what had taken place between them last night or if it was something else.

Emersyn looked up at him. "Stop overthinking it." She said softly.

Noah couldn't help the grin, "that's kind of what I do." He said still smiling.

"I know."

"Here you go." Kelsey handed the phone back to him, "and don't worry we will all watch over each others' places while you're away." Gage moved to put his arm around her and nodded his agreement to what she said.

"Everyone ready?" Calum came back, "Devin's been messaging me every five minutes with more details."

Noah sucked in a breath; the details were good. The more they knew the better this would go. He nodded his head to Gage and then turned to go to the van. He didn't make it a foot before he turned around and grasped Emersyn's hand lightly and pulled her to walk with him.

Gage and Kelsey went back up on the porch and the other couples were already in the van.

He stopped and looked down at her, "anything feels off at any time, you tell Coop or one of the guys, okay?"

She nodded.

"Cooper is going to get the lights put up outside the house, but don't be out there at night working without locking the door, okay?"

She nodded again and then reached up and put her hand over his mouth. "I will be fine. All of us will be. *You* be careful." She stretched up and kissed his mouth when she moved her hand off it.

Noah took a ragged breath, "I will." He stepped back a step and then another and let their hands drop away from each other. If the men weren't watching him, he would have taken a picture of her right now, so he could look anytime he wanted to.

He didn't make it to the van before he was walking back to her. He wanted to pick her up and kiss her but knew one or both of them would have a bad moment if he did that, so when he reached her, he touched her chin so he could kiss her again. "I'll call you when we make the first stop."

She nodded.

He forced his body to turn to go to the van.

"Noah?"

He stopped and turned around but didn't go any closer or he may not go at all.

"You come back here safely—and, Noah, if you see any of the ones responsible," she paused and held his look with something he could only label as fierce, "you do what you have to do to make sure they never hurt anyone again."

Noah dragged a deep breath into his chest and nodded to her. Before he could change his mind, he turned around and climbed into the back of the van, and settled on the back seat. He watched her go over to the porch and stand at the bottom step.

"Did she just tell you to annihilate anyone that's helped Tomas?"

He looked at Blair as he turned in the seat in front of him and nodded.

Blair grinned wide, "damn, I like her style." He bobbed his head. "That looks good on you, by the way." He made a point of looking at Noah's neck then reached over and played with Kobie's hair, "you're a hell of a lot stronger than I am to leave her behind." Kobie turned her head and smiled at him, "I couldn't do it."

"She understands that I have to do this." He said, even though he was thinking he had to keep moving. Noah looked to see Calum glance in the mirror, "what details has Devin been sending?"

Calum smiled and looked at him in the mirror again just before he turned out onto the road, "I'll go over them when we stop, but it's good for us."

Blair bobbed his head and then glanced over his shoulder, "the kind of good that will let your scary one come out and play." Kobie swatted him.

Noah did what he usually did in a vehicle and started thinking about things. It was probably the first time ever that he had some good things to reflect on.

Noah turned and looked out the window, a little surprised with how far they'd driven already, how long had he been zoning out. Then realized he wasn't feeling cramped being in the vehicle. He frowned and checked on his cat and was surprised that he was just there, under the surface as always.

His cat let him know that he was there with him and wouldn't let him down if they found any of the ones their mate had referred to, he would avenge all the innocents.

His phone buzzed in his pocket, he pulled it out and opened it to see it was from Emersyn, he stiffened and opened the message. It was a picture of her and Aspyn smiling. His heart contracted in his chest. He would never let them down. Someone must have helped her send this, he thought. He wasn't good with texting, at all, his vocabulary was too basic to not sound like a robot, and he sure as hell wasn't asking Blair to help. He hit reply and scrolled through the emojis and tapped the heart symbol the hit send. He looked at the picture and then inhaled and closed it. As long as he had them waiting for him back home, he would be able to do this with the teams until every last one responsible for ruined lives, was gone.

Calum's phone rang. He reached over and tapped it. "Jesse, did you manage to get out of there without Thera?" He could see Calum's smirk in the mirror.

"Yeah, we're on our way now."

"What's wrong?"

Noah looked at the phone on the dash and then at the reflection of Calum's dark eyes in the mirror. How did he know something was wrong with one sentence spoken?

Blair leaned forward in his seat.

"You know Tripp Carson, right? How good is he at his job and tracking?"

Calum glanced in the mirror, probably at Blair, "he's special ops, he's better than good. Why?"

Noah leaned forward, not that he needed to, but the tension in the vehicle had just increased a lot and if something was going to go to shit, he wanted to be prepared.

"Amari hasn't checked in the last two times."

"Where was she? There's some big dead zone North…"

"She was back from those." Jesse sounded tense.

"Has Zain tried tracking her?" Calum glanced over his shoulder this time and made eye contact with Blair.

"That's the thing, he has it running all the time now, day or night on all the co-ord team and hers just stopped."

"He won't let Thera and I go look."

Noah didn't have to ask if it was Leah or Evanna with him right now. There was no way Leah would ever want to do such a thing.

"Tripp is on route to her last known location?" Calum was wise not to agree or disagree with what Evanna had said.

"Yes. Shepard called him personally."

Calum nodded, "yeah they know each other pretty well." Calum rubbed his hand on the back of his neck, "if a lot wasn't going on right now, I'd go lend a hand, but if Tripp is on it," he looked over at Shaelan, "he'll find her, you can be sure of that."

"I trust your judgment, Cal," he didn't sound reassured, "It's just, she's female, Alpha, one hell of a bargaining chip."

Noah scowled out the window, his cat was not happy with that at all.

"I feel bad if anyone did try to mess with her, Jesse, it's Amari." Calum's tone was light, but his expression was nothing close to it.

Jesse scoffed, "right. Maybe I should pray for them."

"Keep me up-to-date if you hear anything before, we meet up."

"Will do. We're about forty-five minutes behind, but we'll be there." Evanna said something Noah couldn't make out. "See you then."

"Yeah." Calum reached over and tapped the phone.

"You trust this Tripp person will find her?" Shaelan asked him, concern bleeding from her tone.

Calum reached over and took her hand in his, "if anyone can track her down, it will be Tripp. He's like a ghost in the bush and the last man you'd want to cross."

Blair snorted, "sounds like our kind of person."

Noah turned and looked out the window. Reaching their destination couldn't happen fast enough now. His cat was going to be in a mood the whole ride, just hearing another female had been taken brought some of the darkness, that Emersyn had brightened, back inside them both. The darkness was always going to be there, he understood that now, working with the teams was going to be his outlet to purge it when it was riding him hard. Just as long as he had Emersyn to go back to, all that crossed his path would survive.

KEEP READING FOR AN EXCERPT OF

Pride

Animal Senses Series Book 9

By Jacqueline Paige

Chapter One

Tripp reached in and grabbed his pack. Shepard Addison asking him to do this personally wasn't unheard of, but he had to wonder if this missing female was more important than he was told. Not that all females weren't important—they were, but why have the king ask and not his team leader? Could be he was the closest, but his gut said otherwise, and it was never wrong. Pulling out the map, he opened it on the seat and then checked his phone to see the last location she'd been at.

He stabbed his finger into the map at the location and then dragged it along the map for a few inches. Mountains were close to where she was last tracked. If she'd gone in that direction to head to the meet-up with the teams, it wasn't going to be a good time. If she wasn't just lost and someone did get to her, there were a hundred different ways they could move undetected and vanish, especially with the help of the snow heading that way.

"Shit." Folding the map, he stuffed it back in the pack. It was a long drive from where he currently was. So much for his being the closest theory. He'd wanted to be in on the ops to get more of Konner Flores people out. He smirked, remembering how much spunk Terah had when he'd found them. Curiosity had him wondering if they were all that fast and strong. Now he would never know.

He was going to need enough supplies for a long trek. He looked down at his bare feet, and his boots, those would be a good start. He'd only stopped to go for a quick run and grab a bite to eat before driving to the rendezvous location for the ops.

Walking to the back of his SUV, he opened it up and grabbed his boots. Before he could get the first one done up his phone rang. No number came up. "Carson."

"It's Zain Sanders, I'm the office director for Jesse's team."

Director? aka office guy. Pulling the sock out of his boot, he sat on the bumper and pulled it on.

"I checked your location and have arranged a flight for you to get to Amari's last known location."

He paused for a second and then jammed his foot into his boot. "A flight?" Only one thing in this world turned his stomach, or rather his animal's, and that was flying. Tripp had been in planes, helicopters, even tried cliff gliding and all of them were a big nope. His feet needed to be able to always reach the ground—like a nervous ass noob learning to swim. He clicked his teeth together, it *would* get him there faster, then he might be able to get in on the second wave of the ops. "All right."

"I'll send you the location." This guy's voice told him he was one step from freaking out.

"Can you give me more details on this Amari?" If he could get a sense of what she was like, he might better understand what he was walking into. If she had been taken, would she fight her abductors or just shut down and accept her fate? He'd dealt with both before. He honestly wasn't sure which was the hardest to deal with.

"Like what?" He heard a door close and then boots on tiles. "Sorry, just pissed at myself, I'm the one that told her to start heading to the meet and not wait for one of the incursion team," he snorted, "not that she would have waited."

That explained his next question as to why she was alone. "How long since her trackers went offline?"

"She hasn't checked in for four hours and the trail stops three hours ago."

Shit. Three hours in that area could have her anywhere. He opened his mouth to ask if it was possible she was offline on purpose, but Zain hissed out a deep breath.

"I don't want to have to call her family. It's not going to go well if I do."

Tripp was glad that task was never part of his job. He liked doing his job and someone else dealing with emotional people. "Hopefully you won't have to."

"It will be a shit show if I do." A door slammed and he could hear the echo of traffic now. "The last thing I need right now, that Jesse needs is an angry Alpha all up in his face, not to mention Amari..."

It was like fireworks went off in his head, "Alpha?"

"You weren't told? She's an Alpha's daughter."

Tripp straightened and squeezed the bridge of his nose. "No." She was an Alpha's daughter, which shed some light on the urgency in everyone's tone—light brighter than a thousand-watt lightbulb. He opened his eyes and then stood up, "Okay," he nodded and then shut the hatch. "Any chance she's just lost?" He went back to the front and climbed in, "there's a lot of mountains in that area, the signal could be..."

"No. She's not lost."

Closing the door, he realized he didn't have a direction to go yet. "Can you send me a pic, so I know who I'm looking for?" The chances of seeing a crowd of people in that area were slim, but he still needed a confirmed target. He cringed at his own thought, she wasn't the target...

"Uh, yeah, but she's easy to notice, blond, attitude."

Tripp shrugged; attitude could describe ten different personality types. "Okay, send me the location. I'll head there now."

"Right. Okay." He could hear him running now. "Update me as soon as you get there, so I can let the team know." He swore, "the last thing we need is them distracted."

Tripp nodded. "Will do." It was an automated response and the only one he had right now. When the line went quiet, he looked at the phone and then opened his team leaders' number and typed *123,* and hit send. That was their way of saying, call me if you're able.

An Alpha's daughter. Fucking A, just what he needed.

His phone lit up and he looked down at the information on it. He didn't need to look at the map to figure out where he was meeting his lift in, he'd driven by it a half-hour ago. Jamming his phone into the holder, he started the SUV and turned around.

He didn't get fifty feet before his phone lit up again. That Zain was fast. He liked that. Tapping the screen, he opened the picture and then slammed on the brakes. In the photo was a man and his daughter, all dressed up. He barely looked at her, but the man, he knew all too well.

It was Alpha Vesper Hughes, the leader of one of the two cougar clans in Ontario. Tripp stomped on the gas and would have given himself whiplash if his muscles hadn't already been rock-hard with tension.

Alpha Hughes was an asshole. How did he know this was one hundred percent correct? He'd met the man eight years earlier. It had been a dark and trying time in his life. His father had been killed, for the Alliance and for the protection of another clan. Staying with the clan just brought it all up for his mother over and over again. So, she and his younger sister wanted to leave. Tripp had traveled with them for three weeks, staying off the radar to get them to Ontario only to hit a brick wall at the end of it. That brick wall was Vesper Hughes. He didn't want any outsiders added to his clan unless they were mated in. If it had been up to Tripp, he would have taken his family to Mae's clan instead, but his mother wanted to be with a cousin—he still wasn't sure of the connection, just knew that sometime since the dawn of time their bloodlines had crossed.

When Hughes had called for assistance against the rouge shifter, he met Kenzo Dean. *Rouge shifter,* he sneered. Kenzo was the first man in Tripp's life he'd feared. He smirked, now he worked with him on the same team. He wondered if Kenzo remembered that first meeting too.

Shortly after that, he'd met Shepard Addison and the second man he feared, Calum Dante. He didn't know Calum that well, but since then had worked with him a few times and he respected the hell out of that man, he truly did. He scowled at the picture again, then tapped the screen so it wouldn't go to sleep. The result of that turbulent time was his mother and sister were allowed to be part of that clan and Tripp—was never allowed to step a foot on the clan's land again.

Now—he had to go rescue that man's daughter. He blew out a breath and grabbed the phone. Balancing his wrist over the steering wheel, he enlarged the picture so Alpha Asshole wasn't on the screen. The daughter was wearing some off-the-shoulder dress and smiling like the princess she undoubtedly was. He squinted at it, okay, she was cute as hell with her big, beautiful eyes and pouty lips, but still, she was Alpha Asshole's daughter. "Fuck." He jammed the phone back in the holder and glared at the road. If it weren't for all the ops happening right now, he'd beg one of the others to take over and do this instead of him. Rescuing those held by one-forms was much more rewarding than going in to get some pampered, precious Alpha's daughter. Seriously, what the hell was she doing on one of the Alliance teams? He rolled his eyes, probably whined to daddy, who arranged it and got her the position—and he was going to have to go in a plane to go get her. Knuckles white, he growled at the road in front of him.

KEEP READING FOR AN EXCERPT OF

Mystic Perceptions

Mystic Gifts Trilogy Book 1

By Jacqueline Paige

Prologue

Jacinda didn't remember how she got home. Vague recollections of telling the cab driver her address, but the dizziness had been so bad, she could only focus on not throwing up inside the cab.

Once inside the front door, she slid to the floor hoping her parents weren't home. The pain fueled the dizzy feelings that made her feel as if she was floating. How could her skull be hurting this bad, but her brain feel like it was not attached?

"Jac?"

Her mother's voice was garbled. She tried to lift her head but couldn't find the strength. It happened again Mom, is what she wanted to say, but was afraid if she tried to talk, she would be sick.

"Oh no baby, not again."

She could feel her mother move her off the floor. She was sure she was moving her own feet, but couldn't be certain; she'd have to ask when she came to again. Just please don't let me throw up on my mother, she prayed silently.

"I knew going to such a large, public place was going to be bad. So many people, too many things to touch."

She recognized the worry in her mother's voice and could hear the fear. She'd had to try, just once more to know this would happen to her everywhere, every time. She had only wanted to help an old man get his stuff into his car. The vile thoughts in his mind were hidden behind a warm smile. How could she have ever guessed?

Jac felt her mom's gentle hands touch her forehead, trying to sooth the ache.

"I'll bring you a cool compress to help with the nausea. Just close your eyes and focus on staying calm."

Closing her eyes, Jac took a deep, slow, cleansing breath. Her head was still swimming. I'm such a freak. Wasn't it bad enough when they pulled me out of school? Thirteen and forced to live without a social life. She wondered if her friends really missed her, there hadn't been many phone calls in the last few months. I'll be the ghost no one ever sees.

Rolling slowly and carefully onto her side, not sure which was worse, headache, dizziness, or the urge to throw up all over the place. Her mother's voice carried from the hallway. She'd called her dad, which wasn't surprising. She supposed she was lucky her parents hadn't labeled her a mutant child and put her in some hospital to be studied. They were one of a kind, that much she knew. How many parents would be so accepting of a daughter that saw the past through furniture and other objects? Or that saw someone's emotions by touching them? Not many, she guessed.

"We'll get through this, Jac—no matter what it takes."
She relaxed and let the sleep she was fighting pull her under further. Her mother's words meant everything to her.

1

She stared up at the beams before her eyes rolled closed again, her arms were suddenly so heavy she didn't want to move.

Blinking she watched him as the tightness in her chest increased and her stomach heaved again—she couldn't struggle against it anymore...her face was so hot...so cold...

She focused on him through the blurriness for as long as she could and knew, somehow, they would find him...

Jacinda glared at the phone for a second and then put it back to her ear. "Thanks. Somewhere in the office really narrows it down for me, Sandy." She sighed. "I'll call you later. I am tearing this place apart until I find that stupid receipt." She snarled at the giggle on the other end of the phone.

"Don't get lost in there. You're supposed to meet me in two hours."

Jacinda stood up and studied the office, trying to decide on a starting point. "Yeah, yeah, I'll be there." Hanging up the phone, she put her hands on her hips and surveyed the piles of folders and papers scattered all over the two desks in the small, cluttered space.

Sighing, she grabbed a hair clip off the desk and twisted up her long dark hair. She frowned when it took two attempts to get most of it secured in the clip. One of these times she was going to give in and cut it all off. She rolled her eyes at her own thoughts. Of course, she'd been saying that for most of her adult life, so the chances of it actually happening were not high.

"Okay, so if I were a paid bill, where would I be hiding?" She hefted a box up from the floor. Being short did not help when your desktop reached your waist. Pulling out a handful of envelopes, she started shuffling through them. "Thanks for talking me out of a filing cabinet, Sandy—, boxes are so much more organized…" She smirked. Her friend probably meant for her to actually label the boxes and put them in the large closet. It was on her list of things to do. Eventually.

Halfway through the second box, she was mumbling obscenities for procrastinating with keeping some sort of order. Someday, an amazing client was going to walk through that door and money would fall from the sky. She smirked. Right, you ninny, the dust from the boxes has clogged your brain. Sighing, she pulled out more envelopes. Be careful what you wish for she thought as she dug in again.

By the time she reached the fourth box, she was ready to throw them all in a trash bin and light it on fire. "You'd think if I were one of the few paid bills, I'd be jumping right out of the box to be seen." She slid her hands lightly over the papers. Nothing. "Couldn't have a skill that would be useful when I needed it could I?" She sifted through another pile. "Oh no, I get the ability to see, but never anything I want…"

"Am I interrupting?"

Jacinda spun around towards the door. A tall, tailored blonde woman stood in the doorway. Her eyes were darting all over the messy room. Jacinda straightened up and brushed her hands off on her jeans. "No, of course not." She looked around the room. "Please ignore the mess. I've been—sorting things." The woman looked upset, but Jacinda resisted the urge to touch her and find out for herself if she truly was. "May I help you?" She watched her look down at a small card she held and then glanced around the room.

"I'm, uh, looking for a Jacque Brown."

Jacinda resisted the urge to stomp her foot at the masculine pronunciation of her name, yet again. Was the letter k really that necessary? "I'm Jac Brown." She studied her; there was something vaguely familiar about her. "Do I know you?" The blonde woman looked relieved.

"I'm Amanda Azaire." She held up the card and looked at the shorter woman. "I found your card in my sister's things." She glanced around. "Can—can I come in for a moment?"

Azaire. Why did she know that name? She motioned to the small table and two chairs in the corner. "Please, come in and sit." Azaire cosmetics. That was it. The woman's sister, what was her name? Lonie? Laura? Leslie …

"My sister Lanie is missing."

Lanie. She studied the woman sitting at the table looking suddenly lost and childlike. "Ah, right I helped your sister earlier this year." She sat down and chewed the inside of her lip for a moment. "What do you mean missing?" Large gray eyes looked back at her.

"I haven't been able to reach her for days." She wrung her hands together in her lap. "That's not like Lanie. She's never out of touch. We were supposed to be going away a few days, she would have let me know if—if…"

Not needing any sort of special abilities to know what came next, Jacinda reached over and set a box of Kleenex in front of her. She sat through the sniffling and tears for a few moments. "I don't do that sort of investigating Miss Azaire."

She sniffled again. "Please call me Mandy." She took a slow, shaky breath. "I know you don't, but I've already talked to the police." She took another breath. "And they say I need to file a formal report." She paused, biting her bottom lip for a moment. "To do that, I'd have to tell Daddy and if—if Lanie is just off somewhere, somewhere…"

"Oh, I see." Tell Daddy? She fought the urge to roll her eyes. Well, okay so Daddy running the largest cosmetics industry might run into some serious problems if word got out one of his children were missing, or worse, thought to be missing, when they're just off somewhere being human. "I really don't know what I can do."

She shrugged. "I was desperate and thought, I don't know—maybe you could check places and be a little less noticeable then if I were to do it."

Ah yes, being a nobody would of course be of assistance to someone like her... Jac's mind flew back to the bills that were due. Maybe being nobody sucked, but if she were paid for it, that would be a good thing. "I've never really done this sort of investigative research." She paused when a hopeful look appeared in the younger woman's eyes. "But I suppose I could poke around a bit and see if I can eliminate a few possibilities for you." The not so composed heiress lunged across the table and hugged her tightly.

"Oh, thank you. I don't care what it costs, I'll pay all expenses, just please, please find Lanie for me before Daddy finds out."

The younger woman's emotions flooded into Jacinda's mind, creating an instant tension. Trying to unwrap Amanda's arms, she smiled in a polite way. "Just let me get a pen and paper and I'll get some information from you, okay?" She stifled the urge to jump to the other side of the room out of reach, and shout, 'Don't touch me!' She managed to slowly walk over to her desk and dig out a notebook and pen from the clutter.

Forty-five minutes later, she looked down at the check sitting on top of the notes she'd taken. The photo of Elaine Azaire sat beside it. Now you do missing persons? The number on the check made her feel somewhat shell-shocked. Getting up, she walked over to the phone. Glancing back over to the check sitting a few feet away, she shook her head. The phone rang twice before her friend growled into the other end.

"You're going to stand me up, aren't you?"

Jacinda smirked. "With good reason." There was a chuckle on the other end.

"The only reason good enough would be a tall sexy man."

She grinned. "Or enough money to pay a few overdue bills. You think entirely too much about sex, lady." Sandy shrieked into the phone.

"You've robbed a bank?"

Jac snarled into the phone. "So funny, *ha ha*. No. I have a client and they paid me a lovely deposit."

"A deposit? What are you researching?"

She hesitated. "More of a who than a what."

"A person? You're investigating a person? Jac, you don't do people."

"Well, apparently I do now."

"Who?"

She chewed the inside of her lip. "I can't say."

"What? What do you mean you can't say?"

Jac brushed a pile of envelopes off her chair and sat down. "It's kind of complicated." She glanced at the advanced payment for what had to be the hundredth time. "And they're more or less missing."

"Oh. My. God. You took on a missing person case?"

"Well…" Why did she always stretch out those three words to emphasize her shock?

"I'll be there in ten minutes. Don't move."

She stared at the phone listening to the dial tone. She sighed. She was about to be reminded that people with any sort of ability that were different from the rest of the world were ridiculed and made fun of, or worse, studied like a lab rat.

Having been to a doctor once in her life regarding her special ability, she was examined like she was some sort of contaminated growth. They decided that her brain chemistry was out of balance. The solution, or so she'd been told, was a prescription to restore the balance and prevent the hallucinations. That appointment ended with her telling a rather alarmed doctor that he should tell his wife he was gay and save her the heartache to come.

Hallucinations my butt. She sneered. How could touching someone or an inanimate object bring about a hallucination that revealed emotions and events from the past?

Jacinda sighed and tried to push the feelings aside. It bothered her more than she cared to admit that she couldn't have a normal life, a normal job. She had tried many times and was not interested in putting herself through that again. She could count all the jobs she'd lost because of her gift. Being fired for not showing up or acting weird. Usually from seeing something she wasn't expecting, or the results of seeing something she didn't want. How many times had she regained consciousness with strangers standing over her, looking at her like she was a freak? Too many times.

She took a few deep breaths and brought herself under control. Glancing at the clock, she smirked. She should have timed it to see how quickly Sandy would get here. She loved Sandy, really. Sandy was her external conscience. She kept her from doing one stupid thing after another. She looked at the payment once more. What harm could discreetly looking around for someone cause?

She frowned, admitting to herself she was lying. The last time she had thought like that, things did not turn out well. She ended up having to move. Going through life being able to feel people's emotions and see things, that most times shouldn't be seen, was a hard life. That hard life had left her isolated and alone. She had also learned, the hard way, it was easier to be alone and live privately in a larger city than in a small town.

The last six years had been good, mostly since she met Sandra Gains, but her first thirty years had been trying. Learning to deal with emotions that weren't hers would cause her to be ill, or even pass out. Sandy had helped her find ways to cope, and as long as people didn't suddenly touch her when she wasn't expecting it, she was just fine.

About Jacqueline

Jacqueline Paige lives in Ontario in a small town that's part of the popular Georgian Triangle area.

She began her writing career in 2006 and since her first published works in 2009 she hasn't stopped. Jacqueline describes her writing as *all things paranormal*, which she has proven is her niche with stories of witches, ghosts, physics, and shifters now on the shelves.

When Jacqueline isn't lost in her writing, she spends time with her five children, most of whom are finally able to look after her instead of the other way around. Together they do random road trips, that usually end up with them lost, shopping trips where they push every button in the toy aisle, hiking when there's enough time to escape, and bizarre things like creating new daring recipes in the kitchen. She's a grandmother to nine so far) and looks forward to corrupting many more in the years to come.

Jacqueline also writes under the pseudonym of J. Risk

Jacqueline loves to hear from her readers, you can find her at http://jacquelinepaige.com/

Author note:

Did you enjoy reading one of my books?

If so, PLEASE help spread the word on social media. You can help by sharing on Facebook, tweet about it, post something on Instagram, Pinterest. Posting a review on your favorite book sites go a long way to help authors. With your help in keeping my books "out there", I can continue writing to keep those stories coming.

Writing and promoting can be very time consuming. I love talking to readers, but the hours spent on keeping so many social media outlets current can become overwhelming and time for writing pays the price. If you can take a few minutes to help, that would be awesome. Thank you!